100
MALICIOUS
LITTLE
MYSTERIES

100 MALICIOUS LITTLE MYSTERIES

SELECTED BY ISAAC ASIMOV,
MARTIN H. GREENBERG,
AND JOSEPH D. OLANDER

BARNES
& NOBLE
BOOKS
NEW YORK

This edition published by Barnes & Noble, Inc.,
by arrangement with Martin H. Greenberg.

ISBN 1-56619-922-0

Printed and bound in the United States of America

M   3   4   5   6   7   8   9

Acknowledgments

"Six Words" by Lew Gillis. Copyright © 1978 by Lew Gillis. First published
    in *Ellery Queen's Mystery Magazine* (March 1978). Reprinted by permission
    of the author.
"The Little Things" by Isaac Asimov. Copyright © 1975 by Isaac Asimov.
    First published in *Ellery Queen's Mystery Magazine* (May 1975). Reprinted
    by permission of the author.
"A Matter of Life and Death" by Bill Pronzini and Barry N. Malzberg.
    Copyright © 1974 by Renown Publications, Inc. First published in
    Mike Shayne Mystery Magazine. Reprinted by permission of the authors.
"Perfect Pigeon" by Carroll Mayers. Copyright © 1978 by Carroll Mayers.
    Reprinted by permission of the author.
"The Cop Who Loved Flowers" by Henry Slesar. Copyright © 1966 by
    Davis Publications, Inc. Reprinted by permission of the author.
"Trick or Treat" by Judith Garner. Copyright © 1975 by Judith Garner.
    Reprinted by permission of the author.
"Twice Around the Block" by Lawrence Treat. Copyright © 1956 by
    Renown Publications, Inc. Reprinted by permission of the author.
"An Easy Score" by Al Nussbaum. Copyright © 1973 by H.S.D. Publica-
    tions, Inc. Reprinted by permission of the author.
"The Good Lord Will Provide" by Lawrence Treat and Charles M. Plotz.
    Copyright © 1973 by Lawrence Treat and Charles M. Plotz. Reprinted
    by permission of the authors.

CONTENTS

Snacks

by Isaac Asimov

As a man who constantly battles the upward-edging scale, I am perfectly ready (even delighted) to admit that nothing beats a nice roast duck dinner—or filet mignon—or brook trout—with, of course, all the fixings.

Yet even the best trenchermen among us will admit that there are times during the light-hearted conviviality of a successful cocktail party when nothing beats a carrot stick dipped into something garlicky, the cracker on which a bit of chopped liver or smoked salmon rests, the shrimp dipped in a tangy sauce.

There are, in other words, times for the full dinner and times for the snacks.

And so it is in literature. What is better than a long and exciting mystery novel when we have a day of leisure in which to track down the clues and follow the intricate play of action?

But suppose we need something for just those few minutes before dropping off, or for some minutes of comfort over a sandwich or while waiting for a train? In that case, how about all the excitement, thrills, and surprise of a mystery novel compressed into two thousand words or less? A snack, in other words.

If there's nothing like a snack at the right time, then here in this book are an even hundred of them, every one of them guaranteed by your humble anthologists. (And pray notice that even the introduction is snack-sized.)

P.S. This anthology was inspired by the fact that I had done three previously on short-short science fiction, and I felt the same could be done for mysteries. It is hard, however, to do anything in the realm of the mystery anthology that the master, Ellery Queen, has not already done. In 1969 he published *Mini-Mysteries,* a collection of seventy stories, and this anthology follows in the tradition.

Six Words

by Lew Gillis

The editor looked up in annoyance. There, standing before him, having somehow penetrated to the heart of his cozy editorial sanctum, was—of all things—an author.

Automatically the editor's eyes flicked over the piles of manuscripts on his desk. Perhaps, he thought, this was some outraged author come to claim a treasured story submitted long ago and still grinding—slowly—through the mill of the gods.

But no, this author had come equipped with a manuscript of his own, which he now unceremoniously thrust into the face of the startled editor.

"Publish this!" he said peremptorily.

"Is *that* all?" the editor replied, recovering quickly. "May I remind you, my dear sir—"

"Publish this!" the author repeated, this time more menacingly. He was a large lumpy man with an untidy beard, and he looked as though he meant business.

The editor smiled expansively, playing for time. "There are, of course, many ways," he began, "to get a story published, Mr. . . . Mr. . . .?"

"Gillis," the author stated. "Lew Gillis." He still stood with his manuscript thrust at the editor. "I am aware of the many ways to get a story published," he said flatly. "During the last several years I have had occasion to try them all."

"Really?" the editor rejoined brightly. He was growing bored.

"Without success," said Lew Gillis.

"Ah!" Things were becoming clearer. The man was obviously a disappointed author.

"I have, for example," Lew Gillis said, "submitted my

stories with covering letters calling attention to my previous literary successes." He shrugged. "To no avail."

"Perhaps," the editor suggested, "had these previous literary successes not been figments of your—"

"I have ignominiously scraped acquaintance with published authors, poor wretches of little or no talent, for the sole purpose of using their barely recognizable names to get past secretaries and into the presence of editors," Gillis continued.

"But this device, too," the editor completed the thought, "availed you nothing." He smiled wearily. "And not surprising either, when you consider that editors abhor—"

"Finally," the author went on, "I hit upon a scheme which, during the last year, has brought me considerable success."

In spite of himself the editor was interested. "A scheme?" he repeated.

"An extremely simple scheme," said the author. "Nowadays when I have a story to sell I merely choose an editor, find a way to elude his secretary, hold my manuscript out to him, as I am doing with you now, and speak six words."

"And those six words are . . .?" The editor felt some resentment at having to supply all the straight lines.

"And this six words are"—the burly author paused mischievously—"potent. Yes, yes, certainly potent."

"I imagine they would have to be," the editor acknowledged with ill-concealed sarcasm, "to achieve such remarkable results. Still, I don't understand—"

"The first response to them is invariably derisive," the author admitted, "as yours will no doubt be. Editors, as a class, are preternaturally contemptuous of authors. I would even feel justified in calling them monomaniacally arrogant."

"Surely," replied the editor, "that's a bit of an overstate- —"

"In the end, however, I have managed to convince most of them of the seriousness of my intentions. Those few I have not—" he shrugged. "Well, you would no doubt recognize their names at once. I could easily supply documentation."

"All this is very interesting, Mr. . . . Mr. . . .?"

"Gillis," the author stated again. "Lew Gillis."

"But I'm afraid I must tell you, sir," the editor continued, probing with his foot as unobtrusively as possible for the emergency alarm button beneath his desk, "that there are no circumstances I can think of, no combination whatever of six words I can imagine, that could force me to publish a story, by you or by anyone else, that I did not expressly choose to publish."

For a moment the bearded author made no reply. Then once more, without warning, he thrust his manuscript, its title and author's name—SIX WORDS by Lew Gillis—now clearly visible, into the face of the editor.

"Publish this," he began, with an air of once and for all concluding the business.

"Or—?" the editor inquired.

Gillis grinned savagely. "That," he said, "is the third word."

The Little Things

by Isaac Asimov

Mrs. Clara Bernstein was somewhat past fifty and the temperature outside was somewhat past ninety. The air-conditioning was working, but though it removed the fact of heat it didn't remove the *idea* of heat.

Mrs. Hester Gold, who was visiting the 21st floor from her own place in 4-C, said, "It's cooler down on my floor." She was over fifty, too, and had blonde hair that didn't remove a single year from her age.

Clara said, "It's the little things, really. I can stand the heat. It's the dripping I can't stand. Don't you hear it?"

"No," said Hester, "but I know what you mean. My boy, Joe, has a button off his blazer. Seventy-two dollars, and without the button it's nothing. A fancy brass button on the sleeve and he doesn't have it to sew back on."

"So what's the problem? Take one off the other sleeve also."

"Not the same. The blazer just won't look good. If a button is loose, don't wait, get it sewed. Twenty-two years old and he still doesn't understand. He goes off, he doesn't tell me when he'll be back—"

Clara said impatiently, "Listen. How can you say you don't hear the dripping? Come with me to the bathroom. If I tell you it's dripping, it's dripping."

Hester followed and assumed an attitude of listening. In the silence it could be heard—drip—drip—drip—

Clara said, "Like water torture. You hear it all night. Three nights now."

Hester adjusted her large faintly tinted glasses, as though that would make her hear better, and cocked her head. She said, "Probably the shower dripping upstairs, in 22-G. It's Mrs. Maclaren's place. I know her. Listen, she's a good-hearted person. Knock on her door and tell her. She won't bite your head off."

Clara said, "I'm not afraid of her. I banged on her door five times already. No one answers. I phoned her. No one answers."

"So she's away," said Hester. "It's summertime. People go away."

"And if she's away for the whole summer, do I have to listen to the dripping a whole summer?"

"Tell the super."

"That idiot. He doesn't have the key to her special lock and he won't break in for a drip. Besides, she's not away. I know her automobile and it's downstairs in the garage right now."

Hester said uneasily. "She could go away in someone else's car."

Clara sniffed. "That I'm sure of. *Mrs.* Maclaren."

Hester frowned, "So she's divorced. It's not so terrible. And she's still maybe thirty—thirty-five—and she dresses fancy. Also not so terrible."

"If you want my opinion, Hester," said Clara, "what she's doing up there I wouldn't like to say. I hear things."

"What do you hear?"

"Footsteps. Sounds. Listen, she's right above and I know where her bedroom is."

Hester said tartly, "Don't be so old-fashioned. What she does is her business."

"All right. But she uses the bathroom a lot, so why does she leave it dripping? I wish she *would* answer the door. I'll bet anything she's got a décor in her apartment like a French I-don't-know-what."

"You're wrong, if you want to know. You're plain wrong. She's got regular furniture and lots of houseplants."

"And how do you know that?"

Hester looked uncomfortable. "I water the plants when she's not home. She's a single woman. She goes on trips, so I help her out."

"Oh? Then you would *know* if she was out of town. Did she tell you she'd be out of town?"

"No, she didn't."

Clara leaned back and folded her arms. "And you have the keys to her place then?"

Hester said, "Yes, but I can't just go in."

"Why not? She could be away. So you have to water her plants."

"She didn't tell me to."

Clara said, "For all you know she's sick in bed and can't answer the door."

"She'd have to be pretty sick not to use the phone when it's right near the bed."

"Maybe she had a heart attack. Listen, maybe she's dead and that's why she doesn't shut off the drip."

"She's a young woman. She wouldn't have a heart attack."

"You can't be sure. With the life she lives—maybe a boyfriend killed her. We've *got* to go in."

"That's breaking and entering," said Hester.

"With a *key*? If she's away you can't leave the plants to die. You water them and I'll shut off the drip. What harm? —And if she's dead, do you want her to lay there till who knows when?"

"She's not dead," said Hester, but she went downstairs to the fourth floor for Mrs. Maclaren's keys.

"No one in the hall," whispered Clara. "Anyone could break in anywhere anytime."

"Sh," whispered Hester. "What if she's inside and says 'Who's there'?"

"So say you came to water the plants and I'll ask her to shut off the drip."

The key to one lock and then the key to the other turned smoothly and with only the tiniest click at the end. Hester took a deep breath and opened the door a crack. She knocked.

"There's no answer," whispered Clara impatiently. She pushed the door wide open.

"The air conditioner isn't even on. It's legitimate. You want to water the plants."

The door closed behind them. Clara said, "It smells stuffy, in here. Feels like a damp oven."

They walked softly down the corridor. Empty utility room on the right, empty bathroom—

Clara looked in. "No drip. It's in the master bedroom."

At the end of the corridor there was the living room on the left, with its plants.

"They need water," said Clara. "I'll go into the master bath—"

She opened the bedroom door and stopped. No motion. No sound. Her mouth opened wide.

Hester was at her side. The smell was stifling. "What—"

"Oh, my God," said Clara, but without breath to scream.

The bed coverings were in total disarray. Mrs. Maclaren's head lolled off the bed, her long brown hair brushing the floor, her neck bruised, one arm dangling on the floor, hand open, palm up.

"The police," said Clara. "We've got to call the police."

Hester, gasping, moved forward.

"You mustn't touch anything," said Clara.

The glint of brass in the open hand—

Hester had found her son's missing button.

A Matter of Life and Death
by Bill Pronzini and Barry N. Malzberg

Letter from Herman Skolnick to the Committee for the Divine, Bay City, California:

I have perruzed your recent advertisement in *Astounding Spirits* with great interest. It is absolutely vital that I know the answer to the following question: is there a Life After Death? Please reply by return mail (my address is % General Delivery, Bay City).

P.S. I am quite serious. I must know the answer to this question immediately.

Letter from the Committee for the Divine to Herman Skolnick:

You will find the answer to your question, and many others, in our Course on Celestial Metaphysics, brochures on which are being released to you in conjunction with this letter. Payment of the full enrollment fee is due upon your signing up for the course, but there will be no further charges of any sort.

Letter from Herman Skolnick to the Committee for the Divine:

I do not think you understand the seriousness of my intent, or the necessity of my need for the answer to my question. I am desperate and I have neither the time nor the funds to enroll in your Course. I beg you to answer: is there a Life After Death?

Letter from the Committee for the Divine to Herman Skolnick:

As a result of certain laws of publications and information, regulating our use of the mails for our services, we are unable to reply to your question, the answer to which, as was stated in previous correspondence, will be found in our course on Celestial Metaphysics. We will allow a ten percent (10%) reduction in the price of the Course for immediate enrollment and will guarantee to refund your money promptly if you are not satisfied with the results.

Letter from Herman Skolnick to Elsa Wiggins, The Helping Hand Mission, Bay City, California:
I have heard many good things about the work you've been doing, and am writing to you because I urgently need your help. Please tell me (% General Delivery, Bay City): is there a Life After Death?

Letter from Elsa Wiggins to Herman Skolnick:
Thank you, brother, for your expression of faith in the community service which we at The Helping Hand Mission are so unselfishly performing in offering Hope for the lost, the intemperate, and the mis-directed among us. From your letter, we know that you too are one of those lost souls—but we cannot begin to offer you the proper guidance through correspondence. Won't you come in and see us?

(Our free lunch is served every day at noon; dinner at six p.m. Soup and coffee available at all hours. Liquor and tobacco prohibited. Donations always welcome, large or small.)

Letter from Herman Skolnick to Miss Dorinda, % the Miss Dorinda Answers column, Bay City Express, Bay City, California:
I am desperate to know the answer to this question: is there a Life After Death? No one seems willing to help me. Please, please, won't you tell me the answer (my address is % General Delivery, Bay City).

Letter from Miss Dorinda to Herman Skolnick:
I detected a genuine note of soulful desperation in your recent letter, Mr. Skolnick, and so I'm rushing this reply to you right away (we do have to be careful, you know, since many misguided individuals seem to take great pleasure in playing cruel and heartless practical jokes on selfless servants of the human condition such as myself).

The question of whether or not there is Life After Death is one which has bothered every profound person at one time or another during the course of his life. But to some questions, Mr. Skolnick, there are simply no answers. Can it be you seek guidance in this matter because of some crushing personal crisis? Such as a storm on the bittersweet sea of matrimony? If so, perhaps my new book, *Miss Dorinda Answers: Crises in Marriage*, which was recently published by Nabob Press at $6.95, might contain valuable insights.

I cannot help you otherwise, Mr. Skolnick, unless you confide in me the reasons for your desperate need to know if there is a Life After Death. But I do want to help you, very much, and if you will write to me again, outlining the nature of your personal crisis, I will do everything in my power to re-establish emotional harmony in your life.

Letter from Herman Skolnick to Doctor Franklin Powers, % The Magazine of Psychic Phenomenon, New York City:

I have perruzed your recent column in *The Magazine of Psychic Phenomenon,* in which you offered to respond to any questions from readers on topics of profound significance. I have such a question, Doctor, and I must have the answer as soon as possible. My address is % General Delivery, Bay City, California, and I assure you that I am asking your help with all the earnestness I possess. Help me! I am desperate!

Is there a Life After Death?

Letter from Doctor Franklin Powers to Herman Skolnick:

Thank you for your recent inquiry, Mr. Skolnick.

Ordinarily, I would not undertake to set forth such an opinion as you request; however, I do have definite feelings on the subject, being, if I may modestly say so, an eminently qualified authority on spiritual matters through my close association with Madame Zelda and other recognized mediums. Simply stated, my opinion then is thus: yes, Mr. Skolnick, there is a Life After Death—although even my dear departed aunt, with whom I have had several illuminating conversations through Madame Zelda, is unable to tell me its exact nature.

I hope you will find this response to be of some use, and I would like to hear from you again should you feel inclined.

Just why do you wish so desperately to know if there is a Life After Death?

Suicide note found near the body of Herman Skolnick:
I have feared for my sanity for some time now, and cannot face the prospect of another tomorrow. I would have drunk the ratsbane preparation long ago if I had not been disturbed about the question of Life After Death. I have now obtained sufficient proof, however, that there *is* a Life After Death and thus the final obstacle to the taking of my own life has been removed. I am sorry for all the trouble and inconvenience my death will cause my fiancée, my acquaintances, and of course the police, but I must selfishly think of myself at this moment. I simply cannot go on any longer.

Statement of the Foreman of the Jury at the Coroner's Inquest into the death of Herman Skolnick:
In view of the statements of investigating officers and of the strange nature of the correspondence found in the deceased's possession, we the jury of this inquest are of uniform agreement that Herman Skolnick was mentally disturbed and died by his own hand.

Letter from Robert Claverly to Miss Francine Allard, Bay City:
I realize this is a poor time to attempt to re-establish our once deeply-meaningful relationship, Francie, but you know how I feel about you. I'll be here and waiting whenever you need me. Perhaps, once time has begun to heal your grief and shock at the death of your fiancé, Herman Skolnick, and you have had the opportunity to carefully perruze our relationship in your mind, you will realize that I am and always have been the only man who could ever make you truly happy, and that I stand ready to do anything—anything at all—so that we might always be together. . .

Perfect Pigeon

by Carroll Mayers

At first I didn't favor the idea. I mean, all the odds have to
be on your side for a successful bank hit. But Frankie kept
pressing me. Like: "It'll be a piece of cake, Joe."

"You've checked them all?" I asked.

"Every bank in the city. Security Savings is our best bet."

"Because of one character." I made it a statement, not a
question.

"Exactly," Frankie said. "I've been practically in his
pocket for a week. He's Casper Milquetoast in person."

"Even a worm can turn."

"Not this worm. I *know* him, I tell you."

You've read accounts in the papers where a lone bandit
tries to heist a bank by passing the teller a note threatening
bodily harm, or maybe death, if he or she doesn't give with a
jackpot of cash. Sometimes the bandit scores. Usually he
doesn't. Usually the teller is only momentarily taken aback,
then manages either to cry out or press an alarm button.
Perhaps both. Whatever, it's a fiasco for the heister.

Frankie had in mind the note-passing gambit. The thing
was, he had a refinement. He meant to be particular about
the teller he passed that note *to.*

I couldn't fault Frankie's basic reasoning. If he could tab a
teller, male or female, a real Nervous Nellie who'd be too
scared, too paralyzed, to take any physical action other than
complete compliance, Frankie would be home free—"a
piece of cake."

That was where Frankie's "survey" came in. Checking the
personnel (first by general appearance, then by discreet,
in-depth, after-work surveillance) of every bank in the city,
Frankie had come up with the perfect pigeon.

One Homer Jennings.

Homer was a teller at Security Savings, and the exact type Frankie wanted. Why Homer hadn't been put out to pasture long ago was a mystery. Certainly crowding mandatory retirement, Homer had a physique like Twiggy's and eyesight comparable to Mr. Magoo's. A lifetime bachelor, he lived alone behind triple-bolted doors and seldom went out after dark. More important, he frequently wrote letters to the newspapers deploring "crime in the streets."

Unbelievable? Not really. And he was definitely our man.

However, I still wasn't completely sold. "There's an alarm at Security Savings, isn't there?"

"Sure. A button on the floor at each teller's station."

"And you're saying Homer will be so terrified he'll simply freeze, do nothing but hand over the money? Won't even shift one foot to that button?"

"He won't risk it, Joe. He'll be scared witless, believe me."

It sounded good the way Frankie spelled it out. Also, I'd be going along just for the ride, so to speak. Because I wouldn't be *in* the bank at the moment of truth. I'd be outside, behind the wheel of a souped-up jalopy, ready to do my specialty as a crack wheel-man. Which was why Frankie had latched onto me in the first place.

I finally agreed. "Okay, deal me in," I told him. "You've got a gun to flash along with that note?"

He grinned. "I'll pick up a plastic model at the five-and-dime. With Homer that'll be enough."

But Frankie didn't stop with Homer. For three days before our hit he diligently checked traffic in the bank, determining busy and slack periods. He settled on one-thirty in the afternoon, after the luncheon rush and before the closing surge. He also surveyed the traffic on the streets at that hour and set up my best route to take off when he scooted out with the cash.

So there it was. A real easy score, right?

Wrong. We never racked it up. I managed to wheel clear when the alarm clanged, but Frankie never got out of the bank. An alerted guard's shot shattered his shoulder.

I have to admit poor Frankie had Homer Jennings pegged one hundred percent. The old gaffer *was* terrified—so terrified that when Frankie gave him a glimpse of the toy gun to reinforce the note, Homer fainted dead away and his body collapsed on the alarm button, kicking it off just as neatly as if he'd nudged it with his foot.

The Cop Who Loved Flowers

by Henry Slesar

Spring comes resolutely, even to police stations, and once again Captain Don Flammer felt the familiar, pleasant twitching of his senses. Flammer loved the springtime—the green yielding of the earth, the flourishing trees, and most of all, the flowers. He liked being a country cop, and the petunia border around the Haleyville Police Headquarters was his own idea and special project.

But by the time June arrived, it was plain that there was something different about Captain Flammer this spring. Flammer wasn't himself. He frowned too much; he neglected the garden; he spent too much time indoors. His friends on the force were concerned, but not mystified. They knew Flammer's trouble: he was still thinking about Mrs. McVey.

It was love of flowers that had introduced them. Mrs. McVey and her husband had moved into the small two-story house on Arden Road, and the woman had waved a magic green wand over the scraggly garden she had inherited. Roses began to climb in wild profusion; massive pink hydrangea bloomed beside the porch; giant pansies, mums, peonies showed their faces; violets and bluebells crept among the rocks; and petunias, more velvety than the Captain's, invaded the terrace.

One day the Captain had stopped his car and walked red-faced to the fence where Mrs. McVey was training ivy.

Flammer was a bachelor, in his forties, and not at ease with women. Mrs. McVey was a few years younger, a bit too thin for prettiness, but with a smile as warming as the sunshine.

"I just wanted to say," he told her heavily, "that you have the nicest garden in Haleyville." Then he frowned as if he had just arrested her, and stomped back to his car.

It wasn't the most auspicious beginning for a friendship, but it was a beginning. Flammer stopped his car in the McVey driveway at least one afternoon a week, and Mrs. McVey made it clear, with smiles, hot tea, and homemade cookies, that she welcomed his visits.

The first time he met Mr. McVey, he didn't like him. McVey was a sharp-featured man with a mouth that looked as if it were perpetually sucking a lemon. When Flammer spoke to him of flowers, the sour mouth twisted in contempt.

"Joe doesn't care for the garden," Mrs. McVey said. "But he knows how much it means to me, especially because he travels so much."

It wasn't a romance, of course. Everybody knew that—even the town gossips. Flammer was a cop, and cops were notoriously stolid. And Mrs. McVey wasn't pretty enough to fit the role.

So nobody in Haleyville gossiped, or giggled behind their backs. Mrs. McVey and the Captain met, week after week, right out in the open where the whole town could see them. But he was in love with her before the autumn came, and she was in love with him; yet they never talked about it.

She did talk about her husband. Little by little, learning to trust Flammer, inspired by her feelings for him, she told him about Joe.

"I'm worried because I think he's sick," she said. "Sick in a way no ordinary doctor can tell. There's such bitterness in him. He grew up expecting so much from life and he got so little."

"Not so little," Flammer said bluntly.

"He hates coming home from his trips. He never says that in so many words, but I know. He can't wait to be off again."

"Do you think he's—" Flammer blushed at the question forming in his own mind.

"I don't accuse him of anything," Mrs. McVey said. "I

never ask him any questions, and he hates to be prodded. There are times when—well, I'm a little afraid of Joe."

Flammer looked from the porch at the pink hydrangea bush, still full-bloomed at summer's end, and thought about how much he would enjoy holding Mrs. McVey's earth-stained hand. Instead, he took a sip of her tea.

On September 19th Mrs. McVey was shot with a .32 revolver. The sound exploded in the night, and woke the neighbors on both sides of the McVey house.

It was some time before the neighbors heard the feeble cries for help that followed the report of the gun, and called the Haleyville police. Captain Flammer never quite forgave the officer on duty that night for not calling him at home when the shooting occurred. He had to wait until morning to learn that Mrs. McVey was dead.

No one on the scene saw anything more in Captain Flammer's face than the concern of a conscientious police-man. He went about his job with all the necessary detach-ment. He questioned Mr. McVey and made no comment on his story.

"It was about two in the morning," McVey said. "Grace woke up and said she thought she heard a noise downstairs. She was always hearing noises, so I told her to go back to sleep. Only she didn't; she put on a kimono and went down to look for herself. She was right for a change—it was a burglar—and he must have got scared and shot her the minute he saw her . . . I came out when I heard the noise, and I saw him running away.

"What did he look like?"

"Like two feet running," Joe McVey said. "That was all I saw of him. But you can see what he was doing here."

Flammer looked around—at the living-room debris, the opened drawers, the scattered contents, the flagrant evi-dence of burglary, so easy to create, or fabricate.

The physical investigation went forward promptly. House and grounds were searched, without result—no meaningful fingerprints or footprints were found, no weapon turned up—indeed, they found no clue of any kind to the murderous burglar of Arden Road. Then they searched for answers to other questions: Was there really a burglar at all? Or had Joe McVey killed his wife?

Captain Flammer conducted his calm inquiry into the case, and nobody knew of his tightened throat, of the painful constriction in his heart, of the hot moisture that burned behind his eyes.

But when he was through, he had discovered nothing to change the verdict at the coroner's inquest: Death at the hands of person or persons unknown. He didn't agree with that verdict, but he lacked an iota of proof to change it. He knew who the Unknown Person was; he saw his hateful, sour-mouthed face in his dreams.

Joe McVey disposed of the two-story house less than a month after his wife's death—sold it at a bargain price to a couple with a grown daughter. Joe McVey then left Haleyville—went to Chicago, some said—and Captain Flammer no longer looked forward to spring, and the coming of the flowers, with joyful expectation.

But spring came again, resolutely as always, and despite the Captain's mood of sorrow and resentment at his own inadequacy, his senses began to twitch. He began driving out into the countryside. And one day he stopped his car in front of the former McVey house.

The woman who stood on the porch, framed by clumps of blue hydrangea, lifted her arm and waved. If a heart can somersault, Flammer's did. He almost said Grace's name aloud, even after he realized that the woman was only a girl, plumpish, not yet twenty.

"Hello," she said, looking at the police car in the drive-way. "Beautiful day, isn't it?"

"Yes," Flammer said dully. "Are the Mitchells at home?"

"No, they're out. I'm their daughter Angela." She smiled uncertainly. "You're not here on anything official, I hope?"

"No," Flammer said.

"Of course, I know all about this house, about what happened here last year—the murder and everything." She lowered her voice. "You never caught that burglar, did you?"

"No, we never did."

"She must have been a very nice woman—Mrs. McVey, I mean. She certainly loved flowers, didn't she? I don't think I ever saw a garden as beautiful as this one."

"Yes," Captain Flammer said. "She loved flowers very much."

Sadly, he touched a blue blossom on the hydrangea bush, and started back toward his car. He found that his eyes were filling up, and yet they had seen things clearly.

For suddenly he stopped and said, "Blue?"

The young woman watched him quizzically.

"Blue," he said again, returning and staring at the flowering hydrangea bush. "It was pink last year—I know it was. And now it's blue."

"What are you talking about?"

"Hydrangea," Flammer said. "Do you know about hydrangea?"

"I don't know a thing about flowers. As long as they're pretty—"

"They're pretty when they're pink," Flammer said. "But when there's alum in the soil—or iron—they come up blue. Blue like this."

"But what's the difference?" the girl said. "Pink or blue, what difference? So there's iron in the soil—"

"Yes," Captain Flammer said. "There must be iron in the soil. And now, Miss Mitchell, I'll ask you to please fetch me a shovel."

She looked bewildered, but then she got him the shovel. There was no triumph on Flammer's face when he dug up the revolver at the base of the hydrangea bush, its barrel rusted, its trigger stiff.

He didn't rejoice even when the gun had been identified, as both the weapon that had killed Grace McVey and as the property of Joe McVey. He didn't rejoice when the killer had been brought back to face justice. But while he felt no sense of victory, Captain Flammer admitted one thing: there was a great deal of satisfaction to be derived from the love of flowers.

Trick or Treat

by Judith Garner

I was sitting with my American friend Bambi in our basement kitchen when the front doorbell rang. As the caretaker, I immediately rose to answer it, not for the first time cursing the necessity of taking on this job for the rent-free quarters.

It was October 30, and Mrs. Adams, my niggardly employer, had forbidden fires so early in the season. But already the chill and damp promised a fierce winter. I opened the street door to a grotesque little figure outlined against the yellow fog.

It was a small girl, about eight or nine years old, dressed as a witch in a long black university gown and pointed Welsh hat. She was not one of the tenants of our service flats, but I vaguely thought I had seen her playing in the Gardens with her Nanny and a pram. I had an idea she was an American, that her father had something to do with the Embassy. Not a pretty child, she had an old-fashioned rubber doll in a very dilapidated push-chair.

"Trick or treat?" she asked.

"Treat," I said firmly, thinking I was being offered a choice.

She looked at me expectantly, but when I made no move, she inquired, "Well, where is it then?"

"What?"

"My treat," she said patiently. "If you don't give me a treat, I'll play a trick on you."

"You be off now," I said crossly. "Why, it's extortion! You Americans are all gangsters at heart!"

I closed the door in her hostile little face and went down

to the basement, where Bambi was lighting yet another of her cigarettes.

"Trick or treat," I explained.

"Oh!" she exclaimed. "I didn't know you had that custom in England."

"We don't. What is it, American?"

"Yes, indeed. We always used to go out in costumes trick-or-treating in New York."

"What kind of trick can I expect?"

"Well, my mother used to let us take a sockful of flour. If you hit it against the door it leaves a lovely mark."

"I thought I heard some sort of thud as I came downstairs," I said, "but it didn't sound like a sockful of flour, more like a kick."

"Well, they say things are very unpleasant in the States at Halloween nowadays. How gangs will break your windows or slash your tires if you don't give them at least a dollar."

I thought the custom simply encouraged hooliganism and I said so. "Anyhow, Halloween isn't until tomorrow."

Bambi looked put out at my unfriendliness about her national customs. "Good lord!" she said. "I've been giving away pennies for the Guy for the last month. I do think Guy Fawkes is just as peculiar. Fancy burning a human figure!"

I couldn't see it that way, but I held my tongue. Tonight I resented Bambi; poor though she was personally, I envied her the affluence of her background. Besides, I had always wanted to travel myself.

I poured her another cup of tea, and she reverted to her show-business anecdotes. Then Ron, my husband, joined us, and we played dominoes with the gas money until eleven.

I was up at six the next morning, bringing Ron his tea and stoking up the boiler for the hot water. At 7:30 I went up to the ground floor for the milk. The milkman was just leaving.

"Curious decorations you have around here," he said, gesturing at our front door. It certainly was odd. Nailed to the door was a doll's hand. It had a rubber skin filled with cotton; the stuffing was coming out. It looked ugly and perverted.

"If I'd seen that in Brixton or Camden Town," the man

said, "you know what I would have thought? That someone was practicing voodoo. But you don't get that sort of thing around here. Not in Gloucester Road, you don't."

I pulled the dirty thing off the door and chucked it into an open dustbin. "It's all up and down the Gardens," he continued. "Bits of a doll, nailed to the doors."

Not being superstitious, I just shrugged and went upstairs to distribute the milk. Later, having got my son off to school, I began cleaning the flats and the halls.

I did not associate the mutilated doll with my small visitor of the previous evening until, Mrs. Adams having sent me out shopping, I saw the torso just being removed from Professor Newton's door.

"Creepy, isn't it?" I greeted him.

"It's that wretched Halloween child who did it. Trick or treat indeed! Something disturbing about that family. Too much sibling rivalry is my diagnosis. I shall make a formal protest to the parents. Better yet, I shall write a letter to the *Times*, protesting about the importing of foreign customs—noxious foreign customs!" Having with some difficulty removed the nails, the Professor took the grisly souvenir into the house with him and indignantly slammed the door.

The head of the doll was impaled on the railings at the corner. There I found Lady Arthwaite studying it with interest. "I wonder what the poor thing has done to be decapitated," she murmured to me as I passed. "Positively medieval, isn't it? Or, to be precise, it's—well, I haven't seen a doll like that since before the war. The skin texture is so much more lifelike than this disgusting plastic you get nowadays. I would have liked one like it for my little granddaughter."

But as it was chilly I could not wait around. Nevertheless, her homely words took something of the horror out of the incident. I did my shopping, and made Mrs. Adams' lunch. I worked until it became dark, which was very early.

A storm was brewing. The sky was very dark and threatening. My son got home from school just in time, but I made him a nice cup of hot cocoa anyhow, in case the chill had entered his bones. He is a delicate boy.

The rain came pelting down just after five. Ron was

drenched when he came in half an hour later. "Halloween,"
he said. "I need a drink." I mixed the whiskey and hot
lemonade the way he liked it.

He sat crouching over the newly stoked boiler in his
second-hand smoking jacket. I began preparing the
dinner—chops, chips, and peas, with fruit salad and custard
for dessert.

We began to eat. Suddenly the front doorbell sounded
again. Muttering angrily, I climbed the stairs.

The little American stood there, dressed like a pirate this
time.

"Trick or treat?" she said.

This time she had her baby brother in the push-chair.

Twice Around the Block

by Lawrence Treat

At an hour after midnight, only a handful of people got off
at the subway station that served the huge, sprawling,
small-homes development called Sunny Hills. Harry, big
and handsome and blustery, was by intention the last one
out.

He had the cap, the glove, and the knife, well concealed
under his coat. He was never without them, for he did not
know just when his chance would come. Maybe tonight,
maybe not for two or three weeks. It would come when he
was able to walk past the night watchman's shack without
being seen.

Although Harry's plans had been perfected for some
time, he was smart enough not to push them. He'd stood
Mary for three years, he could wait a little longer. Besides,
she had a part-time job in a department store, and she
handed him her pay envelope every week.

Mary did it meekly, pleased that they were finally building up a savings account. He'd always made good money, but he spent it all on himself. He had flash and style to him, although he hadn't realized how exceptional he was in that respect until Velma moved in next door.

He never could understand why a woman like Velma had landed in Sunny Hills, where even the small, neat houses were so monotonously alike that you could hardly tell them apart. But she spoke vaguely of some trouble she'd been in, and he gathered that she'd been forced to quit her job in the night club where she'd had the hat-check concession.

From the moment they saw each other, they sparked like a pair of high tension wires, and neither of them had tried to resist. Shortly after the first crackle, Harry had managed to get himself transferred to the night shift so that he could see her during the day—without frustrating complications.

But it wasn't satisfying. The nights were what depressed him, going back to the house where he no longer belonged, to the woman he didn't want, the woman he had grown to hate.

"Kitten," he had said to Velma once. "If something would only happen to her. If she could meet with an accident—"

"You could make it seem like an accident," Velma had said in her low, torchy voice.

"If I do, you're going to be part of it."

"Well?"

"Maybe it would be smarter to try and get a divorce."

"You'd have to pay alimony. There wouldn't be much left."

"You like money, don't you?" he'd said. And her black eyes, lifting slowly, practically singed him.

After that, he began his preparations. He bought the roll of film and kept it at home—just in case. He always took the rear car of the subway and was the last one out. Also just in case. And he checked the subway schedule and found out that the night trains ran exactly fifteen minutes apart, and every evening he set his watch by the subway clock. Just in case.

Tonight was no different from the other nights. He came out of the subway exit and looked around to make sure that nobody had noticed him. Except for one cab, with the driver dozing over the steering wheel, the street was deserted.

He crossed the roadway and strode down the long block, and for the hundredth time he thought it over. He put his hand in his pocket and touched the knife. He'd found it in a public lavatory. There was no conceivable way of tracing it and no one except Mary had ever glimpsed it.

As he approached the night watchman's booth he walked fast, the tempo of his pulse lifting. Then he was alongside the cubicle, and his heart gave a sharp, convulsive jerk. Mike Hogan wasn't there. This was it—the one unbelievable chance.

Harry didn't panic. He sidled stealthily over to the shadows, beyond the ornamental gateway to Sunny Hills. He put the cap on, pulling it low, and he raised his coat collar. He left the sidewalk and slunk across the front yards, keeping close to the houses. If anybody saw him, they'd take him for a prowler.

All right. Let them see him, let them tell the police later on that a man had sneaked across the lawns. Wake up, you fools, and take a quick look. Quick, but not careful.

At the corner of his block, he turned and glanced behind him. Stay calm now, make sure. When he'd convinced himself that the coast was clear he started running—quietly, with a low, scuttling stoop. He was chuckling to himself, in silent excitement, buoyed up by the certainty that everything would go right.

He put his key in the door and stepped inside. He was glad it was pitch dark. He might have hesitated and drawn back if he'd seen Mary's face. He wasn't a cruel man, he told himself. He was merely a man who faced facts.

He took out the knife and snapped it open. His palm was wet, but he gripped the rough handle firmly. He flexed his arm once, his features hardening.

He walked swiftly and soundlessly down the familiar hall. He ascended the one step, and opened the door to the right. Her bed was directly behind it.

He struck savagely and repeatedly. This was the part he'd dreaded, but it was soon over, cleanly, effectively. Her breath caught and she moaned, but she didn't even wake up.

He wheeled and went out, circled the house and stopped in front of the bedroom window. He put on the thick, heavy glove and punched once at the glass. There was a brittle, crackling sound—and that was all.

When he came into the room again, later, he'd have time to raise the sash, and the evidence of a marauding burglar would be clinched as far as the police were concerned.

He glanced at his watch again. He was surprised that it had taken him only six minutes, and the precision of his timing gave him added confidence.

He returned to the street and began the long circle of the block, back to the subway station. He ran openly now, deliberately keeping to the concrete sidewalk so that his steps thudded audibly. That was part of the plan. He was willing to be seen, at a distance, to establish the presence of somebody running away.

He took the shortcut through the field and stopped at the rubbish pile, where he discarded the glove and the cap. Squinting in the darkness, he took out his keys. If the police should suspect him—if they should make more than a cursory investigation—he didn't want them to find he had a key to Velma's house. He threw the key away.

He put his key-ring back in his pocket, set his hat firmly on his head, and marched briskly towards the subway exit. He got there with a couple of minutes to spare, and stood for a moment in the shadows of the adjoining newsstand. He took long, slow, deep breaths, and thought it through again—detail by detail.

He'd forgotten nothing; he'd made no mistakes. He could trust Velma not to talk. She had good reason to stay silent, but if she did break, there was no proof. No witnesses—and no overheard quarrels with Mary. No guilt-pointing link between him and the knife.

He heard the rumble of the subway, and two or three passengers came up the steps. He waited a few seconds, then stepped into the light. The lone cab was still there, the driver awake now. Harry waved to him and continued on his way.

He headed for the watchman's shack. Hogan would have to go home with him and be present when he discovered the body. That was vitally important. But Harry had laid the background long ago. He'd stopped here night after night for the past month, not missing a single night.

Hogan stepped out of his shelter, recognized Harry, and grinned. "Evening, Harry," he said. "On the dot, as usual."

Harry smiled. "Sure, right on schedule. And Mike—that roll of film I told you about. I got it at home for you. It won't cost you a cent, either."

"That's damn nice of you, Harry."

"Come on back with me, and I'll give it to you now."

"Thanks," said Hogan. He fell into step with Harry and began grumbling endlessly about his camera problems. Harry hardly listened.

As they rounded the corner of his block, Harry took out his keys. He stopped in front of his house—number forty-eight.

"Come in," he said. "I got them in the bedroom. It won't take me a minute."

He put the key in the lock and tried to turn it. It stuck, and he pulled it out to examine it.

"What's the matter?" said Hogan pleasantly. "Got the wrong key?"

Harry gave him a look of terror and rammed the key back in the lock. The wrong key?

Then the door swung open. Mary, hugging her robe tight around her shoulders, said, "Oh, I'm so glad you're back. I'm so relieved."

Harry straightened up, and stared unbelievingly at his wife. A quick, hard lump seemed to rip at his stomach, and he grabbed the doorway for support—the doorway that was identical with Velma's.

Mary's voice seemed to come from a great distance. "I heard glass break; it woke me," she said. "I'm sure something happened to that woman next door. And I was so scared. Just think—it might have been me."

An Easy Score

by Al Nussbaum

It's impossible to say exactly why the two men chose old Mrs. Hartman for their victim. Perhaps it was her obvious age and frailty. Perhaps it was the fact that she had come out of the bank only minutes before. Perhaps they had been attracted by the oversized shoulder bag she clutched protectively, or the fact that she walked only a block before leaving the busy thoroughfare and strolling along a quiet and deserted side street.

Any combination, or all of these factors, may have influenced them. In any case, they had seen her and marked her an easy score. They had come up behind her and then separated, one going to either side. The one on her left had tripped her and, at the same instant, the other man cut the strap on her shoulder bag and tried to take it away from her. Instead of throwing her hands out to block her fall, as they had expected her to do, the gray-haired old woman grabbed the bag with both hands and gripped it tightly. She fell to the pavement, and there was the sound of an old bone snapping, but she didn't give up her hold on the bag.

One man wrapped the dangling end of the shoulder strap around his hand and tried to wrench the bag free, while the other man kicked the old woman with his square-toed boots. There were no cries for help, no screams. The only sounds were the shuffle of feet and the men's heavy breathing as they tried to force Mrs. Hartman to release her bag. The men were determined to have the bag. Every tug on the strap was accompanied by several kicks to loosen her hold; but her tightly clamped jaws and frantic grip were evidence that she was just as determined not to have it taken from her.

Unfortunately, the woman wasn't a match for even one man, let alone two. It was only seconds before she had been thrust into unconsciousness by pain and exhaustion. They tore the bag from her limp fingers and ran away, leaving her sprawled across the sidewalk.

No one saw the attack and robbery. It was almost fifteen minutes before Mrs. Hartman was discovered by another pedestrian. The police and an ambulance arrived simultaneously, but by then the two men were miles away.

She regained consciousness for a few moments as she was being carried to the ambulance on a stretcher. She turned her pain-filled eyes toward a uniformed policeman who was standing nearby, looking down at her. "My money," she said in a tone so weak he almost missed it. "They stole my purse, and it had all my money in it."

"How much was taken, ma'am?" the officer asked.

She paused a moment, then managed to reply, "Thirty-three thousand dollars," before losing consciousness again.

She hadn't been able to say much, but it was enough to raise the mugging from the level of a relatively minor offense, as such things go, and give it the stature of a major crime. Four detectives were dispatched to the hospital emergency ward to be on hand when she could speak again; and an equal number of newspaper reporters and television newsmen converged upon the hospital, too.

When she was wheeled from the treatment room, Mrs. Hartman looked like a mummy. Both of her arms and one leg were in heavy casts and her head was swathed in bandages. She was awake, though, and able to answer a few more questions. Detective Sergeant Kendris, a burly man in his forties, did all the talking. The people from the news media had to make do with what they were able to overhear and the photos they could take.

"Mrs. Hartman, can you hear me all right?" Kendris asked.

"Yes," the woman replied weakly.

"You told the officer where you were found that you had been robbed of thirty-three thousand dollars. Is that right?"

"Yes . . ."

"How did you happen to have so much cash with you?"

Mrs. Hartman hesitated, as though seeking the right words. Then she confessed, "I'm . . . I'm a foolish old woman. I don't always show good sense. Once every year, and sometimes twice, I draw all my savings from the bank. I keep the money at home for a few days, to look at it and touch it, then put it back in the bank. This time . . ." her voice trailed off weakly " . . . I lost it all."

"Did you recognize the thief?"

"There were two of them, but I'd never seen them before. And I'm not sure I'd know them if I saw them again. It all happened so very fast . . ."

At that point the sedative the doctor had administered took hold and she went to sleep.

"If you have any more questions, Sergeant Kendris," the nurse said, "you'll have to come back tomorrow."

The next afternoon, Kendris stormed into the hospital, looking like an angry bear, but he didn't get to speak to Mrs. Hartman. She slept all day, and the doctor refused to allow Kendris to awaken her.

The following day, Kendris returned again. He had calmed somewhat, but he was still visibly angry. Mrs. Hartman was propped up in bed and a high-school-age hospital volunteer was reading to her from the newspaper. Kendris asked the girl to wait outside while he talked to Mrs. Hartman.

"All right," he demanded once they were alone, "what was the idea of lying to me?"

"I . . . I don't know what you mean," she answered.

"Come off it! You know what I'm talking about—your imaginary thirty-three thousand dollars. The robbery was all over the newspapers and television, but when I went to the bank to see if they had a record of the serial numbers on the money, I learned you've never had an account there. The only time they see you is when, like the day before yesterday, you stop in to cash your Social Security check. Why did you lie?"

The injured woman's hands opened and closed and opened again in a gesture of helplessness. "I didn't want the thieves to get away with it. I . . . I wanted them to pay for what they did to me."

"But you *didn't* have to lie," Kendris persisted. "Don't you know we'd have worked just as hard, made exactly the same effort, to recover your Social Security pension as we did for the larger amount?"

When she didn't reply immediately, Kendris had time to examine what he'd just said and to see how ridiculous it was. As long as it had been believed that thirty-three thousand dollars had been stolen, there had been four detectives assigned to the case, and reporters to record their every move; but now he was the only one officially assigned, and that would last only until he returned to the office and put his report in the Unsolved File. At least he had the grace to be embarrassed.

"Oh, that isn't what I meant! I'm sure the police do their best regardless of the amount lost," Mrs. Hartman said, but to Kendris' ears the words had a hollow ring. It made him all the more ashamed to have this beaten-up old woman show more concern for his feelings than he'd shown for hers.

"Look," he said, cutting the interview short, "let's just forget the whole thing." He began moving toward the door. "If anything turns up, you'll be notified," he said, and then he was gone from the room.

The young hospital volunteer returned. She picked up the newspaper she'd set aside when Kendris arrived, and sat beside the bed.

"Would you like me to read some more?" she asked.

"Yes, please," Mrs. Hartman answered. "Read the part about the murders again."

"But I've already read it four times," the girl protested.

"I know, but please read it again."

The girl cleared her throat and then began. "Police investigated a disturbance in an apartment at 895 Seventh Avenue at about ten last night and found two men, William White and Jesse Bolt, who shared the apartment, dead on the living room floor, the result of a knife fight. Neighbors said the men had been arguing and fighting most of the day, each accusing the other of cheating him out of an undisclosed amount of money. The knife fight in which they killed one another was the climax of the day-long confrontation. Both men had long arrest records. Police are continuing their investigation."

Mrs. Hartman smiled behind her bruised lips. "Please, read it again," she said softly.

The Good Lord Will Provide

by Lawrence Treat and Charles M. Plotz

STATE PENITENTIARY

April 3

Dear Judy,

It's been a whole year now, a whole long year without you. But I been a real good prisoner staying out of trouble like a cat stays away from water. They all say I'll get my parole next April, plenty of time to put in a crop. So hang on, you and Uncle Ike. The only thing bothering me is I ain't heard from you in so long. Why? What's happening?

Judy, it's not like I done anything wrong. All I did was drive that car. I didn't know they had guns and itchy fingers, I didn't even know them good. They was just a couple of city fellas hanging around a bar and I got chinning with them and happened to let drop I was the champeen stock car racer of Hadley County. I done a little bragging maybe. I musta told them I could just about drive a car up the side of a wall and down the other side and if they wanted to see how good I was, why come on out and look. Which they did.

Maybe I was a little stupid but when they allowed they'd pay me right then and there to take them to the bank next day and then on out to the back hills where there was no roads, which they said they wanted to do just for the hell of it—well all I did was ask how much. And when they told me I plumb near keeled over. Because it was almost as much as we needed for that mortgage payment. I figured money was money and if they were taking a lot of it out of the bank, why wouldn't they be generous? What I didn't know was they didn't have no account there.

So I reckon I was real stupid. But stupid or not I sure was lucky because if I'd stayed with that pair much longer I'da got killed too. But they paid me to get them out of town and up into the hills and after I done that I took off and come straight back to you.

When Ike heard the news on the radio he knowed right off it was me at the wheel of the car. Nobody else could have outdrove and outsmarted the cops and I bet I could have got clear off to Mexico or maybe China if I'da wanted to. And if the airplanes hadn't spotted me like they did that pair. But I done what I was paid for, so I come back where I belonged. And if they took fifty thousand like the papers said or a million I wouldn't know. I was waiting out in the car and all the money I ever seen was what I give you. And like I said, I got it the day before and it wasn't stolen from the bank. Not that bank anyhow.

The sheriff kept asking me where the stolen money was. After all the two bank robbers was dead with no trace of the money and all the sheriff had was me. Just a poor dumb farmer with a knack for handling a car.

But I don't want to worry you with all this. I'm real lonesome for you like I said. So when are you coming up here to visit me? And how are you and how's Ike and the farm?

Your loving husband
Walt

R.F.D. 2, Hadley

April 10

Dear Walt

I got your letter and the reason I ain't come to see you is that I just don't have the money for the trip. Besides I got to do all the chores now. Uncle Ike's down with the rhumatiz again and Doc Saunders says he won't be up and around until the warm spring weather sets in and that's not liable to happen until May. And when Ike's feeling puny he wants me around all the time and all he does is complain and tell me everybody's out to take the skin off me. He even tried to chase George off the place when George came around in his new car to ask me out for a ride. And I sure needed to get away from the farm for awhile.

George was real nice to me too. He wanted to know how I was getting along without you and if I missed you much. Well I said it was kind of lonesome, there was things a girl needed sometimes and who was around except Ike? Seems George got my meaning wrong but I straightened him out real good. Afterwards I told him right out that we was liable to lose the farm unless we got that mortgage installment paid and how could I pay it until I got a crop in? And I said that what with George getting promoted to be vice president of the bank he could maybe do something. He said he'd see what he could manage and that was about as far as we got. Anyhow it was nice getting away from Ike for awhile, specially when George took me to dinner at that new place in town.

Walt, I wish you was a banker too.

Your loving wife
Judy

State Penitentiary

April 15

Dear Judy,

I know it's hard on you and with Ike to take care of it's even worse. He's tetchy enough when he feels good but when he's got the aches he's enough to try the patience of a saint. But the good Lord will provide, Judy, and I know what I'm saying.

About George and the bank holding off—you want to get it writ down. So next time you see him you want to ask him about Ruthie Watkins which I found out about from a guy up here named Ernie Taylor. Ernie, his business is selling letters. And like he says, if I got a cow or a bushel of wheat I can sell them, can't I? So why can't he sell letters?

Ernie and me get along fine because the both of us we're

innocent men and we shouldn't ought to be here. But as long as we are we talk about things and Ernie happened to mention some letters he got hold of which George writ to this Ruthie Watkins. So maybe you better mention them to George next time you see him.

Your loving husband
Walt

R.F.D. 2, Hadley

April 22

Dear Walt,

George took me out to dinner again and we talked about a lot of things. And like you told me to I just happened to mention Ruthie Watkins and then I said about the mortgage and how it ought to be writ down. And the very next day I got a letter from the bank promising to hold off until autumn but I don't know what good it's going to do. Because next time I was out with George, Ike got hold of some of that while mule stuff and after that he got the idea he ought to go riding in the tractor. Which he did, as far as that big ditch on the west side. Ike didn't get hurt bad, just a bruise or two that he's relaxing from, but you ought to see what's left of that tractor. So how do I make that mortgage payment in the fall with no crop coming in? And if I don't pay up we got no farm.

I'm tired, Walt. I'm plumb tired and just about at the end of my tether. You said the good Lord will provide—but how? How?

Your loving wife
Judy

STATE PENITENTIARY

April 28

Dear Judy,

You got to be patient like I said and if you're real patient the Lord *will* provide. Because He come to me in a dream and He said that there was something buried in the south field that would take care of us. So you tell Ike to get over that rhumatiz of his. Tell him I only got a year to go and then I'm going to dig up that something in the south field and after that everything's going to be all right.

Your loving husband
Walt

R.F.D. 2, Hadley

May 4

Dear Walt,

I don't know just how to tell you this but I guess I'll just set it down the way it happened.

You know how Ike hates the law ever since they come around and took you away. So when the sheriff and six deputies showed up the day before yesterday Ike tried to chase them away. He got up out of bed and ran all over the place looking for his shotgun, only I had it hid. Then he yelled at them and called them all kinds of names and they finally grabbed him and tied him up for a spell, so he never did see what they done. He's spry again, all that running after the deputies loosened him up and now he's as good as ever. But I don't rightly know what the sheriff come for and you'll never tumble to what those deputies of his done.

Walt, they went down to that south field and the six of them spent the whole day digging and then they come back the next day and kept on until they dug up just about every inch of that field. And I never did see any six men look so tired and they sure was mad. I asked them lots of questions and one of them—I think he come all the way down from the prison—he allowed as how all your mail gets read. Walter, what did he say that for?

Your loving wife
Judy

May 7

Dear Judy,
  Now plant.

Your loving husband
Walt

Boomerang

by Harold Q. Masur

The thin man on the witness stand fumbled with the edge of his necktie. He had been Raynor's secretary and one of the two men present in the district attorney's house the night he'd been murdered.

I asked him: "The day Raynor was killed, didn't he tell you he had enough on the defendant to hang him?"

"Objection!" Sam Lubock, the defense lawyer, had leaped to his feet, thick-jowled face flooded with color.

"Sustained," snapped Judge Martin. He said it without even glancing at me.

That's how it had been all through the trial—Lubock making objections, the judge sustaining them. And this was supposed to be a court of justice. The lady outside, weighing scales in her hand, must have been laughing in her stone throat. Only there was nothing funny about it.

Lubock grinned and sat down beside his client.

I looked at the defendant, and a white sheet of fury blazed through me. There was no doubt in my mind that he had murdered my chief, District Attorney Raynor, the one man I had worshiped and respected.

Judged by certain standards, Frank Hauser was a success. He had made and kept three fortunes, had done it over the sweat and toil and blood of a hundred men. Night clubs, clip joints, slot machines, numbers, protective societies—anything that paid big dividends.

He was a slender man, smooth and oily, cold and deadly as a rattlesnake. He sat there, smiling contemptuously, a stain on the community. Any time he pulled the strings, a couple of politicians danced.

And then, quite suddenly, two months ago, a reform ticket had placed Dan Raynor in the district attorney's office. Dan Raynor was not for sale. Nobody had that kind of money. Alone, Raynor was not dangerous. But teamed with his special investigator, Tom Gahagan, they menaced the organization, the very existence of Hauser's machine.

Gahagan was all cop. Ploddingly, meticulously, he'd piled up the evidence against Hauser, enough to send the man to the gallows, and some half dozen big shots with him.

So of course Raynor had to go. The evidence had to be blown out of the safe. And Gahagan—well, that was the question. Where was Gahagan? The only man who could tie Hauser to this rap.

At the bottom of the river? Bought off? Hiding? I didn't know, and it probably wouldn't do much good if I did.

Because this was one murder case that was fixed. Good and tight. Hauser was going to go scot free.

The jurors had been bought and paid for. I'd known that since the second day of the trial. What's more, Hauser was the man who'd hoisted Martin to the bench. And the judge was going to protect him even if he had to rewrite the rules of evidence. With Gahagan missing there wasn't anything I could do.

What I really wanted though, was to get Gahagan up there on the witness stand. I wanted him to shout his testimony until the bailiffs dragged him from the chair. Sure, it wouldn't hang Hauser, but the spectators would hear it, the reporters would hear it, and maybe the world would learn what was going on in this beautiful city of ours.

You see, Gahagan had been in the district attorney's home that night Raynor was killed. He had been in another room, but at the sound of the shot he'd caught a fleeting glimpse of the car as it rocketed away down the street. He had recognized it as Hauser's.

But—Gahagan—was—missing—

I clenched my fists. Fifty grand! A hundred grand! That kind of money was chicken feed to Hauser. But it might turn the head of even a man like Gahagan.

I know. It had been offered to me. I was still weak from temptation. But if I'd ever accepted a bribe from Raynor's killer, it wouldn't have been much fun living with myself.

The weapon that had smoked down Raynor had been tossed through the window of his study. It was an old Colt army automatic, millions of which had been manufactured, practically impossible to trace. It had already been introduced into evidence. I picked it up and showed it to the thin man on the witness stand.

"When you heard the shot and ran into the deceased's study, where did you find this gun?"

Raynor's secretary wet his lips, his eyes wandered to the floor. He said: "Mr. Raynor was holding it in his hand."

For a brief instant I was shocked into immobility. I just stood there, staring at him, completely stunned. A whisper rippled through the courtroom.

It had happened. They'd bought off Raynor's secretary. They were trying to show that the D.A. must have committed suicide. My own witness had boomeranged. And I was bound by his answers.

I guess what happened then was absolutely unprecedented. I saw red. My face was burning. I took a single step forward and sent my fist crashing full into his face.

Hell broke loose. Judge Martin started banging with his gavel. Sam Lubock was on his feet shouting. Two bailiffs were dragging me back. Hauser's mouth was warped by a thin smile. If I could have got my hands on him at that moment, I would've choked the life out of him.

I waited for the judge to finish his scalding comments. I didn't apologize. I didn't say anything. I just stood there, licked, beaten, ready to give up the fight. And then, suddenly, there was a flurry in the rear of the courtroom.

I turned and the pulse started hammering against my temples. A tall figure, his hands pressed tightly against his sides, was walking in stiff-legged, jerky steps down the aisle.

Tom Gahagan . . .

He didn't look at me. He didn't look at anybody. He went straight to the witness chair, gripped the arms and eased himself into it. His eyes were narrowed, his lips grim and colorless. He seemed tired, almost exhausted. Then his eyes found mine, and I saw a thin sheen of oily perspiration standing out over his whole face.

Lubock vented an audible gasp. Hauser was staring pop-eyed. Both men looked dumbfounded, as if they'd paid Gahagan to go to Africa and were suddenly amazed to find him here. I knew then that they had never expected him to show up.

Excitement quickened my blood. Here was a chance to do something. If only Judge Martin didn't order the bailiffs to throw us both into the clink for contempt of court. I asked Gahagan a few preliminary questions and he answered them in short cryptic sentences. Then I picked up the old Colt army automatic and handed it to him.

"This is the People's exhibit one," I said. "Do you recognize it?"

He turned it over slowly in his hands. You could hear a watch ticking in the courtroom. All eyes were focused upon him. He opened it, peered into the empty chamber, then held it loosely in his lap. He looked up.

"Yes. This is the gun that killed Mr. Raynor."

"Where were you when the shot was fired?"

Gahagan's eyes met mine in a steady look. "I had just opened the door to Mr. Raynor's study."

That was a lie! I sucked in a sharp breath, waiting for Lubock's objection. Gahagan hadn't been near the study. But Lubock was biding his time. I knew then what was going through Gahagan's mind. Probably he felt that if all the other witnesses were perjuring themselves for the defense, he could lie for the prosecution.

A thought struck me and suddenly my hands were clammy, like two lumps of cold dough. What if Gahagan had sold himself? What if he testified that he had seen Raynor commit suicide? Scarcely breathing, I asked my next question.

"What did you see?"

Lubock and Hauser were both leaning tensely forward,

watching Gahagan. Judge Martin sat stiffly at the bench. Gahagan's eyes traveled along the counsel table and came to rest on Hauser. He said in a low voice:

"I saw Hauser standing at the window holding this gun in his hand, pointing it at Raynor, like this—"

And he lifted the gun, sighting along the dull barrel directly at the defendant. Hauser's mouth sagged loosely and he stiffened in his chair. For once in his life I could see that Lubock was speechless. But his neck muscles were taut and he was getting ready to jump up. For the moment, Gahagan's play had caught everyone by surprise.

His eyes were opaque, like blank empty windows. A vein bulged in a blue diagonal across his forehead. His voice came out clearly, almost ringing:

"Hauser pulled the trigger—like—this—"

A shot exploded in the courtroom. And as I watched, a raw red-lipped hole suddenly jumped into the temple above the bridge of Hauser's nose. A split-second of unbelief rioted across his face, then he toppled forward over the defense table.

A woman screamed, high and shrill. Spectators ducked under their seats. The jurymen cowered back against the rear of the jury box. Judge Martin held his gavel poised in midair. Lubock held a horror-stricken look upon his client.

Gahagan dropped the gun. It clattered to the floor. His face, the color of wax, was lighted by a smile, a strange triumphant smile. Unseen, he had slipped a shell into the automatic. I grabbed his arm and dug my fingers into it.

"They didn't want me to testify," he said in a dull voice. "They were holding me in a warehouse."

"Good Lord, man! This is murder. You didn't really see Hauser kill the D.A."

Gahagan coughed. "No, but I saw him kill somebody else down in that warehouse this morning."

I stared at him. "Who?"

"Me," Gahagan whispered hoarsely.

And then he tumbled forward out of the witness chair in a half turn, sprawling to the floor on his back. He didn't say anything more. I didn't expect him to. For his coat had pulled open and in stark crimson relief against the white of his shirt was the jagged tear of a bullet hole.

The Way It's Supposed To Be
by Elsin Ann Graffam

We had so much fun. I don't remember about when I was *real* little, but I'm ten now and I know we had a good time, just the two of us, ever since my father went away.

Mom had his picture on the mantel and she talked about him all the time—how he loved me so much and what he was like and stuff. My Dad was a great guy, on the football team at college and everything. Then he was a stockbroker and married to Mom. Mom was glad he bought stocks for us because that meant she didn't have to go out to work and leave me when he went away.

I was three when he went away and I don't remember him. I tried to when I was little, but I just couldn't. But it was okay. He was sort of alive to me in the picture. Mom would say, "Daddy would be so proud to know you had all A's on your report card," and I'd look at his picture there on the mantel, and he'd be smiling, happy for me. I bet you didn't know that pictures could smile, did you? Well, they can.

People called Mom a widow and I didn't find out until last year what that meant. Dad was an old man. He's got gray hair in the picture and that means you're old. Mom doesn't have gray hair. She's young. And pretty. She's got a lot of fluffy blonde hair around her face and big blue eyes. She's the most beautiful lady in the whole world.

I'll never leave my mother. The other guys, you know, they say they're going down to Florida and dig for treasure or go overseas and look for monsters in some lake. They can't wait to leave home. But not me.

I can't tell them that. I told Billy Earle once that I'd never leave Mom and he laughed at me. But they can't understand. They don't have a Mom like mine. All their mothers have lines between their eyes. That means they frown a lot. My mother never frowns. She's the nicest person on earth. I'll never leave her. I told that to Dad a year ago and he looked down at me from the mantel and said, "You're a good boy, Glenn."

Maybe the guys don't understand, but Dad does.

Everything was real neat until Mr. Knott came along. One night last summer I woke up because I thought the TV was on too loud. I went into the living room to tell Mom to turn it down, and there was a man sitting on the sofa. Mom jumped when she saw me.

"Is anything wrong?" I asked her.

"No, everything is wonderful," she said.

I didn't like Mr. Knott. He was old and he had a big nose.

"Who is he?" I asked her.

She said, "This is Mr. Knott and he's my friend."

I went back to bed but I couldn't sleep. I thought I was the only friend Mom had. I hoped with all my might that Mom would never see him again. But she did. He was over a lot. Mom would say, "Come on, Glenn, just say hello to Mr. Knott."

When my tenth birthday came last October, I shut my eyes real tight when I blew out the candles, and I wished that Mr. Knott would go away and never come back. But it didn't work.

After a while the lady down the street came to babysit me. Mom would go out with Mr. Knott. I'd lie down on my bed the whole time they were away, thinking maybe I'd die of sadness and then Mom would be sorry for what she did. But I never died and Mom kept on seeing Mr. Knott.

Once they were away for a whole weekend. Mom kissed me good-bye that Saturday morning and hugged me real tight. But I didn't care—nothing mattered any more, not after that rotten old man came along. I wanted more than anything else for it to stay that way, just the two of us, Mom and me. The way it's supposed to be.

"Surprise!" Mr. Knott said to me that Sunday night when he and Mom got home. "Your mother and I were married yesterday morning," he said.

Mom said, "That's right, Glenn. I didn't want to tell because we were afraid you wouldn't understand. We're going to be so happy!"

We, we, we! Only the "we" wasn't Mom and me, it was Mom and that old man.

You don't die from crying, or I'd be dead now. I never said a word to him, or looked at him. Mom and he would talk and I'd feel like I was in a deep dark hole. The more days that went by, the deeper and darker that hole got. It was blacker than night there.

Dad didn't like it any more than I did. Sometimes I'd stand in front of the fireplace and look at his picture on the mantel, and you know what? He was *crying*. Big tears came down the glass in the frame. They made a puddle on the mantel.

One night when I was talking to Dad, the puddle ran over and made spots on the rug. Mom came in the room just then and asked me what I was doing.

"Look!" I said. "Dad's crying because you married that man! See?"

She looked at me funny and left the room. Right after that I heard Mom and Mr. Knott arguing. It was the first time in my life I ever heard my mother yell.

The next day I got home from school and threw my books on the sofa. Something was wrong. I looked around the room. Then I saw it. Or, I mean, I didn't see it. There was a blank space where Dad's picture should have been.

"Mom!" I yelled. "Where is it?!"

"Where is what?" she asked. As if she didn't know!

"My Dad's picture is gone!"

And she said, "Well, Mr. Knott thought it was a good idea to put it away since he is your father now."

I banged my head against the mantel and yelled that Mr. Knott was not my father, I had only one real father and he was the man in the picture.

Mom said, "Glenn, you're old enough to realize that a lady needs a husband. Your father has been dead for six and a half years. I was all alone. Now I have somebody to love me. Mr. Knott is my husband and the sooner you accept that the better off we'll all be!"

And she had frown marks between her eyes.

That night the babysitter came over. Mom and Mr. Knott went to the movies. I was glad they were gone. I snuck into Mom's room and opened the top drawer of her dresser. I knew it would be there. I was right.

I took it out and looked at it. In the little bit of light from the hall, Dad's face was more alive than ever. His eyes looked right into mine and he told me exactly what to do.

That was five days ago. I'm out of that dark hole now. Things are fine again. It's just Mom and me, the way it's supposed to be.

Some cops came and talked to me after they took the body away. Mom was crying. "Don't worry," the biggest cop said to her. "They can't touch the boy. He's too young to know what he did."

Mom shook her head until her hair was flying and she said something I don't understand to the cop.

"That's exactly," she cried, "what they told me six and a half years ago!"

Thank You, Mr. Thurston

by Ed Dumonte

They all told me, "Mr. Thurston can help you." When I took my pictures to dealers or collectors or to other artists they all said, "See Mr. Thurston—he will know what to do."

But how could I? Alone and friendless in the city, I had no influence, no channel of communication, to a man of Mr. Thurston's stature and importance. I understand this now. But I wasted many weeks sitting in the anteroom of Mr. Thurston's office. Each morning I rolled up several of my best canvases and went to Mr. Thurston's office to wait.

"Mr. Thurston sees no one without an appointment," the

girl would tell me. Or "Mr. Thurston will be in conference all day."

All the mornings and all the afternoons of all the days I waited patiently, hopefully, and I never got so much as a glimpse of Mr. Thurston. At last my money ran out and I had to take my paintings into the streets again—to display on fences and trees.

But I didn't stop trying to get Mr. Thurston's attention. Everybody knows that an artist has no chance of getting a showing or any critical attention unless he can win the patronage of some great man. Perhaps, I reasoned, if I couldn't speak for my paintings, my paintings could speak for me.

Among my best works were scenes of the city, done soon after I arrived, while the city was still fresh and beautiful to me. One of my impressions was a skyline of vertical lines and planes done in shades of gray. Another, painted at the waterfront, interpreted the warehouses as cubes of dingy brown, the river as a parallelogram of polluted blue, the whole surmounted and spanned by arches of rust. These were two of the pictures I rolled into a tube and mailed to Mr. Thurston.

After a week my paintings were returned . . . unopened. Stuffed into the wrapping was a note: "Mr. Thurston does not examine unsolicited artwork."

I was almost angered by the note. But when I thought about it, I decided it was reasonable. Mr. Thurston was a great and influential man, his name on every tongue. He must receive thousands of requests for help every week, hundreds of paintings from daubers and Sunday artists. He could hardly be expected to give his valuable time to every unknown artist who called on him.

For a time I puzzled over ways and means of getting to see Mr. Thurston. My problem was solved, I thought, by a prosperous-looking gentleman who one afternoon stopped and examined my street display.

He liked my pictures. They showed depth and feeling, he said. Excellent composition, striking colors. When he asked why I didn't have a dealer to represent me or a gallery to hang my pictures, I told him, and he understood.

Although he had no influence himself, he said, he had a friend who would be most interested in seeing my work.

And he wrote me a letter of introduction to Mr. Thurston.

Was it to be that easy, then?

The next day I brushed my suit, applied a bit of black paint to my shoes, and with two paintings under my arm I went back to Mr. Thurston's office. I interrupted one of the familiar excuses to give the secretary my letter. She disappeared into the inner office, returned after a few moments, and handed the letter back to me.

"Mr. Thurston has asked me to tell you that he is acquainted with the writer of this letter, and that his personal distaste for the man is exceeded only by his abhorrence for his judgment of art. Under no circumstances would Mr. Thurston consider sponsoring a piece of work recommended by that man."

As she spoke I flushed with anger; but my anger changed, as I realized what had happened, to my embarrassment and shame. I had been duped, tricked by one of Mr. Thurston's enemies, cruelly used as a pawn in some hideous joke. I fled from the office and ran blindly back to my room.

I lay for hours on my cot, moaning with anguish as the consequences of what I had done became all too clear to me. Foolishly I had let my name be associated with a man whom Mr. Thurston despised, and forever afterward, though innocent of any offense, my name and my work would be attacked by Mr. Thurston as if I too were his enemy.

All that was left to me was to leave the city, leave my oils and brushes, leave my paintings for the janitor's boilers, and try to endure somehow the living-death of the world of non-art. But I was not yet free to go.

If I were ever to know peace I must find *some* way to apologize to Mr. Thurston. Not that he would accept it, for he was a great and important man, and I had offended him beyond endurance. And, too, there was so little I could do. A public apology from a nonentity has no significance. I would gladly have cut off my ear and sent it to him, but he would probably return the package unopened.

The answer came to me in a flash of inspiration. I would do a portrait of Mr. Thurston!—a portrait that would express more clearly than words the respect and admiration I felt for him. A portrait of feeling and sincerity beyond any doubt or question . . .

I immediately started to work, searching newspaper and

magazine files for pictures of Mr. Thurston, rereading his famous articles of criticism and opinion. From these fundamentals of likeness and character I made sketches—ten of fifteen sketches to capture the arch of an eyebrow or the shading of a cheekbone. Forty or fifty sketches to find the proper angle of the head and express the character of the chin. Hundreds of sketches to re-create for all the world to see the soul of this great and influential man.

At last I was satisfied with the sketches, and then slowly, painstakingly, I began to commit to canvas the image I had conceived. For days, without food or rest, I fought with mass and color to put a living man into oil—the massive brow illuminated from within by a brilliant intelligence, the eyes that saw beneath the flat surface of canvas to the heart and soul that gave a painting life, the thin lip that curved into an almost cruel disdain for shoddiness or incompetence, the sweeping line of jaw and chin that bespoke the sensitivity of a true critic and connoisseur . . .

When the painting was finished, I carried it to Mr. Thurston's office and left it propped against a chair. Then, wrung dry by exhaustion and the passion of my work, I returned to my room and collapsed into unconsciousness.

I don't know how much later it was or how it came about, but my next memory is of Mr. Thurston himself standing over me, shaking the portrait in my face and shouting at me.

"I am accustomed to being hounded by every inconsequential dauber in the city," he said. "If you have been the most persistent, I reasoned that it must be because you were the least talented. When I found this—this atrocity—in my anteroom I saw that I was right.

"I do not make a practice of offering constructive criticism for every smear of paint I see. But since to do so in your case may save me the further annoyance of being exposed to your work, I shall make this exception. My critical opinion is: stop painting! If you must paint, study under the proper teachers and you may one day be capable of designing wallpaper. You will certainly never rise above that level.

"Use your eyes and whatever sense you may have and you will see the truth of what I say. Compare this—this portrait!—with its subject, for example. Do the frontal lobes of my brain really peep through a gap in my forehead? Do my eyes indeed dangle out of their sockets? Have I somehow missed seeing in my mirror what is apparently a third eye? Are the bones of my jaw as badly broken and dislocated as this—this execrable—this heinous—this shocking—"

Mr. Thurston went on. And on and on. But I was no longer capable of understanding what he said. The very core and fiber of my being had been torn apart and shredded, as by some mighty internal explosion. With excruciating pain and blinding light the truth of all that Mr. Thurston said burst upon me.

It was futile to try to express thoughts and emotions with abstract forms, as I had been doing. My pictures had to look like the objects they represented. It was really so simple . . .

It goes without saying that it was Mr. Thurston's wise and generous criticism that made my paintings the success they are today. A reporter was with the policemen who broke open the door of my room and his newspaper printed photographs of Mr. Thurston lying beside his portrait. Other reporters, too, were kind in describing the likeness as "uncanny," "startling," "an incredible similarity." Art dealers and collectors have been clamoring for more of my work ever since.

Unfortunately the light here is bad and I am kept too busy shuttling between the courtroom and the doctor's examinations to continue my painting. So the portrait of Mr. Thurston will probably be my last painting. That's the opinion of the lawyer assigned to me by the judge; he believes I have only another six weeks or two months left, and I'm too exhausted to complete a major work in that time.

But that's all right. The portrait is my masterpiece.

Thank you, Mr. Thurston.

Funeral Music

by Francis M. Nevins, Jr.

As he wrote the confession he could hear the laughter of children playing in a distant meadow.

Hydrangea bushes, deep blue and soft white, swayed in the light summer breeze outside the study windows. He bent over the steel typing table and tapped out the confession with slow precision, using only the middle finger of his right hand. From the stereo speakers mounted on wall brackets above the desk came the softly haunting strains of the Baudelin *String Suite No. 2* as the words slowly filled the sheets of cream bond paper under the printed heading: H. JOSHUA HAWES.

"Before I take my life I must write this. Paul Baudelin's second wife did not die by her own hand but by mine.

"I will not repeat at length what I established in my book, *The Life and Music of Baudelin,* and what has been confirmed for me each day of the seven years I have lived with the Master as his business manager, biographer, and shield against the blows of everyday existence. Before his first marriage he was simply one of many competent young composers in a milieu dominated by his betters—Stravinsky, Shostakovich, Hindemith, Poulenc, Milhaud.

"Then in 1947 he met Claudette and within hours he was savagely, passionately in love. And on their honeymoon in Spain that winter occurred that famous freak accident in contemporary music history—the sudden collapse of a decaying and condemned building as she happened to be walking along the street, so that within moments Mme. Claudette Baudelin was crushed beneath tons of rubble, and Baudelin, who had been so full of the joy of love, was desolate.

"It was the shadow of that lost love, snatched away by sudden blind chance, that filled, one might almost say obsessed, his music from that day, and lent to his compositions a fullness and poignancy, a sense of the merciless randomness of the universe. It is to the fate of Claudette that we owe the four great Symphonies, the second Suite for Strings, the cycle of Death Songs—all the major works of Baudelin's second period which established him as the foremost French composer of the generation.

"And then last year he fell in love again. He was in New York City to conduct the Philharmonic in his Third Symphony. Elana Nassour was second violinist, and her musicianship was superb. It was her rendition of the sublimely difficult passage at the end of the *lento* movement that first stirred his heart, Baudelin told me. The night after the performances of the Symphony they slept in each other's arms.

"Suddenly he was like a boy of eighteen again, this fifty-year-old titan of world music. The universe revolved around Elana and he was soaringly happy. The sense of unutterable loss that was the hallmark of his second period vanished. He almost ceased composing, and what little he wrote was no longer worth hearing. I couldn't stand to see that happen. I loved his work too much.

"And so, four months after they were married—I allowed him that much time of happiness—I mixed an overdose of sleeping pills into the thick Turkish coffee she drank each night before bed.

"I was both careful and lucky. There has been much speculation whether her death was accident or suicide, but no suggestion of murder. And in the year since her death, out of his grief at the loss of her, Baudelin has begun to compose great work again. If she had lived, the Fifth Symphony and the tone poem *La Mort de Dieu* would never have been. That is my justification.

"But it is not enough. I have come to see that no work of art is worth a human life, not even a masterpiece by Baudelin. I have committed a great wrong which can be expiated in only one way. And so I shall go upstairs and take the revolver from my night table drawer and place the barrel in my mouth and squeeze the trigger.

"Baudelin, old friend and benefactor, do not curse my memory, I beg you."

The string suite on the stereo came to an end, and the record player shut itself off with a sharp click. He tugged the third sheet of paper out of the typewriter—it began with the words "can be expiated"—and reread the confession with infinite care.

When he was satisfied he swiveled to the oak desk and placed the final sheet of cream bond on the blotter, above the last page of a signed copy of the management contract between Paul Baudelin and H. Joshua Hawes.

And then Baudelin picked up one of the felt-tipped pens with which Hawes customarily wrote, and boldly traced the signature of H. Joshua Hawes at the end of the suicide note, deliberately permitting variations, remembering that no two signatures by the same person are ever exactly the same.

When he compared the result with Hawes's genuine signature, he gave a little gasp of delight: the forged signature, he was sure, would deceive an expert. He put the contract away in a drawer, slipped the protective lid over the typewriter, and fastened the sheets of the confession together with a paper clip. He then crossed the rooms of the spacious Connecticut farmhouse they had rented for the season.

The perfect murder, he reflected, is not so difficult after all; in fact it requires far less skill than the composition of a symphony. He sprang up the staircase two steps at a time and slipped into Hawes's room without knocking.

His manager-biographer-buffer was sprawled in a wing chair with his huge belly bulging beneath his scarlet dressing gown and his slippered feet resting on the edge of the bed. On the little teakwood table beside the chair there was a water tumbler half full of thick apricot brandy. A bright-jacketed detective novel lay open on Hawes's lap.

Baudelin sauntered casually across the room until he was within one step of the night table where he knew Hawes kept his revolver.

"What's up?" Hawes glanced up half irritated and spoke in a foggy mutter.

Touching only the end of the paperclip, not the papers themselves, Baudelin set the three sheets of the suicide note on top of the book on the other's ample lap. "You might find this document more interesting than the detective story."

As Hawes began reading, Baudelin backed toward the night table and eased the drawer open noiselessly, but kept his eyes fixed on Hawes as his fingers hunted for the weapon. First the musicologist's mouth puckered in a whistle of amusement; then as he read more and more of the confession his face seemed to turn paste-white and his thick lips trembled in sudden terror. At the moment Hawes saw the forgery of his own signature on the last page, Baudelin snatched the revolver out of the drawer and pointed it at the other. Hawes's mouth fell open in fright and disbelief.

"Wider, please." Baudelin smiled bleakly and curled his finger around the cool metal of the trigger.

And suddenly H. Joshua Hawes began to roar with laughter. Great uncontrollable waves of mirth shook his huge frame and he rocked back and forth in the wing chair as if the revolver barrel were the most outrageously funny joke in the world. He groped blindly for the tumbler of apricot brandy, lifted the glass toward Baudelin like a salute, and gulped the drink down in a single swallow.

"Oh," he mumbled, his face dripping with sweat. "What a scheme, what an absolute love of a scheme! You were right, you know. Much better than this novel."

Baudelin was laughing too, but more quietly. He returned the revolver to the night table and shut the drawer tight. "I imitated your writing style well, no? Just the right touch of the pompous and the artificially dramatic." He was delighted at the way Hawes bit down on his lower lip at his touch of criticism. "And not only your style did I capture, but your typing touch as well! You are a trained ten-finger typist, so to match your even touch on the keyboard I typed the entire confession with my one finger."

"Clever of you," Hawes admitted. "I missed that. But you did make one very bad mistake." He folded his arms in a gesture of patronizing superiority.

Baudelin lifted his graying brows in disbelief. "And what might that be?"

"The note's too damn *long*. No one would believe it was really written by someone who was about to kill himself. It rakes up too much past history. You wrote that confession as if there were a huge audience of readers out there who'd never heard of you or Claudette or Elana, so you had to tell them everything they needed to know to follow the story. That isn't the way anyone would write a suicide note."

The composer shook his head right and left. "I disagree with you most profoundly. You are a former music critic for a newspaper, so your instinct is always to write so that the great audience can follow what you are saying. Besides, my friend, your style *is* long-winded, even when you write about me."

Hawes lifted himself out of the wing chair, crossed to Baudelin, and kissed him lightly on each cheek like a French dignitary awarding a medal. "I won't argue it any further. Round Number Thirteen—this is the thirteenth round, isn't it?—goes to you. I can afford to give you one round, I think. The score is now nine to four in my favor, if I'm not mistaken?"

"Nine to four," Baudelin conceded. "But you were always a good manipulator, you know, while I am simply a guileless old naif who scribbles funny marks on music paper. Should I not have what you call a handicap?"

"You old fraud," Hawes chuckled, "you're as devious as I am any day and you know it, and just as adept at the game of plotting against me as I am at plotting against you. So no handicap. The first to take eleven rounds is the winner. I'll make my move within our usual week's time, and I warn you now that I plan to do something especially fiendish to repay you for this clever one."

"As you please." Baudelin shrugged. "Then I leave you to hatch your scheme in peace." With two fingertips he retrieved the confession he had drafted and silently left the room.

He could not restrain his excitement as he descended the stairs. It had worked! The look on Hawes's face as he read the confession had betrayed him. He had never seen such a look of terrified guilt in his life. It had been the sudden numbed panic of a person with a monstrous secret who without warning and beyond human expectation has been exposed. There was no other way of interpreting Hawes's reaction.

True, he had recovered quickly, but not quickly enough. H. Joshua Hawes had murdered Elana in the manner and for the reason Baudelin had written in the confession. His face had given him away, as Baudelin had been praying it would when he set this trap. What was it Hamlet had said? "The play's the thing wherein I'll catch the conscience of the king?"

He was not sure when he had begun to suspect—four months ago, perhaps five. He had never believed his adorable Elana could have killed herself, without explanation, without leaving a note or even a hint. And he could not accept that she had died by accident, for in that case he himself must be some kind of accursed creature, whom no woman could love without paying with her life. And so her death had to be murder, and the only person who lived with them, the only one who could have put the sleeping pills into her Turkish coffee, was Hawes.

Like an evil god Hawes had been manipulating Baudelin's life for seven years, managing his business affairs, publishing interpretations of his music, taping their conversations for use in his books—in the maze of the musical milieu Hawes was the researcher, and Baudelin the experimental rat. He had wanted Baudelin to continue the doom-haunted works of the second period, and so Elana had to die. The only difference between the typed confession and reality was that, in fact, Hawes felt no remorse at all.

Baudelin knew he could prove none of this in a court of law, that there was no way he could make that stare of blubbering terror reappear on Hawes's face for the benefit of a judge and jury. But he didn't need a judge and jury for what he intended to do.

In the study, as sunset turned the distant hills violet and orange, he reread the confession. When he had reassured himself, he swiveled to the steel typewriter table and fed a fresh sheet of cream bond into the carriage and rewrote the third page.

". . . can be expiated in only one way. And so I shall go to the liquor cabinet and pour myself a final snifter of apricot brandy, mixed with an overdose of sleeping pills. It is at least a fitting way to die.

"Baudelin, old friend and benefactor, do not curse my memory, I beg you."

He forged Hawes's signature again at the end of the

confession which now was conveniently marked with Hawes's fingerprints, and put the three sheets away in a desk drawer beneath a sheaf of sketches for a concerto. Then he took the original third sheet into the downstairs bathroom, tore the sheet into tiny bits, flushed them down the toilet, took the bottle of sleeping pills out of the medicine cabinet, brought it into the kitchen where he crushed the tablets to powder, and poured the powder into the decanter of apricot brandy. When he was finished he replaced each thing where he had found it, cleaned his work space carefully, and went back to the study to wait for the sounds of Hawes stumbling downstairs to refill his glass.

Somewhere in a distant meadow he could still hear the laughter of children playing.

Murder Will Out

by Edward Wellen

VICTIM: Here he comes, oozing crocodile tears. Could I but throw off this illness and grow pert once more, they would be real tears. Still, he will weep sincerely when he finds the vaults bare. I have spent all to buy future life. But now my heart is faint, my belly writhes, my hands clutch at the sheet as if it were the thread of life, and all my members fall to trembling. My throat is choke-full of dust. This is the taste of death.

MURDERER: *Now he dies. The sun will not sink below the horizon, I think, before he is gone and all falls to me. But I must show grief even as I rejoice in my heart. Wealth and mastery are now mine, and I will ram through great works and far outbuild him. Set your mind at rest, I keep telling myself: for the tomb will mask it. What I have done will remain forever hidden.*

DETECTIVE: Ha! Then I'm right. The state of the mucous lining and a rough chemical analysis of the skin confirm my hunch. Later I'll hike over to the lab for more conclusive tests. But I can tell you now how you met your end. Someone fed you arsenic. Unfortunately, it's a bit late for an official autopsy report in your case, you poor old bundle of rags, you poor old mummy.

An Insignificant Crime

by Maxine O'Callaghan

When the shop bell rang, I looked up from the account books and groaned. I had enough trouble managing the old man lately without that woman coming around to ruin things completely.

He watched her grimly, his mouth thinned to a tight, self-righteous line—judge, jury, and executioner. I closed the books and hurried to the end of the counter.

"Father, please," I said.

"Please, nothing. I meant what I said. If that woman steals something today, I'll turn her over to the authorities."

I kept my voice low, but his was rising in agitation. "Let's go back into the office and talk," I urged quietly. A glassed-in area lay directly behind the counter where it was possible to work and watch the aisles at the same time. He hung back stubbornly, but I coaxed him in and closed the door.

"There's no reason to discuss it," he said.

"There's every reason. Her father has a lot of influence in this town. If you think you can humiliate him without reprisal, you're dangerously mistaken. If she takes something, why can't you simply charge it to his account as you've done in the past?"

"Because it's wrong, that's why. I've compromised my principles long enough."

I began to sweat. The room was oppressively hot, but that was only partly the reason. I was shaking with inner rage. The old fool couldn't see beyond the end of his thin quivering nose. He would sacrifice the business and our future, his daughter's and mine, and feel smugly sanctimonious. And for what? An insignificant little crime that would hurt nobody.

"You mustn't judge the poor woman," I said, trying to think of a way to avoid the clash that was sure to come. "Her father says it's a sickness."

"Rubbish. She's a thief, and worse, she makes no attempt to hide it." His jaw set obstinately. There was not a drop of perspiration on that cold forehead. "I tell you I have my principles, though your generation wouldn't understand that. All you value is the dollar."

You should talk, I thought grimly. I've worked for him long enough to know how he cheats his customers. Nothing big or obvious—just a niggling penny here and there or merchandise a bit substandard. My one comfort was that he could not live forever. My wife was his only child, born late. If I hung on, the store would eventually be mine—a starting point for the ideas and plans that churned impatiently inside my head. I couldn't allow him to throw everything away because of his single-minded morality.

He kept watch like a hangman waiting on the scaffold, but I began to feel a little hope. She walked up and down the aisles fingering things and dropping them back in the bins. Perhaps the whole thing would blow over. She didn't *always* steal. It's the weather, I told myself. For weeks the heat had clamped down like the lid on a boiling pot, shredding nerves and stroking tempers. Go away, I pleaded silently; make your purchase and get out of here.

It was too late for prayers. Her plump fingers had chosen their prize for the day, bold as brass. The old man sucked in his breath sharply and prepared to charge out of the office, but I grabbed him.

"I won't let you do this," I said.

"You can't stop me." He tried to shake me off, but I hung on tenaciously. "This is my store. I know you're waiting anxiously for me to die so you can get your hands on it, but at present I am very much alive and I'll do as I please."

"Go ahead then," I said recklessly, "but listen carefully. If you do this, I'm leaving. You spend a lot of time belittling me, but you're not a stupid man. You're crafty enough to recognize the amount of work I put into this store. The truth is, you can no longer handle the business alone."

"Don't be ridiculous," he snapped, but he hesitated.

"I have another opportunity." It was a blatant lie, but I was desperate. "I'll take it tomorrow. You'll lose not only my help but your daughter and grandson as well."

He licked his lips, but I could read nothing in those hooded, fish-gray eyes. It took every ounce of my will power to fold my arms and lean casually against a desk, to pretend I could breathe the hot soggy air.

"Well," I said. "Exactly how much are your principles worth to you?"

He didn't answer, just turned his back on me and went out to the counter where the woman waited with a few pennies' worth of nails to legitimatize her visit. I thought his walk seemed slower than usual and his shoulders drooped, but I couldn't be certain. I followed him with my heart thudding painfully against my ribs, convinced that I had made a ghastly mistake and ruined my future.

He accepted payment without a word or a look at her large shopping basket where the hatchet handle was plainly visible. He even managed a stiff nod and a "Good afternoon, Miss Lizzie," while I breathed a shaky, victorious sigh and made a note to charge the stolen ax to Mr. Borden's account.

The Stray Bullet

by Gary Brandner

There were plenty of empty stools in Leo's, it being the Monday after Easter, but the kid followed Hickman all the way to the end of the bar and sat down next to him. Normally, Hickman would not have minded having company, but on this Monday evening he was tired and would have preferred to sit alone.

The kid looked to be about twenty-two or twenty-three, and he needed a shave. Hickman shifted his stool a fraction of an inch farther away and concentrated on the glassy stare of the deer's head mounted behind the bar.

"Quiet night," the kid said.

"Yeah," Hickman grunted. He motioned to the bartender who was pulling on a red vest. "One of the usual, Leo."

The bartender dropped ice cubes into a squat glass and poured whiskey over them. He set the drink in front of Hickman and turned to the kid.

"What'll it be?"

"I'll have a glass of beer," the kid said.

"How about a sandwich, Mr. Hickman?" the bartender asked while he filled a glass from the beer tap.

"No, thanks, Leo. I'm trying to lose a few pounds."

The bartender patted his own stomach. "That's what I ought to do, but I'd rather be fat and happy than thin and miserable. As long as the girls don't complain, right?"

"Sure," said Hickman.

Leo picked up the money for the drinks and went down the bar to ring it up.

"This is my first trip to Los Angeles," the kid said. "I'm from Oregon."

"Nice state," Hickman said. "Green. Rains a lot, though."

The kid leaned over and peered intently into Hickman's face. "Look, do you mind if I tell you a story? I have to tell it to somebody all the way through just one time. If you're a hunter it should interest you. It's a story about a stray bullet."

Hickman studied the kid for a few moments. He was thin, almost frail, under the too-heavy checkered jacket. He had an unruly shock of brown hair and was overdue for a shave. His eyes had a pinched, hurting look.

"Okay," Hickman said, "Let's hear it."

The kid signaled for Leo to bring each of them another drink, and began to speak in a tight voice.

"My name is Wesley Mize. Last September I was married in Portland to a girl named Judy who I knew ever since we were in grade school. She was blonde and cute with sky-blue eyes the size of half dollars.

"For our honeymoon I took a week off from my job in a sporting goods store. We planned to just drive around our own state. On the second day we were headed out Highway 58 east of Eugene when Judy spotted an old logging road leading off into the woods. She was sure there would be wild blackberries, which she loved, up that way, so I turned off the highway and drove as far as I could before the brush got too thick.

"We got out of the car and, sure enough, wild blackberries were everywhere. Judy laughed and danced around like a little girl. She got a plastic bucket out of the car and ran ahead of me to fill it up with the berries.

She went running up on top of a little rise then, and she turned to wave for me to come on. She said, 'Hurry, Wes, come see what I found.'

"I started up to where she was waiting for me, but I never did see what she found. Just as I got to the rise where she was standing, a bullet went through her head and killed my wife of two days."

"Hey, that's terrible," Hickman said, feeling that he should say something.

"I just about went crazy," the kid went on. "I never heard the shot that killed her, but then there were three more in quick succession. I didn't see where they hit. I just started running at the sound like I was chasing the devil. My foot got caught in some roots and I fell. It broke two bones in my right leg. Somehow, I don't know how, I must have crawled back to Judy's body, because that's where they found me in shock about six hours later. If a patrolman hadn't seen where our car turned off the highway and gone up to investigate, we might both still be there."

"That was lucky, anyway," Hickman said.

"Was it?" Wesley Mize let the question hang between them like smoke. "I spent the next five months in the hospital while they tried to fit my leg back together. There wasn't a single hour of those one hundred and forty-seven days that I didn't wish it was me who died instead of Judy."

"Couldn't the police tell anything about who fired the shots?"

"Not much. They knew it was a 30-06 deer rifle. An empty whiskey bottle was found where the shots came from. They guessed the guy was shooting at an old sign-post where the logging road turned off. Just having a little target practice. He hit the post three times. His first shot was the stray that killed Judy. He never even knew he hit anybody. There was a screen of brush right there and you couldn't see to the road."

"That's really a tough break," Hickman said. "It's too bad you didn't at least get a look at the guy's car."

"Oh, but I did. I not only got a look at his car, I read the California license number, and I saw the man who did the shooting. I saw his fat drunken face as he threw the bottle out and drove away. He was weaving all over the road. Probably didn't remember a thing the next day. I was running after the car when I caught my foot and fell."

"Then why couldn't the police locate the man if you knew his license number and what he looked like?"

Wesley Mize stood up and wiped his mouth with a paper napkin. "I'll tell you the rest of the story when I get back," he said.

As the kid limped toward the Men's Room, Leo came over to Hickman and leaned on the bar.

"That guy's getting kind of loud," he said. "Is he giving you any trouble?"

"No, I think he's all right. He's all unstrung about

something that happened to his wife. I think he just wants to get the story off his chest."

"If he starts to get out of line give me the high sign. I heard him say he's from Oregon, and those people don't much like us Californians. For my money they can keep their state."

"It does rain a lot," said Hickman.

The kid came back and sat on his stool. Leo gave him a hard look and sidled away down the bar.

"The reason the police didn't catch the guy," the kid said, picking right up on his story, "is that I didn't tell them about seeing him."

"What would you do that for?" Hickman asked. "Didn't you want him punished?"

"That's exactly why I did it. I want him *punished,* not slapped on the wrist. As soft as the courts are these days, they would probably let him off with a suspended sentence. That man destroyed the most beautiful thing in my world. There is only one punishment for what he did. He's got to die.

"During those long months when I was in the hospital there was just one reason for me to live—so that I could come after the man who took my wife . . . and kill him."

"You mean you're going to try to find the guy yourself?"

"I mean I *have* found him. It was easy. I wrote to the California Department of Motor Vehicles and gave them the license number. They wrote back the name of the car's owner. It turned out he lives here in Los Angeles."

Hickman felt a sudden clutch of fear. "You have his address?"

"That's right. I went to his house today. I waited until I saw him come out to make sure he was the one, then I followed him right here to this very bar."

Hickman looked down and saw that the kid was holding a .45-caliber service automatic in his lap.

"Wait a minute, son," Hickman cried, "you're making a mistake!"

"No mistake," the kid said.

As their voices rose, Leo came hurrying up the bar. When he reached the spot across from the seated men, Wesley Mize raised the big pistol and shot him in the face. Leo was knocked back against the rows of bottles, then he pitched foward, smacking against the bar as he fell.

Hickman sat as though welded to the bar stool. Wesley Mize laid the automatic on the damp surface of the bar and pushed it toward him.

"I won't need this any more," the kid said. "The stray bullet is home now."

A Night Out with the Boys

by Elsin Ann Graffam

The lights were dim, so low I could hardly make out who was in the room with me. Annoyed, I picked my way to the center where the chairs were. The smoky air was as thick as my wife's perfume, and about as breathable.

I pulled a metal folding chair out and sat next to a man I didn't know. Squinting, I looked at every face in the room. Not one was familiar.

Adjusting my tie, the stupid, wide, garish tie Georgia had given me for Christmas, I stared at the glass ashtray in the hand of the man sitting next to me. The low-wattage lights were reflected in it, making, I thought, a rather interesting pattern. At least, it was more interesting than anything that had happened yet that evening.

I was a fool to have come, I thought, angry. When the letter came the week before, my wife had opened it.

"Look!" she'd said, handing me my opened mail. It was a small square of neatly printed white paper.

"It's from that nice man down the block. It's an invitation to a meeting of some sort. You'll have to go!"

"Go? Meeting?" I asked, taking off my overcoat and reaching for the letter.

"You are Invited," the paper read, "to the Annual Meeting of the Brierwood Men's Club, to be Held at the

Ram's Room at Earle's Restaurant, Sunday evening, January 8, at Eight o'clock."

It was signed, "Yours in Brotherhood, Glenn Reynolds."

"Oh, I don't know," I said. "I hardly know the guy. And I've never heard of that club."

"You're going!" Georgia rasped. "It's your chance to get in good with the neighbors. We've lived here two whole months and not a soul has dropped in to see us!"

"No wonder," I thought. "They've heard enough of your whining and complaining the times they've run into you at the supermarket."

"Maybe," I said, "people here are just reserved."

"Maybe people in the East just aren't as *friendly* as the people you knew back home," she said, sneering.

"Oh, Georgia, don't start that up again! We left, didn't we? I pulled up a lifetime of roots for you, didn't I?"

"Are you trying to tell me it was *my* fault?! Because if you *are,* Mr. Forty and Foolish, you've got another think coming! It was entirely your fault, and you're just lucky I didn't leave you over it!"

"All right, Georgia."

"Where would you be without Daddy's money, Mr. Fathead? Where would you be without me?"

"I'm sorry, Georgia. I'm just tired, that's all."

She gave a smug little smile and went on. "You *are* going," she nodded, making her dyed orange hair shake like an old mop. "Yes indeedly. You can wear your good dark brown suit and that new tie I gave you and . . ."

And she went on, planning my wardrobe, just as she'd planned every minute of my last fourteen years.

So the night of the eighth I was at the Annual Meeting of the Brierwood Men's Club. Totally disgusted. What crazy kind of club had a meeting annually? A service club? Fraternal organization? Once a year?

It was almost eight when the men stopped filing into the room. They were, with hardly an exception, a sad-looking lot. I mean, they looked *depressed.* A gathering of funeral directors? A club for people who had failed at suicide and were contemplating it again?

"I think this is all of us, men," Reynolds said, standing at the dais. "Yes. We can begin. Alphabetical order, as always. One minute."

A sad, tired-looking man in his fifties stood up and went to the platform.

"Harry Adams. She, she . . ."

He wiped his brow nervously and went on.

"This year has been the worst ever for me. You've seen her. She's so beautiful. I know you think I'm lucky. But I'm not, no, no. She's been after me every minute to buy her this, buy her that, so she can impress all the neighbors. I don't make enough money to be able to do this! But she threatened to leave me and take all I've got, which isn't all that much any longer, if I don't give in. So I took out a loan at the bank, told them it was for a new roof, bought her everything she wanted with the money. But it wasn't enough. She wants more. A full-length mink coat, a two-carat diamond ring. I'll have to go to another bank, get another loan for my roof. I'm running out of money, I'm running out of roofs . . ."

"One minute, Harry."

Dejected, the little man left the platform and another took his place.

"Browning. She invited her mother to live with us. The old dame moved in last April. I could hardly put up with my wife, but now I've got two of them. Whining, nagging—in stereo, yet. You can't imagine how it is, guys! I get home from work five minutes late, I've got two of them on my back. I forget my wife's birthday, my mother-in-law lets me have it. I forget my mother-in-law's birthday, my wife lets me have it."

He looked over at Reynolds, sitting on the platform.

"More?"

"Ten seconds, Joe."

"I just want to say I can't stand it at home any longer! I'm not a young man any longer! I—"

"Minute, Joe."

And it was another's turn. I sat there rigid with fascination. What a great idea! Once a year, get together to complain about the wife! Get it out of the system, let it all out! And to think I hadn't wanted to come!

Some guy named Dorman was on next. His wife had eaten herself up to two hundred and eighty pounds. And Flynn, his wife had gone to thirty doctors for her imagined ills. Herter, his wife refused to wear her false teeth around the house unless they had guests, and Klutz, his wife had wrecked his brand-new sports car three times in the year, down to Morgan, whose wife gave all of his comfortable old clothes to charity.

And then it was *my* turn. It wasn't, you understand, that I wanted to *impress* anybody—but to be able to actually say it, to tell the world what she'd done to me—heaven!

I took my place on the dais and looked at Reynolds.

"You can begin now," he said kindly.

"Freddie Nerf. Her name was Jennie and she was my secretary and she was twenty-three and I loved her more than anything else on earth and knew I always would and my wife who is cold like you wouldn't believe found out and told everybody on the west coast what I'd done and said we'd have to move thousands of miles away from 'that tramp', only Jennie wasn't a tramp and I'll never in my life see her again and I still love her so much and my wife keeps bringing the whole thing up and I try to forget because it hurts so much, but I know I'll never be able to, especially with my wife reminding me all the time."

"One minute, Fred."

"I CAN'T STAND MY WIFE!" I yelled into the microphone as I left the platform.

Never in my thirty-nine and three-quarter years had I felt so good. Almost laughing from the pure pleasure of getting it out of my system, I took my seat and half-listened to the others. Owens, whose wife told his kids he was a dummy, and Quenton, whose wife had gone back to college and thought she was smarter than he was, and Smith, whose wife slept until noon and made him do all the housework, all the way down to Zugay, whose wife made all of his clothes so he went out looking like a hold-over from the Depression. Which he certainly did.

One guy, who hadn't spoken, interested me. He was smiling. Actually sitting there with a big grin on his face. I was staring at him, wondering if I knew him, when Reynolds spoke.

"All right, men. Time to vote. George, hand out the paper and pencils, okay?"

"Vote?" I asked the man sitting next to me, whose wife hid his hairpiece when she didn't want him going out.

"Sure. Vote for the one who has the lousiest wife."

I scribbled down the name Freddie Nerf. After all, I did have the lousiest wife.

Glenn Reynolds collected the slips of paper and sorted them. In a few minutes he turned to face the men.

"For the first time, men" he said, "a new member has won. Fred Nerf. The one with the wife, you remember, who called his nice girlfriend a tramp."

I half-rose as he congratulated me, feeling somewhat foolish and yet proud. It was indeed an honor.

And then all of them, all the sad-faced, beaten-down men gathered around me and shook my hand. Some of them actually had tears in their eyes as they patted me on the back.

Later, as we all went to the lounge to have a drink before going home, I found Reynolds at the end of the bar and went over to him with my drink.

"This is some deal!" I said. "It really, *really* felt good to get it out of my system! Whose idea was this club?"

"Mine," he said. "We've met once a year for the last five years. I control the membership and I wanted you to be included this year. That wife of yours is really something, isn't she?"

"Yes," I agreed. "She sure is. How come you didn't speak? Because it's your club?"

"Oh, no. My wife passed away four years ago."

"I'm sorry," I said, feeling suddenly awkward. "That guy sitting over there, the one who's had the big smile on his face all evening, who the heck is he?"

"Gary McClellan? He's a plumber."

"Oh, *sure*. Say, didn't my wife tell me that McClellan's wife died last year in some sort of horrible accident?"

Reynolds smiled broadly and patted me on the arm. "Of *course*, old man! McClellan was *last* year's winner!"

Office Party

by Mary Bradford

Everett Willis left the main entrance of the industrial controls department at dusk after the Thanksgiving party at the office. He had hated being there, but it was the annual turkey-and-basket-of-cheer raffle and he had to oversee it. He had tried to stop the practice this year but everyone protested. Now the party was over—but the night wasn't.

It was sleeting a fine coat of ice on the vast parking lot for three hundred company cars. Everyone else had gone home. Willis stayed to the end to make sure no one had passed out behind the Xerox machine. It was always a little lonesome finding your car the only one left, he thought, and a little eerie. His car was parked in the middle of the lot.

But one thing had been a master stroke this night. He smiled to himself. And it was all wrapped up inside the small gray cardboard box he was carrying close to this side. The box contained the kickback payoffs from the shipping crew he had caught selling company goods after circumventing inventory records. The office party had been the perfect night to split the cash he knew they'd received that afternoon. Now he could meet his new car payments and the mounting credit card bills that snowballed in each month.

The sodium lights cast a strange pall over the lot as he hurried toward his car. He waved goodnight to the security guard as he passed by the old man whose head was bundled up in a scarf against the biting cold. It would be three-quarters of an hour before he got home where his wife was waiting dinner and his eldest son was waiting impatiently for the car.

His son would leave early, and after dinner his wife would

walk the two blocks to Walnut Lane to baby-sit for her sister for a few hours. His two younger children, as usual, would be glued to the TV set in the family room. Willis would put the money in the metal box in the locked cabinet above his tool bench in the basement.

He opened the door on the driver's side, placing the box carefully on the back seat. He started to slide into the seat when he noticed a large woman slumped on the passenger seat. Startled, he jumped back out.

"For God's sake, who are you? What are you doing here?

The woman pulled herself up to a sitting position. She had a wild, unkempt black hair and was wearing a green polyester pantsuit which she overflowered like molten lava. She had on a green parka jacket with a hood of ratty-like fur framing her face. She was very, very drunk. "You take me where I want to go or I'll scream. I'll scream that Everett Willis attacked me in the plant's parking lot, and the security guard'll come running."

"Who the hell are you?" he demanded, getting back into the car out of the hard-driving sleet and wind.

"Who am I? That's a good question. Whom am I?"

She turned full face toward Willis, who recoiled from the smell of cheap alcohol.

"I don't know who I am. But I know where I want to go. Mr. Boyd of marketing put me in this car. Mr. Boyd said you were a great guy and would see that I got home. That was not a nice thing to do," she broke out tearfully. "He should have taken me home himself, he should have. You take me to Mr. Boyd's house, and we'll tell him so, the two of us."

Willis swore under his breath—Stan Boyd, the office clown. He'd get even with Boyd if it was the last thing he did. My God, he thought, of all nights for this to happen. He had the box with him. He had to get it home. And now that clown, Boyd, had dumped this on him.

"Why didn't someone take you home? What happened?"

"We were having a party like yours in Building A, waiting for the raffle drawing, and some drinks were passed around. You know how it is at those parties. And they had the raffle and you know I never won anything in my whole life, not even when I was a kid, and you know what, Mr.

Willis of industrial controls? Yes, I know you. I read the employees' newsletter faithfully, *very faithfully.* You are in charge of shipping, you coach a Little League baseball team, you're on the industrial controls bowling team, and you're a Sunday school teacher. You have a wife and three children—one, two, three—and you have been with the company for ten years—one, two, three, four . . ."

Willis exploded. "Okay, you know all about me. What about you? I don't remember seeing you around, Miss, or is it Mrs.? What's your name and why did that clown, Boyd, bring you here?"

"I was telling you. I had never won anything in my whole life and you know what—I had to win that damn turkey! Now what the hell do I want with a twenty-pound turkey. I live alone. I don't need a twenty-pound turkey. I need . . ."

She tossed her head back and laughed. "You know I left that turkey on top of the file case and after this three-day holiday it will be a little ripe, don't you think so, Mr. Willis of industrial controls? Say, let's go get him. Let's go get Mr. Boyd of marketing. Now, let's go now. If you don't, I'll scream. You want to hear me? I can scream good and loud. I've had lots of practice."

Willis sat back in the seat and rubbed his face in his hands. He felt hot and his throat was dry. The sleet was coming down heavier, and the windshield was icing up. He started the car to defrost the windshield.

"No cabs," she said. "Don't go back and call me a cab. Take me to Boyd or I scream."

"I don't know where the s.o.b. lives! And I'm expected home by six o'clock!"

"I know where he lives. It's in Lakewood at the corner of Mulberry and Vine."

It was hot and oppressive in the car. The alcoholic fumes and the stale aroma of cheap perfume were overwhelming. God, what can I do, he wondered. I could take her up to the night watchman, but I don't want this to get around. No, it's up to me to take care of it. I'm the senior official. It's my responsibility. If I take her to Boyd's, it will embarrass his family. His wife and mine are good friends.

"Look, I'll take you to Boyd's. But you stay in the car. I'll do the talking. Is that understood?"

"Yeah, let's go to Boyd's." She had a self-satisfied smile on her face, and she sunk lower in the seat. Willis opened the window on the driver's side. The cold, biting air felt good against his hot, dry skin and the dryness of his throat.

"Remember, you stay in the car," he ordered.

She looked at him through half-closed eyes.

"You know, Mr. Willis of industrial controls, I'm a woman who was never meant to be a career woman. I liked being a dumb housewife. Yeah, you're looking at a liberated woman, Mr. Willis. I've got a lot to thank women's lib for. My husband liberated me. He didn't want to stand in the way of my development.

"That Boyd is a so-and-so. He had no right to put me in your car. I thought he was taking me home. I guess I got a wee bit drunk—or stoned—and I was slumped against the file case, and when he was closing up the place he found me. He was really swearing. He picked me up and brought me outside, and I thought he was going to take me home. That's what I thought, Mr. Willis. That he would take me home. But, instead, he put me in your car and drove off in his own. And that was not a nice thing to do, was it?"

Willis drove the streets of Lakewood through the northwest residential section. He came to the corner of Mulberry and Vine. It was an area of large, pleasant homes. Boyd's house was a two-story brick with green shutters and a two-garage. It was handsome and impressive.

Willis got out of the car. The sleet was coming down hard now, and he moved slowly across the slick flagstone walkway. The woman remained inside.

Boyd's wife came to the door and invited him in. "No," Willis said evenly, "if Stan could just come to the door, please. I have something to discuss with him."

Boyd wasn't home. Willis swore under his breath. What am I going to do now, he thought grimly as he returned to the car.

"Now what?" he said to the woman. "He's not home. Now, look, whoever you are. This is not my fault. I have nothing to do with this. I should be home right now, not driving around with a . . . I've got to take you home or someplace. Do you live in an apartment, a house? Just tell me. Do you have any friends you could go to?"

She sank farther down in the seat. "I'm gettin' cold. Let's stop at Marty's Coffee Shop and get some hot black coffee."

The coffee shop was empty except for two men at the counter sitting on stools. A young waitress slowly wiped off the table tops of the booths. Willis guided the woman into a booth where she wedged herself into the corner. She seemed to be a little more manageable. The drunkenness was wearing off a bit, he hoped fervently.

The waitress brought them mugs of hot black coffee. The woman sipped the coffee slowly, much to Willis' relief.

"Look, I've got to call home. I'll be right back," he said. The phone booth was at the front of the coffee shop. He saw the woman get up and go to the ladies' room at the back of the shop. He put the box of cash beside the telephone.

His wife's voice was frantic. "Where are you? What's happened?" She listened attentively and patiently, as he knew she would. He explained slowly and carefully all that had happened. She was understanding but apprehensive.

The woman was sitting in the booth when he came back from the phone. She had straightened up considerably. She seemed much younger. Her hair was combed, her face freshly made up, and the dark green print scarf at her neck was tied in a fashionable bow.

She lit a cigarette and looked evenly at Willis.

"I do a pretty convincing drunk, don't I? I've had enough practice. I can also be a salesclerk, a garden club president, a mother-in-law waiting for her kids to show up, and a new clerk in the accounting division of a large company. I'm one of twelve women in this state licensed to be a private investigator. I'm fifty-five years old, a grandmother, and being an old lady is no stumbling block in this work."

Willis' face had gone ashen white.

That box you have with you, Willis. Mr. Boyd and another company man are coming in the front door now. And if it's cash payments for all those company machines and supplies you and the shipping crew have been funneling off on the side, you'll have to explain it to them."

Her face was calm and serene—and smiling. Now she looked like what she really was—somebody's sweet old grandmother.

Comes the Dawn

by Michael Kurland

The sun was just sending its slanting rays over the mountains to the East, etching the pattern of the adobe rooftops into the walls of the buildings across the street, when the first daylight patrol of the *Guardias Municipales* found the twisted body of what had been a man lying in the dust. At first they thought it was just another looter. . . .

Civil insurrection, even in a country where it is almost the normal pattern of life, is always an ugly thing. Whether it is right or wrong, good or evil, necessary or irrelevant, it is the handmaiden of chaos. Looting, raping, fire, and death are always within its domain. Its borders spread, and are not sharp or distinct. Unconnected events are swept before it as flotsam before the ocean tide.

Manuel Hispoza Forgas had a brother. This brother's name was Philippe. Manuel did not like Philippe; a feeling which was reciprocated. These brothers lived in widely separate parts of the city and saw each other but seldom. Philippe's dislike for his brother remained fairly constant through the passing years, he preferred to just not ever think about Manuel. Manuel's feeling festered and grew into a supreme, blinding hatred; he could not help but think about Philippe constantly.

Philippe and Manuel shared jointly in their father's estate. Philippe prospered with his portion, establishing a small furniture shop which grew into a major store over the years. Manuel tended to try more speculative ventures: mostly at the racetrack and cockfight. As Philippe's fortunes rose, Manuel's fell; and Manuel's dislike of his brother increased.

It is incidental, perhaps, that Philippe married the very girl that Manuel, on afterthought, decided he would have liked to marry. It is predicatable that, of all the houses in the city, Manuel was most fond of the one in which Philippe happened to live.

Manuel's hatred of his brother drove him to thoughts of murder. Shooting, strangulation, poison, defenestration; murder by axe, knife, car; all these fancies and more took up a large part of his imagination. He planned accidental deaths, locked room murders, and murders of passion. He read detective stories, true crime books, and medical journals. He became cognizant of every famous killer from Cain to Torquemada, from Richard III to Lizzie Borden. That he restrained from committing that most horrible and fascinating of all crimes can be attributed only to one fact—Manuel's extreme cowardice. These famous murderers, Manuel would reflect when reading about Mrs. Simms or Doctor Crippen, became famous not because they committed murder, but because they got caught. Manuel didn't have a very high regard for the local police, but if there were the slightest chance—however small—of hanging for his crime, Manuel would keep it a secret dream.

The wonderful idea came to Manuel on the second day of the insurrection. On the evening of the third day he went to find Philippe to tell him about it. Philippe, who as usual was working late in his store after the clerks had gone home, let Manuel in when he knocked.

"You want something?" Philippe asked.

"Don't be unfriendly," Manuel replied. "I've come here this evening out of concern for you. The riots in this part of the city are horrible: looting, burning, killing."

"I'm touched that you have such concern for me," Philippe commented, and went back to his desk. "But you could have seen me at the house, I have to be leaving soon."

"Ah, yes. The curfew starts shortly, doesn't it?" Manuel asked.

"It does. And I don't want to have to spend the night here."

"If the riots start again tonight, aren't you afraid the store will be looted, or perhaps burned?"

"I should think that would please you," Philippe commented. "I think the *Guardias Municipales* have the situation well under control. Besides, I carry heavy insurance."

"Ah!" Manuel shrugged. "Insurance, of course." He sat down on the desk Philippe was working at, and leaned over Philippe. "Before you leave," he said, "I want to tell you of the brilliant idea I had yesterday. I've been thinking about it for two days, and it seems perfect. Perhaps you can find a flaw in it?"

Philippe threw down his pencil. "You're sitting right on the papers I've been trying to work on. I don't give a fig for your ideas—get up and get out of here!"

"Ah, but this idea concerns you," Manuel said. He took a large, heavy revolver from under his shirt, and pointed it at his brother.

Philippe jumped up, upsetting his chair. "What's this?" he demanded shrilly.

"A revolver," Manuel told him. "It's quite old, but I think it will work. I'm going to kill you with it."

Philippe straightened the chair, and sat down again: slowly, as though he were sitting on a case of eggs. "Kill me? You wish to kill me?"

"I've wished nothing else for many years."

"They'll hang you," Philippe said.

"I think not," Manuel answered. "And I've been thinking about it quite a lot. Let me explain."

"You're insane," Philippe said.

Manuel went on as if he hadn't heard. "The trouble, of course, is the police," he explained. "They find a body, and they start searching for a murderer. They check for clues; they try to find witnesses; they try to establish a motive. They slowly close their net until they find their killer. It is almost inevitable."

"Yes, yes. Inevitable. If you kill me, they will find you and hang you." Philippe pounced on the thought. "You don't want to be hanged. Now leave here, and we'll forget all about it. I promise you, I shall not say a—"

"The trick," Manuel went on, as if his brother had said nothing, "is to stop this process before it starts. And I've found a way. It came to me while I was listening to the radio. It's a clever idea, but very simple. What bodies do they find that do not cause them to search for a murderer?"

Philippe said nothing.

"I will tell you. Now, in this part of the city, during the riots, there is much looting going on at night. The *Guardias* shoot anyone they find looting. Such bodies are buried without question. If one of the bodies happens to be the owner of a store instead of a looter, a regrettable mistake has been made, and that is the end of it. You see how simple it is?"

Manuel took the revolver in both hands and pointed it at his brother's head. "Bang," he said.

"You're crazy," Philippe said, starting to shake uncontrollably.

"You see something wrong with the plan?" Manuel asked.

"They'll hang you."

"How are they going to catch me?"

Philippe did not answer.

"Turn around," Manuel said.

"What?"

"Turn around. I'm going to tie you up. When I hear some shooting, so I know the *Guardias* are out, I'm going to drag you outside. Then, bang! The *Guardias* never come up the street to see the looters they've shot until morning, for fear of ambush, so you'll lie there until daylight. Of course, I'll untie you before I leave. Regrettable accident. I shall cry when I hear the news."

Manuel tied and gagged his brother with rags that wouldn't leave marks, and continued sitting on the desk staring at Philippe. Philippe tried to meet his brother's stare with a defiant look. "Bang," Manuel said softly, and Philippe looked away.

Manuel took a thick, black cigar out of a box on the desk, and lit it with a wooden match from his pocket. "Would you also like a cigar?" he asked his brother politely. Philippe shook his head.

Time passed. Manuel lit another cigar from the stub of the first one, and then a third from the stub of the second. The street outside was dark and silent. Suddenly there was the sound of breaking glass, and then of running feet. A loud cracking sound was heard, and the feet stopped running.

"It's almost time," Manuel said.

From a few blocks away there were new noises, and then more gunshots. Soon the siren of a fire-engine filled the night with its wail.

"Time," Manuel announced. He dragged his brother to the door of the shop, and then outside to the slightly set-in doorway, and propped him up against the wall.

"Good-bye, Philippe."

Manuel took three steps away from the doorway, turned and raised his pistol as though he were engaged in a duel. He took a last, deep drag on the cigar, and . . .

At first they thought it was just another looter. "There he is," one of the *Guardias* said to his partner, "the one I shot at last night. I told you I saw a burning cigarette."

"Cigar," the second one said, looking down.

"Look over here," the first one called, "there's someone tied up in this doorway."

Acting Job

by Richard Deming

The man was tall and pale, with a wooden expression and hooded eyes. He would have been perfect in the movie role of Jack-the-Ripper. Myrna Calvert hesitated before letting him in, then seemed to decide it was silly to let his appearance bother her.

"Come in, Mr. Moore," she said coolly, stepping aside to let him go past her into the apartment and closing the door behind him.

He glanced around the actress' front room, approving its tasteful furnishings. When she invited him to sit, he gave his head a nearly imperceptible shake.

"I won't be here that long," he said, barely moving his lips.

"I'll just say what I have to say and leave. But first, I didn't quite tell you the truth over the phone."

The woman's green eyes narrowed. "You don't really have any life-or-death information for me?"

"Oh, that part was the truth. Only my name isn't Moore. I'm not going to tell you my real name."

Myrna's lovely features were marred by a frown. She studied him suspiciously.

He said, "Before I explain just what this is all about, I want you to know why I'm telling you. I've seen every play you've ever been in, Miss Calvert. I think you're the finest actress and the loveliest woman who ever walked on a stage."

Myrna's back stiffened. "If this is just some trick to get an autograph—"

"It isn't," he interrupted. "I just don't want you to be scared of me. You would be if I told you why I'm here before letting you know how I feel about you. I want you to know I wouldn't harm you for anything."

The actress looked surprised. "Why should you harm me?"

"It's my business," he said dryly. "I belong to an organization which disposes of people for a handsome fee."

Myrna's eyes gradually widened until they were enormous. In an incredulous tone she said, "You mean you've been hired to kill me?"

"My organization has. I've been assigned the job. I don't intend to do it."

After a period of shocked silence, she asked faintly, "Who wants me dead?"

The man raised his eyebrows. "I figured you'd know that. I was just given the job, not the reason."

Myrna paced to a sideboard, took a cigarette from a box and lit it. "Why have you risked telling me this, Mr. whatever-your-name-is? Won't your organization be angry with you?"

"I don't plan on them finding it out."

"Suppose I called the police and asked for protection? Wouldn't they know then?"

He shrugged. "You could probably get me killed, if you're that ungrateful. Are you?"

She studied him with an undecided expression on her face. "You're taking this risk just because you're a fan of mine?"

"A little more than that, Miss Calvert."

"Oh? What?"

"I've been in love with you for five years," he said quietly. "Don't let it upset you. It's from a distance and I never expected to meet you. I don't plan to bother you. When I walk out of here you'll never see me again. I just don't want you dead."

After contemplating him for a time, she said, "I'm flattered. And very lucky too, I suspect. You look like an efficient killer."

"I am," he said dryly.

She took a quick, nervous puff on her cigarette and stubbed it out. "You don't know any details of this plot?"

"There was a condition attached," he said. "I'm supposed to tail you. If you caught a plane for Europe tonight, I was supposed to forget it. If you didn't, I was supposed to move in and do the job."

Her nostrils flared. "Max Fenner!" she said.

"The theatrical producer?" he inquired.

She gave a jerky nod. "I knew he hated me, but I didn't think he'd go this far. He must be mad."

"What's his beef?"

"He's over a barrel," she said viciously. "I want the lead in his new play. He's already signed Lynn Jordan, and he knows she'll sue his pants off if he reneges on the contract. But I'm in a position to cause him even more trouble if he doesn't play ball."

He said, "I thought I read you were supposed to make some picture in France."

Myrna made an impatient gesture. "That's peanuts compared to the lead in *Make Believe*. Max knows I have no intention of catching that plane. I told him yesterday if he didn't bring around a contract by this evening, I'd talk to his wife."

He examined her curiously. "You're blackmailing him into giving you the part?"

"This is a cutthroat business, mister. You get to the top any way you can. Lynn Jordan signed her contract on Max's casting couch. I'm in a position to wreck his marriage if he doesn't break the contract and sign me. There isn't an actress on Broadway who wouldn't use that position in the same way I am. It isn't amoral, because there aren't any morals in the theatrical business."

He shrugged. "It's nothing to me. You ought to know something, though."

"What?"

"You're not off the hook just because I'm turning down the job. The organization will assign somebody else. And maybe he won't be a secret admirer."

Myrna paled a little. "They won't just forget it when you back out?"

He shook his head. "Not a chance."

"And if I ask for police protection, they might kill you?"

"Uh-huh. It wouldn't save you anyway. You'd get by tonight, maybe, but the cops can't guard you forever. They'd get to you eventually. I doubt that the cops would believe you anyway. They'd think it was a publicity stunt. And I'm not about to back up your story. Tipping you off is as far as I can afford to go."

Nervously she lit another cigarette, immediately punched it out again. "What do you think I ought to do?"

"You could save everybody trouble by catching that plane. I wouldn't even have to turn down the job if you did that. I could just report that you caught it."

"And miss the best part I ever had a chance at?"

He shrugged again. "My outfit is pretty efficient. You won't star in anything if you're in the morgue."

Myrna paced back and forth. "Suppose I hired you as a bodyguard?"

He gave her a bleak smile. "I might as well commit suicide. They'd just get both of us."

She stopped pacing, lifted another cigarette from the box, then dropped it back again without lighting it. "You don't think I have a chance?"

He gave his head a slow shake.

Biting her lip, she considered. "But if I catch that plane, nothing at all will happen?"

"That's right," he said tonelessly. "You make your picture in France without a care in the world."

"All right," she decided. "Tell your people I'm on my way to France."

His wooden expression momentarily relaxed into the barest suggestion of a relieved smile. "Thanks, Miss Calvert. That will keep both of us out of bad trouble."

When the tall, pale man entered Max Fenner's office, the fat, bald-headed producer eyed him worriedly.

"How'd it go, John?" he asked.

"Like shooting fish in a barrel," the pale man said, sinking into a chair. "She's catching the plane."

"She didn't suspect you were a phony?"

The pale man looked pained. "I told you I do the best gangster act in the business."

"Yeah, but are you sure she didn't recognize you?"

"Where would she see me? I've been ten years with the Cleveland Players. She doesn't even catch off-Broadway shows, let alone out-of-towners. I tell you she swallowed it hook, line, and sinker."

Max Fenner breathed a sigh of relief. "That's a load off my mind. If she'd ever played those tape recordings for my wife—" He paused to shudder. "John, if you ever carry on an affair with an ambitious actress, make sure her apartment isn't wired for sound."

"How could anybody blackmail me?" the character actor inquired. "I can't hand out parts in Broadway plays."

"I guess you wouldn't have the same problem," the producer agreed. "You're going to follow up by being at the airport to make sure she doesn't change her mind, aren't you?"

"Sure. You can phone me at my rooming house about nine P.M. I'll be back from the airport by then."

Max Fenner nodded. "I won't forget this, John. The minute you tell me she's on that plane, you've got a part in *Make Believe.*"

When the character actor came to the phone, Fenner asked, "Did she make it?"

"Yeah," Blake said. "She's gone. I told you there was nothing to worry about."

"Good job," Fenner said with relief. "Drop by tomorrow and we'll draw up your contract."

"What sort of message is it?" Fenner asked dubiously.

"I told you it has to be delivered personally," the man said in a patient tone. "May I come up?"

"All right," Fenner agreed. "You know the apartment?"

"Uh-huh. See you in five minutes, Mr. Fenner."

When the doorbell rang five minutes later, Fenner found a plump, middle-aged man standing in the hall. The man had a round, pleasant face and a deferential manner.

"Mr. Fenner?" he inquired.

"Yes. You're Howard Smith?"

The man nodded. Letting him in, Fenner closed the door behind him. Howard Smith glanced around the front room.

"You're alone?" he asked.

"Yes. What is this message?"

The plump man smiled. "Miss Calvert resented what you did to her today, Mr. Fenner. She was really quite frightened."

Fenner said coldly, "I don't know what you're talking about."

"Hiring a professional killer to work on her, Mr. Fenner. She wasn't sure whether the man actually was sincere when he said he couldn't kill her because he admired her so, or was merely subtly warning her that he would kill her if she didn't catch that plane. But she was too frightened to risk not catching it. I suppose you know she's on her way to France."

"You're saying nothing which makes sense to me, Mr. Smith," Fenner said in the same cold voice. "I haven't hired any professional killer."

"Of course you did, Mr. Fenner. But I won't press the point. What Miss Calvert wanted me to tell you was that she has contacts too. You've heard of Vince Pigoletti, I suppose?"

"The racketeer?"

Howard Smith nodded. "He's a great admirer of Miss Calvert. He is one of the numerous men with whom she has had—ah—romantic alliances, I understand. Mr. Pigoletti was kind enough to put her in touch with the organization I represent."

Fenner frowned. "What organization is that?"

"We don't advertise its name, Mr. Fenner. But it's a competitor of the one you engaged. Miss Calvert resented your action so much that she decided to retaliate in kind. Ordinarily we don't explain things like this, but she stipulated that she wanted you to understand exactly what was happening."

Fenner's face gradually paled. "I don't think I follow you," he said faintly.

"I think you do," the plump man said.

He drew a silenced revolver from beneath his coat. Staring at him in fascination, Max Fenner realized that this was no character actor.

Myrna Calvert had hired the real thing.

The Last Smile

by Henry Slesar

The arrogance went first. The clanging of the death-cell door drove it out of Finlay the first day. Then he turned sullen, uncooperative, his young face taking on the protective coloration of the cement block that lined his prison. He wouldn't eat, talk, or see the chaplain. He snarled at his own lawyer, muttered at the guards, and kept his own company. A week before the scheduled execution, he began to cry in his sleep. He was twenty-one years old, and with the aid of an accomplice, had mercilessly beaten and slain an aged storekeeper.

On the morning of the fifth day, he woke out of a nightmare in which he had been sentenced to die. Finding the dream sustained by reality, he began to scream and hurl himself against the steel bars. Two guards came into his cell and threatened him with mechanical restraints, but they failed to quiet him down. An hour later, the prison chaplain, a silver-haired, stocky man with the pained face of a colicky infant, looked in on him and said the same old things. This time, however, there was an air of pleading that made Finlay listen harder.

"Please," the chaplain whispered. "Be a good fellow and let me come in. It's important, really."

"What's important?" he said bitterly. "I don't want you praying over me."

"Please," the chaplain said in a curious, begging tone. The boy in the cell wondered at it, and wearily gave his permission. Once the chaplain had been admitted, however, he regretted the decision. The silver-haired man took a small black book from his pocket.

"No!" Finlay yelled. "None of that! I don't want no Bible reading!"

"Just look at it," the chaplain said, his face reddening. "Here, take a look."

Finlay took the small thick volume from the plump fingers. Outside the cell, a guard with a comfortable paunch stood profiled against the hall light. Finlay looked at the open page, marked *Revelation,* and then at the tiny slip of white paper that had been stuck into the binding of the book. The handwritten message read:

Trust me.

Finlay blinked at it rapidly, and then looked at the cherubic face of the man beside him. The round chin fitted the turnabout collar like an egg in an eggcup, and the expression on the baby features was impassive.

"Now can we talk?" the chaplain said cheerfully. "There's so little time, my son."

"Yes," Finlay said vaguely. "Listen, what's the—"

"Shush!" A chubby finger crossed the chaplain's lips. "Let us not speak any longer, son. Let us pray." He placed his palms together, and closed his eyes. Bewildered, Finlay mimicked him, and the chaplain droned on in a convincing monotone about salvation and redemption. When he was through, he beamed at the prisoner and took his leave.

Finlay didn't see the chaplain again until late that evening. This time, there wasn't any hesitation about admitting the chubby little man to his cell. As soon as he was inside, Finlay whispered hoarsely at him:

"Listen, I gotta know. Was it Willie sent you? Willie Parks?"

"Shush," the chaplain said nervously, looking at the strolling guard. "Let us not speak of earthly matters . . ."

"It *is* Willie," Finlay breathed. "I knew Willie wouldn't let me down." As the chaplain opened his little black book, he grinned and leaned back on the cot. "Go on, pal, I'm listening."

"The Bible tells us to have courage, my son," the chaplain said meaningfully. "The Bible tells us to keep faith in ourselves, our friends, and our Lord. Do you understand?"

"I understand," Finlay said.

That night, he slept well for the first time since his imprisonment. In the morning, he asked for the chaplain again, and the guard raised an eyebrow at the sudden conversion. When the little man arrived, Finlay smiled broadly at him and said: "What's the Bible say this morning, chaplain?"

"It speaks of hope," the chaplain said gravely. "Shall we read it together?"

"Sure, sure, whatever you say."

The chaplain read a lengthy passage, and Finlay began to stir restlessly. Then, just as he was about to explode with impatience, the chaplain handed the small book over, and Finlay saw the written message in the binding:

Everything's set.

The chaplain smiled at the prisoner, patted his shoulder, and called the guard.

On the beginning of what was officially his last day on earth, Finlay was visited by his attorney, a small man with a perennially moist upper lip. He had nothing to offer in the way of hope for commutation of the sentence, and Finlay gathered that his visit was merely to satisfy the contract. He seemed surprised by the condemned man's congeniality, a sharp contrast to the hostility he had shown before. In the afternoon, the prison warden came by and asked Finlay again if he cared to reveal the name of his accomplice in the murder of the storekeeper, but Finlay merely smiled and wanted to know if he could see the chaplain. The warden pursed his lips and sighed. At six that evening, the chaplain returned.

"How's it gonna work?" Finlay whispered to him. "Do I crash outa here, or—"

"Shush," the little man warned. "We must trust a Higher Power."

Finlay nodded, and then they read the Bible together.

At ten-thirty that night, two guards entered Finlay's cell and performed the ugly duties of shaving his head and slitting the cuffs of his trousers. The ceremony made him nervous, and he began to doubt that his escape was ordained. He started to rave and demanded to see the chaplain; the little man appeared hurriedly and talked to him in quiet, firm tones about faith and courage. As he spoke, he placed a folded slip of paper into the boy's hands; Finlay swiftly hid it under the blanket of his cot. When he was alone once more, he opened the note and read it. It said:

Last-minute escape

Finlay spent the rest of the time tearing the note into the tiniest possible shreds and spreading them around the floor of the cell.

At five minutes to eleven, they came for him. The two guards flanked him, and the warden took up the rear. The chaplain was permitted to walk beside him all the way to the green metal door at the end of the corridor. Just before they entered the room, with its silent audience of reporters and observers, the chaplain bent toward him and whispered:

"You'll be meeting Willie soon."

Finlay winked and allowed the guards to lead him to the chair. As they strapped him in, his features were calm. Before the hood was dropped over his face, he smiled.

After the execution, the warden asked to see the chaplain in his office.

"I suppose you heard about Finlay's accomplice, Willie Parks. He was shot and killed this afternoon."

"Yes, I did. Rest his poor soul."

"Strange, how Finlay took it all so calmly. He was a wild man before you started working on him. What did you do to that boy, chaplain?"

The chaplain put his fingertips together, his expression benign.

"I gave him hope," he said.

Grief Counselor

by Julie Smith

I started to give Sidney Castille my usual rappity-rap. "This is Jack Beatts," I said, "with the Grief Protection Unit of the county coroner's office . . ."

That was as far as I got before he hung up.

Sidney's wife, Dawn, had died two days before in a freak accident. He'd found her with a broken neck and her copy of *Vince Mattrone's 30-day Yoga Actualizing Plan* lying on the floor beside her. It was open to the section on headstands.

I'd called him because it was my job. After the death certificates are signed, they're sent to me or one of the other grief counsellors so we can get in touch with the victim's families.

As soon as Sidney hung up, I knew he was out of touch with his feelings. He was in the first phase of the grief cycle—what we psychologists call the stage of "disbelief and denial." He was refusing to deal with death.

That's normal and that's okay, but I wanted Sidney to know he had alternatives. I had things I could share with him. So I decided to pay him a visit.

I meditated a few minutes to get myself centered and then I drove my Volkswagen over to Sidney's house on Bay Laurel Lane. It was a typical northern California redwood house set back from the road in a grove of eucalyptus. Smoke was coming out of the chimney.

As I got closer, I could see the living room through sliding glass doors that opened onto a deck. Several cats prowled in the room like tigers in a forest. Dozens of plants hung from the ceiling and took up most of the floor space as well. There was nothing to sit on but oversized cushions.

On the far wall of the room was a fireplace with a pile of

books in front of it. A man was squatting there, burning the books, feeding them one by one into the fireplace.

"Sidney?" I said. "I'm Jack Beatts from . . ."

"Oh, yes, the man from the coroner's office."

He let me in and waved me to a cushion, but he didn't seem pleased about it. In fact, he went right back to feeding the fire.

"Sidney," I said, "I'm going to be up front with you. When you hung up, I sensed I'd better get over here right away."

"Yeah, that's what I thought. I guess I panicked when you said 'coroner's office.' "

"A lot of people are uptight about that. But I'm going to ask you to forget about the bureaucracy and just be open with me."

"I guess we may as well get it over with." He put a copy of *Zen Flesh, Zen Bones* in the fireplace and turned around to face me. A tear rolled down each cheek.

"That's it, Sidney," I said. "Flow with it. Experience your feelings."

"You talk like Dawn."

"I know how it is, Sidney. Everything reminds you of her, doesn't it? But that's okay at this stage. I don't want you to be negative about it."

"Negative!" he snorted. "What am I supposed to . . ."

"I'll bet those are Dawn's books you're burning." He nodded. "And it looks like you're about to take the cats to the pound. You're getting rid of everything that reminds you of Dawn, aren't you?"

Tears came into his eyes again. "I couldn't take it any more, Mr. Beatts. I never should have married her in the first place."

"I know where you're coming from, Sidney. You felt inadequate because you were a lot older than Dawn, right?"

"She was twenty-two," he said, "and looking for a Daddy. A rich daddy. And I was just lonely, I guess. I picked her up hitchhiking on my way out here from Ohio after my first wife died." He winced. "But *she* died of natural causes."

"Death *is* natural, Sidney. I mean life is a circle, you know? I want you to choose to recognize that. And if burning books is what's happening for you, I don't want you to feel guilty behind it. Just acknowledge that it's okay."

"Look, are you going to take me in or what?"

"Take you in? Oh, you mean to the Grief Center."

"Is *that* what they call it in California?"

"For sure. We can rap anywhere you like if the vibes are wrong here."

"What is a vibe, Mr. Beatts? If I heard Dawn use that word once I . . ."

"Now stay loose, Sidney. I hear what you're saying and I sense you're uptight behind it. You couldn't relate to Dawn's lifestyle, right?"

He began picking up cats and taking them to the carriers on the deck. I didn't want to blow the energy we had going, so I followed along beside him.

"She was all caught up in what they call the human potential movement," he said. "Transactional analysis, transcendental meditation, self-actualization, bioenergetics, biofeedback . . ."

"She must have been a heavy lady."

"She talked funny. Like you. And she cooked things like wheat germ soufflé. And she wanted the house to be 'natural.' You couldn't go to sleep without a cat curled around your neck, or a spider plant tickling your nose. It got so every time I saw her do that crazy yogurt . . ."

"Yoga."

He closed the last carrier and we went back into the house.

"I used to call it yogurt to annoy her," he said, squatting by the books again. "Anyway, when she started to stand on her head, she'd do it first with her feet against the wall and then she'd let go of the wall and stick her legs up in the air. Well, every time I saw her with her feet like that, getting little toeprints all over the paint, I'd think how easy it would be just to grab her and . . ." He stopped.

"And what?"

"And snap her neck."

I nearly clapped him on the back I was so relieved. At last he'd gotten his energy flowing in a positive way! "I have to acknowledge you, Sidney," I said. "It's really a far out thing to see someone being so open about his fantasies."

Sidney tried to speak, but he couldn't. He took out a handkerchief and blew his nose. Sometimes you have to hurt people to help them so I took a chance.

"You killed her, didn't you, Sidney?" I said.

He kept his eyes down as he put the handkerchief back in his pocket. "You knew all along," he said finally.

"For sure," I said supportively. "Self-recrimination is very common in the first stage of the grief cycle, and I want you to know that it's okay."

"Okay?" he said. "I don't understand."

"A lot of people get on that kind of trip when something like this happens. You and Dawn weren't getting along and you feel guilty about it now, right? You think she died because of something in your karma."

The way Sidney looked at me I could tell he was surprised. He didn't really expect anyone else to understand. He started to speak, but I stopped him.

"That's okay," I said. "You know? Because it's only the first part of the cycle. You know what's next? Personality reorganization! Sidney, you've got a really positive thing to look forward to."

Sidney sat down on one of the cushions and started to laugh. It doesn't happen often that somebody really flashes on the whole cycle like that, and it was a far out thing to see.

"Mr. Beatts," he said. "I don't remotely understand where you're coming from . . ."

"Don't try, man."

"But I think I can flow with it."

The Best Place

by A. F. Oreshnik

Dr. Jason Whitney saw the two federal agents enter the crowded restaurant. Their rumpled suits and stubble-covered cheeks betrayed the fact that they had been too busy to think of appearances for some time. They moved wearily toward him along the line of booths against the wall, looking for an empty one. When they reached the booth where the young doctor was sitting alone, he spoke to the agent he recognized, a deceptively soft-looking man in his forties.

"Hello, Tom. Have a seat." He indicated the place opposite him with a sweep of his hand. "There probably aren't any empty booths at this hour. A lot of people stop here for breakfast on their way to work."

Tom Campbell slid heavily into the booth and was followed by his look-alike companion. "I'd like you to meet my partner, Joe Moffet, Dr. . . . Dr. . . ." Campbell snapped his fingers, trying to dislodge the name from his memory.

"Whitney. Jason Whitney," the doctor offered with a smile, not the least offended at not being remembered.

"Yeah, that's right," Campbell acknowledged with a nod as Joe Moffet and the young doctor clasped hands briefly.

"You men look like you've had a hard night," the doctor said.

"You can say that again," Campbell answered. "We haven't been out of our clothes in two days. Just brought a man back from Spain."

"Extradition?"

Campbell gave a wry smile. "You could call it that. Our man was staying in Andorra, that little postage-stamp country on the border between Spain and France. They'd have let him stay there until his money ran out, which would've taken a couple of thousand years or so. We have no treaty with them."

"So what happened?"

"The usual. We pretended we'd lost interest in him and waited for him to get careless. When he made the mistake of taking a walk too close to the Spanish border, we were ready. Next thing he knew, Joe and I each had one of his arms and were marching him past the Spanish custom-house. We tossed him into a car and rushed him to a plane we had waiting at one of our bases. The Spanish authorities pretended they didn't see a thing."

"Seems like a lot of trouble and expense over just one man," Dr. Whitney said.

"It was Henry Hammond." Campbell had a touch of pride in his tone.

A waitress came to take their breakfast orders. As soon as she was gone, the doctor repeated the name. "Henry Hammond . . . It *does* sound a bit familiar. Should I know the name?"

"He's the big-shot financier who jumped bail and skipped the country a couple of years ago. He'd built himself an empire, using phony balance sheets and illegal manipulations. He got away with just about every nickel from his companies' treasuries."

"Oh, yes, now I remember. It made quite a splash in the papers at the time. What did you do with him?"

"Dropped him off at your place ten minutes ago," Campbell said.

The second agent, Joe Moffet, had been sitting quietly, but now he twisted his face into a puzzled expression and said, "Huh?"

Campbell turned to him. "The doctor is in charge of the infirmary at the Federal House of Detention on West Street," he explained. "He'll probably be giving our friend a physical examination today."

"I check all new prisoners," Dr. Whitney agreed.

The waitress returned with their orders. They didn't say much until they had settled back to enjoy their coffee. Then the conversation returned to Henry Hammond.

"Do you think he'll return the money he stole?" the doctor asked.

"That's something you'll have to ask Hammond. We couldn't get a word out of him all the way across the Atlantic. He probably has it safely stashed away in a couple of dozen Swiss banks. One thing's sure—no one will ever see it again unless he wants them to."

"I wonder what makes a man decide to be a criminal?" the doctor mused.

Campbell shrugged. "Who knows? People don't always do the things you'd expect, or fit into patterns the way you think they should. Take yourself, for instance. What's a bright young guy like you doing in the Public Health Service? There's no military draft anymore, so you didn't choose it as an alternative service the way doctors and dentists have in the past. I'll bet you could have had your pick of the private hospitals."

"Yes, I probably could have, but I'm happy where I am. I think it's the best place for me. If I didn't, I'd go somewhere else or do something else. That's the way you feel about your job, isn't it, Tom? That active police work is the best occupation for you?"

"You certainly have Tom figured out," Joe Moffet said. "And you put it into words better than he does, too. He's turned down two promotions in the last year. He could have a comfortable desk job in D.C., but he prefers to transport fugitives. Everyone thinks he's crazy, but he says he's happy where he is."

They exchanged small talk for a few more minutes, then left the restaurant together. They paused to say good-bye on the sidewalk outside, and Tom Campbell's face clouded with confusion and embarrassment. "I'm terribly sorry, Doctor, but I—uh—I've forgotten your name again."

Jason Whitney smiled. "That's all right. You'd be surprised how many people have trouble remembering me. The next time you're at the House of Detention stop by my office to say hello. I always have a pot of coffee on the hot plate." He turned to the other agent. "That goes for you, too, Mr. Moffet. Stop in any time. It's been nice meeting you."

Jason Whitney waited until ten that morning before

having Henry Hammond called to the infirmary. He chose that time because the morning sick call had been taken care of by then, and his assistants were enjoying a coffee break.

"Good morning, Mr. Hammond. I'm Dr. Whitney, the Chief Medical Officer here. I'm in charge of the health and physical well-being of you and the other prisoners. It's my job to examine each new arrival and determine whether or not he'll require treatment of any kind."

Hammond nodded his understanding. He had dark circles under his eyes and stood nervously in the doorway of the infirmary. He clenched and unclenched his right fist in an uneven rhythm, and his eyes swept back and forth, taking in all the cabinets and equipment. It was obvious his sudden arrest and transportation to the United States had been a severe shock.

"Step this way, please," Whitney said, leading the way to a side room.

Here there were bare white walls and the only furniture was an examination table for the patient. There was nothing that might prove distracting.

"Lie down, please. I'm going to take your blood pressure. I'm sure you've had it done before."

The doctor wrapped the instrument around Hammond's arm, and squeezed the bulb to pump air into it.

"Be as quiet as you can. I want the lowest reading possible. Relax as much as you can and try not to think of anything in particular."

Whitney busied himself with the instrument.

"Your reading is a bit high, Mr. Hammond. I think you're a little too tense. I you don't mind, I'll show you how to re-lax. Just close your eyes. That's right, close your eyes and relax the eyelids. I think you can get the feeling of complete relaxation if you'll follow my suggestions. Relax your eyelids completely. Now turn your attention to your arms. Let them become completely limp. Think of them as a pair of limp rags and when I lift them let them fall back to the table just as a couple of limp rags would. That's very good. Now we'll do the same with your legs. See, you're much more relaxed and at ease now.

"I'll just take your blood pressure again and see how well you've done. Oh, that's very good. That's very, very good.

You're far more relaxed than before. Let's try it again, Mr. Hammond, and this time keep your eyes closed all the while. That will aid the relaxation process.

"Okay, now, relax your eyes. Now your arms. Let them become as limp as rags. Now your legs. Relax them. Just relax your whole body. Let your whole body go limp. Let your whole body become heavy. Get completely comfortable. Now, if you are truly relaxed, you will find that your eyelids won't open. Relax your eyelids and body completely. When you feel you're completely relaxed you may try to open your eyes. If you are completely relaxed, they won't open. If you cannot open your eyes, you will be completely relaxed. That's fine. Now try to open your eyes. See—you cannot open them. You are completely, deeply relaxed and you cannot open your eyes. Your arms and legs are heavy and limp and you cannot lift or move them."

As quickly and easily as that, without once using the words sleep or hypnosis, Dr. Jason Whitney placed Henry Hammond into a deep trance.

In the next half hour he deepened the trance still further, then extracted from Hammond the code numbers and balances of ten secret bank accounts. Immediately before allowing the man to wake up, he directed Hammond to forget forever that the secret accounts had ever existed. "And you will never be able to remember my name," he told him.

That reminded Whitney of Agent Tom Campbell. When he had hypnotized Campbell a year before and instructed the man to keep him informed about criminals with hidden money, he had neglected to order him always to come to the restaurant alone. He would have to rectify that oversight at the first opportunity.

As Hammond left the infirmary to return to his cell, Dr. Whitney watched him walk away and felt a wave of satisfaction. This *was* the best place for him. He didn't have to work the long hours a hospital might have demanded, and he was collecting far, far more money in a single year than his professional hypnotist parents had earned in their lifetimes.

Dead End

by Alvin S. Fick

What a surprise it was to see Sweets yesterday—and not altogether a pleasant one.

By the time I got my chair turned around in the kitchen after I heard him knock and rolled through the arch into the living room, he had walked in.

It was just like Sweets to do that, just walk in. He stood there in the center of the room looking around, his pudgy face divided by a wide toothless grin that made his head look like a Bender melon split by a cleaver. Not a bad idea, that.

I had come back from a ride down to the Heron Valley overlook just before his car pulled up in front. "You've put on weight, Sweets," I said. I looked at the bulge above and below his narrow belt. He eased into a rocker facing the couch. Aside from my bed and a dresser, that's about all the furniture left in my house. When you live in a wheelchair, that's the first move you make—you get rid of all the road hazards.

"It's been near four years, old buddy," Sweets said. He shifted his weight in the rocker. It creaked in protest. I noticed that the pressure within had tested every fiber in his soiled chino pants. The stitching down the front had surrendered in the struggle and the zipper was exposed, a silver snake that caught the light from the west window. It was like Sweets to go around that way. My distaste for him spilled over into my voice.

"Don't 'old buddy' me, Sweets. What do you want? What are you after now, after all this time? I have nothing left."

"That ain't no way to talk to an old friend. Ain't I the one who told the boys they should build the ramps for you?

Ain't I the one who said you need a low counter in the kitchen for cooking and eating? Ain't I the one who hung those bars on chains in the bathroom so you could get in and out of the tub—take care of yourself?"

I couldn't help but mimic him. "Yeah, and ain't you the one that got careless setting off that dynamite charge in the quarry that put me in this chair for life?"

Sweets wriggled his button nose as if he smelled something bad. It twitched side to side, a pink crabapple adrift on a sea of bread dough.

"That was a accident. That was five years ago. You shouldn't oughta hold a grudge like that. Lord knows I wouldn't hurt a flea."

Wouldn't hurt a flea. When he was eleven, after having been punished by his father for beating his dog, Sweets had let a mean bull out of its stall into the barnyard. There it gored and killed the old man, who was patching a watering trough. Everybody thought the bull had broken the tie rope, but a few days later in school I heard him bragging how he had cut the rope and rubbed dirt on the frayed ends.

Wouldn't hurt a flea. I remembered how Sweets used to catch flies when we were kids in the one-room country school we both attended. He'd pull off their wings, then tie a thin thread to one leg.

"See my pet," he'd say. He would draw a blob of ink from the inkwell with his pen and wet the fly with it. Then he'd walk the fly across the paper on his desk, or on the nice white collar on the dress of the girl in front of him.

"Chinese writing," he used to say, and his laugh shook fat even then.

Why the girls took to him so, I never understood. But if I did not understand then, his success with women when he grew older was even more of a mystery to me. He'd had three wives—my Norah among them. His first, Charlene, fell from a boat and drowned when the two of them were fishing in Heron River. Ellie hung herself from a rafter tie in the attic of their house. I stopped taking the *Heron Falls Gazette* when I read Norah's obituary six months after she left me for Sweets. The story said she fell down the cellar stairs with a load of laundry in her arms and hit her head on a protruding rock in the fieldstone foundation.

Sweets. What a name. Did I tell you how he got it? His last name is Sharger, but the kids in school found it hard to say and seeing it was so close to the kitchen staple and how the girls loved him, they hung Sweets on him.

My life has always been tied to his in some way. My dislike for him, begun in boyhood, hardened into something deeper long before he hit the switch that sent a piece of rock into my spine, long before he took away my Norah. I never held anything against her for leaving half a man. The bitter part was her going to Sweets.

"You still in the quarry?" I said, desperate for any topic to get my mind off Norah.

"Yep." Sweets brightened. "Been foreman ever since Jeff Bellins died."

"Jeff's dead? He was younger than either of us."

"One of those things. An accident. You know better than most that stone quarries is dangerous places." He stared at my wasted legs.

"How did it happen?"

Sweets' voice turned slick and oily. "He was careless. I seen it all happen. He was standing by the big flat belt that drives the crusher. He must of leaned over to look at something and the belt caught his clothes—pulled him kerspang right into the pulley. Tore him up fierce. I was only a step away but I couldn't do anything for him. Poor guy. He yelled just once."

"How long ago was this? How did Debbie take it?" I remembered Jeff's slender little auburn-haired wife. She was nearly as pretty as Norah and ten years younger.

"Yes, Debbie. I felt terrible sorry for Debbie. Guess I understood better than most how lonely she was. Let's see, that was a couple of months after Norah passed on, and we both—me and Debbie—took to leanin' on each other. We had happy times together so we up and got married."

"Is she out in the car? Is she with you? I'd love to see her."

The corners of Sweets' mouth turned down and for a moment I thought I detected a hint of moisture in his eyes.

"I wish I could. Sure wish I could. But she took sick less than a month back. Got off her feed and just kind of pined away." Sweets seemed genuinely moved. "I buried her two weeks ago."

"I'm sorry to hear that, Sweets."

"Well, we got to go on living." His mood changed. "I just came over to see how you're getting on. It don't pay to lose touch with old friends. That's the way I've always felt about your family. A day or two ago I got to thinking on it, the way I haven't seen you in years. Then I got to wondering about your brother, Harry. He moved to California, didn't he?"

I nodded.

"And Hester, your younger sister, where is she now? I suppose she's off and married with a slew of kids."

"No, Hester isn't married. She's up in Augusta. She has a job with the state." The moment the words were out I wished my tongue had been paralyzed too.

"Say! I bet she's on Debbie's Christmas-card address list I threw out when I was cleaning her dresser this morning." He brushed away an imaginary tear. "I haven't burned that trash yet. When I get home I'll dig that list out and sit right down and write Hester a letter. Maybe I'll phone her. That would be nice."

My insides felt knotted and cold. I hoped he hadn't noticed the way I'd gripped the arms of the wheelchair.

He rambled on. "I ought to drop in on her someday just for old times' sake. She was just a pretty little snippet when we was getting out of school, but I bet she's a real lady now."

The fear in my belly was a coiled cold serpent. "Sweets, why don't you wait a day or two?" My mind raced in search for something to delay him. "I have some pictures of Hester taken when she and some of her girl friends were on a swimming party last summer." I struggled to keep my voice calm. "She's a real beauty."

Sweets heaved his bulk out of the chair. "Are they in your bedroom? I'll go and get them. What drawer are they in?"

I rolled my chair across his path.

"That's not necessary. I have them in a box somewhere in the closet. Tell you what. You come by tomorrow and I'll have them out to show you. We can call Sis on the phone from here. It will pave the way for your visit if I tell her you're coming to see her."

"Good!" Sweets rubbed his hands together. "I'll bet little Hester is a livin' doll." He gave me a good view of pink gums and a tip of tongue wetting his lips.

"And, Sweets, as long as you're coming over tomorrow, could you bring a load of wood in your pickup for my

Franklin stove? Do you still have the old pickup? It's getting toward fall and I could use some firewood." I added, "I just got my disability check. I'd pay you well for some wood."

He stood by the door with his hand on the knob. "Well, I don't know. The brakes ain't so good on the pickup."

Sweets paused while the cold coil in my belly turned slowly.

"I guess if I'm your friend I can haul a load of wood for you. After all, we're almost family." The quality of reeking old motor oil was back in his voice.

"Good, then. I'll see you tomorrow," I said to his back as he walked out the door.

As soon as he was gone, I rolled down the front ramp to the sidewalk and on out to the narrow blacktop road. I live around a bend on this dead-end highway, the last house on the road the town extended a quarter of a mile some years ago to a small picnic area. It's beside a scenic view that looks out over Heron Valley and the mountains beyond. I'm about the only person who goes there any more. Every day, weather permitting, I wheel down to the overlook, poking here and there among the grass and weeds with the stout walking stick I always carry across my lap. It's like an extension of my arms.

The seclusion and beauty of the place have been my joy, and the exercise has given me tremendous arm and shoulder development that makes getting around in the house easy. Even swinging on the bars in the bathroom seems like play to me.

The town paved a turn-around area at the end of the road and erected posts and crossbars around it. The dropoff at the ledge is perhaps six hundred feet. It's so abrupt no trees grow on its face to obscure the view. Grass and weeds grow in the cracks in the amesite. The wood posts are rotten at the base. They cracked ominously when I set the brakes on my wheelchair and pushed against them.

When I got back to the house I had a sandwich. A little later I drank a glass of scotch over ice before I went to bed. I slept well.

This morning I brought the bottle and a couple of glasses into the living room. I think Sweets and I should have a few drinks to celebrate our renewed friendship. Today I feel calm and at peace with my narrow world as I wait for

Sweets. Surely he'll be so happy at the prospect of seeing Hester that he won't mind giving me a ride in his truck down to the scenic overlook where we can admire the view across Heron Valley.

While I wait, I've been jamming my stick against the baseboard by the front door. I'm certain it's just the right length to reach a pickup gas pedal.

Pure Rotten

by John Lutz

May 25, 7:00 A.M. Telephone call to Clark Forthcue, Forthcue mansion, Long Island:

"Mr. Forthcue, don't talk, listen. Telephone calls can be traced easy, letters can't be. This will be the only telephone call and it will be short. We have your stepdaughter Imogene, who will be referred to in typed correspondence as Pure Rotten, a name that fits a ten-year-old spoiled rich brat like this one. For more information check the old rusty mailbox in front of the deserted Garver farm at the end of Wood Road near your property. Check it tonight. Check it every night. Tell the police or anyone else besides your wife about this and the kid dies. We'll know. We mean business."

Click.

Buzz.

Snatchers, Inc.
May 25

Dear Mr. Forthcue:

Re our previous discussion on Pure Rotten: It will cost you exactly one million dollars for the return of the merchandise unharmed. We have researched and we know this is well within your capabilities. End the agony you and your wife are going through. Give us your answer by letter. We will check the Garver mailbox sometime after ten tomorrow evening. Your letter had better be there.

Sincerely,
A. Snatcher

Snatchers, Inc.
May 26

Mr. Snatcher:
Do not harm Pure Rotten. I have not contacted the authorities and do not intend to do so. Mrs. Forthcue and I will follow your instructions faithfully. But your researchers have made an error. I do not know if one million dollars is within my capabilities and it will take me some time to find out. Be assured that you have my complete cooperation in this matter. Of course if some harm should come to Pure Rotten, this cooperation would abruptly cease.

Anxiously,
Clark Forthcue

Dear Mr. Forthcue:
Come off it. We know you can come up with the million. But in the interest of that cooperation you mentioned we are willing to come down to 750,000 dollars for the return of Pure Rotten. It will be a pleasure to get this item off our hands, *one way or the other*.

Determinedly,
A. Snatcher

Snatchers, Inc.
May 27

Dear Mr. Snatcher:
I write this letter in the quietude of my veranda, where for the first time in years it is tranquil enough for me to think clearly, so I trust I am dealing with this matter correctly. By lowering your original figure by twenty-five percent you have shown yourselves to be reasonable men, with whom an equally reasonable man might negotiate. Three quarters of a million is, as I am sure you are aware, a substantial sum of money. Even one in my position does not

raise that much on short notice without also raising a few eyebrows and some suspicion. Might you consider a lower sum?

Reasonably,
Clark Forthcue

Dear Mr. Forthcue:
Pure Rotten is a perishable item and a great inconvenience to store. In fact, live explosives might be a more manageable commodity for our company to handle. In light of this we accede to your request for a lower figure by dropping our fee to 500,000 dollars delivered immediately. This is our final figure. It would be easier, in fact a pleasure, for us to dispose of this commodity and do business elsewhere.

Still determinedly,
A. Snatcher

Snatchers, Inc.
May 29

Dear Mr. Snatcher:
This latest lowering of your company's demands is further proof that I am dealing with intelligent and realistic individuals.

Of course my wife has been grieving greatly over the loss, however temporary, of Pure Rotten, though with the aid of new furs and jewelry she has recovered from similar griefs. When one marries a woman, as in acquiring a company, one must accept the liabilities along with the assets. With my rapidly improving nervous condition, and as my own initial grief and anxiety subside somewhat, I find myself at odds with my wife and of the opinion that your 500,000 dollar figure is outrageously high. Think more in terms of tens of thousands.

Regards,
Clark Forthcue

Forthcue:
Ninety thousand is *it! Final!* By midnight tomorrow in the Garver mailbox, or Pure Rotten will be disposed of.

You are keeping us in an uncomfortable position and we don't like it. We are not killers, but we can be.

A. Snatcher

Snatchers, Inc.
May 30

Dear Mr. Snatcher:
  Free after many years of the agonizing pain of my ulcer, I can think quite objectively on this matter. Though my wife demands that I pay some ransom, ninety thousand dollars is out of the question. I suggest you dispose of the commodity under discussion as you earlier intimated you might. After proof of this action, twenty thousand dollars will accompany my next letter in the Garver mailbox. Since I have been honest with you and have not contacted the authorities, no one, including my wife, need know the final arrangements of our transaction.

Cordially,
Clark Forthcue

Forthcue:
  Are you crazy? This is a human life. We are not killers. But you are right about one thing—no amount of money is worth more than your health. Suppose we return Pure Rotten unharmed tomorrow night? Five thousand dollars for our trouble and silence will be plenty.

A. Snatcher

Snatchers, Inc.
May 31

Dear Mr. Snatcher:
  After due reflection I must unequivocally reject your last suggestion and repeat my own suggestion that you dispose of the matter at hand in your own fashion. I see no need for further correspondence in this matter.

Clark Forthcue

Snatchers, Inc.
June 1

Clark Forthcue:
There has been a take over of the bord of Snatchers, Inc. and my too vise presidents who haven't got a choice agree with me, the new president. I have all the carbon copys of Snatchers, Inc. letters to you and all your letters back to us. The law is very seveer with kidnappers and even more seveer with people who want to kill kids.

But the law is not so seveer with kids, in fact will forgive them for almost anything if it is there first ofense. If you don't want these letters given to the police you will leave 500,000 dollars tomorrow night in Garvers old mailbox. I meen it. Small bils is what we want but some fiftys and hundreds will be o.k.

Sinseerly,
Pure Rotten

Grounds for Divorce

by James Holding

The power failure lasted less than five minutes—but it came at an awkward time.

John Marcy, soup spoon in hand, was seated at the dining table ready to start his dinner. He was hungry.

Angela, his wife, who had just carried the filled soup plates in from the kitchen and taken her own seat across the table, was reaching out a hand toward the cracker dish when the house lights flickered once, then winked out.

"Oh, dear!" Angela said, startled. "Now what? Look out the front window in the living room, John, and see if the neighbors' lights are out, too. Maybe it's just ours."

John put down his soup spoon obediently, groped his way into the living room, and looked out the front window. "Even the street lights are out," he reported over his shoulder. "It's a general power failure, I guess."

He could hear Angela moving in the darkness of the dining room behind him. "I've got candles," she said in a moment, "if you'll get the matches from the coffee table in there."

John cautiously located the coffee table in the blackness and explored its surface for the book of matches always kept near the ashtray. As his hand closed on it, a match flared in the dining room, and a second later two candles set in silver candlesticks on the table were dissipating the darkness.

"Never mind, John," Angela called, "I found a match in the buffet drawer. Come on and eat your soup now. It'll get cold."

Before John got back to his chair at the table, the electric lights came on again.

"Ah," said Angela with relief. "That's better." She didn't blow out the candles.

John picked up his soup spoon and then, with a distraught air, put it down again. He looked across the table at Angela whose gentle blue eyes were regarding him anxiously. "Is the soup cold, dear?" she asked. She took a sip of her own. "Mine isn't."

He shook his head. How lovely she is, he thought, and what a heel I've been to go running after those other women. His conscience was suddenly tender. An unaccustomed pang of shame caused him to lower his eyes.

"No," he said, "I don't suppose it's cold, darling, but I'm not very hungry tonight."

"It's yellow pea soup, John. You love it."

"I know." He raised his head. "And I love you, too, Angela. You know that, don't you?"

Her eyes filled with tears. "Let's not go into that again," she said, trembling.

John said, "I'm an All-American heel, Angela, I admit it. A woman-crazy, middle-aged wolf who ought to know better. And I'm genuinely sorry for it."

Angela brushed aside her tears with the back of a flexed

wrist, a somehow pathetic gesture. She stood up. "Now you've spoiled *my* appetite," she said. She picked up the two soup plates and carried them out to the kitchen.

"So I want to divorce her," John Marcy told his lawyer quietly the next day.

Bartley, the lawyer, aimed a faintly disapproving glance at his client and friend. "Divorce her?" he echoed. "*You* want to divorce *her*?"

"Yes."

"Don't make me laugh, John. It's common gossip in town that *she* ought to divorce *you*. And I know the score, John, so don't try to kid me. I haven't forgotten those breach-of-promise suits and the paternity action I had to settle for you, John."

"I'm not forgetting them either. I just want to divorce Angela, that's all. And I need your advice on how to go about it. That's simple, isn't it?"

"Not all that simple, no. Why?"

"Why what?"

"Why do you want to divorce her all of a sudden after letting things drift along like this for years?"

"Because she won't divorce me, that's why. And I want to be free of her."

"Yes, but why won't she divorce you? Some foolish idea that this way she can punish you for your past peccadillos?"

"No. You'll think I'm even more insufferable than you do now if I tell you the true reason."

"Try me and see."

John hesitated. Then he said, "Well, it's my considered opinion, knowing Angela as I do, that she won't divorce me because she still loves me."

"That's no reason," Bartley said.

"It is if she doesn't want another woman to get her hooks into me permanently," John said. "She knows how vulnerable and—uh—undiscriminating I am." He paused. "You realize it isn't easy for me to talk like this, Bart."

"Go on," Bartley said, and with the privileged candor of long friendship he added, "Everybody knows you're a heel, John. No need to be embarrassed in front of me."

Marcy flushed and plowed on doggedly. "Angela has

decided that if she can't enjoy my full-time love and loyalty, no other woman will get a chance at it, either."

"Is that what Angela says?"

"Not in so many words, no. But I'm positive it's how she feels."

"How can you be positive about a thing like that?"

"From her actions, Bart. From her attitude lately."

"And you want to charge mental cruelty, is that it?"

"No, you don't understand at all." Marcy sighed.

"I'll say I don't. But I might remind you, John, that even in these enlightened times you need stronger grounds for divorce than a simple statement that your wife loves you and you're sure of it."

John said, "Don't clown with me, I'm serious. I tell you I want to divorce Angela."

"I'm not clowning. But you've got to have grounds. Angela's got plenty—but you haven't. Understand?" Bartley didn't wait for an answer. He went on, "Exactly when did you decide you had to divorce Angela? Maybe that'll help."

Resignedly John said, "Last night. At the dinner table."

"What happened?"

"We had a power failure in our neighborhood. The lights went out."

"Well, well." Bartley lit a cigarette and examined his client's glum face with interest. "That certainly explains a lot."

"It did to me," John said, "even if you think it's some sort of joke."

Exasperated, the lawyer leaned back in his swivel chair. "Nothing about divorce is some sort of joke, as you call it," he snapped. "So be serious about this, John! Tell me about the lights going out, if you think it's important."

"It's important, all right. The lights were out for only a couple of minutes, but during that brief period of total darkness I suddenly found out Angela's true feelings for me, Bart." John was dragging out the words reluctantly. "I'm being honest with you."

"Good," Bartley said. "So in the dark you had this great revelation of Angela's true feelings. What did she do—try to seduce you, or what?"

Marcy shook his head. "I'm sorry to make you pry it out of me like this, Bart," he apologized. "But I was pretty surprised at the time, and I'm not over my confusion yet."

"Obviously. But let's have it. You're stalling."

"I suppose I am," Marcy admitted. He took a deep breath. "Well, you've got to get the picture. Angela had just brought in our soup. We were ready to begin eating. And it was at that instant, with our soup plates on the table before us, that the lights went out."

"All right. What then?"

"Then," Marcy said, "then I saw that Angela was trying to kill me."

"Kill you!" Bartley dropped his cigarette on the rug and swore as he stamped it out.

"That's what I said. Kill me. Poison me. She had poisoned my soup."

Bartley stared at him, shaking his head. "But in the dark—" he began.

"If the lights hadn't gone out, I'd be dead. I'd have eaten that damned soup and gone where no waitress or chorus girl could ever give me the come-on again." For the first time Marcy smiled. "My soup was loaded with yellow phosphorus."

"How did you know?"

"High school chemistry. When the lights went out, my soup glowed in the dark like a plate of incandescent paint."

After a dazed moment Bartley managed to whisper, "Attempted murder."

"Is that grounds for divorce?"

"Should be enough for a starter," Bartley said, swallowing.

"Angela, poor darling, tried to distract my attention from the soup," John went on. "She got candles lit as soon as she could, to hide the soup's phosphorescence." He paused. Then he said, "Understand, Bart, I'm telling this to nobody but you. If you go to Angela and tell her you know all about her attempt to murder me last night, I think that out of shame she'll consent to divorce me for the old-fashioned reasons. But I don't want the police to hear a word about this."

"Why not?" asked the lawyer. "After all, attempted murder—"

"Because Angela still loves me, as I told you—enough to want to kill me, if that's the only way she can keep me straight. And in my own stupid way I still love her—now more than ever, perhaps. I don't want the police hounding her."

Bartley hunched his shoulders in pure bafflement. He said, "If you and Angela still love each other so much, why not stay together? Why not go on through life hand in hand, as the poet says? Why a divorce?"

John Marcy stood up. He gave the lawyer a crooked grin. "Everybody knows I'm a heel," he said. "But that's a little different from being a fool. There might not be a power failure the next time."

Inside Out

by Barry N. Malzberg

I've got to start stacking the corpses in the bedroom now.

The living room, alas, is all filled. It was bound to happen sooner or later. Still, it's a shock to realize that the day of inevitability has come. There is simply no room any more. Floor to ceiling in four rows the bodies are stacked except for the little space in the corner I've left for my chair and footrest. Even the television set is gone. It was hard to sacrifice the television set but business is business. I put it at the foot of my bed, dreading the time when I'd have to start putting the bodies where I slept. But I must face up to reality and the living room is finished. *Fini. Kaput.* Used up. Cheerlessly I accept my fate. If I am to go on murdering I will have to bring the bodies, as the abbess said to the bishop, into the boudoir. And I am, of course, going to go on murdering.

When I do away with Brown the superintendent tonight, therefore, his corpse will go in the far corner beside the dresser. Virgin territory to be exploited—not that there is any sexual undertone to this matter. None whatsoever. It is what it is. It is not a metaphor. It is not a symbol. It is the pure sad business of murder.

Brown rolls the emptied garbage cans across the lobby, filling my rooms with a sound from hell. He also refuses to clean the steps more than once a week. Time and again I have asked him to desist from the one and do the other, but the man is obdurate. He pretends not to know English. He pretends he doesn't hear me. He pretends he has other duties. This morning I saw four disgusting orange peels on the third-floor landing, already turning brown. There is no way that a man of my disposition can deal with this any more, but I'm not able to move out. For one thing, what would I do with my bodies? It would be such a job to transport them all.

Therefore Brown, or what is left of him, will repose in the bedroom tonight. *Au boudoir.*

The murders are fictive, of course. I am not actually a mass murderer. These are imaginary murders, imagined corpses that have slowly filled these quarters since I began my difficult adjustment about a year ago. Abusive peddlers, disgusting street persons, noxious fellow employees in the Division. In my mind I act out intricate murders, in my body I pantomime the matter of conveying the corpses here, in my heart all of the dead stay here with me, mild in their state. It is a fantasy that enables me to go on with this disgusting urban existence; if I could not banish those who offend me I would be unable to go on. It is of course a perilous coupling, this fantasy, since I might plunge over the fine line someday and actually believe I've done away with these people, but it is the only way I can continue in circumstantial balance.

Giving the fantasy credence, however, demands discipline and a good deal of scut work. It is with regret that I have given up all of my living room except for the chair and footrest, but also out of simple respect for will. If I were not to make reasonable sacrifices in order to propitiate this accord it would be meaningless. One cannot play the violin well without years of painful work with wrists and hands acquiring technique. One cannot be a proper employee of the Division without studying its dismal and boring procedures. One cannot be an imaginary mass murderer without taking responsibility for the imaginary bodies.

The derelict who wipes my windshield with a dirty rag at the bridge exit is still there, of course, although I murdered him six months ago. This morning he cursed me when I gave him only fifteen cents through the cautiously opened window. His rag hardly infiltrated my vision, his cursing fell upon a benign and smiling countenance. How could I tell him, after all, "You no longer exist. Since I did away with you half a year ago your real activities in the real world have made no impression upon me. Your rag is a blur, your curses a song. I drove a sharp knife between your sixth and seventh ribs in this very street before witnesses, threw your body into the trunk, and conveyed it bloodless to my apartment where it now reposes. The essential you lies sandwiched in my apartment between the waitress from the Forum Diner who spilt a glass of ice water in my lap and the medical social worker from the Division who said I had no grasp at all of schizophrenia. I possess you, do you understand that?"

No, I don't think he would understand that. This miserable creature, along with the waitress, the medical social worker, and many others, cannot appreciate the metaphysics of the situation.

I did away with Brown in his apartment two hours ago. "Mr. Brown," I said when he opened the door, "I can't take this any more. You're totally irresponsible. It's not only the orange peels, the hide-and-seek when the toilet will not flush, and the terrible smells of disinfectant when you occasionally wash the lobby. That would be enough, but it's your insolence that degrades my spirit. You do not accept the fact that I am a human being who has a right to simple services. By ignoring my needs you ignore humanity." I shot him in the left temple with the delicate .22 I use for extreme cases. The radio was playing Haydn's Symphony 101 in D Major loudly as I dragged him out of there, closing the door firmly behind. I would not have suspected that he had a taste for classical music, but this doesn't mitigate his situation. He now lies at the foot of my bed. Now and then he seems to sigh in the perfectitude of his perfect peace.

The medical social worker commented today during a conference upon my abstracted attitude and twice she tapped me on the hand to bring me back to attention. I know she feels I'm exceedingly neurotic and not a diligent caseworker, but how could I possibly explain to her that the reason my attention lapses during these conferences is that she was smothered several weeks ago and has not drawn a breath, even in my apartment, since?

Brown's corpse is curiously odorous. This is a new phenomenon. I am a committed housekeeper and can't abide smells of any kind in my apartment (other than pipe and coffee, of course), and my corpses are aseptic. Brown's, however, is not. It is progressively foul and disturbed my sleep last night. Heavy sprays of household antiseptics don't seem to work. The apartment was even worse when I came home tonight.

I knew it was a mistake opening up the bedroom for disposal, but what choice did I have? There is simply no room left outside of here and I refuse to have corpses in the bathroom. There are, after all, limits. I'll just have to do the best I can. After a while either I'll get used to it or the smell will go away.

I should get rid of Brown's body—the smell is impossible now—but I am reluctant to do so. It would set a dangerous precedent, it would break a pattern. If I were to dispose of his body he would not then be symbolically dead, and if I did it with him might I not then be tempted to do it with one of the others? Or with succeeding victims? My project would become totally self-defeating—I would have accomplished nothing.

It has of course occurred to me to call the real Brown to help me dispose of the body of the imaginary Brown, but I won't do that either. It would be a nice irony but one he would not understand. I will either have to do the job myself or hold on.

Besides, I have not seen the foul man here in days. . .

It's all too much. I couldn't deal with it any more and accordingly dragged Brown's body to the landing for pickup tomorrow morning. That should solve the problem, although I'm concerned at the rupture of my pattern and also by the curious weight of his body as I lumbered with it, fireman-carry fashion, to the stairwell. He's the most unusually corporeal of all my victims. Even in imaginary death he seems capable, typically, of giving me real difficulties.

Two policemen at the door in full uniform, with grim expressions, demand entrance to the apartment. Behind them I can see a circle of some tenants from the building.

I seem to be in some kind of difficulty.

At my very first opportunity during this interview I intend to distract the police and kill them—put an end to this harassment—but I have a feeling that won't work.

I should never have abandoned the living room as a disposal unit. That was my only mistake. I should have begun disposing of old corpses as they were replaced by the new. It would have been sufficient.

But it's too late now, the police say.

The Bell

by Isak Romun

I'm standing here on the stairwell, waiting. He comes by here every evening, usually the last one out of the office. He takes this stairwell because it lets him out into that part of the parking lot where his car stands alone.

Not tonight, though. He'll never make it to the lot. The steps are sharp, angular. And hard, made of unyielding metal. When he comes down, I'll be waiting, a hello on my lips, an arm raised in greeting. A strong arm, an arm that will send him bouncing and bruising down the stairs. If that doesn't kill him, I'll simply finish the job by smashing his head against the angle of a step. An accident. That's what it will look like. Something that could happen to anyone hurrying down these stairs.

It started early this morning with the forlorn shape of Yuddic—an old Gaelic name, he told me one time—with Yuddic McGill slouching against my desk. Mac isn't a pushy sort, and it took me a few moments to become aware of his presence and a few more to note the worried look on his face.

"Talmage, I've got bad news."

"Bad news?" I remarked unconcernedly. Mac was always blowing things out of proportion, so I rather pointedly kept on with my job of sorting and posting vouchers.

"Yes. Stromberg just fired me."

Now, this gave me a turn, caused me to look up, perhaps feel a twinge of fear—you know, don't ask for whom the bell tolls, it tolls for thee, and that sort of thing. Always believed in it. Well, I thought, who diminishes old Yuddic diminishes me. If Stromberg could get away with this arbitrary action, then the old domino theory might come into play and who knew who'd topple next?

Besides, the figure Mac cut was one to invite compassion. He was a diminutive, retiring, almost ridiculous man. Atop his sloping shoulders resided a head on which was impressed a face of such undistinguished features as to foster the belief that the die of character had been applied too lightly, or had been nudged at the precise moment of contact. Around this was arranged a head of listless, squirrel-gray hair allowed, mod fashion, to grow to his jawline, intimating a spirit to which the remaining cut of his Establishment jib lent the lie.

Mac's news, matched with the sympathy that the image of Mac himself always evoked, goaded me. I jumped from my seat and said to him earnestly, "He can't do that to you, Mac! You're one of the key men in this outfit. Have you gotten the formal notice?"

"I'll get written notice later today. The old pink slip. He called me into his office for a little oral preview so I wouldn't faint dead away later on."

"Well, that's good. It's not official until you receive the slip. You can't let him get away with it, Mac. You've got to do something."

"What's to do?" He shrugged and stood there, a pitiable, defeated sight.

"March right back in there and let him know what'll happen if he lets you go. Give him a picture of the impact that the loss of your expertise will have on this organization."

"Oh, Tal, I can't do that. I can't blow my own horn," he said despairingly. "He wouldn't believe me as much as he would someone else."

"By God, then I'll do it!" I exclaimed, not unaware of the admiring attention I was receiving from the other workers sitting nearby. "I'll go in and lay it out for Stromberg. Don't worry, Mac, you'll still have your job at the end of the day."

Then to the silent huzzas of the people in the outer office I marched down the long aisle formed by two rows of identical desks to the ominous green door behind which sat the equally ominous Stromberg. I tell you it took nerve and I won't say I didn't look back. I did once and was confirmed in my resolve when I saw the glimmer of hope spreading across the face of my little buddy, Yuddic McGill.

I pushed myself forward, ignoring the protest of Miss Frisby, Stromberg's secretary, and threw open the door. Stromberg looked up from a pink form in front of him and smiled inquiringly as if he had been expecting me (the man has spies everywhere). I recognized the form and noticed it was still blank. Talk about timing!

I moved into the office, slammed the door, and before Stromberg could say one word, was all over him.

"Mr. Stromberg, if you fill in that pink slip you're getting rid of one of the best men we have. McGill's a man of unquestioned ability. Firing him will be like slicing off your right arm. Accounts Receivable will pile up a week's backlog in two or three days. He's the real strength in this department."

And I went on with much more of the same puffery, but that gives you the idea. All the time Stromberg just sat there silently and smilingly taking it in. When I paused to catch my breath, he said crisply, "Thanks. Appreciate it." Then he picked up the phone and pressed an intercom button.

Miss Frisby came on and Stromberg barked, "Ring McGill's desk!" A pause during which he smiled some more at me. "That you, Mac? Forget what I told you earlier. Right, you're not fired. Good God, man, stop blubbering and get back to work!"

He slammed down the instrument and looked at me. I'm sure my face showed real gratitude as I said, "You won't regret it, sir. McGill will give you a fair shake. Nine for every eight you pay him, I'm sure."

"Took a lot of courage coming in here," Stromberg said briefly and then went back to the pink form in front of him and began filling in the spaces.

What's this? I thought. Was it all some sort of unfeeling joke played on poor Mac?

I was wrong. Stromberg handed me a copy of the completed form. *My* name was on it. There I had it, my two weeks' notice. *I was fired!* I could hardly keep myself from strangling the man right there at his desk.

"It was either McGill or you," Stromberg explained. "It was McGill until you barged in here and did a good selling job on him."

"Oh, sir," I whined, all the starch gone from my voice, "won't you please reconsider?"

"Sure, if you can get McGill to quit," Stromberg said and cackled cruelly.

In the outer office I joined the others in congratulating Mac on his deliverance and in accepting accolades for my part in it. I didn't tell anyone that I'd gotten the ax, particularly not Mac. I couldn't spoil his good news with my bad; nor could I make the ridiculous request that he decline Stromberg's benevolence so that I'd be kept on.

Instead, I put on a good face and only let it slip when my eye chanced on the green door at the end of the aisle. Then and there I devised a course of action that, while precipitate, would be extremely satisfying.

That's why I am waiting now on this stairwell. My character is repulsed at what I have resolved to do, but a spirit of survival possesses me. I've finally learned that, these days, the bell tolls only for the guy going to his own funeral. A bystander's got to close his ears to the ding-dong.

He's up there in the office, concluding the conscientious extra hour he always puts in. Stromberg left some time ago. Only Mac and I are in the building.

Sorry, little buddy.

The Box

by Isak Romun

Working for Stromberg was like being locked in a box. No matter how you tried, you couldn't get out. That's how I felt—as if I were in a box, and only Stromberg had the key.

But one day I found another key, one that would unlock the lid of the box just as effectively as Stromberg's key. Which he would never use. So I would use my own.

My key was death.

Once I had made the decision, I found it quite easy to live with. With something like gusto I attacked the matter of a plan—how I would kill Stromberg. It should not be something complex or difficult. Simple plans are usually the safest. But I had no experience.

Oh, certainly, I had read mystery stories, had even in my mind concocted ways and means of putting to rest the fictional victims I met on the printed page. And with more panache than many of their creators! But there's a difference between a cold, paper thing and a warm, pulsing human organism. Not that Stromberg could be called warm and pulsing. He was like a fish, and it was my intent to hook that fish.

But how to hook him? I thought of poison. Traceable. A hit-and-run accident. Unpredictable—Stromberg might not die. A gun. Noisy and messy. Besides, none of these methods passed the test of simplicity. I determined to use materials and circumstances at hand.

I was evaluating the merits of a push down a stairway when Hopkinson came up to me. "I'll need two dollars from you," he said. I asked why. "Stromberg's farewell gift. He's put in for retirement. Lucky you. I hear he said you were the only man to fill his shoes." Did I hear right? Was it true?

It *was* true! Suddenly I was outside my box. I would not have to kill Stromberg. Matter of fact, he began to look quite human to me. I realized with remorse that what I thought were constraints on me were, in reality, his way of testing me, of training me. That good fellow really had my best interests at heart. At his retirement bash we posed for a parting photo, smiling, each with an arm about the other's shoulder.

I've been chief now for almost five years. But don't think it's been all fun. By no means. When you become a supervisor, you take on something called responsibility. Something only you have. It's up to you to see that the job gets done, that your section functions smoothly.

I swear, though, there are times I throw up my hands in despair. I'm pressured to produce, but with what must I produce? A bunch of incompetents who'd rather hang around the water cooler than do an honest day's work.

The worst is Hopkinson. He said a strange unsettling thing to me the other day. He said working for me is like being locked in a box.

Perhaps I should check with the personnel office about retirement.

The Physician and the Opium Fiend

by R. L. Stevens

The lamplights along Cavendish Square were just being lit, casting a soft pale glow across the damp London night, as Blair slipped from the court behind Dr. Lanyon's house. It had been another failure, another robbery of a physician's office that yielded him but a few shillings. He cursed silently and started across the Square, then drew back quickly as a hansom cab hurried past, the horse's hoofs clattering on the cobblestones.

At times he wished it could end this easily, with his body crushed beneath a two-wheeler. Perhaps then he might be free of the terrible craving that growled within him, forcing him to a life of housebreaking and theft.

William Blair was an opium fiend. He still remembered the first time he had eaten opium, popping the little pill of brown gum into his mouth and washing it down with coffee as de Quincey had sometimes done. He remembered the gradual creeping thrill that soon took possession of every part of his body. And he remembered too the deadly sickness of his stomach, the furred tongue and dreadful headache that followed his first experience as an opium eater.

He should have stopped the diabolical practise then, but he hadn't. In three days' time he had recourse to the drug once more, and after that his body seemed to crave it with increasing frequency. It was his frantic search for opium which now led him nightly to the offices of famous physicians, to the citadels of medicine that lined Cavendish Square. He had broken into ten of them in the past fortnight, but only two had yielded a quantity of opium sufficient to ease his terrible burthen.

And so it was in a state bordering desperation that Blair entered the quiet bystreet that ran north from the Square. He had gone some distance past the shops and homes when he chanced to note a high, two-storey building that thrust forward its windowless gable on the street. He was familiar enough with doctors' laboratories in this section of London to suspect that here might be one, hidden away behind this neglected, discoloured brick wall. But only a blistered and disdained wooden door gave entry into the building from this street, and the door was equipped with neither bell nor knocker.

Hurriedly he retraced his steps to the corner, avoiding a helmeted bobby who was crossing the street in the opposite direction. He waited until the police-officer had disappeared from view, his hand ready on the dagger in his pocket. As he moved on, a few drops of water struck his forehead. It was beginning to rain.

Round the corner he came upon a square of ancient, handsome houses. Though many were beginning to show the unmistakable signs of age, the second house from the corner still wore a great air of wealth and comfort. It was all in darkness except for the fanlight, but the glow from this was sufficient for him to decipher the lettering on the brass name-plate. He had guessed correctly. It was indeed a doctor's residence. He set to work at once as the rain increased.

It took him only a few moments of skillful probing with the dagger to prize open one of the shuttered windows. Then he was through it and into a flagged hall lined with costly oaken cabinets. The doctor was obviously wealthy, and Blair hoped this meant a well-stocked laboratory. He moved cautiously along the hall, fearful of any noise which might give the alarm. The house could have been empty, but it was possible the good doctor had retired early and was asleep upstairs.

Blair made his way to the rear of the first floor, heading in the direction of the windowless gable he had observed from the street. He passed into the connecting building and through a large darkened area that, by the light of his Brymay safety-matches, appeared to be an old dissecting room, strewn with crates and littered with packing straw, and dusty with disuse. Blair moved through it to a stairway at the rear. This would lead to the second floor of the windowless gable, his last hope of finding a supply of opium.

The door at the top of the stair was a heavy barrier covered with red baize, and it took him ten minutes ere he finally forced it inward with a loud screech. The disclosed room proved to be the small office-laboratory he sought— his work had not been in vain! The remains of a dying fire still glowed on the hearth, casting a pale orange glow about the room. The laboratory had been in use that very night, and in such a home the storage shelves would be well stocked.

It took him but a brief search to discover, amidst the chemical apparatus, a large bottle labeled LAUDANUM. This was a tincture of opium, he knew, and no less an authority than de Quincey had reckoned twenty-five drops of laudanum to be the equivalent of one grain of pure opium. Yes, this would satisfy his need.

His hand was just closing over the bottle when a voice from the doorway rasped, "Who is there? Who are you?"

Blair whirled to face the man, the dagger ready in his hand. "Get back," he warned. "I am armed."

The figure in the doorway reached up to light the gas flame, and Blair saw that he was a large, well-made, smooth-faced man of perhaps fifty, with a countenance that was undeniably handsome. "What do you want here, man? This is my laboratory. There is no money here!"

"I need—" began Blair, feeling the perspiration collecting on his forehead. "I need opium."

There was a sharp intake of breath from the handsome doctor. "My God! Have conditions in London come to this? Do opium fiends now prowl the streets and break into physicans' homes in search of this devilish drug?"

"Get out of my way," returned Blair, "or I will kill you!"

"Wait! Let me—let me try to help you in some way. Let me summon the police. This craving that obsesses you will destroy you in time. You need help, medical treatment."

As he spoke, the doctor moved forward slowly, forcing Blair back towards the far wall of the room. "I don't want help," sobbed the cornered man. "It's too late to help me now."

The doctor took a step closer. "It is never too late! Don't you realize what this drug is doing to you, man? Don't you see how it releases everything that is cruel and sick and evil in you? Under the influence of opium, or any drug, you become a different person. You are no longer in command of your own will."

Blair had backed to the wall now, and he could feel its chill firmness through his coat. He raised the dagger menacingly. "Come any closer, Sawbones, and I swear I will kill you!"

The doctor hesitated a moment. He glanced at the darkened skylight above their heads, where the rain was now beating a steady tattoo upon the glass. Then he said, "The mind of man is his greatest gift. To corrupt it, to poison it with drugs, is something hateful and immoral. I hope that I am never in a position where I lose control of my free will because I have surrendered to the dark side of my nature. You, poor soul, are helpless in the grip of this opium, like the wretched folk who smoke it in the illegal dens, curled upon their bunks and oblivious of the outer world."

"I—I—" began Blair, but the words were lost in his throat. The physician was right, he knew, but he was beyond caring now, beyond distinguishing between right and wrong. He only knew that the doctor had forced him further from the bottle of laudanum.

"Let me call the police," urged the doctor, softly.

"No!"

The physician's hand moved, all in a flash, seizing one of the bottles from the shelf beside him and hurling it upwards through the skylight. There was a shattering of glass and a shower of silvery white pellets from the bottle. Then a sudden violet flame seemed to engulf the entire skylight, burning with a hissing sound that ended almost at once with a burst of explosive violence.

Terrified, Blair tried to lunge past the doctor, but the large hands were instantly upon him, fastening on his coat and wrist, forcing the dagger away.

They were still locked in a life-and-death, silent struggle when, moments later, a helmeted bobby burst into the laboratory. "What's happening here, sir? I saw the flame and heard the explosion—"

"Help me with this man," shouted the physician. "He's trying to steal opium!"

Within seconds Blair was helpless, his arms pinioned to his sides by the burly police-officer. "Take me," he mumbled. "Take me and lock me up. Help me."

Another bobby arrived on the scene, attracted by the noise and flame. "What was it?" he asked the doctor.

"I had to signal you somehow," he told them. "There were potassium pellets in the bottle and I took a risk that enough rainwater had collected on the skylight to set off a chemical reaction. Potassium reacts even more violently with water than does sodium."

"You were successful," returned the second policeman. "I heard that boom two streets away."

The doctor was busy moving some of his equipment out of the rain which was still falling through the shattered skylight. "I think with treatment this man can be saved," said he. "It is his addiction that has led him into a life of crime."

"I would not worry too much about him, sir. He could have killed you with this dagger."

"But I do worry about him, as I would about any human being. As for myself, I was much more fearful that he would wreck my laboratory. I have been engaged in some important experiments here, relating to transcendental medicine, and I feel I am on the verge of discovery."

The first police-officer pulled Blair towards the door. "Then we will leave you alone to clean up, sir. And good luck with your experiments." He was half-way out the door when he paused and said, "O, by the by, sir, I will need your name for my report. I did not have time to catch it on the brass outside."

"Certainly," replied the physician, with a smile. "The name is Jekyll. Doctor Henry Jekyll."

Over the Borderline

by Jeff Sweet

"Don't you see? He had to be stopped."

"Stopped, Mrs. Sutherland? Stopped from doing what?"

"If I hadn't acted she would have died. He would have killed her."

"Who, Mrs. Sutherland? Who would he have killed?"

"You're looking at me like you don't believe me, Lieutenant Foley. You think I'm just a batty old lady, don't you? An old lady who's lost her marbles."

"No, I don't. Really, I don't."

"Like crazy Mrs. Jessup who's always calling the police or the F.B.I. about enemy agents hiding under her bed. I'm right, aren't I? That's what you think."

"I swear, Mrs. Sutherland, I don't think that at all."

"Then why don't you believe me?"

"Well, I'll tell you, Mrs. Sutherland, it isn't that I don't believe you. It's just that I—well, I guess I really don't *understand.* I mean, I don't have the full picture."

"I've tried to answer all your questions, Lieutenant."

"Yes, and I appreciate that, Mrs. Sutherland. But still—"

"What?"

"Look, I have an idea. Why don't you tell me about it again, from start to finish? I promise you I won't interrupt."

"From start to finish? Yes, maybe that would be best, and I suppose the best place to start would be with Cora and Jim. Cora and Jim Franklin. Such a nice couple. They remind me of the late Mr. Sutherland and myself when we were young. A very nice couple, the Franklins. Of course, they have their problems. More than their share. She was pregnant when they got married, you know. That's not always the best way to start a marriage, especially since the baby wasn't Jim's. That awful Harrington Furth."

"Uh, Mrs. Sutherland—"

"Lieutenant, you promised you wouldn't interrupt."

"I know, Mrs. Sutherland, but I'm afraid I'm a little lost. Who is Harrington Furth?"

"Lieutenant, if you will hold your horses I'll get to that, I promise you. All in good time. But you mustn't interrupt."

"Yes, Mrs. Sutherland."

"Where was I?"

"Harrington Furth."

"Oh, yes, Harrington. A very rich, very irresponsible young man. His father is the president of Furth Electronics, you know—a very distinguished man. But Harrington, I'm afraid, doesn't take after his father. Or should I say Harrington *didn't* take after his father? Oh, well, you understand my meaning, I'm sure. It must have been very hard on old Mrs. Furth, having a son like Harrington. Always racing around in his fancy cars, always getting into trouble. And his father always coming to the rescue. I swear, if it had been me, I would have let that young man stew in his own juice! It might have taught him a sense of responsibility. And the way he drank!

"Anyway, there was poor Cora. She hadn't married Jim yet, you know. Jim was going with the Stanton girl then—the one with the big false eyelashes and all the teeth. What Jim saw in her I don't know. But like I say, there was poor Cora. Her mother had just died on the operating table and Cora was all alone. She was scared and vulnerable. And that awful Harrington saw this and—well, he took advantage of the situation, and when he'd gotten what he wanted he left Cora flat. Not too long after she found out she was pregnant."

"You mean with Furth's child?"

"That's what I said, didn't I? Really, Lieutenant, you must learn to listen. Anyway, around this time the Stanton girl left Jim and took up with young Harrington, which in my opinion served them both right. Meanwhile, Jim was desperate, almost suicidal, and then, one day, in came Cora. Did I tell you Jim was an obstetrician?"

"No."

"Well, he was, and all the girls on the staff at the hospital thought he was the handsomest doctor around. But he didn't pay any attention to them. And then, as I said, in came Cora and he told her she was pregnant and she just stood there, very bravely, fighting back the tears. But, of course, it wasn't any use. Before you could blink an eye she was in his arms, crying like a little girl. And he was holding her so tenderly. It was love from that first moment, I could tell. I could tell right off because it was just like that when Mr. Sutherland and I met. Except I wasn't pregnant and Mr. Sutherland wasn't an obstetrician.

"What I'm talking about is the way you—well, you know in your heart when someone's just right for you. You don't think about it, you just *know*. That's the way it was with Mr. Sutherland and me. And that's the way it was with Cora and Jim.

"I'll never forget the day Jim proposed. She was in her eighth month then and he'd been seeing a lot of her. 'Marry me,' he said. 'No,' she said, 'I couldn't do that to you. I couldn't make you part of my shame,' she said. I remember how difficult it was for me to keep from shouting out to her, 'Don't be a fool, Cora! He loves you! Don't give up this chance for happiness!'

"But I needn't have worried because that's just what he said to her himself. 'I love you,' he said. 'You give my life purpose. If you don't say yes, I don't know what I'll do.' To make a long story short, she did say yes and they were married soon after. He even delivered the baby."

"Mrs. Sutherland, what has this got to do with—"

"Lieutenant, please!"

"Sorry, Mrs. Sutherland."

"As I said, they were married and were so happy, and the baby didn't look a bit like Harrington. But I could tell they weren't over the worst of it. I knew in my bones that tragedy was going to strike, but for the longest time I didn't know how.

"To tell you the truth, I was having an awful time sleeping. I finally had to go to Dr. Sumroy and get a prescription for sleeping pills. I'd never used them before because I've heard so many stories of old people accidentally taking an overdose. And not just old people. Young people, too. It's supposed to be especially bad if you take them when you've been drinking, though in my case that was no problem. But I was having so much trouble sleeping because of all my worrying about Cora and Jim that I just *knew* something tragic was going to happen even though I didn't know what.

"Then, suddenly, it came to me. I can't tell you how it came to me because I honestly don't know how to explain such things. Call it woman's intuition, if you like, but I knew what was going to happen. *Harrington was going to kill Cora in an automobile accident!* It was inevitable. He'd just bought a new sports car—one of those fancy foreign things that makes a lot of noise, and it was common knowledge he was speeding recklessly all over town. So you see, it was logical.

"Of course, I couldn't let it happen. I remember how heartbroken I was when Mr. Sutherland died in an accident, only he wasn't killed by a foreign car. I was so miserable, I nearly died. So what was I supposed to do? I knew what would happen if something weren't done, and I couldn't just sit quiet and *let* it happen. I had to do something. But what?

"Then, today, an amazing coincidence brought me the answer. I came into the city to shop on Fifth Avenue for my nephew's birthday, and I stopped into a restaurant on Forty-Seventh Street. Not too far away from Radio City and Rockefeller Center, you know the area? And who was in the restaurant but young Harrington!

"I went up to him, and I said, 'Mr. Furth?' He smiled. I'll say that for him, he had a nice smile. 'Mr. Furth,' I said, 'I want to talk to you.' He stood up, a little woozy from all the liquor he'd been drinking, and offered me a seat, which I accepted. 'Mr. Furth,' I said, 'I'm going to speak plainly. I know what's going to happen.' 'What's going to happen?' he said, still smiling. 'I know you're going to kill Cora Franklin with that fancy foreign car,' I answered.

" 'How did you find out?' he asked, obviously surprised. 'Never you mind how I found out,' I said. 'What I'm saying is so, isn't it? You're going to kill her with your sports car, aren't you?'

" 'Yes,' he said, 'that's so.'

"He admitted it! With a smile! There wasn't a trace of

regret anywhere on his devilish face. He actually seemed happy about it! I knew I was in the presence of great evil.

"He excused himself and went to the men's room. I suddenly knew what I had to do. I opened my handbag and took out the sleeping pills I had got from Dr. Sumroy, and I dropped something like two dozen of them into his coffee. I left, waited until I was sure it was all over, then came here to turn myself in. And that, Lieutenant, is my confession."

"I see."

"Do you believe me?"

"Yes, I believe you, Mrs. Sutherland."

"One thing you have to know—I did this for them, Lieutenant. For Jim and Cora and the baby. You have to realize that it was the only way. You do understand, don't you?"

"Yes, Mrs. Sutherland, I think I do."

A few minutes later, after Mrs. Sutherland had been led away, Lieutenant Foley turned to Sergeant Warren, who was standing a few feet away. "Well, that settles that," he said.

"Lieutenant, maybe I'm some kind of an idiot," said the sergeant, "but I don't see that it settles anything. Her story about the overdose in Maxwell's coffee jibes, and she matches the waiter's description, but I'll be damned if I can figure out why she kept calling Taylor Maxwell by the name Harrington Furth."

"Sergeant, Taylor Maxwell was an actor."

"I still don't get it, sir."

"I've just been looking at his résumé. For the past few years he's been a regular on an afternoon TV soap opera called *The Will To Live*," explained the lieutenant. "The name of the character he played was Harrington Furth."

It Could Happen to You

by John Lutz

I never dreamed something like this could happen; or rather, I'd always thought something like this could happen only in a dream. But looking back on it piece by piece, it's easy to understand how it did happen. It was just a chance combination of circumstances, none of those circumstances so unbelievable by itself. It's the sort of thing that could happen to anybody; to you.

There'd been some mix-up in the flight schedule, so here I was with a six-hour layover in a city a thousand miles from home. It was a big city, and a nice summer night, so I decided to take a little walk around the downtown area, just to look things over.

That was at eleven o'clock, maybe too late for that kind of walk on a week night. And there wasn't much happening downtown, only a few night spots here and there open; or maybe I'd just picked the wrong part of town.

I strolled innocently along, my light raincoat slung over my arm against any threat of rain. I'd stopped in a few places that looked fairly respectable, staying in each for only one drink and a few words of conversation before going back outside and resuming my wandering. Walking around and sort of taking in the atmosphere of strange cities is a habit of mine. My job keeps me traveling just enough not to get bored with it, so I'm usually interested in new places. And I knew I'd probably never get back to this city.

It was almost one o'clock when I noticed my wallet was missing. I was on Nineteenth Street at the time, idly walking along and looking in the windows of the closed shops.

A lost wallet. Nothing so unusual about that. You've

probably lost your wallet at some time and felt that sudden rush of helplessness. Well, that feeling's even stronger in a strange city, in case you've never had the experience. Everything that gave me a sense of identity or security was in that wallet—my driver's license, my folding money, my credit cards . . .

For a moment I stood in bewilderment, checking my other pockets, but of course the wallet wasn't in any of them. A wallet's the sort of thing you automatically return to the right pocket. I hurried back along the almost-deserted streets toward the Posh Parrot on Twelfth Avenue, the last cocktail lounge I'd been in, all the time keeping my eyes to the ground on the off-chance I might see the wallet where it had fallen from my pocket.

The Posh Parrot was closed, the neon sign in its window dull and lifeless, the window itself throwing back a pale reflection of my worried self.

I told myself it didn't matter. If I had lost the wallet in the lounge and someone had picked it up, he'd probably taken it with him. But I distinctly remembered sliding the wallet back into my hip pocket after paying for my drink; I even remembered folding the corner of a fifty-dollar bill to mark it from the smaller denominations. I began retracing my route back to Nineteenth Street, figuring the wallet must have slipped out of my pocket somewhere along the way.

No luck. What was I going to do? What would you do?

Even the ticket for the last leg of my trip home was in that wallet. I felt suddenly like a vagrant, a trespasser. I realized what a difference a dozen credit cards and a few hundred dollars' cash make in our society.

The only thing I could do was phone Laurie, my wife, and get her to wire me some money. I felt in my other pockets, and among keys, comb, and ballpoint pen, could muster only a nickel and two pennies. So much for that inspiration.

To make me feel worse, a light drizzle began to fall. I hurriedly slipped on my raincoat and turned up the collar.

I was walking forlornly, head down, hands jammed in my coat pockets, so I didn't see the man walking the poodle toward me until we were only about a hundred feet from each other.

My awkwardness and embarrassment about trying to borrow money from a stranger, combined with the short period of time I had to come up with what I was going to say, made my throat suddenly dry. You'd feel the same way.

I stopped directly in front of the man, a little guy with wire-framed glasses and a droopy mustache, and he stood staring at me with alarm.

"Would it be possible for you to lend a stranger some money?" is what I meant to say, and then I was going to explain the reason to him. I was ill at ease, as nervous as the little man appeared, and my voice croaked so I guess he only heard the last part of my sentence, the word "money." He backed up a step, and his poodle sensed his fear and my nervousness and began to growl.

The man's droopy mustache trembled. "I don't have much . . ." he said, "honest . . ." I saw his eyes dart down to the bulge of my right hand in my raincoat pocket, and I understood.

"Wait a minute," I started to say, but I saw him glance off to his right and his eyes grew wider behind his thick glasses. I looked and saw the cop almost on us.

"Trouble?" the cop asked. He was young and rangy, built more like a cigarette-ad cowboy than a cop.

"In a way, Officer," I said.

"He was trying to hold me up!" the little man almost screamed, and his poodle started growling again.

"I thought so," the cop said. "I was watching from across the street."

I felt my heart fall like a meteor. "Hey, no, wait a minute!" I was shoved roughly so that I had to support myself against the side of a building with both hands.

"Be careful!" I heard the little man shout. "He's got a gun in his right coat pocket!"

The cop's hands searched me the way they'd been trained in the police academy, and I knew by his unsteadiness that he was nervous. All three of us were standing there frightened. Even the dog was frightened.

"He was bluffing you," the cop said. "They do that." He jerked me up straight and held onto my arm.

"Bluffing? . . . I was only trying to borrow some money! . . ."

The young cop let out a sharp laugh. "A polite mugger, huh?"

"This is insane!" I said.

The cop shrugged. "So plead that way in court."

"I'll press charges!" the little man kept saying. "You can be sure of that!"

But the cop was ignoring him now, reciting my rights in a low monotone. He was even ignoring me somewhat as he droned on about my "right to remain silent." He was really going to do it! I might really be going to jail! And even if I wasn't convicted, what would the arrest mean to my family, my friends, and my job?

I panicked then, and in what seemed at the time a lucky break, a bus turned the corner and lumbered toward us. I remember one headlight was out and the wiper blades were swinging back and forth out of rhythm. The bus was only doing ten or fifteen miles an hour, and when it was almost even with us I jerked out of the cop's grip and darted in front of it, around it. The front bumper even brushed my pants leg, but I didn't care.

Now the bus was between me and the law, and I had a few precious seconds to run for freedom. The bus driver helped me by slamming on his brakes, probably stopping the bus directly in front of the cop so he had to run around it. I was running down an alley, not looking back or even thinking back, when I heard the shot. In my state, the bark of the gun only made me run faster. I turned the corner, flashed across the rain-slick street and cut through another alley. That alley led to a parking lot, and I ran through there to the next street. I slowed then, listening, but hearing no footsteps behind me. I knew I wouldn't have much time, though. The cop was probably calling in for help right now.

I walked for three more blocks before I saw a cab. It scared me at first; I'd thought the lettering on the door signified a police car. Then I saw that the light atop the car was blue, and there was a liquor advertisement on the trunk. I waved to the cab and climbed in with deliberate casualness when it stopped to pick me up.

"Regent Hotel," I said, trying to keep my breathing level. Didn't every city have a Regent Hotel?

"Torn down," the cabby said, glancing over his shoulder. "You mean the Regency?"

"That's it," I said, and we drove on in silence.

After about ten minutes I saw an all-night drugstore ahead of us, and I had the cabby pull over.

"I'll only be a minute," I told him. "I want to see if they'll fill an out-of-town prescription for insulin."

"Sure." He settled back in his seat and stared straight ahead.

It was a big drugstore, with a few other customers in it. The pharmacist behind the counter gave me a funny look, and I smiled and nodded at him and walked over to the magazine rack. After leafing through a news magazine, I replaced it in the rack and walked over to a display of shaving cream as if it interested me. From there I walked out the side door.

I walked until I was clear of the drugstore's side display window and ran for three or four blocks. I turned a corner then and started walking at a fast pace, but slow enough so that my breathing evened out.

I must have walked over a mile, trying to think things out, trying to come up with some kind of an idea. The agonizing thing was that nothing that had happened was really my fault. You could be in this same kind of mess sometime, just like me. Anybody could.

If only I had some money, I thought, I could get a plane or bus ticket. The police didn't watch bus terminals or airports for every fleeing street-corner bandit. If I could get out of this city, get back home a thousand miles away, I'd be safe. After all, no one had my name or address. The cop hadn't gotten any identification from me when he searched me because I wasn't carrying any. It would be as if none of this had ever happened. Eventually Laurie and I would joke about it. You and your spouse joke about that kind of thing.

Right now, though, things were a far cry from a joke! If I didn't get out of town fast, I might well wind up ruined, in prison!

I was in more of a residential part of town now, wide lawns, neat ranch houses, and plenty of trees. The moon was out and it had stopped raining, and I saw the man walking toward me when he was over a block away, on the other side of the street. The desperation surged up in me, took control of me. You can understand how I felt. There was no time to make phone calls or wait for money. I had to get away fast, and to get away fast I needed money. I stooped and picked up a white grapefruit-sized rock from alongside someone's driveway.

Crossing the street diagonally toward the man, I squeezed the rock concealed in my raincoat pocket, smiling when I got close enough for the man to see my face.

He was carrying enough money for a plane ticket to a nearby city, where I had Laurie send me enough to get home. At home, though, where I'd thought I'd be safe, I still think about it all the time.

I'd never had any experience in hitting someone's head with a rock, so how was I to know? I was scared, like you'd be, scared almost out of my senses, so I struck harder than I'd intended—much harder.

Think about it and it's kind of frightening. I mean, here's this stranger, on his way home from work on the late shift, or from his girl-friend's house, or maybe from some friendly poker game. Then somebody he's never seen before walks up and for no apparent reason smashes his skull with a rock. It could happen to you.

Class Reunion

by Charles Boeckman

The banner across one wall in the Plaza Hotel banquet room welcomed "Jacksonville High, Class of '53." The crowd milling around in the room was on the rim of middle age. Temples were graying, bald spots were in evidence.

Tad Jarmon roamed through the crowd. At the bar, he found his old friend, Lowell Oliver, whom he had not seen since graduation. "Hello, Lowell," he said.

Oliver drained his glass. "Hi, ol' buddy," he said with a loose grin. He shoved his face closer in an effort to focus his eyes. Suddenly, he became oddly sober. "Tad Jarmon."

"In the flesh."

"Well . . . good to see you, Tad. You haven't changed

much." He held his glass toward the bartender for a refill. His hand was shaking slightly.

"We've all changed some, Lowell. It's been twenty years."

"Twenty years. Yeah . . . Twenty years . . ."

"Have you seen Jack and Duncan?"

"They're around here someplace," Oliver mumbled.

"We'll have to get together after the banquet and talk over old times," Tad said.

Oliver stared at him with a peculiar expression. Beads of perspiration stood out on his forehead. "Old times. Yeah . . . sure, Tad."

Tad Jarmon meandered back into the crowd. Soon he spotted Jack Harriman with a circle of friends in another corner of the room. Jack looked every inch the prosperous businessman. He was expensively dressed. His face was deeply tanned, but he was growing paunchy. He'd put on at least forty pounds since graduation.

"Hello, Jack."

Harriman turned. His smile became frozen. "Well, if it isn't Tad Jarmon." He reached out for a handshake. "You guys all remember Tad," he said, a trifle too loudly. His hand felt damp in Tad's clasp.

One of their ex-schoolmates grinned. "I remember how you two guys and Duncan Gitterhouse and Lowell Oliver were always pulling off practical jokes on the town."

"Yeah," another added. "If something weird happened, everybody figured you four guys had a hand in it. Like the time the clock in the courthouse steeple started running backward. Took them a week to figure out how to get it to run in the right direction again. Nobody could prove anything, but we all knew you four guys did it."

The group chuckled.

"I saw Lowell over at the bar," Tad said to Harriman. "I told him we should get together after the banquet and talk over old times."

"Old times . . ." Harriman repeated, a hollow note creeping into his voice. "Well . . . sure, Tad." He wiped a nervous hand across his chin. "By the way, where are you living now?"

"Still right here in Jacksonville, in the big old stuffy house on the hill. After my dad died, I just stayed on there."

Tad excused himself and went in search of Duncan Gitterhouse. He soon found him, a man turned prematurely gray, with a deeply lined face and brooding eyes.

"Well, Duncan, I guess I should call you 'Doctor' now."

"That's just for my patients," Gitterhouse replied, his deep-set eyes resting somberly on Tad. "I was pretty sure I'd be seeing you here, Tad."

"Well, you know I couldn't pass up the opportunity of talking over old times with you and Jack and Lowell. Maybe after the banquet, the four of us can get together."

The doctor's eyes appeared to sink deeper and grow more resigned. "Yes, Tad."

The banquet was followed by speeches and introductions. Each alumnus arose and told briefly what he had done since graduation. When the master of ceremonies came to Tad, he said, "Well, I'm sure you all remember this next guy. He and his three buddies sure did liven up our school years. Remember the Halloween we found old Mrs. Gifford's wheelchair on top of the school building? And the stink bombs that went off during assembly meetings? They never could prove who did any of those things, but we all knew. How about confessing now, Tad? The statute of limitations has run out."

Tad arose amid laughter and applause. He grinned and shook his head. "I won't talk. My lips are sealed . . ."

After the banquet, the four chums from high school days drifted outside and crossed the street to a small, quiet town-square park. Jack Harriman lit an expensive cigar.

"It hasn't changed, has it?" Duncan Gitterhouse said, looking up at the ancient, dome-shaped courthouse, at the Civil War monument, the heavy magnolia trees, the quiet streets. "It's as if everything stopped the night we graduated, and time stood still ever since."

"The night we graduated," Jack Harriman echoed. He pressed a finger against his cheek, which was beginning to twitch again. "Seems like a thousand years ago."

"Does it?" Tad said. "That's odd. Time is relative, though. To me it's just like last night."

"We don't have any business talking about it," Duncan Gitterhouse said harshly. "I don't know why I came here for this ridiculous class reunion. It was insanity."

"Don't know why you came back, Duncan?" Tad said softly. "I think you do. You couldn't stay away. None of you could. You had to know if anyone ever suspected what we did that night. And you wanted to find out what that night did to the rest of us, how it changed our lives. We shared something so powerful it will bind us together always. I was sure you'd all come back."

"Still the amateur psychologist, Tad?" Harriman asked sourly.

Tad shrugged.

"It was your fault what we did that night, Tad," Lowell Oliver said, beginning to blubber in a near-alcoholic crying jag. "You were always the ringleader. We followed you like sheep. Whatever crazy, sick schemes you thought up—"

"We were just kids," Gitterhouse argued angrily. "Just irresponsible kids, all of us. Nobody could be held accountable—"

"Just kids? We were old enough in this state to have been tried for murder," Tad pointed out.

There was a heavy silence. Then Tad murmured slowly, "I used to go past the place on the creek where old Pete Bonner had his house-trailer. For years you could see where the fire had been. The ground was black and the rusty framework of the house-trailer was still there. It was finally cleared away when the shopping center was built, but every time I go by that place I think about the night old Pete Bonner died there. And I think about us. A person acts; the act is over in a few minutes. But the aftermath of the act lives on in our emotions, our brains, perhaps forever. We committed an act twenty years ago. The next day, they buried what was left of old Pete. We're stuck with that for the rest of our lives."

They fell silent again, each thinking back to that night. It was true that Tad had been the ringleader of their tight little group, and the night of their graduation, it was Tad who thought of the final, monstrous prank: "Let's set Pete Bonner's trailer on fire."

"But Pete's liable to be in the trailer," one of the others had said.

"That's the whole point," Tad had grinned, then explained, "After tonight, we'll be going different directions.

Duncan is going into medical school. Lowell's going into the Army. Jack's going to business college. I'll probably stay here. We need to do something so stupendous, so important, that it will weld the four of us together forever. So, we'll roast old Pete Bonner alive."

Tad had pointed out to the rest of them that Pete was the town drunk, an old wino who had no family. It would be like putting a worthless old dog out of his misery.

Because of the hypnotic-like hold Tad had on the others, they had agreed—sweating and scared—but they'd agreed.

That night after graduation exercises, Tad led them to Pete Bonner's trailer with cans of gasoline and matches. As they ran away from the blazing funeral pyre, the screams of the dying old wino followed them.

"I can still hear that old man screaming," Duncan Gitterhouse said, his hands shaking as he chain-lit another cigarette.

"Tad, you said we're stuck with what we did for the rest of our lives," Jack Harriman sighed. "It's true. I've made a pile of money, but what good is it? I can't go to sleep without pills. I eat too much. My doctor says I'm going to have a coronary in five years if I don't quite eating so much, but I can't stop. It's an emotional thing, a compulsion. Look at poor Lowell there. He's spent the last five years in and out of alcoholic sanitariums."

Duncan Gitterhouse nodded. "My practice is a success. Compensation, I guess. I have the idea that if I save enough lives, I'll make up for the one we took. I do five, ten operations a day. But my private life is a shambles—my wife left me years ago; my kids are freaked out on drugs." He turned to Tad Jarmon. "I suspect you didn't get off any better than we did, Tad. You never married. You're stuck here, in the home you grew up in. I don't think you *can* leave . . ."

They sat in the park for a while. Then they got up and went off to their respective motel rooms—Tad to his big, old-fashioned house with white columns.

In his study, Tad took down one of his journals from a bookshelf. In his neat, precise hand, he carefully described the events of the evening, recording in detail all that Jack, Duncan, and Lowell had said. Following that entry, he added his prognostication for their future. "I would estimate that Jack will be dead within ten years, probably suicide if he doesn't have a stroke first. Lowell will become a hopeless alcoholic and spend his last years in a sanitarium. Duncan will keep on with his practice, but will have to turn to drugs to keep himself going."

He sat back for a moment. Then as an afterthought, he added, "I will continue to live out my life here in this old house, on the inheritance my father left me, eventually becoming something of a recluse. Duncan was right; I can't leave. It is a psychological prison. But I am reasonably content, keeping busy with my hobby, the study of human nature, that will fill volumes when I am through."

He put the journal away. Then he turned to another bookcase. It was lined with similar neatly bound and dated journals. He went down the line until he found one dated 1953. He opened it and flipped the pages, stopping when he came to the date of their graduation, then he started to read:

"Tonight being graduation," he had written, "I decided we must do something spectacular. A crowning achievement to top any previous prank. Early in the afternoon, I stopped by Pete Bonner's trailer. I had in mind giving him a few dollars to buy us some whiskey for the evening. Being underage, we couldn't go to the liquor store ourselves, but Pete is always ready to do anything for a small bribe. I was surprised, indeed, when I walked into Pete's trailer and found him sprawled out on the floor. He was quite dead, apparently from a heart attack. If I hadn't found him, he'd probably have stayed there for days until someone accidentally stumbled upon him as I had done. I immediately got a brilliant idea for a colossal joke and a chance to test a theory of mine. They say time is relative. If someone believes he has committed an act, it's the same to him as if he *has* committed the act. The consequences, as far as they affect him, should be the same.

"This time the joke would be on Jack, Duncan, and Lowell. They're so gullible, they'll do anything I tell them. I hurried home and swiped the wire recorder out of Dad's study. I recorded some agonized screams and put it under Pete's trailer, all hooked up so it would take only a second to turn it on. I then went over to talk to Jack, Duncan, and Lowell. I convinced them it would be a great idea to burn up Pete's trailer and roast Pete alive. Of course, they had no way of knowing Pete was already dead. Tonight, after graduation, we slipped down to Pete's trailer with gasoline and matches. I went around the other side, pretending to slosh my gasoline around, and reached under the trailer and switched on the wire recorder. As soon as the flames shot up, we began hearing some very convincing screams. It will be most interesting, in future years, to see what effect tonight's act will have on the lives of Jack Harriman, Duncan Gitterhouse, and Lowell Oliver."

Tad Jarmon closed the journal and leaned back with a cold, thoughtful smile.

The Way It Is Now

by Elaine Slater

When they were first married right after graduation from college, he had never been able to spend enough time with her. They bought a small cabin in the North Woods with no communication to the outside world, and spent every weekend there, walking hand in hand, sitting by a roaring fire, lost in each other—that is, when they weren't chopping wood or hauling water from the brook, huffing and laughing at the unaccustomed exertion.

But lately things had changed. Business commitments kept him occupied on Saturdays. He could no longer find the time to escape to the cabin. When she spoke to him, he was never quite there. His reading moved gradually from the *Partisan Review* to the *Wall Street Journal*, and endless market reports. He still sat through the arty movies— Fellini, Truffaut—but when she tried to probe their murky depths, he never contributed a word.

"Where *are* you?" she would ask in exasperation. "Am I talking to a stone?"

"I heard you," he would reply, jumping slightly as though she had caught him at the cookie jar. "Your last words were precisely 'and the dog, of course, symbolizes the eternal evil in man.' "

She would sigh. He was listening evidently, but still . . . he wasn't all there. His mind was on other things, and not all the newly acquired luxuries that his business success brought could compensate for the loss of her young, playful, loving husband. His sense of humor seemed now to be reserved for his business associates, who told her how he broke them up at the Board meetings. He worked several nights a week and came home bone-weary. How could a man that tired exercise a sense of humor, or talk, or, for that matter, make love?

Now they had a house in the suburbs and a housekeeper. She read the magazine advertisements and decided there was a ready remedy at hand. She bathed at twilight, perfumed herself, donned an expensive dressing gown, lit candles, and made a mixer of martinis. When he arrived home, his favorite Mozart concerto was playing. He looked mildly surprised at her outfit, commented that she smelled good, said he preferred a bourbon on the rocks to a martini which gave him indigestion, suggested more lighting over dinner because he couldn't see what he was eating, picked up the latest *Barrons Report,* and fell asleep on the sofa. His own snoring woke him up and he stumbled up to the bedroom.

If she had suspected another woman, she would have had a better idea of how to fight back. But how does one fight the overwhelming commitment to Business? She read Betty Freidan and decided to get a job, but even that didn't fill the gaping void in her life. She thought about taking a lover, and had lunch with one of the young men with whom she worked. He showed an extraordinary interest in her husband's stock portfolio, and shuddering at the thought of a preoccupied lover, she decided she hated all men.

She began to brood. Her friends had children on whom they could vent their frustrations. She had no one. She mulled over the idea of suicide, but her other self kept calling out rebelliously.

"Why should *I* die? *I'm* perfectly capable of laughter, of life, of love! It's *he* who is dead already and doesn't know it. It's not fair for you to kill me."

The *Evergreen Review* slipped out of her lap, and she stared for a long time at her hands.

When he came home that night, she made no attempt to share with him the boring day's activities. He didn't seem to notice the deathly silence, although the housekeeper became so nervous that she broke a rare Minton plate. When the telephone rang just as they were having their coffee, he jumped up to answer it.

His suddenly animated voice was saying, "Harry! How did it go in Toronto? I've thought of nothing else all evening."—as she walked thoughtfully upstairs.

When he came into their bedroom, he was jubilant. He caught her around the waist and shouted, "The Toronto deal is going through! Can you beat that? After two years of negotiating it's finally going through. Bigness is the only thing that talks these days, and we're going to be *BIG!* If only Harry was here right now, would I love to hear all the details. I'd—"

She interrupted him quietly. "Let's celebrate. Let's go to the cabin this weekend. We haven't been there in months. The road will soon be impassable and we won't be able to go again until spring."

"This weekend?" He looked dubious.

"Yes—we'll have a second honeymoon. We could find each other again."

"Have you lost me? Or have I lost you?" he asked in his old teasing voice. "Okay, honey, if you want a second honeymoon you'll have it. But I'll have to cancel two meetings on Saturday. How about putting it off for a week or two?"

"No," she said firmly.

He was too triumphant at the thought of the successful Toronto deal to argue; so on Friday they drove up to the cabin.

It was just as they had left it. No one ever came near the place. There was a pile of wood in the snow by the ax. The wood was not too wet and they quickly made a smoky fire to warm the little room.

She bounced on the squeaky brass bed a few times, and gazed about her happily. All the old warmth and affection began to return. Perhaps here they would find what they had lost. Perhaps here he would look *at* her again, not *through* her. Perhaps here he would once again be interested, if only for a weekend, in her, in her life, in her love—and forget the business world which consumed him. Yes, she was ready to settle for a weekend.

He gazed into the fireplace, at the crackling blue and orange flames. There was a distant, even wistful look on his face. She watched him tenderly, feeling the old love for that tired worn face. She sat opposite him in the shabby old chair that they had bought together in a country junk shop, and had loaded hysterically onto the pickup that he had driven in those days. The front seat was so loaded with their gear that she had ridden the whole day to the cabin seated on that chair in the back of the truck amid a clutter of second-hand household goods.

How funny that had been! Everyone on the road had turned to look, laugh, and wave. And when they arrived at the cabin after an unbelievably bumpy trip—over miles of isolated dirt roads with low overhanging branches that clawed at her face and battered the truck—she had jumped into his waiting arms. Happily he had carried her to the threshold, where he discovered he had to drop her unceremoniously in order to get at the key which was hanging on a rusty nail. They had laughed together until they couldn't stand up, but they had clung to each other for support. Yes, clung to each other . . .

She was deep in nostalgia. He lifted his head and gazed at her. She gazed back into his eyes, trying to guess his thoughts. Were they as far away as hers? He started to speak, and she leaned forward, a slight smile on her lips.

"You know—" he began wistfully.

"What?" she interrupted flirtatiously.

"—Central American Tobacco has just merged with Amalgamated Biscuit."

She buried the bloodstained ax in the snow and went back to sit by the fire—to lose herself in nostalgia before she had to go look for the shovel.

The Hot Rock

by James McKimmey

A sharp, chilling wind blew fog across London. The portly man, wearing a dark duster-length overcoat with a fur collar and a homburg fitted squarely on his bald head, closed the door of his small shop on Chandos Place and locked it. When he had escorted the mink-clad woman into the waiting cab, the fog had obliterated the gold lettering on the door of the shop, which read: *Henry Thornwall Esq., Jeweler.*

Henry leaned forward, patting an inside pocket to make certain that he had not, in the tension of what they were doing, forgotten his examining glass, then gave the driver an address near the Thames. He leaned back with a sigh.

Street lamps flashed against the face of his companion. She looked young from a distance, but on closer examination it was obvious that she was middle-aged, heavily made up, rich, and, right now, very excited.

She put a hand on Henry's plump wrist, squeezing fingers glittering with rings. "How dangerous is this, Henry?"

Henry shook his head, "I wish I knew, Madam. It's not my . . . ah . . . accustomed . . . well, you know."

"I know," she said softly, a waver in her voice. "But the Sional, Henry!"

"Shhh." He looked ahead at the driver.

"For twenty thousand pounds!" She tapped her large purse. "And it's worth double that!"

"Shhh, shhh," went Henry.

The cab moved ahead, the driver making his way through the murk as though by magic. Henry leaned sideways and put his mouth close to her ear. "It's all happened so quickly. Tell me again what he said on the telephone."

"He *whispered,* Henry," she said softly.

"Yes, quite," Henry nodded. "What did he whisper, then?"

"That he had the Sional Diamond and would sell it to me for twenty thousand pounds if I would meet him at the address you've given the driver—with the money."

Henry nodded again. "And that name he gave himself?"

"The Cockroach." She shuddered. "I said I'd do what he asked if I were allowed to bring you to examine the stone. But why do you suppose he has chosen me, Henry?"

Henry shrugged. "Mrs. Peter Sterling-Bahr?"

"I suppose it's obvious, isn't it? Peter would die if he knew. But he won't find out. He never pays any attention to *my* money. Unless something happens that . . ."

Henry put a hand into the right pocket of his coat and pulled out a small chrome-plated pistol. It reflected lights they were passing as he checked it.

"*Henry!*" the woman said.

Henry returned the pistol to his pocket. "Chaps like this . . . I don't know. They whisper so you can't get a good chance at their accent so you might know something that way. They constantly run underground like sewer rats. I, well, thought it might prove comforting."

The woman touched Henry's hand again. "I never thought of you as being so heroic, Henry. I'll make it up to you. I promise."

"*Ma*dam," Henry said gently. He smiled. Then the smile disappeared. "And we are here, I'm afraid."

They moved toward an old warehouse in the wind-driven fog as the cab's taillights abruptly disappeared.

"Shouldn't we have kept him?" Mrs. Peter Sterling-Bahr asked.

"I shouldn't think so," Henry said. "His license may already have been observed. We wouldn't want you followed to the hotel where you're going to put it, you know."

"Of course. Oh, Henry," she said, hugging his arm, "what would I do without you?"

"Let's, ah, complete the business first, Madam. Then . . ."

His voice trailed away as they stopped before a closed wooden door. Henry put his hand on the latch, paused, took a breath, then opened it. There was a yellow crack of light far across a large high-ceilinged room. Henry dug into the left-hand pocket of his coat and produced a small flashlight.

"You thought of everything, didn't you, Henry?" the woman whispered.

"I rather hope so, anyway," Henry said as they moved forward following the small beam of light.

"I'm trembling, Henry."

He squeezed her hand.

They arrived at the door where light was escaping below on the dusty wooden floor. Again Henry took a breath, then turned the handle. They looked in at a small figure seated at an old desk beneath a naked light bulb hanging from the ceiling of a small room; long and greasy-looking hair with streaks of gray hung shoulder-length; metal-rimmed glasses with tinted lenses decorated a face that looked surprisingly boyish; the suit was wide-shouldered, gray and pin-striped; delicate hands rested on either side of a wide-brimmed fedora placed on the desk.

Henry and the woman stood in absolute silence, staring.

"Madam Sterling-Bahr?" came the throaty whisper. "I am The Cockroach."

The woman managed to nod.

The Cockroach curled a slender finger and motioned them forward. They went to the desk and stood looking at the tinted glasses reflecting light from the bulb above. The Cockroach removed a small revolver from a pocket. The woman turned in alarm just in time to see that Henry had also gotten out his pistol. The two weapons pointed at each other.

"No nonsense, you understand," Henry said in a controlled voice, and adoration showed in the woman's eyes.

The Cockroach stared at the chrome pistol for some time, then drew out from a pocket a small object wrapped in velvet. The fabric was worked loose, exposing a magnificent briolette-cut diamond. The woman drew her breath in, blinking. Henry's eyes narrowed. "May I?" he asked.

The Cockroach shrugged, and Henry carefully placed his pistol in the woman's hand, saying, "Don't hesitate to pull the trigger, my dear, if he should become cute in any fashion."

"Oh, Henry," the woman breathed, but she held the pistol firmly as Henry got out his jeweler's loupe and fitted it to his eye and examined the stone at length. Finally he nodded. He returned it to the velvet and put away his examining glass. "Yes, indeed." He reclaimed his pistol from the woman.

"*Is* it?" she asked.

"Most assuredly."

"Money," The Cockroach whispered.

When the transaction had been completed and the diamond was in the woman's purse, Henry said, "Shall we, then?"

He began backing toward the door, pistol in hand, and the woman went with him. In the large outer room, they made their way through darkness. "I'd use the torch," Henry said quietly, "but I shouldn't want him to go out the back door of that room and up into the loft somewhere where he could shoot at it."

"Dear God," the woman whispered.

They finally fumbled their way outside into a shroud of cold. Then they hurried along the sidewalk. It seemed an eternity, but at last they were able to find a free cab. As they got in, Henry gave the address of a club near Piccadilly Circus. He put an arm around the woman's fur-covered shoulders, feeling her trembling.

"Foolish place to go, rather," he said. "Too many theatrical types, and worse. But I do have a membership."

"Must we go there?" she asked. "Can't I simply go straight to the hotel, then—"

He shook his head. "Beggar might be following. Best to put him off."

"Of course," she said. "I think I'm falling in love with you, Henry."

"Mr. Peter Sterling-Bahr would not like that, I suspect."

"But I shouldn't care," the woman said, holding Henry's hand tightly.

They went upstairs to an informal room which hummed with conversation as members stood and sat about. Henry ordered a gin and orange for both of them. The woman sipped hers, face looking pale.

"Henry," she said, "the Sional! In my purse!"

"Yes, Madam. We seem to have done it."

"Not madam, Henry. Not ever again. Elizabeth."

"Elizabeth," Henry nodded, testing the sound of it. He repeated it.

She had removed her coat, and it was spread on the sofa beside her. Her dress was black, her jewelry was notable, and her legs looked much younger than the rest of her as she crossed them and gave Henry that same look she'd shown in the warehouse near the river.

"You couldn't go with me to the hotel?" she asked.

"I should rather like to, certainly," he said.

"You couldn't come after I've checked in—please, dear Henry!"

"I should like that, indeed, Elizabeth. But—"

"Later, then?" she said. "Some other day or night?"

"I shall require you to remember that."

"I shall. And how do I do it at the hotel, again?"

"Ask them to put the item you have in your purse into safekeeping for the night."

"But if I went home instead—"

He shook his head. "With your husband on business in Paris—"

"But the servants," she said. "Surely—"

"Blighter may already be in with one of them. I would rather trust the Ritz, my dear," he said positively. "A formidably reliable establishment. Then, tomorrow, I shall accompany you to the vault. I think we might go now, if you've finished your drink," he suggested.

They returned to the street where Henry obtained yet another cab. He directed it to the misty glitter of Piccadilly Circus and said to the woman, "Much better if you get out and walk to the hotel rather than taking another cab. If someone should be following this one, they'll continue, I think. When we next stop with the traffic, simply get out and join the crowd on the sidewalk. I'll call you at the hotel the second I've gotten home."

"I do hate leaving you, Henry."

Henry smiled. "I hate leaving you, Elizabeth." He touched her, then said, "Now, my dear."

She got out swiftly and hurried toward the crowded sidewalk where neon cut through swirls of reflecting fog.

The cab moved on, and Henry looked through the back window just as a small figure in a pin-striped suit, wearing tinted glasses and a wide-brimmed fedora over long greasy hair, came up to Elizabeth. An arm was put around her waist, and she was drawn toward a dark doorway. Her mouth opened as though she might be screaming, but Henry, looking away and settling back in his seat, guessed that she wasn't making a sound.

When he reached his flat, the telephone was ringing. He lifted it, saying, "Henry Thornwall here."

"Oh, Henry!" Mrs. Peter Sterling-Bahr said in anguish. "How could it have happened!"

"Are you all right?" he asked with concern.

"Not hurt. Not physically. But he just came up on me on the sidewalk the minute I got out of the cab. He put his arm around me and whispered he had his gun pointed at me and made me go into a doorway where he got the stone out of my purse and ran off! What could I do! It's stolen! I couldn't . . . Oh, Henry! How could he have followed us? In the fog? Two cabs? The club? And yet be there on the sidewalk, waiting . . . Henry?"

"I don't *know* how," Henry breathed. "I rather . . . thought I'd been so clever. But I guess I'm no good at that sort of thing. Oh, damn, Elizabeth. Dreadful, altogether."

"Dreadful, yes," she said limply. "Yes, it is. What do I do now, Henry?"

"Go home, I should think. Have something to drink. Try to forget it."

"It that really all there is for me to do now?" she said wearily. "Henry, is that all?"

"I rather think," he said slowly, "that it is."

Twenty minutes later, Henry's door buzzer sounded. When he opened the door, he saw no one on the stoop. Then he looked behind the bushes and saw the small figure wearing the wide-brimmed hat and tinted glasses standing beside the wall. Henry reached out and pulled the figure in and closed the door. "And here you are, my dear," he said fondly, then kissed a boyish forehead.

The sound of the shower stopped in the bath off Henry's comfortable bedroom. Henry stood in the adjoining study by the bar mixing two Scotches with soda. When his visitor, an extraordinarily beautiful creature with thick blonde hair, came out of the bedroom, he could see the suit, hat, glasses, and wig on the bed beside the carelessly dropped currency. The girl was dressed now in a satin negligee. She smiled beautifully as she crossed to Henry and put her arms around his neck.

"Oh, darling," she said, "it was so smooth, wasn't it?"

"Practice makes perfect, doesn't it?" he said, kissing her boyish forehead again.

A Puff of Orange Smoke

by Lael J. Littke

Bill O'Connell knew all about the way his wife Alice liked to have Paul Newman in the kitchen with her when she washed the dishes. He didn't mind. After all, didn't he sometimes have Raquel Welch snuggled by *his* side as he drove home from work?

Everyone was entitled to his own private fantasies, and certainly a pretty girl like Alice must occasionally yearn for something a little more spectacular than an ordinary, slightly homely, not-very-tall guy who made an adequate but not fancy living in an insurance firm, a guy who was totally untalented except for a real flair for emptying the garbage.

Bill knew he was neither handsome nor suave, and definitely not the dashing romantic type. But Cortland Marshall was, and, confound him, he was coming through Los Angeles on his way to Washington, D.C. from his most recent diplomatic post in Thailand, an exotic spot if Bill ever heard of one. He couldn't blame Alice for being all agog over the fact that Cortland was coming to dinner. Cort had never married and liked to keep in touch with Alice, even though she had married. When he wrote that he was coming through L.A., Alice had written back insisting that he stop and visit.

So now the kids were packed off to Grandma's, the house was shining with wax and polish, the rib roast in the oven was giving off an aroma which could tempt any man to give up his bachelorhood, and Bill was cautioned to "be nice to Cort."

It wouldn't have been so bad if Cortland had been a plumber or a grocery clerk; but a man with a glamor job like his could set a girl's heart to thumping even if he was bald and hollow-chested, which Cortland was not. It had never been quite clear to Bill why Alice had married him—Bill—when she could have had Cort. But then she was the type who yearned over stray kittens and wept for starving dogs, and she said she fell in love with Bill because he looked as if he needed someone to take care of him.

The big question was, could that kind of love withstand the strain of Cortland showing up once or twice every year still obviously smitten with his old flame? Certainly Alice seemed perfectly happy—but what was it then that made her cheeks glow when she ran to open the door in answer to Cortland's knock?

"Cort!" she cried, and then giggled happily as Cortland engulfed her in a bear hug. Right in front of Bill. As if Bill did not exist.

"Alice, honey," he said. "You haven't changed a bit."

"Neither have you, Cort," Alice-honey said.

Bill had to admit she was right. He had been away almost a year this time, but his well-tailored clothes and close-cropped dark hair were as attractive as ever. And he absolutely oozed charm.

Finally Cortland noticed Bill. "Well, Bill," he said affably, "howza boy?"

Bill wanted to snap his teeth and snarl, but instead he pasted on a wide silly grin and said, "Fine, Cortland. How are you, buddy?" Immediately he felt like a clod, which was how Cortland always made him feel.

His duties to his host taken care of, Cortland turned back to Alice. "Tell me what you've been doing to stay so beautiful," he said.

Alice giggled again. "Oh, Cort, I've just been a housewife. Come on out in the kitchen and talk to me while I finish fixing dinner."

Cortland put his arm around Alice's shoulders and they walked into the kitchen, leaving Bill alone with his bad thoughts. He wished that Cortland, in the time since Alice last saw him, had lost his teeth or his hair or something so that he didn't look like every housewife's dream of romance.

Not that he was afraid Alice would run off with Cortland or anything like that. Or would she? Even if she didn't, she might start imagining it was Cortland standing by her side each time she washed the dishes. Bill could put up with Paul Newman in the kitchen. But Courtland Marshall — *NO!*"

"Oh, Bill," Alice sang out, "come on in and join us."

You bet he would join them. He'd go in there and sit and watch and if Cortland got fresh with Alice he'd poke him in the nose. Or at least he would think about it hard.

"Bill," Cortland said as he walked into the kitchen, "we've just been going over old memories."

Bill wished viciously he could wipe out those memories. Or better still, wipe out Cortland. Just a flick of the magic finger, folks, and poof, he's gone!

Bill flicked his fingers at Cortland and said aloud, "Poof, you're gone!"

There was a poof of orange smoke and Cortland was gone.

Bill stood in rigid silence for almost two minutes. Then Alice said in a matter-of-fact voice, "All right, boys, that was a nice trick. But dinner is almost ready. Come on back, Cortland."

Bill swallowed. "Alice," he said. His voice was a high squeak.

Alice went on stirring the gravy. "Bill, show Cort where he can wash his hands."

Bill tried again. "Alice," he squeaked. "I think Cortland *is* gone."

"Where'd he go?" Alice asked. "This is a fine time for him to go somewhere."

Bill collapsed on a kitchen chair. "I think I made him disappear."

"Well, make him reappear."

Bill shook his head. "I don't know how. I don't even know how I made him *dis*appear."

Alice stopped stirring the gravy. "Bill, are you sick?"

"I sure am," Bill groaned. His scalp felt tight and his eyes were so large he didn't think he could close the lids over them. "I've got to call the police," he whispered.

Officers Magee and Smithson were big, burly, and jaded. They had heard everything. Many times. Bill noticed, however, that they still had spirit enough to glance appreciatively at Alice.

"Sure," Officer Magee said when Bill had told his story. "You just flick your fingers and some guy disappears."

Bill gave them a sickly grin. "I know it sounds crazy, but that's what happened."

Officer Magee sighed. "Maybe we better search the premises," he told Smithson. "See if there are any signs of a struggle. Maybe he really did do away with this guy."

Magee looked again at Alice, who gave him a warm smile. Bill could almost hear the wheels in the officer's head grinding out, "Pretty wife, jealous husband, so goodbye, boy friend."

The two policemen conducted a thorough search of the house and back yard, poking around in the flowerbeds—for signs of digging, Bill thought.

"Okay," said Officer Magee when they returned. "Now tell us the truth. We're busy men, Mac. Our next call is a complaint about a billygoat who whistles *Yankee Doodle*."

Officer Smithson guffawed.

Bill stood up and drew himself to his full five feet seven inches. He glared straight into the eye of his own reflection in Officer Magee's shiny buttons. He slumped down again. "I did tell you the truth," he mumbled.

"Well, tell us again," boomed Officer Smithson.

Bill licked his dry lips. "You see," he began, "Cortland was standing just about where you two are now. All I did was flick my fingers like this." He flicked his fingers. "And I said, 'Poof, you're gone!' "

There was a poof of orange smoke and Officers Magee and Smithson were gone.

Bill gulped. "Aw, come on back, you guys," he said weakly.

"Bill," Alice said. "Is that *all* you do? Just flick your fingers and someone disappears?"

Bill scarcely had the strength to nod as he sank onto a chair.

"I didn't know you could do that," Alice said with admiration. "You're quite a guy. No wonder I love you so much." She kissed him on top of the head. "I think I'll put dinner on now. Or maybe I should wait until Cortland gets back. When *will* he be back?"

Bill shook his head.

"Let me know when he gets here," Alice said. "I'll go put the finishing touches on the dining room." She left.

Bill wasn't at all sure that Cortland would get back. Or the two officers, either. He found himself wondering if Magee and Smithson had families. Maybe right now several little kiddies were crying for their daddies to come home. Bill stared bleakly at the spot where the three men had stood.

"I've got to turn myself in," he said to himself. "I'll call and tell them to come get me."

He wasn't sure just what he would say. As he waited for his call to be transferred to the police lieutenant, he tried to formulate something that wouldn't brand him immediately as an absolute nut. What could he say? "See, I've got these magic fingers—"

"Lieutenant Hargrove," said a gruff voice on the wire. There was a pause.

"Lieutenant Hargrove," repeated Bill. There was another pause.

"I'm Lieutenant Hargrove," the voice said, a wary note coming into it, as if Lieutenant Hargrove were girding himself to deal with an addled brain.

Bill cleared his throat and considered hanging up. "Well, you see, Lieutenant Hargrove," he said, "these two officers came to my house to investigate a strange occurrence, and I don't know what happened to them."

Lieutenant Hargrove asked quickly, "Which two officers was that?"

"I believe their names were Magee and Smithson."

"Oh, those two loonies," said Lieutenant Hargrove.

"They just called from Palm Springs. Said they didn't know how they got there. Couple of nincompoops. Get lost crossing the street."

Bill clutched the phone. "Palm Springs, you say? Are they all right?"

"Sure," said Lieutenant Hargrove. "Physically, at least. Say, did you get that strange occurrence taken care of?"

"Yes," Bill said hastily. "Yes. Oh, yes. Thanks." He hung up quickly. No reason to be thought a nut if everyone was all right. Of course there was still Cortland. But he would undoubtedly show up somewhere. San Francisco, maybe. Probably figure the State Department sent him on a rush mission or something.

Bill started to whistle. He walked to the mirror that Alice kept on the wall just inside the kitchen door. He *was* quite a guy, he thought, peering at his reflection. But he didn't look any different. He sort of thought he might, considering his newly discovered talent. And what a talent! Just let Alice's old boy friends come nosing around now. Just a flick of the fingers, and away they'd go. Even Paul Newman couldn't do that.

Bill smiled at himself in the mirror. Just let them come. He could take care of them. He flicked his fingers at his reflected image. "Poof," he said, "you're gone!"

"Bill," Alice said, coming in from the dining room. "I think we'd better go ahead and eat before the roast dries out."

She looked around the empty kitchen. "Bill?" she said. "Bill? Where are you?"

The Chicken Player

by Joe L. Hensley

Jamie pulled the dusty, black T-bird onto the shoulder of the road he'd been cruising and sat there waiting. The radio was off because on a still day he could hear a car from further away than he could see it.

In that hour of cruising he'd checked the road carefully. It wasn't in top condition, but it was all right, better than many he'd played the game on, and it had the advantage of sparse traffic, perhaps too sparse. The only other car he'd seen during that hour of driving was an old Chevy, worn out, down at the springs, driven by a man with white hair. Not very good prey, but a possible. The old man had driven by without a glance, moving very slowly. Jamie was still debating with himself whether to follow when he'd seen a child's curious face appear in the rear window of the old car.

That had ruined it. He was superstitious about kids and there'd been enough bad luck recently. Thursday, he'd almost been arrested by a State Trooper, but had managed to outrun him. Friday, the transmission had gone out of the T-bird and he'd been dismounted the whole weekend. Now, deep inside, he felt he'd about worn out this part of the country and it was time to move on. People were starting to look familiar to him, remind him of people he'd known before in other places and at other times. It was kooky how so many faces reminded him of Mr. Kelly. Mr. Kelly was thousands of miles away, back in New York State. Mr. Kelly was five years before in time.

Jamie remembered with narcissistic nostalgia that he'd been an amateur then, just learning the game. Then it had been a game of half-grown kids, played on deserted roads, with sentries out to warn if police came near. The Chicken Game. God, it had grabbed him even then.

The run at Mr. Kelly's car had been a lark, an impulse, a broadening of the game to include the world around Jamie. He'd have gotten away if he hadn't blown a tire at the critical moment. That had thrown him into the Kelly car when he thought himself safely past and it had jumbled his hopped up Ford into a junk pile, but he'd scrambled out unhurt.

He would not have thought that a kid could scream as much or as long as the Kelly boy had. Mr. Kelly had been thrown clear and he was unconscious, so only Jamie had to listen to the screams from the burning Kelly car. He had listened and felt strange inside and when the screams stopped he'd giggled a little.

After awhile there'd been lots of police and questions.

"I lost control," he told them. "The tire blew and I lost control." He repeated it and repeated it, and stubbornness and the good lawyer his Aunt hired made the difference. The jury turned him loose.

Only Mr. Kelly knew. Jamie remembered the eyes that had burned right through him during the trial.

When it was done and Jamie was free, he moved on. It was an act of protection, not fear. By that time he'd played again and again and without the game there was nothing. No angry, vengeful man was going to take the game away.

So now he was twenty-three years old and he'd been playing the game for a long time. It was now a professional thing, done carefully, accomplished at rare, safe intervals when the desire became overpowering. The game was more than anything else, more than the sum total of all the rest. It was more than love, greater than sex, better than drugs, and stronger than the fear of death.

Sometimes when Jamie was around other people who were his age, he could have screamed. The talk was mundane, the pleasures crude, and there was an eternal sameness to each scene. Sometimes he was sure that the only time he was really alive was when he was behind the wheel of the T-bird, alone, hunting. The rest of it was just the scene, all papery and fragile.

The game was simple, but there were rules. The other car was the mark. You passed it and accelerated away, making sure the highway was clear. A mile or so ahead you turned and came back at the mark, twisting right lane to left lane until the mark saw you. Then you took his lane, going straight for him, foot deep in the accelerator, forcing the mark to turn away, to chicken.

The rest of the game was of his own variation. When the mark turned away, Jamie followed, while the brutal, delicious fear rose within him.

Sometimes other drivers froze and stopped dead in the road, and that filled Jamie with contempt. More often they came on erratically until he forced them from the road. Two months back, he'd run a lone, male driver down a steep hill and seen him roll, metal shrieking, against rocks and trees until all sound stopped. That had been a very good one.

The game took nerve and a sure knowledge of the condition of the highway and an instinctive feel for what a car would do, but the shuddery exultation was worth all of it.

He'd not played the game for two weeks now and the last time had been a washout. He leaned back in the T-bird's bucket seat and thought and let the heat of anticipation wash over him. Vaguely he remembered his mother and father. They'd died when he was ten years old. It had been an accident on the Turnpike. A truck had smashed their car to nothingness. In a way he was a child of speed. The insurance had made him nearly rich and he lived frugally now, except for cars. An indulgent, adoring Aunt had raised him, given him his first car, protected him first from angry neighbors and, later, the police.

A sound brought him back to awareness. He heard a faraway motor, and then he saw the tiny, fast-moving car in his rear-view mirror. He started the T-bird and listened to the sweet motor, the best that money could buy. He fastened his seat belt. Once he would have snarled at the idea of wearing a seat belt, but now the game was so precious that he took no chances and the belt held him firmly as he twisted back and forth.

He waited the other car out and it came past, moving fast, on the borderline of speeding. He caught a furtive glimpse of a lone, male driver who sat stiffly upright, appearing to be almost drawn back against the seat.

He gunned the T-bird out behind and passed the other car and was elated when it speeded up as he went around it. He could almost envision the other driver cursing him as he cut in sharply and pressed the accelerator down. There was no riding passenger in the other car. There was only the driver.

A perfect mark. *Oh, Heat that lives within me: Make this one of the good ones.*

Jamie made his turn when the distance was right. There was no car behind the mark and nothing in his own rear-view mirror. The heat began to build.

He let the engine wind up until the speedometer read ninety, and he eased, right lane, then left lane.

He saw dust puff from the rear tires of the other car and something inside him screamed: *No! Don't quit on me!* The other car came on and Jamie smiled.

At three hundred feet away he slid the T-bird into the left lane, dead at the other car, anticipating what would happen. The other driver would panic now, move out of the path of Jamie's hurtling car. Then the variation. Jamie would follow, forcing the other driver away from the traveled road, onto the tricky shoulder.

At this moment Jamie liked to see the oncoming driver's face. He lifted his eyes, and the face he saw seemed vaguely familiar and smiling, but that was impossible. Savagely, with hate, Jamie floorboarded the T-bird.

At fifty feet the other car cut sharply left and Jamie corrected happily, for this was as anticipated, but then the other car cut right again and there was no time to recover. The T-bird was caught slightly broadside. Jamie heard the thunder of the crash and fought the wheel and got the T-bird straightened as his wheels bounced on the shoulder, but one of the wheels hit a rut and he felt the T-bird going. He bent desperately into the seat, felt the top hit on the parched ground, heard the renewed tearing of metal and then it was a roll that seemed endless. The door came away beside him, but the belt held him firmly until all of the crazy, loud motion stopped and there was silence. Jamie reached then very quickly for the ignition, smelling the gasoline smell, breathing as hard as if he'd run a mile.

He could see the other car out of his starred windshield.

Its right front end was smashed. The driver had the door open and he was unhooking a complicated safety harness that ran from a roll bar in the car over his shoulders and waist. It was the harness that had given him the stiff look, Jamie calculated.

Jamie unhooked his own seat belt, but the steering wheel was still in the way and his left leg was caught somewhere. He felt the beginning of pain, and the warmth of blood running down his injured leg brought a leaping panic.

"Help," he called.

The other man came slowly up to the jumbled T-bird.

"Hello, Jamie."

"I remember you," Jamie said incredulously. "You're Mr. Kelly."

"Can you make it out?" Mr. Kelly asked.

Jamie shook his head. "It's my leg."

Mr. Kelly's eyes sparkled.

Jamie looked at the other man, unable to read him, fighting away fear. "You like the game?"

Mr. Kelly smiled. "Enough to learn to play it. I trained in sports cars and drove dirt track for awhile after my boy died and before I came after you."

"Maybe . . ."

Mr. Kelly held up his hand. "If they put you away you'd be back." He nodded. "There isn't any way to break you, Jamie."

"We could play again," Jamie said. "I've never had anyone before who could really play." He searched within. "It was better than it's ever been." And it had been.

"Not ever again, Jamie," Mr. Kelly said gently.

The fear came up in waves. "If you do anything they'll find out somehow. You prosecuted me once. They'll catch you."

"Not about us," Mr. Kelly said. "You've changed your name too many times."

Jamie laughed and the fear went away and he was exultant with triumph. "My fingerprints haven't changed. They took them then. They'll take them again. They'll use them and find out."

Mr. Kelly smiled a curious smile and sniffed at the gasoline fumes.

"I thought about that, too."
He lit a match.
When the screaming was all over, Mr. Kelly giggled.

Nothing But Bad News

by Henry Slesar

Dillon whirled and shot the bully for the fifth time. Pauline clenched her teeth and said *Miss, you bastard,* but the marshal didn't, his accuracy guaranteed by rerun inexorability. Arnold Summerly breathed a fifth sigh of relief, and Pauline said, "For God's sake, Arnold, didn't you *know* how it was going to turn out?" but Arnold was narcotized now by the commercial following the shoot-out.

Pauline reached out to tune in the seven o'clock news, but Arnold's hand beat her to the dial and spun it to the local channel; it was their own shoot-out, re-enacted every night.

"Arnold, please!" Pauline said. "Let's watch the news for once, just *once.* Anything could be happening. Greenland could have declared war on us. The world may be coming to an end. Anything!"

"If it happens, we'll hear about it," Arnold said.

"How? How? You never watch the news. You never read a paper. You care so little about the world, what difference would it make if it *did* come to an end?"

"This beer is warm," Arnold said. "You've been putting the beer in the refrigerator door again. How many times do I have to tell you to put the beer inside?" The screen divided itself into the shape of a heart, and Arnold forgot his pique. The prospect of Lucy in the twentieth year of her pregnancy erased all rancor.

"You're a vegetable," Pauline said. "Do you know that, Arnold? You're an office machine in the daytime and a vegetable at night. A head of lettuce sticking out of a shirt collar."

At least he had the decency to get angry.

"All right! All right! You want to know why I don't watch the news? Why I don't read the paper? Because it's all *bad* news. Nothing but *bad* news. That's the reason so many people turn mean and rotten, they get to hear nothing but *bad* news from morning till night. There's not one nice, decent, cheerful thing you ever hear about, not one thing you can feel *good* about. That's why!"

"It's not true," Pauline said. "Maybe it seems that way, but it isn't."

"Yeah? Yeah? You want to bet? You want to bet, like, that new fur coat you want so bad? You want to bet that, Pauline, huh?"

"What do you mean, bet?"

"You heard me. Put your money where your big mouth is. You turn on the news, go ahead. And you hear one real *good* piece of news, you can quit saving for that fur coat, I'll buy it for you. Tomorrow. You won't have to wait another year, I'll put it on your back right now!"

The coat was an ebony mink. Pauline's Holy Grail.

"And if there *isn't* any good news?"

Arnold grinned.

"You give me that money you been saving and we take the fishing trip."

Pauline hated fishing trips. So she hesitated.

Arnold chuckled, both at her and at Lucy. Lucy thought the baby was coming. Desi was panicked. Pauline was simultaneously sickened at the thought of dead fish and exhilarated at the thought of mink.

"All right," she said. "OK, Arnold. Turn on the news."

Arnold gave Lucy a regretful smile and wrenched the dial.

Jensen looked so grim that Pauline's heart wrenched, too.

"The prospect for a major conflict in the Middle East intensified tonight, after an Israeli commando raid into Lebanon followed a series of bombings in Tel Aviv that claimed ten lives. . . ."

Arnold sucked loudly on his beer bottle.

"A new threat to the Vietnam truce was posed tonight as reports of a buildup. . . ."

Arnold burped and chuckled and chortled.

"And now, here's a film report on the fire that destroyed the ocean liner Marianna and cost the lives of thirty passengers and crewmen. . . ."

Arnold enjoyed the account of the disaster almost as much as *I Love Lucy*.

"The strike of longshoremen, now in its third week, may cripple the economy of the entire Eastern Seaboard, according to a new study. . . ."

Arnold basked in the blue light of the set.

"Another charge of corruption in Government came today from a high-placed official in the Justice Department. . . ."

"After a week-long search, the mutilated body of seven-year-old Sharon Snyder was discovered in an abandoned tenement. . . ."

"A tax rise forecast by bóth Federal and state economists brutally slain in apartment-house elevator the highest increase in food prices in ten years accident total now five hundred but expected to rise as floods sweep tornadoes struck hurricane winds rising to thirteen children dead twenty injured as train strikes school bus and protesters arrested on steps of mugging victim dies as new strain of flu virus thousands homeless as assassin forecasts rain for holiday weekend. . . ."

Arnold was having a very good time.

"Well, how about it, how about it?" he said. "How's about the news, Mrs. Current Events, you enjoying the show? And how's about that fishing trip, you going to throw up again, like you did the last time, when I bring home the catch?"

"It's still on," Pauline said gratingly. "The news is still on, Arnold; will you at least let the man finish?"

"Sure," said Arnold, smiling.

"And now," said Jensen, not smiling, "repeating our first item, the state health authorities have issued an urgent warning concerning the danger of botulism in the canned mixed vegetables packed by Happy Lad Foods. Any can of Happy Lad mixed vegetables marked five-L-three is known to contain these deadly bacteria and should be destroyed immediately or returned to the place of purchase. . . ."

The credits were beginning to roll and Pauline couldn't bear Arnold's chuckling noises a moment longer. Tears blurred her path between living room and kitchen. In the center of the tiled floor, she fought a wave of nausea (smell of dead fish, nonsmell of mink), and then she went to the cupboard and looked through her canned-food inventory, searching the labels for a can of Happy Lad mixed vegetables, series 5L3. Suddenly, she realized that all the news wasn't bad that night. She had one.

The Quick and the Dead

by Helen McCloy

She was a remarkable woman. Basil Willing recognized that the moment he saw her.

She opened the door of his beach cottage without knocking. Behind her a jagged streak of lightning split the night and vanished. Thunder roared above the steady drumming of the surf. An edge of white foam thrust its way up the sand; beyond, the ocean was a blackness—as void as if nothing were there, and never had been. Thunderstorms were rare in California, but when they came they were, like most things California, larger than life.

She was like a storm herself, all darkness and suddenness, all flash and tumult. Basil remembered that the words hurricane and houri have the same root.

"Sorry to bother you." Her voice was rich, deep, warm. "My telephone is dead. May I use yours? I live next door."

"Of course. Over there by the stairway."

She wore a silk sheath, shrill yellow like a flame in the dimly lighted room. Her sandals were gilt; her only jewel was a big round brooch on one shoulder, bits of coral and turquoise pieced together to form the image of a Nepalese god. An artful woman to combine yellow-pink and yellow-blue with yellow.

"Damn! Your phone is dead too! What am I going to do now?"

"What's the trouble?"

"I'm Moira Shiel."

"The singer? Max and Moira?"

The team specialized in folk songs and satirical sketches. They were famous for their quickness in picking up each other's cues when they ad-libbed, as they often did, even on television. Moira was the better actor; Max, the better musician—he had perfect pitch.

She nodded. "I just had a phone call from the Santa Barbara police. Max's father was found dead there an hour ago, at nine o'clock. He lived alone. A neighbor heard his dog barking and called the police. They said he had died of a heart attack about eight thirty.

"They called me because they couldn't locate Max. They had tried the studio in Burbank first, but the night staff said that Max had left there alone, in his car, at six, telling everyone that he was driving to Santa Barbara to have dinner with his father. The police had also tried to call Max's house in Santa Cristina, a hundred miles south of Burbank, but there was no answer. His wife should have been there, but she wasn't.

"I don't want Max to hear this news suddenly, on his car radio. He adored his father. The shock would prostrate him for weeks, perhaps months. I got the Santa Barbara police to promise they would not release the news until I found Max, but they can't hold it back indefinitely. What shall I do? If your phone is also not working it means the line is down all along Malibu Beach. I may not be able to reach him for hours."

Basil glanced at his watch. "Ten after ten now. If he left Burbank at six, he should certainly be in Santa Barbara by this time. I suppose you could drive to Burbank, or to Los Angeles, and find a telephone that's working and—"

"I wouldn't dare leave my house for so long. The line may be fixed at any moment. A call might come through from Max and I'd miss it."

"Then why don't I take you home and drive to Los Angeles myself? I can give Max the message, if you'll tell me the most likely numbers to call."

There was a fire already burning on the hearth in her living room. She stood before it turning the pages of a small black address book. "First, his home number. That's one I always forget—I suppose, because I so rarely have occasion to use it."

"I always assumed you and Max were married," said Basil.

"Oh, no. He was married when we teamed up. Katie, his wife, is nice, but—"

She stopped at the sound of a car on the road that runs above the beach houses at Malibu. In a few moments footfalls were noisy on the wooden steps that led down to her house. She ran to the front door.

"Miss Shiel?" The man in the doorway was stocky and curt. The police. How could you always tell, even without the uniform?

"I'm Carson Dawes, Lieutenant, Los Angeles Police." He smiled at Basil. "Good evening, Dr. Willing. You probably don't remember me, but I've been attending your lectures on forensic psychiatry at the University."

"Dr. Willing?" Moira whirled to look at Basil. "You're a sort of policeman, too!"

"Sort of. I'm really a psychiatrist."

"Sorry to trouble you, Miss Shiel," Dawes went on. "But I couldn't reach you by phone from Los Angeles, so I came out to the beach."

"My line is down. The storm."

"I'm looking for your partner, Max Weber. Do you know where he is?"

"No, I was trying to reach him myself when the line went down. His father, Abraham Weber, died suddenly of a heart attack this evening in Santa Barbara."

"I know," Dawes said. "When I called Mr. Weber's number, trying to find Max, a Santa Barbara policeman answered the phone and told me all about it. They were trying to locate Max, too, he said. They had just talked to you and promised you they'd not release the news until he was found. That was when I tried to call you and discovered your line was down. The studio people in Burbank had told me Max was in Santa Barbara with his father. But he wasn't. Interesting. If he had been, it would have given him an alibi."

"An alibi? For what?" asked Moira.

"His wife, Katie, was murdered this evening."

"But who would want to kill poor Katie?"

"Who but Max? They were on the verge of divorce—as you probably know."

"I didn't."

"The Santa Cristina police called us a little while ago and asked us to bring Max in for questioning. Under California community property law, Katie would get half of everything if there were a divorce. That seems to be very inconvenient for Max just now—as I understand it, he wants to start his own recording company and needs all his capital. Don't tell me you didn't know about that?"

"Of course I knew. That's business. We're partners."

"Katie Weber was in the Santa Cristina house this evening, sitting beside a picture window. According to medical evidence it was about eight thirty when someone fired a shot through the window and killed her instantly. No one heard the shot. Her body was found by her housekeeper, who had left the house at eight, when Katie was still alive, and returned at nine to find her dead. Where was Max at eight thirty?"

"I don't know, but he would never kill Katie."

Dawes looked at her skeptically. "Tough luck for a murderer to have his only alibi-witness die a natural death while he's committing murder and so blow his carefully planned alibi sky-high."

"How dare you assume that Max and his father would plan a cold-blooded murder together?"

"Before Abraham Weber retired, he was a lawyer for the racketeers. He never committed a crime himself, but he was not exactly punctilious about the letter of the law. And he loved his son. The heart attack suggests that the old man knew what was going on tonight and the excitement was too much for him. If I'm right—if Max did plan to use his father as an alibi-witness—the Lord hath delivered him into our hands."

"What do you mean?"

"You asked the Santa Barbara police not to release the news of Weber's death until Max was found, so Max cannot possibly know his father is dead. When we pick him up, he'll undoubtedly claim he was in Santa Barbara with his father at eight thirty, the time of the murder, never suspecting that his father was already dead at eight thirty. That will prove that Max was not at his father's house at all tonight. We'll hardly have to question him. We can just sit back and let him talk himself into the gas chamber."

"That's horrible!" cried Moira. "You're setting a trap for him!"

Again there was the sound of a car on the road above the beach. Moira was already at the door. Dawes drew her back, almost roughly.

"That may be Max Weber now. I left word with the highway police to bring him here if they picked him up within an hour of the time I left Burbank. Miss Shiel, if you try to warn him in any way, I'll have you charged as an accessory after the fact. You must not speak to him at all—not a single word. Understand?"

"Yes." She moved like a sleepwalker to the piano bench and sat down. Basil offered her a cigarette. She took it with trembling fingers. It was Dawes who opened the door when the knock came.

The first man to enter was slender, frail, shy. Basil had an impression of intelligence and sensitivity but without strength—always a dangerous constellation. He was followed by a uniformed highway policeman, who spoke to Dawes.

"We picked him up on the grass verge beside the freeway, Lieutenant. He was just outside Burbank, headed south. He said he was on his way home to Santa Cristina."

Basil knew what the Lieutenant was thinking: Max could have driven to Santa Cristina instead of Santa Barbara when he left the Burbank studio, shot his wife, and then returned to Burbank, so he would re-enter Santa Cristina from the north, as if he had driven south from Santa Barbara. He'd find some witness on the road between Burbank and Santa Cristina to confirm his driving south at that hour—possibly a filling station man, whom he'd talk to when he stopped for gas.

"Moira!" Max ignored the others. "Have you heard the radio? Katie is dead—murdered—"

He started toward Moira, but Dawes put a hand on his arm.

"You are Max Weber?"

"Yes, but—"

"I'm Lieutenant Dawes, Los Angeles Police, and I must talk to you before anyone else does. Where have you been?"

Moira crushed her cigarette in an ashtray on top of the piano. Her restless fingers strayed across the keyboard.

"Miss Shiel, I know you're nervous, but this is no time for playing the piano. Mr. Weber, where have you been?"

"Santa Barbara. I had intended to dine with my father but—"

"But you didn't? Why not?"

"My poor father." Max dropped into a chair and covered his face with his hands. "Dad died all alone. He must have died just before I got there at eight thirty. He was still warm."

"You called his doctor?"

"No. I should have, shouldn't I? But I didn't. It was such a shock, I went kind of crazy. I drove around for a while, trying to realize what it would be like to live in a world without Dad. At last, I headed for home."

"Still without notifying a doctor?"

"I was going to do that as soon as I got home. It didn't seem to matter, really. Dad was gone. The—the thing lying there had nothing to do with him now . . . I was on the freeway, just south of Burbank, when I heard about Katie on the radio. It was just too much, coming on top of Dad's death. I couldn't drive. I pulled off onto the grass and a few minutes later the cops picked me up and brought me here."

"I guess that lets you out." Dawes couldn't hide his disappointment. "I must apologize for—"

"Apologize?" Basil's voice was sharp. "Lieutenant, are you assuming Max Weber was in Santa Barbara tonight solely because he knows his father is dead?'

"Yes. No one knew about Mr. Weber's death except the neighbor who called the police and the police themselves and Miss Shiel and you. It wasn't on the air, because Miss Shiel made the police promise they wouldn't release the news until Max was found. She couldn't have telephoned Max about his father's death, because her line went down right after the Santa Barbara police called her and told her the news. I know, because it was then I tried to reach her myself. Obviously, she had no opportunity to tell Max that his father was dead before I arrived."

"True, but Miss Shiel did have an opportunity to tell Max Weber that his father was dead after you arrived."

"What do you mean? She didn't say a single word to him!"

"Words are not the only means of communication."

"You're thinking of some sort of code?"

"I suppose it could be called a code." Basil stepped over to the piano. Slowly he played seven notes. "Do you recognize those notes?"

Dawes looked blank, but the young highway policeman gazed at Basil with awe. "Well, I'll be damned! Key of C natural. It would have to be. You must have perfect pitch, too."

"No, I was watching her hands, as you were watching mine just now."

"What are you two talking about?" demanded Dawes.

"These are the seven notes Miss Shiel struck on the piano: A B E D E A D. *Abe dead.*"

"I hate you!" Moira screamed at Basil. "What business is it of yours? Why didn't you leave it alone?

"It's all right, Moira," said Max gently. "I might as well give myself up—I haven't a chance without Dad to alibi me. The police will dig and dig until they trace the gun back to me."

"Then . . . you did do it?" Moira's voice was now a whisper.

"Yes, I killed Katie. For you as much as for the money. Moira, I love you so much . . ."

"Why the key of C natural?" Dawes asked Basil, later that evening.

"The enharmonic factor. On the keyboard, B sharp is also C natural, C flat is also B natural, E sharp is also F natural and F flat is also E natural. You can't tell which note of these pairs is indicated unless the notes are written and the key indicated. C natural is the one exception—the one key that has no sharps or flats.

"Max Weber was quick to realize that if Moira's playing was a message in code, it would have to be in the key of C natural—otherwise, he would have no way of identifying the notes—that is, the letters. Because he had perfect pitch, not just relative pitch, he was able to do what few people can do—identify a single note, or a small group of notes, played alone.

"Moira took advantage of Max's gift on the spur of the moment. She was quick, but he was even quicker. They were quite a team, justly famous for picking up each other's cues at an instant's notice . . . I hope you're not going to charge her as accessory?"

"I should," said Dawes slowly. "But I won't. Max's punishment will be punishment enough for her . . . But I'm glad you were here, Dr. Willing—she fooled me completely."

An Exercise in Insurance

by James Holding

When three masked men walked into the bank with sawed-off shotguns that afternoon and calmly began to clean out the tellers' cash drawers, I wasn't even nervous. I was sure they weren't going to get away with it. I was perfectly certain that five straight-shooting policemen, strategically placed, would be waiting for the robbers outside the bank door when they emerged.

That's the way it would have happened, too, if it hadn't been for Miss Coe, Robbsville's leading milliner.

As proprietress and sole employee of a hat shop, just around the corner from the bank and felicitously called *Miss Coe's Chapeux,* Miss Coe fabricated fetching hats for many of the town's discriminating ladies. She was an excellent designer, whose products exhibited a fashionable flare, faintly French, that more than justified her use of the French word in her shop name.

Miss Coe was middle-aged, sweet, pretty, methodical, and utterly reliable. Indeed, her dependability was often the subject of admiring comment from local ladies who had become somewhat disillusioned by the unreliability of other tradesmen. "You can always count on Miss Coe," they frequently told each other. "If she says she'll have the hat ready on Tuesday at eleven, she'll have it ready. She'll be putting in the last stitch as you come in the door." I had even heard remarks of this kind at my own dinner table, since my wife was one of Miss Coe's steady customers.

But perhaps you are wondering what Miss Coe, a milliner—reliable and methodical as she undoubtedly was—could possibly have to do with the robbery of our bank?

Well, you may remember that some years ago, several of the companies that insured banks against robbery agreed to reduce the premium rates on such insurance if the insured bank was willing to conform to a certain security arrangement.

This meant, simply, that to win the lower insurance rate, a bank must maintain a robbery alarm system somewhere *outside* the bank itself; that in the event of a robbery, a warning bell or buzzer must sound elsewhere so that police could be instantly alerted without interference, and arrive on the scene in time to prevent the robbery and even, hopefully, to capture the bandits in the act.

In those days of rather primitive electrical wiring, the insurance companies did not insist that, to meet this security requirement, the outside alarm be necessarily installed in the police station itself. Any other location where the ringing of the alarm would unfailingly initiate instant action would serve as well.

The potential savings on insurance premiums made possible in this way were quite substantial. Our bank accordingly decided to take advantage of them. As Cashier, I was entrusted with the job of selecting a suitable outside alarm site, preferably somewhere near the bank, since the installation charges would thus be minimal.

After some thought, and with the memory of my wife's recent words to a bridge partner, "You'll find Miss Coe utterly dependable," fresh in mind, I went around to see the milliner on my lunch hour one day.

After introducing myself, I explained to her that the bank intended to install an alarm buzzer somewhere in the neighborhood. I explained the alarm's purpose. Then I went on diplomatically, "Miss Coe, I have never heard you referred to among the ladies of my acquaintance without some warm testimonial to your complete reliability, to your calm, methodical turn of mind."

"How nice," she murmured, pleased. "I do try to be precise and methodical about things, it's true. I find life less complicated that way."

"Yes. And that's exactly why I am going to ask you to permit us to install our alarm buzzer in your shop."

"Here?"

"Right here. You are always in your shop during banking hours, are you not?"

"Of course. I carry my lunch, so I'm not even away at lunch time."

"Good. With your penchant for doing exactly what is needed at exactly the right time, I am certain that our alarm buzzer, although placing a new responsibility on your shoulders in the unlikely event of a bank robbery, will in no way discommode or harm you. And I might add that the bank will naturally expect to pay you a small stipend for your cooperation."

She flushed with pleasure. "What would I have to do?" she asked.

"If the alarm buzzer should ever ring, you merely go at once to your telephone there, Miss Coe . . . ," I indicated her telephone on a counter at the back of the shop, ". . . and place an emergency call to the police, giving them a prearranged signal. That is all. Your responsibility then ceases. You see, it's very simple."

"I'm sure I could do that, if that's all there is to it," Miss Coe said, glancing at her wall clock a little guiltily, as though she feared she were three stitches late on a hat promised a customer one minute from then. "And I won't say that a bit of extra income won't be more than welcome."

By the end of the week the buzzer was installed in her shop. The system was thoroughly tested, and it worked perfectly. On our first "dry run", the squad of police arrived at the bank just four minutes from the time they received their telephone call from Miss Coe. The insurance people, satisfied with their inspection of the system and my recommendation of Miss Coe, granted us the lower insurance rate forthwith.

Since a daily test of the wiring circuit, to assure its constant readiness, was specified in our insurance agreement, I arranged with Miss Coe that at exactly three o'clock each day, I would press the button under my desk at the bank and ring the buzzer in her shop. That was as far as the daily test needed to go; it was expected that Miss Coe's telephone would always be operative but if, in the event it were out of order or in use when the buzzer should ring, Miss Coe could merely nip into the shop next door and telephone the police from there.

For two years it seemed that Miss Coe would never be called upon to display her reliability in behalf of the bank's depositors. We had no bank robbery, nor even an attempted one. I tested the alarm buzzer each day at three; Miss Coe continued to make fetching hats for Robbsville's ladies undisturbed; and each month I mailed her a small check for her participation in the bank's alarm system.

You can readily see now, I am sure, why I had no qualms whatever when our bank robbery finally did occur. This was the event for which the police, Miss Coe, and I had so carefully prepared. This was the actual happening that our rehearsals had merely simulated. I knew that our outside robbery alarm was in perfect working order. I knew that Miss Coe was in her shop, ready to act, as dependable and unfailing as the stars in the heavens.

So, far from being startled or apprehensive, I really felt a certain pleasurable excitement when I looked up from my desk, just before closing time that afternoon, and saw the three masked bandits presenting their weapons to our staff and terrified patrons. In common with the other occupants of the banking room, I slowly raised my hands over my head at the robbers' command. Simultaneously and unnoticed, however, I also pressed my knee against the alarm button under my desk.

I could picture clearly the exact sequence of events that would be set in train by that movement of my knee. Miss Coe's buzzer would sound. She would perhaps sit immobile for a shocked second at her work table. She would drop the hat she was working on and cross speedily to her telephone. She would place her emergency call to the police with splendid calm. And then she would wait confidently for the news from me that our bank robbers had been circumvented or captured.

Unfortunately, as I found out later, Miss Coe did none of these things.

What she did do, when the alarm buzzer sounded in her shop, was merely to glance at the clock on her wall, rise impatiently from her sewing stool and cross the room, and there (bless her methodical heart!) push the minute hand of the wall clock ahead ten minutes so that it pointed to exactly three o'clock.

The Old Heap

by Alvin S. Fick

August 8, 1975

Acme Parking Plaza
2135 Congress St.
Akron, O.

To whom it may concern:

This afternoon when I picked up my car at your parking garage I discovered that all four hubcaps were missing. Obviously they were stolen during the day, because I'm sure all of them were on the car when I left it on C level, the one you reach from the Orville Avenue ramp.

I spoke to one of the attendants about this, but all he did was shrug his shoulders and say probably the hubcaps fell off on the way in this morning and I didn't notice. Impossible—not all four, anyway. He said the office was closed and wouldn't even give me his name, so I am writing this letter expecting a reply which will enable me to get an adjustment on this.

> Yours truly,
> Dennis Daggett
> 14 Pepper Lane
> Chatham, O.

August 12, 1975

Mr. Dennis Daggett
14 Pepper Lane
Chatham, O.

Dear Mr. Daggett:

Your letter of August 8 has been brought to my attention. On behalf of Acme Parking Plaza, I express sincere regret for the loss of hubcaps from your car which occurred, you say, while your vehicle was parked at our facility. In view of the activity in the garage section of our Plaza, I find it difficult to believe this could have happened on C level, or anywhere else on our premises, to be quite candid. We employ an ample staff of trained, dependable and reputable attendants who constantly monitor all areas.

We trust you will have no problem in obtaining reimbursement from your insurance carrier under the terms of your comprehensive coverage.

Again, sorry you incurred a loss.

> Cordially,
> Elroy R. Kent
> Customer Relations
> Acme Parking Plaza

August 15, 1975

Mr. Elroy R. Kent
Customer Relations
Acme Parking Plaza
2135 Congress St.
Akron, O.

Dear Mr. Kent:

I have your letter, and I don't like your Doubting Thomas attitude. I have been parking at Acme Plaza for three years, and I don't like the way you imply I am lying about this matter.

I only use my car going back and forth to work. It never sits on the street. It is parked in my garage—locked, by the way—when I am home. I have always used your indoor parking area instead of the big outdoor lot on the Congress St. side. I do this because I take great pride in the way I take care of my car. I have never left it outdoors in the weather.

Don't talk to me about comprehensive insurance. The money that would cost I have been putting into the cash register of Acme Parking Plaza, just so I wouldn't need comprehensive. Why do you think I paid your outrageous indoor fee if not to protect my property?

I am checking on the cost of replacement hubcaps. I will be sending you the bill.

> Yours truly,
> Dennis Daggett
> 14 Pepper Lane
> Chatham, O.

August 19, 1975

Mr. Dennis Daggett
14 Pepper Lane
Chatham, O.

Dear Mr. Daggett:

In view of the low cost of comprehensive insurance, it seems a little foolish of you not to have it. But that is your business, shortsighted though it may be. It would be pointless for you to send us a bill for your replacement hubcaps, which I doubt you will be able to obtain anyway in view of the age of your car. I spoke to the C level attendant to whom you complained on August 8. He tells me you drive a 1949 Kaiser.

Really, Mr. Daggett, you can't hope to find hubcaps for *that!*

> Cordially,
> Elroy R. Kent
> for Acme Parking Plaza

178

August 20, 1975

Mr. Kent:
   You are damned right that it is *my* business whether or not I carry comprehensive insurance, and it certainly is none of *your* business to call me foolish because I don't. And just what the hell do you mean, "It would be pointless for you to send us a bill"?
   You have a responsibility in this matter, and I aim to see that you fulfill it.
   The tone of your letter of August 19 makes me madder than spit. Who in blazes are you to call me shortsighted? How many shortsighted people do you know who have nursed along, loved and cared for a single automobile for twenty-five years? Let me assure you I can and will find hubcaps. They will cost you a pretty penny, because I am going to charge you for the time I spend searching, and when I find them I expect they may be dented and rusty. Repair, including re-chroming, will be part of the bill.
   On August 19 I stopped in at your office to discuss this matter in person, but your secretary said you were out, and she said she didn't know when you would be back. Bull! Or were you too busy writing that goddamned letter dated the 19th to see me? There's no need for me to ask why I got the same answer from her every time I tried to reach you by phone.
   I expect an immediate reply by return mail that you will honor the bill for my new hubcaps. Don't phone about this. I want it in writing. I don't trust you.

                                                     Dennis Daggett

P.S. Needless to say, I have found another place to park my car.

August 22, 1975

Mr. Dennis Daggett
14 Pepper Lane
Chatham, O.

Dear Mr. Daggett:
   It pains me that I find it necessary to warn you about the

intemperate language you are using in your letters. I understand perfectly well the circumstances surrounding the loss of hubcaps from your old car.

It strikes me that, for a person who parked in our facility for three years, you were remarkably unobservant, even singularly inattentive to the prominently posted stipulations regarding vehicles left on our premises. There was not a day you parked at Acme when we at Acme Parking Plaza carried a single iota of responsibility for your vehicle or, for that matter, your person.

It's as simple as that. We have no responsibility. Period.

Cordially,
Elroy R. Kent
for Acme Parking Plaza

P.S. If your vision is so bad you couldn't see the three-by-four-foot signs stating in letters two inches high THE MANAGEMENT IS NOT RESPONSIBLE FOR LOSS OR DAMAGE FROM ANY CAUSE TO VEHICLES, CONTENTS, DRIVERS OR PASSENGERS—well, in that case you shouldn't even be on the road with your old heap.

August 25, 1975

Kent:

There is only one way you can avoid a lawsuit. I stated in my letter of August 20 that I do not trust you. Double that. Prove to me that you and the rest of your crew at Acme are not a bunch of crooks and I may even forgive your insult to my fine old Kaiser. I'll have you know it is a choice and carefully preserved part of automobile Americana. I can accept anything in the way of insults, but you went too far when you called my Kaiser an old heap.

If you wish to prove your point, take down one of those "prominent" signs next Tuesday and bring it to Rose's Cafe across from your Congress St. entrance. Be there at 6:15 P.M. Don't make me wait, because I have lost my patience. If this keeps you from your 9-to-5 routine, count it as small cost to get me to drop this affair without other courses of action.

I don't recall seeing the signs you mention. You better not bring a freshly painted, trumped-up version, and you know damned well I'd never set foot on Acme property to see one.

Don't forget: September 2 at 6:15 sharp.

Dennis Daggett

P.S. Confirm our appointment in writing, and don't be late.

August 28, 1975

Mr. Dennis Daggett
14 Pepper Lane
Chatham, O.

Dear Mr. Daggett:

Your request of August 25 is ridiculous, but I am going to humor you just so I can see the silly look on your face when you read the sign. I will bring one from the open parking lot rather than one from the inside area. That way you will be able to see the weathering for yourself.

I say I will show up to humor you. Closer to the truth is my desire to get a look at the priceless pile of old tin and rust you call auto Americana.

Aside from the fact I will be carrying a big sign, you will have no problem identifying me. I will be the one who is laughing—probably uncontrollably after seeing the Kaiser at the curb.

See you on the 2nd, Dennis.

Cordially,
Elroy R. Kent
for Acme Parking Plaza

September 17, 1975

Mr. Dennis Daggett
14 Pepper Lane
Chatham, O.

Dear Mr. Daggett:

Just this morning I reviewed for the first time the correspondence of Elroy R. Kent. I note that you and he exchanged letters during the month of August. Obviously, there was a strong disagreement between you and Acme Parking Plaza regarding the loss of hubcaps from your car while it was parked on C level of our garage.

To the regrets expressed by Mr. Kent I wish to add my own. Further than that, I think it might be in order for me to apologize on behalf of Mr. Kent for his failure to keep the appointment he had with you on September 2. I do not know if you read the Akron papers, since you are a resident of Chatham, but Mr. Kent met with a tragic accident which kept him from meeting you. As you already know, he was planning to bring with him one of the signs from the parking area—a rather unusual agreement on his part, but perhaps in keeping with the strange nature of the correspondence the two of you conducted.

As he was crossing the street, Mr. Kent was struck by a hit-and-run car. I add with personal sorrow that he died on the way to the hospital without regaining consciousness.

The police have theorized that the sign obscured Mr. Kent's vision, and that he stepped in front of the car which hit him. However, there is so little traffic on Congress St. at that hour I cannot understand how the driver missed seeing Mr. Kent. How could he have missed seeing a man carrying a three-by-four-foot sign? I devoutly hope the police find him.

No one in the cafe saw the accident, and apparently no pedestrians or other drivers witnessed it. As I said above, the street is not very busy at 6:15 of a summer evening.

Perhaps you wondered why Mr. Kent failed to keep the appointment. The police interviewed everyone in the cafe, and took names. Since you were not on that list, I can only assume you were late for the meeting in spite of your insistence on Mr. Kent's punctuality.

My primary reason for writing this letter is to settle the disagreement which culminated in Mr. Kent's untimely death. I must apologize for the manner in which your loss was handled. I cannot say for sure until I read some of his old files, but I do not believe it was customary for Mr. Kent to be quite so caustic. I'm sure you understand, however, that he had to be firm in his capacity as arbiter in customer problems.

Mr. Daggett, Acme Parking Plaza wishes to make full

financial restitution for your loss. We will do so, although I am obliged to reiterate that Mr. Kent was accurate in his assessment that we are devoid of responsibility. Please stop in to see me with your bill, and I will personally hand you a check to cover it.

> Sincerely yours,
> Robert Winsett
> Vice President
> Acme Parking Plaza

September 19, 1975

Mr. Robert Winsett
Acme Parking Plaza
2135 Congress St.
Akron, O.

Dear Mr. Winsett:

Isn't that a shame about Mr. Kent!

Thanks for the offer to buy my hubcaps, but that won't be necessary. I had a little accident with my Kaiser several days ago, and you know how hard it is to get parts for an old heap like that—especially such things as grills, lamps and so on.

I figured the best thing to do was get rid of it, so I drove it to an auto junkyard. They would only give me $20!

A couple of days ago I stopped to see if I could check the glove compartment for a pen I think I missed when I emptied the car. One of the guys in the yard said they had put my car through the crusher and shipped it out for scrap the day before.

I suppose it's on the way to Japan already.

> Yours truly,
> Dennis Daggett
> 14 Pepper Lane
> Chatham, O.

P.S. Seeing you are in the automobile business in a manner of speaking, I sure would appreciate your dropping me a line if you ever learn of anyone with a 1956 Hudson Hornet for sale—in nice shape, that is.

As the Wheel Turns

by Jane Speed

Paula Thorpe drank three cups of coffee, slowly, without being interrupted by so much as a glance from her two breakfast companions. There they sat, the pair of them: Howard, her husband of six months, poring over *Art Treaures of Ancient Syria;* and his mother, a fat little mountain of a woman squeezed into a wheel chair, applying herself assiduously to the one pursuit which fully engaged her interest—eating.

Paula slammed her empty cup down into its saucer. Mother Thorpe lifted her head at the sound like a startled rabbit and hastily snatched the last blueberry muffin from the bun warmer. Howard merely shifted in his chair and murmured, without looking up, "Excellent breakfast, my dear."

Paula sighed, gathered up a stack of dishes, and carried them out to the kitchen.

From earliest memory Paula had yearned for the company of artists. She had not been able to coax forth any noticeable talent of her own, so she had set her sights on what seemed the next best means of entry into the charmed circle—to be the guiding genius of some creative spirit.

And then, at a cocktail party last fall, she met Howard Thorpe. His gaunt, tousle-haired good looks and his habit of protracted, brooding silences made him appear a romantic figure of Byronic proportions. And when Paula learned that his field was art (he "earned his bread and butter" by teaching art at a small New England college) and that he was in New York to discuss the possible publication of a book he was working on, she could hardly be blamed for feeling that here indeed was the embodiment of the chance she'd been looking for.

They were married quietly in New York the day after Thanksgiving and set out immediately for his home in Vermont. Howard's teaching schedule and his modest Assistant Professor's salary precluded any honeymoon, but Paula didn't mind in the least. She had embarked on this marriage willing, even eager, to starve in a garret (or the small college-town equivalent) for the sake of her very own struggling artist.

She had plunged with fanatical zeal into her new role. His mother's welfare seemed a matter of prime importance with Howard, therefore it became so with Paula, too. Great plans were afoot for the celebration of the good lady's sixty-fifth birthday which was to occur late in the spring, and Paula fell in with these plans enthusiastically, adding many small refinements of her own to make the occasion more festive.

And every clear day since the first real thaw she had dutifully pushed Mother Thorpe in her rickety wheel chair to the fat little woman's favorite spot, the top of a steep rise which commanded an impressive view of the neat, stone-walled campus. Here, beneath the shade of an ancient elm, Paula, who didn't trust the brake on the venerable contraption, carefully settled one wheel of the chair into a rut. Then she sat patiently while the old woman droned on and on until she finally talked herself into her morning nap.

Mother Thorpe was touched by Paula's devotion and often in her rambling monologues she reiterated her regret that she couldn't do more for her dear Howard and his dear wife. Howard's father, she would explain vaguely, though a dear man, had been a bit of an eccentric and had tied up his sizeable fortune in a complicated trust fund which she herself didn't altogether understand.

"But never you mind, dear," went her favorite refrain as she patted Paula's shoulder with her pudgy hand, "you shall have it all one day, and soon."

But the days dragged into weeks and the weeks into months, and Paula found herself pinning her hopes increasingly on her mother-in-law's words. For the harsh truth was, there was very little else to pin them on.

It had by this time become painfully clear that the

perpetual frown which drew Howard's brows down at his nose in such a devilishly attractive way was not a sign of the outrage of a gifted rebel but of a mildly fussy disposition; he was essentially a silent man for the simple reason that he had very little to say; and his teaching of art history at this small college was not a means to the end of being recognized in his field, but rather an end in itself. In short, Howard was not an artist, but a schoolmaster.

And the book? Paula had clung to this long after her other illusions about Howard were dashed. True, it was to be a scholarly text, hardly destined for a place on the best-seller lists. Still, Paula had rather counted on being able to refer casually to "Howard's book" when she wrote to her friends back in New York. But just yesterday had come a letter from the publisher informing Howard that another house was bringing out a work on substantially the same subject and therefore it would be inadvisable to go ahead with the tentatively proposed publication. So even that satisfaction was to be denied her.

"Well, dear," said Howard, appearing at the kitchen door, "I'm off to the wars." Paula offered her cheek for his husbandly peck—and waited. Without fail, he added, "Lovely day." And then, as though a bright new thought had just occurred to him, "Why don't you take Mother up to the hill this morning?"

But you know I take her every day, Paula opened her mouth to protest. Then she closed it. What was the use? He'd say the same thing tomorrow anyhow. She merely nodded silently and went on with the dishes.

Half an hour later she was trundling the old lady up the hill. She settled the chair into its accustomed place and flung herself down on the ground nearby. The view of the well-trimmed campus surrounded by its stone wall seemed to Paula like nothing so much as a neat, orderly trap. She paid even less attention than usual to her mother-in-law's monotonous prattle, catching only, "You shall have it all one day, and soon."

The familiar words made Paula ache with restless longing. If only "soon" could be right now. Money, she had always piously maintained, wasn't important; and yet, when one had nothing else—

With enough money she could pry Howard out of his

narrow little life; a year in Paris, then perhaps Rome; maybe they could finally live in Switzerland as so many people were doing. It just might make all the difference. There might still be some hidden spark to be struck in Howard if only he could be freed from the deadening influence of this dismal town and its suffocating college.

A gentle snoring from the wheel chair brought Paula rudely back to reality. Not a chance, she thought bitterly. The famous sixty-fifth birthday was only a week away, and the old woman, sleeping peacefully in the shade, looked fit for another fifteen years at least. Oh, it just wasn't fair!

Paula yanked her sleep-numbed leg out from under her and extended it sharply. Her foot accidentally struck the wheel of the chair. She gasped as the chair, loosened from its place, rolled forward a few feet and came to a stop precariously near the beginning of the long downward slope.

For a few seconds Paula sat rigid, hardly able to breathe. And through it all, like an idiotically benign counterpoint, the snoring continued unbroken. The old woman apparently slept as wholeheartedly as she ate. Paula relaxed at last, exhausted from fear. What a close call!

And then, insidiously, a second thought crept into her consciousness. How *easy* it had been. Almost before she realized what was happening, Paula found herself sliding forward along the ground. She stretched her leg out cautiously, and with her foot gave the chair another shove. It moved only a few inches this time and then held, caught by a rut at the very edge.

Again Paula waited, her heart pounding. And again there was no sound except the snoring, and no movement from the woman in the wheel chair.

Paula rose silently. She seemed to have lost all sense of what it was she was trying to do and was filled only with a determination to accomplish it. She grasped the back of the chair with both hands. Gently she eased the front wheels and then the back ones over the obstructing spot. Then with a strong thrust she sent the chair forward.

It started down the grade slowly, then gained momentum. The fat little woman, squeezed in so tightly, didn't even waken fully enough to cry out. There was scarcely any sound at all till the distant, splintering thud as the chair with its heavy passenger crashed into the solid stone wall . . .

It was more than three hours later when Howard finally came out of his mother's room. Paula, sitting in the hall outside, knew by his face that the old woman was dead. The tension in which Paula had spent the intervening hours broke suddenly and she gave way to hysterical sobbing.

"Oh, dear," murmured Howard, distressed. He came to her quickly and sat beside her. "Paula, you mustn't . . . Don't blame yourself, my dear. It was a dreadful accident, that's all." Then, as her sobbing continued unabated, he went on nervously. "Please, dear, try to look at it this way. These last few months have been the happiest Mother has ever known, thanks largely to you. Really, she remarked many times about your great kindness to her."

Paula buried her face even deeper in her hands to hide the blush that flared up in her cheeks. It was several painful minutes before she could control her sobs enough to mumble, "She didn't even get to have her birthday party."

"That's true," said Howard with a sad smile. "Poor Mother. That would be her only regret, I think. She had so counted on being able to turn over Father's money to us."

Paula lifted her head at this and stared at Howard through a blur of tears. "What do you mean?" she asked finally.

"Why—didn't Mother explain to you about Father's will?"

"Not—very clearly," Paula managed to say. Her mouth felt dry.

"Well," Howard began, settling comfortably into his classroom manner, "although Father became quite a wealthy man in his lifetime, he always retained a strong Yankee fear of the corrupting influence of money not earned. He felt that Mother spoiled me and that if he left the money to her outright she'd turn it over to me immediately and I'd become a wastrel. And he may have been right, you know. Dear Mother, she found it very hard to deny me anything. At any rate, Father made out a will leaving the money in trust, allowing Mother only a monthly income until she should reach the age of sixty-five."

"Sixty-five?" Paula echoed stupidly.

"I don't know why sixty-five exactly. Perhaps he felt that by that time I'd be forty and have acquired the habit of earning my own keep."

"But—" Paula was struggling to make sense of Howard's words. "But how could he be sure she'd live to be sixty-five?"

"He couldn't, of course. And," he added with a sigh, "as it turned out, she didn't."

Paula closed her eyes. She could hardly bring herself to ask it. "What—what happens to the money now?"

"Oh—that." Howard frowned in an effort to recall the exact wording. "In the event of her death before attaining the age of sixty-five," he recited with maddening accuracy, "the money automatically goes to the college." Here he permitted himself a dignified chuckle. "Like so many people with very little formal schooling, Father had the greatest respect for institutions of higher learning."

Up to this point Howard had fastidiously avoided looking directly at his wife, on the charitable assumption that her initial excessive outburst had been as embarrassing to her as it was to him. As he turned to face her now, he was shocked to see the crushing effect his words had been having on her.

"Oh, my dear Paula," he hastened to reassure her. "Surely you don't think I mind about the money? How can I miss something I've never had? We lived very frugally even when Father was alive. Why, I have my work, a good wife, our little home—what more could I possibly want? You'll see, my dear, our life will go on quite as usual. Except that poor Mother is no longer with us, nothing has changed at all."

Knit One, Purl Two . . .

by Thomasina Weber

Flo Connelly put her lunch wrappings in the large tote bag beside her camp stool. "You'd think they would have a garbage can here," she said to her new acquaintance of the morning.

"I don't think they encourage eating in the courthouse corridors," replied Mrs. Frisbee.

"Tough. I've attended every hearing held in this courthouse, and if you're not up front when they unlock the doors after lunch, you don't get a seat."

"I had no idea so many people attended preliminary hearings," said Mrs. Frisbee.

"They don't always. But for one like this, where the sweet innocent broad knocks off her husband, they come to hear the dirt."

Mrs. Frisbee moved slightly away from the smaller woman. "They don't know for sure that Delcey Clark killed her husband," she said.

Flo Connelly laughed as she extracted from her bag a pair of knitting needles with five inches of a blue, unidentifiable something on them. "All you gotta do is look at that wide-eyed baby face and that shiny red hair, and you can see it right off. What would she want with a sick, crabby old husband other than his money?"

"How could a young girl like that kill a sick old man?"

Flo's knitting needles moved swiftly. "How could a young girl like that *marry* a sick old man in the first place?"

"Some people are dedicated to helping others."

"Horsefeathers."

Mrs. Frisbee clucked. "You seem to lack compassion, my dear."

Flo looked at the woman scornfully. "And you seem to be the kind who judges a book by its cover."

"A capacity for love can never be concealed."

Amen, thought Flo, returning to her knitting. The corridor was beginning to fill up. The people were forming a line along the wall, but new arrivals were congregating in little knots of two or three beside the line and although they seemed engrossed in conversation, their feet were edging toward the doors. Pointed looks, like poisoned darts, were directed at them by those in line, but no one challenged them.

Flo was interestedly watching the approach of one, a sweating man in dark trousers, dirty white shirt, gaping shoes minus laces and no socks. By the time he had inched up to Flo, she was ready for him.

"Where do you think you're going?" she demanded loudly.

"I'm in line, just like you," he said.

"Oh, no, you're not. You got here seventeen minutes ago and you belong twelfth from the end of the line, which is about fifty feet south of here."

"Who died and made you boss, sister?"

She stood up, her eyes on a level with his third shirt button. Shielded from the others by his broad body, Flo lightly pressed the point of her knitting needle against his abdomen. "If I were you, mister, I'd go to the end of the line." He went to the end of the line.

Twenty minutes before opening time, Flo packed her knitting and her camp stool in the tote bag and turned to face the doors. As if an invisible whistle had sounded, the mob began to move forward until it was a solid unit pushing ahead with nowhere to go.

"Mercy's sakes," gasped Mrs. Frisbee, dismayed at the crush, "you'd think they were giving away something free!"

When the doors were finally opened, Flo made good use of her elbows, netting herself and Mrs. Frisbee seats in the third of the four rows of chairs.

"Were you here this morning?" asked the woman on Flo's other side. She was fat with kinky white hair, wearing a straining green shift with a huge yellow daisy blooming obscenely on her stomach.

"Yes," replied Flo, mentally dubbing the woman Daisy. "Were you?"

"You bet. You don't think I'm going to sit in my hot little

trailer and read magazines when I can sit with air-conditioning and watch the real thing, do you?"

Flo took out her knitting. "What do you think of the pharmacist?"

"Oh, he's cute. Reminds me of my son when he was that age."

"They make a cozy couple."

"You got it all wrong. The whole thing was her idea. He didn't have anything to do with it."

"Don't be ridiculous," said Flo. "They're lovers, and he's the one who got her the drug to give the old man."

"You can't make me believe that. Why, my son used to look just like him, except that his hair is brown instead of blond."

"That's a stupid thing to base an opinion on," said Flo.

"Everybody rise!"

There was a unified surge upward as the judge entered. He was slightly built and his dark-rimmed glasses seemed too large for his handsome face. "Be seated," he said.

Delcey Clark, red-eyed and ghostly without make-up, sat at the table with her attorney, a well-built man in his early forties, at ease in his faultlessly tailored suit. His arm, across the back of her chair, rested so that his hand touched her white nylon shoulder.

"She's got her attorney right where she wants him," Flo whispered to Mrs. Frisbee.

"What's that you're saying?" asked Daisy.

"I must warn the spectators to refrain from making audible comments," said the judge, looking directly at Flo. She held his eyes until he turned to the business at hand, whereupon Flo resumed her knitting.

"Isn't that judge a doll?" said Daisy.

"I'd hardly call him that," said Flo.

"He's the one who will decide whether there's enough of a case to try her for murder," said Daisy.

"He's still a man," said Flo. "All she has to do is hike her skirt up a little and he'll be chewing on his gavel."

"Sh-h," said Mrs. Frisbee. "The judge is looking at you again."

"He's always looking at me," said Flo. "He's used to me by now."

The prosecutor called his first witness of the afternoon, a

neighbor who testified to seeing Delcey and the pharmacist together in a car in front of her house on one occasion. Under cross-examination by the defense, he admitted he had seen no embrace between them. The defense subsequently established the fact that Delcey had been in the drugstore picking up her husband's medicine when it began to rain. Since it was closing time, the pharmacist had driven her home. The pharmacist readily admitted that he was in love with Delcey Clark but insisted he was willing to wait until she was free, "even if it's years until your husband dies," he had told her.

"There are still some good people left in the world," murmured Mrs. Frisbee.

Flo laughed. People turned in their seats to see who had interrupted the proceedings. The judge frowned at Flo. "If the spectators cannot control themselves," he said, "I will be forced to clear the court."

"Hmph!" said Flo under her breath, her knitting needles flying faster than ever. "Young smart aleck! Just because he's sitting up there in a black robe, he thinks he's God Almighty."

"This judge is highly respected," said Mrs. Frisbee.

"He hasn't made a right decision yet, as far as I'm concerned," said Flo. "I don't see how one man can make so many wrong moves."

"Just because you don't agree with his decisions doesn't mean they are wrong," said Mrs. Frisbee gently.

"What's that you said?" asked Daisy, leaning across Flo.

"I said they ought to have women judges if they want justice done," said Flo.

William Clark's physician took the stand and testified that he had been in South America when he learned of the death of his patient and the arrest of Delcey Clark. He had caught the first plane back. While he respected the confidential relationship between doctor and patient, he said the patient was now dead and another life was at stake. Since Dr. Fleischman took very seriously his oath to preserve human life, he felt that his responsibility was to the living, the living in question being Delcey Clark.

The doctor further testified that William Clark, knowing he had less than a year to live, an increasingly pain-ridden year, had insisted this information be kept from his wife. The doctor said he was convinced Clark had hoarded his pain-killing drug to use in one fatal overdose. The doctor then produced his notes taken during consultations with William Clark confirming the deceased's statement that he would take his own life rather than be a burden to anyone else.

The courtroom began to buzz. The prosecutor was out of his chair, the judge was pounding his gavel.

"Very neatly done," said Flo acidly. "Anything to make it look good when they free her."

"Order, order," said the judge in a calm voice which was somehow heard above the clamor. A hush fell immediately, letting Flo's words ring out, "—the usual whitewash." She looked up to meet the cold blue eyes of the judge. He gazed at her for a long moment, then struck his gavel one more time.

"Will counsel please approach the bench," he said. There followed a sotto voce conference and finally the judge said, "In view of the testimony and supporting evidence presented by Dr. Fleischman, a witness for the defense, the case against Delcey Clark is dismissed." He rose and left the courtroom.

Flo stuffed her knitting into the tote bag and pushed her way out the door, ignoring Mrs. Frisbee and Daisy, who were left to talk to each other. She walked determinedly down the corridor to the judge's office, opened the door and stepped inside.

The judge looked up as she entered. "What are you doing in here?"

"I am here as a taxpayer and a citizen of this community, to tell you what I think of you."

"Didn't you cause enough disturbance in the courtroom?"

"It is a taxpayer's right to attend public hearings, isn't it?"

"Of course."

"And there is such a thing as freedom of speech, isn't there?"

"Yes."

"So that means I can attend all the hearings I want and say anything I please. Isn't that a fact?"

"No, it is *not* a fact. There is also such a thing as contempt of court, with which you flirt every time you come into my courtroom."

Flo was standing in front of him now, holding her knitting bag between them. He was not much taller than she.

"Do you understand what I am saying?" he asked.

"I hear you," she replied, reaching into the bag and taking out her knitting, her eyes never leaving his face.

"Of course, you hear me," he said, "but do you understand me?"

"Certainly. I may not have had a college education like you, but I'm not stupid." She unfurled the knitting from its core of needles and raised a needle to his shoulder, the work dangling free.

"You are not listening to me," he said. "Let me tell you this. If I see you in my courtroom one more time, I am going to have you forcibly evicted, taxpayer or no taxpayer."

"Well!" she said, jamming the knitting back in her bag. "Just see if I finish this sweater for you!" She marched toward the door, put her hand on the knob, and turned back to look at the judge. "Such a way to talk to your own mother!"

The Paternal Instinct

by Al Nussbaum

Big Ben came up to me near the side entrance to Leavenworth Penitentiary's B-cellhouse. Everyone calls him Big Ben because he tips the scales at 250 pounds and his first name is Benny. The nickname has nothing to do with time, or the famous London clock, despite the long sentence—thirty years—he's serving.

"Hey, Bill, ya know anythin' about boids?" Ben asked.

"What kind?" I answered, as if it made a difference.

"Sparrows."

"No, sorry." I looked around to make sure no guards were close. "You have one?"

"Yeah, look."

I'd noticed that he had his right hand cupped. Now he held it out to me and opened it. There on his palm huddled the most ugly little creature I'd ever seen. It was about an inch and a half of naked flesh and the head was all beak. There were no feathers.

"*That's* a bird?" I asked.

"Sure. He's just a baby. What d'ya think I should feed him?"

"Where'd you get it?"

"Found him outside. A nest was blew down an' all busted up. I waited a while, but there wasn't no mama boids around, so I picked him up."

Hearing Big Ben say "mama boids" was comical. I almost smiled—but I didn't. I didn't want to take the chance of having him think I was laughing at him. "Birds eat worms; bread, too. Guess you could feed it bread and worms," I offered.

That was on Friday afternoon. I didn't see Ben again until the following Monday. We both were assigned to the Education Building—Ben as an orderly, and I as a helper in the library—and I met him on the way to work. "Still got the bird?" I asked.

"Yeah—see?" He opened a cigar box he was carrying and thrust it proudly under my nose. He had lined the inside with soft rags and the tiny bird was nestled in the center of them.

"You taking it to work?" I asked incredulously.

"Yeah, sure. Can't leave him in my cell. I gotta feed him. 'Sides, they might shake-down and find him. Pets ain't allowed, ya know."

"What're you going to do with it?"

"Gonna put the box on one of the windowsills of A-cellhouse. He'll get lotsa sun an' air, an' I can come out an' feed him every chance I get."

And that's just what he did. Several times that day I looked from a side window of the Education Building. Once

I saw only the cigar box on a window ledge of the building thirty feet away; the other times Ben was out there feeding the bird and whispering to it.

The next day I noticed that two pieces of corrugated cardboard about eighteen inches square were lying on the grass plot between the Education Building and A-cellhouse. This was unusual because trash doesn't get a chance to accumulate at Leavenworth. You seldom see an empty cigarette package, let alone large pieces of paper. I was wondering how they had been left there when Big Ben appeared.

He knelt, lifted a corner of one of the squares, and quickly reached under it. He got to his feet with a pink worm dangling from between his thumb and index finger and went to the cigar box.

I went outside to see what was going on. I heard Ben say, "Ya wants another woim, Baby?" as I approached, but he stopped talking to the bird when he saw me.

"I saw you get a worm from under the cardboard," I said. "How d'you do it?"

"Tore a couple of pieces from a box, soaked 'em in water, an' put 'em on the grass," he said. "Woims come outta the groun' under the paper last night. They didn't go back into the groun' when it got light. They don't move fast an' I can catch 'em."

I stood there watching. Ben fed three large worms to the bird, and it continued to open its beak and scream for more. When there were no more worms to catch, Ben took small pieces of bread, dipped them in water, rolled them into little balls, and then dropped them into the bird's open mouth. The bird would be quiet for a few seconds while it swallowed the bread, then it would open its beak and yell: "Cheep! Cheep!"

"He sure likes to eat," Ben observed fondly.

After that it seemed as though every time I looked out of the window I saw Ben feeding Baby. It wasn't difficult to see why Leavenworth or any prison would outlaw pets. If they were all as demanding and insatiable as Baby, no work would ever get done. Pets would quickly disrupt all order and discipline.

But they would fill a need, too.

It became clear to me that just as woman has a maternal instinct, man has a need to care for and protect a fellow creature. I could see proof of this every time I looked out the window. Big Ben, who wouldn't hesitate to break your jaw if he suspected you were slighting him, thought nothing of gently nursing a tiny bird. I suddenly realized that the empty feeling in my stomach wasn't hunger; I wished I had a skinny, ugly bird to nurse, too.

No one in prison pays much attention to time unless scheduled to get out soon. A week or two, or a month or two, passed. Then I looked out one morning and spotted Ben near the walk at the front of the building. He was on one knee in the classic crapshooter's pose. He opened his hand and released a small, mud-colored bird.

It was hard to believe that this was Baby; he had grown so. He wasn't as big as an adult bird, but no one would have any trouble recognizing him as a bird. The little guy beat his wings frantically and fluttered from side to side, then landed on the soft grass about twenty feet from where he'd been launched. Big Ben lumbered over to where the bird lay on the grass and scooped him into his hand. I could see his lips moving and I knew he was muttering praise and encouragement to the bird.

I watched a few more flights from the window. Baby kept flying increasingly greater distances but wasn't getting much altitude. Several officers entered and left A-cellhouse through its side door. Each glanced at Big Ben and his bird, then quickly looked away. None wanted to enforce the regulation against pets, so they pretended not to notice. After a while Ben stopped giving the bird flying lessons, and I left the window and went back to work.

I looked out the window several times in the next few days, but I must've picked the wrong times because I didn't see Ben. Other guys kept telling me about Big Ben and his bird and how well it could fly and how it came to him when he whistled for it. Baby became the chief topic of conversation around the Education Building. A couple of men joked that they wished Big Ben would teach them to fly—they wanted to see what's on the other side of the prison's thirty-five foot wall.

Then one day I saw Big Ben sitting alone on the steps of

A-cellhouse. I sensed that something was wrong and went over to him. "How's Baby?" I asked.

"He's gone," Ben said. "Flew away. Sat up there," he motioned vaguely toward the wall, "and looked back once, then flew away."

"Maybe he'll come back."

"Naw, he won't come back." His voice held notes of both pain and anger. "Boids is like people. When they don't need ya no more, they forgets ya."

I remembered that someone had once told me Big Ben hadn't received a letter in two years. "Maybe Baby just decided to look around," I said as cheerfully as I could. "Birds do that all the time. It wouldn't surprise me if he came back. The swallows *always* return to Capistrano."

Ben gave me a cold look, then ignored me, so I went inside; but I was a little worried and kept going to the window to keep an eye on him. That's how I happened to be around when the bird returned a few hours later and perched on his shoulder. He cupped it in his huge hands and sat talking to it for a long time. Tears ran down his cheeks, and his back shook. I watched as he touched the bird gently with his lips, then squeezed the life from it.

What Kind of Person Are You?
by Bill Pronzini and Barry N. Malzberg

I arrived at Quality Supermarkets' Fairfield branch promptly at nine o'clock Monday morning and went immediately into the office to check the weekend receipts. A roving district manager with twelve stores and nearly one hundred employees to monitor cannot afford to waste time; I work on a very tight schedule.

At 9:40 I stood and walked quickly into the store proper, to where Franklin was working at Register Three, his regular post. I waited until he finished serving a customer and then motioned him to close down and join me. When he had done that, I took him back into the office and told him to sit down.

He sat poised on the edge of the chair, hands picking nervously at each other; he was about twenty-four, red-haired and gangly, and he reminded me somewhat of my son Ronald. I did not say anything for a time, watching him. He fidgeted under my scrutiny, eyes touching mine, flicking away, flicking back. But he always seemed to be nervous in my presence; I had a reputation as a somewhat stern and uncompromising supervisor.

"I'll get directly to the point," I said. "I have just been over the weekend receipts and register slips, and you're seventy dollars short, Franklin—fifty on Saturday and twenty on Sunday."

His eyes grew wide and his face paled visibly. "Seventy dollars?" he said.

"Exactly seventy dollars. That is a considerable amount, Franklin, as I'm sure you realize."

"Are you *certain*, Mr. Adams? I mean, couldn't you have made a mistake. . ."

"I do not make mistakes," I said stiffly. "The mistake here, if that is what it is, rests squarely on your shoulders."

"I . . . I don't know what to say. I've never been short before, I'm always careful—"

"Indeed?"

"I haven't been off a penny in the two months I've been working here," Franklin said. "You know that, sir."

"I do know it, yes," I said, "but the fact remains that you are seventy dollars short for this past weekend—exactly seventy dollars, not a cent more or less. The question now is what kind of person are you, Franklin?"

"Sir?"

"What kind of person are you?" I repeated. "An honest and fallible one, whose only crime is making careless errors in mathematics? Or a foolish and culpable one who succumbed to the obvious temptation?"

His mouth opened, as though in shock, and he blinked rapidly several times. "Mr. Adams, you don't think I *stole* that money?"

"Did you?"

"No. No!"

I held up a hand. "I am not accusing you of anything, Franklin. I am merely trying to ascertain the truth of the situation here."

"I'm not a thief," he said desperately. "You've got to believe that, Mr. Adams. I don't know how I could have made a seventy-dollar mistake, but that's all it was—a mistake. I swear it."

"I would like to believe that."

"You've *got* to believe it," he said, "it's the truth."

I picked up my pencil and tapped the eraser on the sheaf of papers spread out in front of me. "Embezzlement of funds is a serious offense, you know. I could have you arrested, or at the very least summarily fired."

"Please, Mr. Adams—I didn't steal that money!"

"Have you ever been in trouble before? Any kind of trouble?"

"No, sir, never. Never."

I sighed. "Very well, then. I am not a harsh man, and I have a son about your age; I see no reason not to give you the benefit of the doubt, particularly in view of your prior work record. If you're willing to replace the seventy dollars, and assuming something like this does not happen again, I suppose I am willing to drop the matter entirely."

Relief made him slump on the chair. "I'll replace the money, sure," he said eagerly, "I know I'm responsible for it. I don't have seventy dollars with me, but I can have it by tomorrow; I'll borrow it from my father—"

"That won't be necessary, Franklin. I will accept ten dollars now and ten dollars per week for the next six weeks, assuming again that there are no further shortages and you continue to do your job properly."

"I will, Mr. Adams, I'll be extra-careful. It'll never happen again, I promise you that."

"For your sake," I said, "see that you keep that promise."

He nodded and produced his wallet and handed me a ten-dollar bill. I took it and laid it carefully on the desk. "You can go back to work now," I said.

"Yes, sir. Thank you, Mr. Adams."

When he was gone I sat for a moment looking at the register receipts, the branch ledger-books. Then I finished my work, closed everything into the safe, put Franklin's ten-dollar bill into my own wallet, and left the store to continue my rounds. . .

I arrived at the Essex branch at precisely noon and spent nearly an hour checking the weekend receipts. At 12:50 I went out into the store proper and brought Trowbridge—another young man in his early twenties, tall and thin like Ronald—back to the office and told him to sit down.

"I have just been going over the weekend receipts," I said, "and you're seventy dollars short—fifty on Saturday and twenty on Sunday."

He stared at me incredulously.

"The question now is," I said, "what kind of person are you?"

At eight the following Friday night, I arrived at the Dunes Motel on the outskirts of the city, knocked on the door of Unit Eight, and was admitted.

"Right on time," Cobb said.

"I am always punctual." I opened my wallet and laid two hundred and fifty dollars on the bed.

He picked it up and counted it twice. "O.K., Adams," he said. "That takes care of the first installment. Six more weeks and Ronnie and I will be square." He chuckled. "Unless he decides to borrow another thousand to pay off some more of his gambling debts."

"Ronald will never borrow another dime from you," I said, "I'll see to that. And he is not gambling any more."

Cobb smiled wisely. "Sure—whatever you say, Adams. Just make sure you're here with the second installment next Friday. I'd hate to have to send one of my boys out to pay Ronnie a little visit."

A sudden rush of anger made me clench my fists. "What kind of person are you to prey on decent people this way?" I said. "What kind of *monster* are you?"

Cobb's laughter rang in my ears all the way out to the car and all the way home to my son.

Shatter Proof

by Jack Ritchie

He was a soft-faced man wearing rimless glasses, but he handled the automatic with unmistakable competence.

I was rather surprised at my calmness when I learned the reason for his presence. "It's a pity to die in ignorance," I said. "Who hired you to kill me?"

His voice was mild. "I could be an enemy in my own right."

I had been making a drink in my study when I had heard him and turned. Now I finished pouring from the decanter. "I know the enemies I've made and you are a stranger. Was it my wife?"

He smiled. "Quite correct. Her motive must be obvious."

"Yes," I said. "I have money and apparently she wants it. All of it."

He regarded me objectively. "Your age is?"

"Fifty-three."

"And your wife is?"

"Twenty-two."

He clicked his tongue. "You were foolish to expect anything permanent, Mr. Williams."

I sipped the whiskey. "I expected a divorce after a year or two and a painful settlement. But not death."

"Your wife is a beautiful woman, but greedy, Mr. Williams. I'm surprised that you never noticed."

My eyes went to the gun. "I assume you have killed before?"

"Yes."

"And obviously you enjoy it."

He nodded. "A morbid pleasure, I admit. But I do."

I watched him and waited. Finally I said, "You have been here more than two minutes and I am still alive."

"There is no hurry, Mr. Williams," he said softly.

"Ah, then the actual killing is not your greatest joy. You must savor the preceding moments."

"You have insight, Mr. Williams."

"And as long as I keep you entertained, in one manner or another, I remain alive?"

"Within a time limit, of course."

"Naturally. A drink, Mr. . . .?"

"Smith requires no strain on the memory. Yes, thank you. But please allow me to see what you are doing when you prepare it."

"It's hardly likely that I would have poison conveniently at hand for just such an occasion."

"Hardly likely, but still possible."

He watched me while I made his drink and then took an easy chair.

I sat on the davenport. "Where would my wife be at this moment?"

"At a party, Mr. Williams. There will be a dozen people to swear that she never left their sight during the time of your murder."

"I will be shot by a burglar? An intruder?"

He put his drink on the cocktail table in front of him. "Yes. After I shoot you, I shall, of course, wash this glass and return it to your liquor cabinet. And when I leave I shall wipe all fingerprints from the doorknobs I've touched."

"You will take a few trifles with you? To make the burglar-intruder story more authentic?"

"That will not be necessary, Mr. Williams. The police will assume that the burglar panicked after he killed you and fled empty-handed."

"That picture on the east wall," I said. "It's worth thirty thousand."

His eyes went to it for a moment and then quickly returned to me. "It is tempting, Mr. Williams. But I desire to possess nothing that will even remotely link me to you. I appreciate art, and especially its monetary value, but not to the extent where I will risk the electric chair." Then he smiled. "Or were you perhaps offering me the painting? In exchange for your life?"

"It was a thought."

He shook his head. "I'm sorry, Mr. Williams. Once I accept a commission, I am not dissuaded. It is a matter of professional pride."

I put my drink on the table. "Are you waiting for me to show fear, Mr. Smith?"

"You will show it."

"And then you will kill me?"

His eyes flickered. "It is a strain, isn't it, Mr. Williams? To be afraid and not to dare show it."

"Do you expect your victims to beg?" I asked.

"They do. In one manner or another."

"They appeal to your humanity? And that is hopeless?"

"It is hopeless."

"They offer you money?"

"Very often."

"Is that hopeless too?"

"So far it has been, Mr. Williams."

"Behind the picture I pointed out to you, Mr. Smith, there is a wall safe."

He gave the painting another brief glance. "Yes."

"It contains five thousand dollars."

"That is a lot of money, Mr. Williams."

I picked up my glass and went to the painting. I opened the safe, selected a brown envelope, and then finished my drink. I put the empty glass in the safe and twirled the knob.

Smith's eyes were drawn to the envelope. "Bring that here, please."

I put the envelope on the cocktail table in front of him.

He looked at it for a few moments and then up at me. "Did you actually think you could buy your life?"

I lit a cigarette. "No. You are, shall we say, incorruptible."

He frowned slightly. "But still you brought me the five thousand?"

I picked up the envelope and tapped its contents out on the table. "Old receipts. All completely valueless to you."

He showed the color of irritation. "What do you think this has possibly gained you?"

"The opportunity to go to the safe and put your glass inside it."

His eyes flicked to the glass in front of him. "That was yours. Not mine."

I smiled. "It was your glass, Mr. Smith. And I imagine that the police will wonder what an empty glass is doing in my safe. I rather think, especially since this will be a case of murder, that they will have the intelligence to take fingerprints."

His eyes narrowed. "I haven't taken my eyes off you for a moment. You couldn't have switched our glasses."

"No? I seem to recall that at least twice you looked at the painting."

Automatically he looked in that direction again. "Only for a second or two."

"It was enough."

He was perspiring faintly. "I say it was impossible."

"Then I'm afraid you will be greatly surprised when the police come for you. And after a little time you will have the delightful opportunity of facing death in the electric chair. You will share your victims' anticipation of death with the addition of a great deal more time in which to let your imagination play with the topic. I'm sure you've read accounts of executions in the electric chair?"

His finger seemed to tighten on the trigger.

"I wonder how you'll go," I said. "You've probably pictured yourself meeting death with calmness and fortitude. But that is a common comforting delusion, Mr. Smith. You will more likely have to be dragged. . . ."

His voice was level. "Open that safe or I'll kill you."

I laughed. "Really now, Mr. Smith, we both know that obviously you will kill me if I *do* open the safe."

A half a minute went by before he spoke. "What do you intend to do with the glass?"

"If you don't murder me—and I rather think you won't now—I will take it to a private detective agency and have your fingerprints reproduced. I will put them, along with a note containing pertinent information, inside a sealed envelope. And I will leave instructions that in the event I die violently, even if the occurrence appears accidental, the envelope be forwarded to the police."

Smith stared at me and then he took a breath. "All that won't be necessary. I will leave now and you will never see me again."

I shook my head. "I prefer my plan. It provides protection for my future."

He was thoughtful. "Why don't you go direct to the police?"

"I have my reasons."

His eyes went down to his gun and then slowly he put it in his pocket. An idea came to him. "Your wife could very easily hire someone else to kill you."

"Yes. She could do that."

"I would be accused of your death. I could go to the electric chair."

"I imagine so. Unless. . . ."

Smith waited.

"Unless, of course, she were unable to hire anyone."

"But there are probably a half a dozen other. . . ." He stopped.

I smiled. "Did my wife tell you where she is now?"

"Just that she'd be at a place called the Petersons. She will leave at eleven."

"Eleven? A good time. It will be very dark tonight. Do you know the Petersons' address?"

He stared at me. "No."

"In Bridgehampton," I said, and I gave him the house number.

Our eyes held for half a minute.

"It's something you must do," I said softly. "For your own protection."

He buttoned his coat slowly. "And where will you be at eleven, Mr. Williams?"

"At my club, probably playing cards with five or six friends. They will no doubt commiserate with me when I receive word that my wife has been . . . shot?"

"It all depends on the circumstances and the opportunity." He smiled thinly. "Did you ever love her?"

I picked up a jade figurine and examined it. "I was extremely fond of this piece when I first bought it. Now it bores me. I will replace it with another."

When he was gone there was just enough time to take the glass to a detective agency before I went on to the club.

Not the glass in the safe, of course. It held nothing but my own fingerprints.

I took the one that Mr. Smith left on the cocktail table when he departed.

The prints of Mr. Smith's fingers developed quite clearly.

Out of Order

by Carl Henry Rathjen

The kid got it in the back at seven-thirty that evening.

He'd answered the service station's inside phone, listened, then covered the mouthpiece and said to Jim Daly, "Duck! It's The Sniper. I'm going to call his bluff."

"Don't," Jim had warned, feeling exposed with glass on four sides of the office.

But the kid ran out to call the police from the phone booth near the driveway. A customer, driving in, made him swerve, slipping on a glob of grease. So there was no telling whether the slug got him before or after he began twisting down. No telling from which direction it came. And no sound of a shot either.

Jim Daly, with hair as black as the grease on big knuckles he kept rubbing into a palm, told all that to Whitehead, the squat, blond detective who came in the second police car while the ambulance guys were covering the kid with a canvas.

"So that's an out for you, I suppose," Daly added.

This was the seventh such robbery of a service station. Somebody phoned and said, "You're covered with a gun, every move. Put a clip or rubber band on the bills from the till. Drop them over the wall behind the air hose, then go on with your work. Don't get nosey or call the police. You'll be covered every moment." Seven of them, and the police, as usual, said they were working on it. Now the kid was dead. The first killing.

Whitehead's square face got a little white, then he spoke quietly. "Seeing anybody killed is hard to take, but was he something special to you?"

Jim Daly looked toward the canvas, a hub for a ring of morbid stares being held out of the station by uniformed police.

"He tried to hold me up once," said Daly. "I talked him out of it and gave him a job."

Whitehead stared. "Instead of calling us."

"All he needed was a break," snapped Daly.

"That's all we need too," Whitehead murmured. His partner, a thin man with razor-sharp gaze, said nothing.

"In other words," Daly charged, "you haven't done a damn thing. Now a good kid's dead, murdered. He never had a chance."

Whitehead seemed to sort words before he spoke. "You'd know better than I would how many service stations there are in the metropolitan area. Close to a couple thousand, isn't it?"

"All right," said Daly. "You can't stake out every one of them. But you guys are supposed to know how to run down these killers."

"It takes time," Whitehead began.

"I can't get away with that in my business," Daly declared. "I'm expected to trouble-shoot a customer's car in five minutes."

Whitehead nodded, staring around at apartments across the avenue, store windows facing the sidestreet with a slice of night sky showing in the alley.

"And the customer," he said with a slight smile, "expects it because he thinks it's easy, doesn't know the problems of your job. That works two ways, Daly. If you were a policeman, you'd know."

"I tried to know once." Daly pressed his lips.

Whitehead faced him curiously.

"Why'd they turn you down?"

Daly answered defiantly, staring at a fist making his thumbnail white as the blood squeezed back. "I did time once when I was a kid."

Whitehead studied him. "That's why you gave this one a break."

Daly nodded. "That's why I'm sore, damn sore. A guy

sees he's made a mistake and more than makes up for it. Then someone louses it up for him, and you hand me the usual hogwash alibi. Save it for somebody else. I'll find who got him."

"Take it easy," Whitehead began.

"That's the trouble. I have, waiting for you to do something."

Daly pulled off his coveralls.

But he was still in the station at midnight, though not open for business, when Whitehead drove in with his partner.

"Got it solved, Daly?" he asked, neither sarcastic nor hopeful as he leaned against the desk, hands in the pockets of his topcoat.

Daly poked a thick finger in a cigarette pack that looked as though it had been sat on. "It's like tracking down a miss in a car. I've found out where it can't be from."

"I know what you mean," said Whitehead. He waited. Daly carefully straightened out a bent cigarette, then thumbnailed a wooden match. He waited too. Whitehead sighed, and smiled. "All right, I'll tell you. We know where it couldn't have come from too, but being police, we had to check it out anyway. The shot couldn't have come from the apartments or stores. They've all been occupied a long time. No stick-up artist is going to have friends living in the vicinity of every place he plans to knock over. He wouldn't be on a roof either. Couldn't watch his victim at the phone. We know that from other jobs that have been pulled where he mentioned what the victim was doing while being warned."

Daly blew smoke toward the door. "You don't have to be a cop to figure that out."

Whitehead looked at the No Smoking sign, glanced at the locked gasoline pumps, then got out his own cigarettes.

"And it doesn't take a police officer to figure it took two of them to pull these jobs. One to make the phone call, the other to watch from a dark parked car."

Daly took a long drag, then gestured with his thumb toward the side street. "My guess is the car was parked up there."

Whitehead's partner shifted to peer in that direction,

then turned to look where the kid's body had been. Whitehead just leaned against the desk.

"Police officers have one advantage over citizens who think we're not doing our job. Take the chip off your shoulder and listen, Daly. We looked up records. When the kid tried to hold you up, it wasn't the first job he'd pulled, nor the last."

Daly closed his eyes and took another long drag. "I wish you hadn't told me." He looked up suddenly. "You think he was in on these sniper jobs?"

Whitehead nodded. "And he wanted a larger split. That's why he was shot."

Daly frowned. "But they tried to hold me up."

"That's what doesn't fit," said Whitehead. "They hit only stations doing a good business. We've checked on gasoline purchases with the wholesaler. You haven't been doing so well here since the freeway pulled traffic away. A lot of nights it's not even been worth staying open."

"It was a phony stick-up then," Daly growled. "Just to get the kid."

"A phony, sure," Whitehead agreed, "because we figure the kid was shot in the back, dying out there while he staggered, running to get away from *you!*"

Daly straightened. Whitehead's partner suddenly had a gun in his hand. Whitehead took his hands out of his pockets. One of them held handcuffs.

"You overplayed it, Daly. Too positive we were going to be dumb cops. Too dumb to wonder what happened to the supposed customer who made the kid swerve so you couldn't tell where the shot came from. Too dumb to thoroughly check everything out, records of all kinds, the possible and the impossible. We were even so dumb we tried the phone company, even though we figured the call couldn't be traced. It couldn't, because the kid forgot to tell you—or didn't have time to—that he'd reported earlier this evening the phone was out of order."

Daly expelled smoke. "What does that prove? I might have been confused by the shock of his being killed. I guess he took the call on the outside phone."

"The same as you were so confused," Whitehead suggested, "you forgot to rub grease on your thumbnails when we arrived. So confused you told us yourself that we had killers, not just one man, to run down on these hold-ups. You also thought we were too dumb to have men watching you while you pretended to begin tracking down the kid's killer. There's a crew opening the sewer now to retrieve your silenced gun."

He put the cuffs on Daly and guided him toward the car.

"You know," he said, "it doesn't bother us that people think we're dumb. It takes time, but we find in the long run that we meet plenty who are dumber. You'll have a lot in common with them, Daly . . . in prison."

The Handy Man

by Marion M. Markham

"I am so lucky to have a handy man like you living on the island," Thelma Norburton cooed. Thelma always cooed when she wanted someone to do something for her. She cooed at Arthur frequently. It was cheaper than paying a repair man to fix her vacuum cleaner switch, or her television set, or her toilet valve.

"I just don't *know* what I'd do *without* you. Ever since *poor* Henry passed on I've been *so lost*. You don't *know* how *difficult* it is to be a widow. *Everyone* tries to take *advantage* of me and *cheat* me."

Arthur heard only half of the cooing, as his head was under Thelma's pink kitchen sink. It was the third time in a month that his head had been under Thelma Norburton's kitchen sink. First it was a leak in the pipe leading to the dishwasher—then the garbage disposal jammed—now the diamond ring in the drain. Today he was under there longer than usual, and his back was aching badly. In addition, he had twice bumped his head against the garbage disposal unit.

"Since *you* and Millie moved in next door my *life* has been so much *easier.* You can't *think* how *relieved* I was. The house was empty for *so long,* while the will was being contested. And sometimes I saw *strange* lights at *night.* But, *of course,* the *police* never paid any *attention* to my calls. And then *you* moved in, and I felt so much *safer.*

"I wasn't scared to *death* that I'd be *murdered* in my bed after *you* came. And to find out that you can fix *absolutely* anything. I mean, I certainly am the *luckiest* widow in Florida. I *told* Millie that *just* yesterday. Millie, I said, I am *absolutely* the *luckiest* widow on the Gold Coast to have two of the *cleverest* people in south Florida for neighbors."

Arthur had heard all about that conversation from Millie before.

"Now she wants you to re-upholster a bedroom chair for her," Millie recounted. "And she'd like me to make new drapes to match. Is this what retirement is all about, Arthur? Making drapes for my neighbor? I made my own for years, and hung my own wallpaper, and re-covered our dining room chairs myself just so we could save enough money to retire. I don't want to spend that retirement making Thelma Norburton's drapes.

"Tell her you won't do it."

"Arthur, you know how she is. So forceful and pathetic at the same time. She can afford to have an interior designer make new drapes every month, but she still manages to make me feel guilty if I say no to her. I think it's the neighborhood. We don't belong with all these wealthy people. And Thelma knows how I feel and uses it to make me feel like a servant."

"You're not Thelma's servant. You're my wonderful wife, and you belong here as much as she does. Two million is hardly poverty."

"But it shows—all the years I washed my own dishes and made my own clothes. It shows in my hands and the way my shoulders are bent. It shows, too, that you used to wind your own condensers—or whatever those things were you worked on every night when Alice was a baby and the business just starting.

"It doesn't show. We're as good as anyone else on this island."

"Then why did Thelma ask you to put up a new shelf in her garage just two days after we moved in?"

"I'll speak to Thelma tomorrow and tell her you won't make her drapes and I won't re-cover her chair. I won't have her making my wife feel like a servant." He kissed her gently. "I promise you, I'll take care of it tomorrow."

Arthur tried to speak to Thelma the next morning. When he opened his mouth, Thelma cooed at him about how her *diamond* ring that *dear* Henry had given to her on their *last* Christmas *together* had gone down the kitchen drain, and would Arthur mind *terribly* getting it out for her?

So Arthur lay on his back under the pink sink, while Thelma sat at the glass-topped wrought iron kitchen table —also pink. She sipped grasshoppers, never offering anything to Arthur, and cooed.

"My *goodness,* Arthur. I never thought it would take *this* long to get a little old diamond ring out of a little old *sink* drain. I'm playing *bridge* at two. I mean, you fixed the *washing machine* in an hour, and you had to take it *all* apart. Remember how I bet you *wouldn't* get it all back *together* again? But you *did.* You really are so *marvellous* with your *hands.* I don't believe there's *anything* you can't do.

"Does Millie *appreciate* you? *Really* appreciate you, I mean. If she ever gets tired of you, you just come *right* over here. You *understand?* Henry Bejaman Norburton may have inherited *twenty million* dollars. But he couldn't hold a *candle* to you when it comes to *electricity* and *plumbing.* I really *am* the *luckiest* woman to have a *strong, intelligent, clever* man like *you* around.

"Almost finished," Arthur said, giving a last twist to the thin copper wire he was working with. He handed out the diamond ring that looked too small for Thelma's pudgy fingers.

"You still have time to make your bridge game." He slid out from under the sink and began gathering up the wire cutters, voltage tester, and other tools.

"I just don't *know* how to *thank* you, Arthur. Would you like a glass of *water?*"

"No, thanks, Thelma. It's almost two, and Millie will wonder what's become of me."

"Well, I do *appreciate* it. You really *are* the *cleverest* man. Is there *anything* you can't do?"

"Not once I set my mind to it, Thelma" he said proudly.

Arthur felt real pride later that evening, when he saw the

sudden eerie glow in the kitchen next door, and then total darkness. He'd never wired a garbage disposal before.

Continuous feed disposal units were dangerous, he had always said, what with water running and women pushing things through the metal sink ring with wet hands. If ever the fuse on the unit didn't cut off right, if something happened to short the motor and send an electric current up to that metal ring. . .

Of course, it was probably a one-in-five-hundred-million chance—unless a handy man knew how to fix it just right.

Nightmare

by Elaine Slater

One minute the sun was out, and the next it got all gray and dark. I saw lightning 'way far off in the direction we were going, but I couldn't hear any thunder yet. A wind came up from nowhere and all the leaves on the bushes and trees did a belly-flop.

I looked at Mom, but she was driving perfectly calmly as if nothing was happening. She looked too young to be my mother, and for a second I felt sorry for her, but then I hated her again.

She was taking me to this summer vacation camp, and I didn't want to go. Cripes, how I didn't want to go! She'd showed me this brochure and it had a picture of the Director and all the campers posed outside of bunks with their Counsellors. The Director was a bald, beefy guy with a silver tooth, smiling something awful. The Counsellors were great big jerks in white ducks and open shirts. They all looked too damn proud of themselves.

But the kids! I tell you it was the kids who tipped me off. There they were, standing in front of their bunks, their shorts hanging down, their shirts out, their hair practically growing over their eyes. And I'm telling you there was a look of such dumb misery on their faces, it'd give anyone the shakes. One kid in particular—Bunk 9, I think he was—was practically screaming a warning at me out of that picture. "Stay away from here, kid," he was saying, "this is Hell."

But my Mom was determined that I got to go to camp. And when Mom makes up her mind!

I begged Dad. I said, "Just look at those faces in the brochure. You can tell it's a crumby place."

My Dad has a fierce temper, but still he's an easier mark than Mom. But this time all he said was, "Your Mother and I have talked about this and you must trust us to do what we think is right for you."

He couldn't see those faces like I could, and I was ashamed to tell him the truth. I was scared. Cripes, I was scared!

I tried everything. First I tried persuasion. I argued with them all the time. I told them it was no good sending me there because I wouldn't stay. I told them they couldn't make me go if I didn't want to. Finally I got sent from the table so many times, I decided to go on a hunger strike. I had nothing to lose, I wasn't getting much to eat anyway. But that didn't last long.

Next I ran away. I didn't get far—my bike blew a tire. Then I tried to be as good as I knew how to be, so they'd want me around all summer. I must admit that worked the best. I helped Mom with everything, and when Dad came home I helped him wash the car and mow the lawn. I never even mentioned camp, but I could tell as the time grew closer that they were beginning to look at each other and then at me. They thought I wasn't looking, but I sure was.

Then the whole idea blew. We had a bang-up fight about my fingernails of all things! I don't know what happened to me. I guess all that helping was getting on my nerves. Anyway, I started yelling and fighting, and boy, two days later I was packed into the car with Mom and was headed for camp.

We'd just reached this rickety sign, "Happy Days Camp," when I heard the first thunder rumbling in the distance.

The storm was coming fast. A few drops hit the windshield as we bumped down this long dirt road, and I thought, "My God! She's really going to do it. She's going to leave me here"—and suddenly I knew as sure as shooting I was gonna die here. I was screaming inside, but my Mom was still perfectly calm, concentrating on this lousy dirt road.

The Director was there waiting for us with one of the Counsellors. He grinned at me just like in the photograph, and I swear behind his fat face and sweaty glasses, I could see a death's-head. He took my hand to lead me over to the Counsellor, but I grabbed it away. His hand was like ice even though the rest of him was all sweaty. I looked up at this big Counsellor and I almost dropped right there.

"This is Archie," the Director said, "Counsellor of Bunk Nine. Your bunk."

I sidled up to that big jerk and I whispered, I think I whispered, "I'm gonna kick you in the head."

Cripes! He only smiled down at me, a smile that said, "Anything you can do I can do better, and harder, and *MORE*."

Then there was this huge clap of thunder, and rain began to fall in buckets as we stood there on this weedy parking lot.

I began to shake all over. I couldn't stop shaking. I was gonna die if I stayed here—I knew it. But nobody would believe me, most of all the people I loved best and the ones who were supposed to love me best.

I was shaking all over and had my eyes screwed shut . . . Then there was this sound like a bell screaming in my ears. I awoke shaking with cold. It was dark with just a thin edge of light coming over a distant freezing horizon, but the alarm clock was jangling insistently.

"Turn that damn thing off," my wife's voice said thickly. She was lying in the other bed in a stupor, her eyes closed, her mouth hanging open like a dead fish, and her hair in those great big curlers.

I looked at her in sudden revulsion and my trembling stopped. By God! She looked like my Mother in the dream. I pulled myself around and got out of bed. I picked up my pillow and stood over my snoring wife.

When I was finished she still looked like a dead fish, only this time she really was. Dead, that is. Then I smashed the goddam alarm clock and climbed back to bed. This was one morning I wasn't going to appear at her beefy father's plant or take any more goddam orders from her lousy brother, Archie.

Recipe for Revenge

by Jane Speed

It was a recipe for heartbreak: her love was forever, his only for a while.

She knew this, of course. She was not a fool. But forewarned is forearmed, she told herself.

Brave words, false words. His goodbye, as lightly given as his love, left her stunned and desolate.

Outwardly all went on as before. Her husband, who never suspected, continued to invite business associates to dinner to show off her charming skills; she was an excellent cook and an impeccable hostess. And she did not once fail him, though it seemed to her now a daily act of courage just to stay alive.

Why did she bother? What was she waiting for?

"By the way, my dear," her husband said one evening, "there'll be two guests for dinner on Saturday. Remember that pleasant young man who came here so often last year? Couldn't seem to get enough of your cooking. Well, he's just back from his honeymoon, so I've invited the newlyweds over for dinner. I didn't think you'd mind. You do that sort of thing well."

"Not at all," she assured him. And, smiling a Borgia smile, she set about planning her ultimate menu.

Sweet Fever

by Bill Pronzini

Quarter before midnight, like on every evening except the Sabbath or when it's storming or when my rheumatism gets to paining too bad, me and Billy Bob went down to the Chigger Mountain railroad tunnel to wait for the night freight from St. Louis. This here was a fine summer evening, with a big old fat yellow moon hung above the pines on Hankers Ridge and mockingbirds and cicadas and toads making a soft ruckus. Nights like this, I have me a good feeling, and I know Billy Bob does too.

They's a bog hollow on the near side of the tunnel opening, and beside it a woody slope, not too steep. Halfway down the slope is a big catalpa tree and that was where we always set, side by side with our backs up against the trunk.

So we come on down to there, me hobbling some with my cane and Billy Bob holding onto my arm. That moon was so bright you could see the melons lying in Ferdie Johnson's patch over on the left, and the rail tracks had a sleek oiled look coming out of the tunnel mouth and leading off towards the Sabreville yards a mile up the line. On the far side of the tracks, the woods and the run-down shacks that used to be a hobo jungle before the county sheriff closed it off thirty years back had them a silvery cast, like they was all coated in winter frost.

We set down under the catalpa tree and I leaned my head back to catch my wind. Billy Bob said, "Granpa, you feeling right?"

"Fine, boy."

"Rheumatism ain't started paining you?"

"Not a bit."

He give me a grin. "Got a little surprise for you."

"The hell you do."

"Fresh plug of blackstrap," he said. He come out of his pocket with it. "Mr. Cotter got him in a shipment just today down at his store."

I was some pleased. But I said, "Now you hadn't ought to go spending your money on me, Billy Bob."

"Got nobody else I'd rather spend it on."

I took the plug and unwrapped it and had me a chew. Old man like me ain't got many pleasures left, but fresh blackstrap's one; good corn's another. Billy Bob gets us all the corn we need from Ben Logan's boys. They got a pretty good-sized still up on Hankers Ridge, and their corn is the best in this part of the hills. Not that either of us is a drinking man, now. A little touch after supper and on special days is all. I never did hold with drinking too much, or doing anything too much, and I taught Billy Bob the same.

He's a good boy. Man couldn't ask for a better grandson. But I raised him that way—in my own image, you might say—after both my own son Rufus and Billy Bob's ma got taken from us in 1947. I reckon I done a right job of it, and I couldn't be less proud of him than I was of his pa, or love him no less either.

Well, we set there and I worked on the chew of blackstrap and had a spit every now and then, and neither of us said much. Pretty soon the first whistle come, way off on the other side of Chigger Mountain. Billy Bob cocked his head and said, "She's right on schedule."

"Mostly is," I said, "this time of year."

That sad lonesome hungry ache started up in me again—what my daddy used to call the "sweet fever." He was a railroad man, and I grew up around trains and spent a goodly part of my early years at the roundhouse in the Sabreville yards. Once, when I was ten, he let me take the throttle of the big 2-8-0 Mogul steam locomotive on his highballing run to Eulalia, and I can't recollect no more finer experience in my whole life.

Later on I worked as a callboy, and then as a fireman on a 2-10-4, and put in some time as a yard-tender engineer, and I expect I'd have gone on in railroading if it hadn't been for the Depression and getting myself married and having Rufus. My daddy's short-line company folded up in 1931, and half a dozen others too, and wasn't no work for either of us in Sabreville or Eulalia or anywheres else on the iron.

That squeezed the will right out of my daddy, and he took to ailing, and I had to accept a job on Mr. John Barnett's truck farm to support him and the rest of my family. Was my intention to go back into railroading, but the Depression dragged on, and my daddy died, and a year later my wife Amanda took sick and passed on, and by the time the war come it was just too late.

But my son Rufus got him the sweet fever too, and took a switchman's job in the Sabreville yards, and worked there right up until the night he died. Billy Bob was only three then; his own sweet fever comes most purely from me and what I taught him. Ain't no doubt trains been a major part of all our lives, good and bad, and ain't no doubt neither they get into a man's blood and maybe change him, too, in one way and another. I reckon they do.

The whistle come again, closer now, and I judged the St. Louis freight was just about to enter the tunnel on the other side of the mountain. You could hear the big wheels singing on the track, and if you listened close you could just about hear the banging of couplings and the hiss of air brakes as the engineer throttled down for the curve. The tunnel don't run straight through Chigger Mountain; she comes in from the north and angles to the east, so that a big freight like the St. Louis got to cut back to quarter speed coming through.

When she entered the tunnel, the tracks down below seemed to shimmy and you could feel the vibration clear up where we was sitting under the catalpa tree. Billy Bob stood himself up and peered down towards the black tunnel mouth like a bird dog on a point. The whistle come again, and once more, from inside the tunnel, sounding hollow and miseried now. Every time I heard it like that, I thought of a body trapped and hurting and crying out for help that wouldn't come in the empty hours of the night. I shifted the cud of blackstrap and worked up a spit to keep my mouth from drying. The sweet fever feeling was strong in my stomach.

The blackness around the tunnel opening commenced to

lighten, and got brighter and brighter until the long white
glow from the locomotive's headlamp spilled out onto the
tracks beyond. Then she come through into my sight, her
light shining like a giant's eye, and the engineer give
another tug on the whistle, and the sound of her was a
clattering rumble as loud to my ears as a mountain
rockslide. But she wasn't moving fast, just kind of easing
along, pulling herself out of that tunnel like a night crawler
out of a mound of earth.

The locomotive clacked on past, and me and Billy Bob
watched her string slide along in front of us. Flats, boxcars,
three tankers in a row, more flats loaded down with pine
logs big around as a privy, a refrigerator car, five coal
gondolas, another link of boxcars. Fifty in the string already, I thought. She won't be dragging more than sixty,
sixty-five.

Billy Bob said suddenly, "Granpa, look yonder!"

He had his arm up, pointing. My eyes ain't so good no
more and it took me a couple of seconds to follow his point,
over on our left and down at the door of the third boxcar in
the last link. It was sliding open, and clear in the moonlight I
saw a man's head come out, then his shoulders.

"It's a floater, Granpa," Billy Bob said, excited. "He's
gonna jump. Look at him holding there, he's gonna jump."

I spit into the grass. "Help me up, boy."

He got a hand under my arm and lifted me up and held
me until I was steady on my cane. Down there at the door of
the boxcar, the floater was looking both ways along the
string of cars and down at the ground beside the tracks.
That ground was soft loam and the train was going slow
enough and there wasn't much chance he would hurt
himself jumping off.

He come to that same idea, and as soon as he did he flung
himself off the car with his arms spread out and his hair and
coattails flying in the slipstream. I saw him land solid and go
down and roll over once. Then he knelt there, shaking his
head a little, looking around.

Well, he was the first floater we'd seen in seven months.
The yard crews seal up the cars nowadays and they ain't
many ride the rails anyhow, even down in our part of the
country. But every now and then a floater wants to ride bad

enough to break a seal, or hides himself in a gondola or on a loaded flat. Kids, oldtime hoboes, wanted men. They's still a few.

And some of 'em get off right down where this one had, because they know the St. Louis freight stops in Sabreville and they's yardmen there that check the string, or because they see the run-down shacks of the old hobo jungle or Ferdie Johnson's melon patch. Man rides a freight long enough, no provisions, he gets mighty hungry. The sight of a melon patch like Ferdie's is plenty enough to make him jump off.

"Billy Bob," I said.

"Yes, Granpa. You wait easy now."

He went off along the slope, running. I watched the floater, and he come up on his feet and got himself into a clump of bushes alongside the tracks to wait for the caboose to pass so's he wouldn't be seen. Pretty soon the last of the cars left the tunnel, and then the caboose with a signalman holding a red-eye lantern out on the platform. When she was down the tracks and just about beyond my sight, the floater showed himself again and had him another look around. Then, sure enough, he made straight for the melon patch.

Once he got into it I couldn't see him because he was in close to the woods at the edge of the slope. I couldn't see Billy Bob neither. The whistle sounded one final time, mournful, as the lights of the caboose disappeared, and a chill come to my neck and set there like a cold dead hand. I closed my eyes and listened to the last singing of the wheels fade away.

It weren't long before I heard footfalls on the slope coming near, then the angry sound of a stranger's voice, but I kept my eyes shut until they walked up close and Billy Bob said, "Granpa." When I opened 'em the floater was standing three feet in front of me, white face shining—scared face, angry face, evil face.

"What the hell is this?" he said. "What you want with me?"

"Give me your gun, Billy Bob," I said.

He did it, and I held her tight and lifted the barrel. The ache in my stomach was so strong my knees felt weak and I could scarcely breathe. But my hand was steady.

The floater's eyes come wide-open and he backed off a step. "Hey," he said, "hey, you can't—"

I shot him twice.

He fell over and rolled some and come up on his back. They wasn't no doubt he was dead, so I give the gun back to Billy Bob and he put it away in his belt. "All right, boy," I said.

Billy Bob nodded and went over and hoisted the dead floater onto his shoulder. I watched him trudge off towards the bog hollow, and in my mind I could hear the train whistle as she'd sounded from inside the tunnel. I thought again, as I had so many times, that it was the way my boy Rufus and Billy Bob's ma must have sounded that night in 1947, when the two floaters from the hobo jungle broke into their home and raped her and shot Rufus to death. She lived just long enough to tell us about the floaters, but they was never caught. So it was up to me, and then up to me and Billy Bob when he come of age.

Well, it ain't like it once was and that saddens me. But they's still a few that ride the rails, still a few take it into their heads to jump off down there when the St. Louis freight slows coming through the Chigger Mountain tunnel.

Oh my yes, they'll *always* be a few for me and Billy Bob and the sweet fever inside us both.

The Magnum

by Jack Ritchie

Amos Weatherlee clutched a magnum of champagne in one hand and a hammer in the other.

He paused in the wide doorway of the hotel bar.

At this hour of the afternoon, the barroom was nearly empty except for the three women in one booth with Pink Ladies and a middle-aged man alone in another.

Weatherlee approached him and extended the hammer. "Pardon me, but I would regard it as an extreme favor if you would smash my bottle."

Harry Sloan studied him warily. "Don't you think that would make quite a mess?"

Weatherlee's silver-gray hair was somewhat disheveled and he spoke with a slight slur. "I never thought of that. You don't suppose that the bartender has a basin or something like that we could use?"

Sloan sipped his whiskey and soda. "If you're really set on smashing that bottle, why don't you do it yourself?"

Weatherlee sighed. "I tried. I really tried. Captain O'Reilly did too. So did Carruthers and Larson and Cooper and I don't know how many more. It was quite a wild night."

"What was?"

"Our club meeting a year ago."

Sloan's attention was distracted by the procession of a dozen elderly men filing through the hotel entrance. At least half of them walked with canes. They moved slowly across the lobby toward the open doors of a private dining room.

Sloan showed some interest. "Who in the world are they?"

"Our club," Weatherlee said. "It's our annual reunion.

The members just finished a sight-seeing bus tour of the city and now we're going to have dinner." He watched as the group entered the dining room. "We were all members of the same National Guard Company. We formed the club right after the war."

"World War I?"

"No," Weatherlee said. "The Spanish-American War."

Sloan regarded him skeptically.

"That's Captain O'Reilly," Weatherlee said. "Wearing the broad-brimmed campaign hat." He sat down. "How old do you think I am?"

"I haven't the faintest idea."

"Ninety," Weatherlee said proudly. "I was eighteen when I enlisted."

"Sure," Sloan said. "And I suppose you were a member of Teddy Roosevelt's Rough Riders and charged up San Juan Hill?"

"No. Actually our outfit never got beyond Tampa before the war ended. Our only casualties were to yellow fever."

"You look pretty spry for ninety."

"I am," Weatherlee said firmly. "I take a brisk half-hour walk every day and I'm still in full possession of all my faculties. In full possession."

"Sure," Sloan said. "Sure."

"Of course we weren't all the same age when we formed the club. Captain O'Reilly, for instance, our oldest man, was thirty-six. Twice as old as I at the time. He joined the club more in the spirit of good-fellowship, rather than really expecting to drink the bottle."

Sloan eyed the magnum of champagne. "What kind of a club was this?"

"A Last Man club. Perhaps you've heard of them? We founded ours in 1898. Right after the war ended and we were waiting to get shipped home. We wanted one hundred members, but actually we could get only ninety-eight to sign up."

"And those are the survivors? What's left?"

"Oh, no. Those are only the members who could make it. The others are in hospitals, old age homes, and the like."

Sloan did some mental arithmetic. "You said that Captain O'Reilly was thirty-six when the club formed in 1898?"

"Yes."

"Are you telling me that Captain O'Reilly is now one hundred and eight years old?"

"That's right. Our oldest man."

"And at ninety, you're the youngest?"

"Yes," Weatherlee said. "And I'm Custodian of the Bottle. According to our by-laws, the youngest surviving member is Custodian of the Bottle."

Sloan finished his drink. "Just how many club members are still alive?"

"Ninety-five."

Sloan stared at him for a few moments. "You mean to tell me that only three of you people have died since 1898?"

Weatherlee nodded. "There was Meyer. He died in a train accident back in 1909. Or was it 1910? And McMurty. He stayed in the Guard and worked himself up to full colonel before he was killed in the Argonne in 1918. And Iverson. He died of acute appendicitis in 1921."

Sloan considered his empty glass and then sighed. "Care for a drink?"

Weatherlee smiled affably. "I guess one more won't hurt. I'll take whatever you're having."

Sloan caught the bartender's eye and held up two fingers.

Weatherlee leaned forward and lowered his voice. "Actually this isn't the original champagne bottle. I broke that in 1924."

Sloan studied it again.

"It happened at our convention that year," Weatherlee said. "I was riding the elevator at the time. In those days they didn't operate as smoothly as they do now. There was this sudden jerk as the operator stopped at my floor. The suitcase I was carrying sprang open and the bottle dropped to the floor. Couldn't have fallen more than a foot, but there it lay, shattered on the floor."

Weatherlee shook his head at the memory. "I was absolutely panic-stricken. I mean here I was the custodian of the club's bottle—a great responsibility—and there it lay, shattered on the elevator floor. Luckily I was the only passenger on the elevator at the time. No one but the operator knew what had happened."

"So you went out and bought another bottle?"

"No. I didn't see how I could duplicate it anywhere. The bottle was quite distinctive. Purchased in Tampa, twenty-six years before."

Sloan indicated the bottle. "Then what is that?"

"It was the elevator operator who saved me," Weatherlee said. "He went out and got an *exact* duplicate."

"How did he manage to do that?"

"I haven't the faintest idea. He seemed a little evasive, now that I remember, but I was too overjoyed to press him. He was really most apologetic about the accident. Most solicitous. Took care of the mess in the elevator and brought the new bottle to my room fifteen minutes later. Wouldn't even let me pay for it. Claimed that the entire incident was really his doing and wouldn't accept a cent."

Sloan took his eyes from the magnum. "You said something about Captain O'Reilly trying to break the bottle?"

"Yes. Last year at our meeting. I still don't know exactly why he tried it. But I do remember that he kept staring at the bottle all evening. That year I was the Treasurer and I'd just finished reading my report. We had $4,990 in the treasury. Our dues are actually almost nominal, but still after all those years and compounded interest, it reached that sum."

The bartender brought the drinks. Sloan paid him and took a swallow of his whiskey and soda. "So what about O'Reilly?"

Weatherlee watched the bartender leave. "Oh, yes. Well, just as I finished, he rose suddenly to his feet and began slashing at the bottle with his cane and shouting, 'That damn bottle! That damn bottle!' And then it seemed as though nearly everyone else went mad, too. They shouted and cursed and smashed at the bottle, some even with chairs. I really don't know how it would all have ended if the waiters hadn't rushed in and restrained them."

"But they didn't break the bottle?"

"No. It was most remarkable. The blows were really resounding, and yet it didn't break. I thought about that all year. All this long year."

Weatherlee took a deep breath. "I arrived here early this morning. I am not a drinking man, but on impulse I bought a pint of whiskey and took it up to my room. I just sat there drinking and staring at the bottle. I even forgot all about the bus tour. And then I don't know what came over me, but I picked up an ashtray—one of those heavy glass things that are practically indestructible—and struck the bottle. Again and again, until finally the *ashtray* broke."

Weatherlee took the handkerchief from his waistcoat pocket. "I was in a perfect frenzy. I rushed out of my room with the bottle, and down the hallway I found one of those maintenance closets with its door open. There was a hammer on one of the shelves. I put the magnum of champagne into the stationary tub in the cubicle and struck it again and again with the hammer."

"But the bottle still didn't break?"

Weatherlee dabbed lightly at his forehead with the handkerchief. "But what was most ghastly of all was that all the time I was trying to smash that bottle, I had the feeling that someone, somewhere, was *laughing* at me."

He glared at the magnum. "And then suddenly, the *conviction,* the *certainty,* came to me that neither I, nor *anybody* in the club could destroy that bottle. If it were done, it had to be done by someone on the outside."

Sloan frowned at his drink. "Just *why* do you want to destroy that bottle in the first place?"

Weatherlee sighed. "I don't know. I just know that I *do.*"

They were both silent for almost a minute and then Sloan said, "This elevator operator. What did he look like?"

"The elevator operator? Rather a distinguished sort of person. I remember thinking at the time that he wasn't at all what one would expect of an elevator operator. Rather tall. Dark hair, dark eyes."

One of the doors of the dining room across the lobby opened and a waiter stepped out. He came into the bar. "Mr. Weatherlee, we're serving now."

Weatherlee nodded. "Yes. I'll be there in a moment."

Sloan waited until the waiter was out of hearing. "When did you say you broke the original bottle?"

"In 1924."

"And nobody's died since then?"

"Nobody's died since 1921. That was when Iverson got his acute appendicitis."

Sloan stared at the bottle again. "I'd like to join your club."

Weatherlee blinked. "But that's impossible."

"Why is it impossible?"

"Well . . . for one thing, you didn't belong to our National Guard company."

"Do your by-laws say anything about members having to belong to that particular company? Or any company at all?"

"Well, no. But it was *assumed*. . . ."

"And you did say that you never did fill your membership quota? Only ninety-eight people signed up? That leaves a vacancy of two, doesn't it?"

"Yes, but you are so much younger than any of the rest of us. It would be unfair for us to have to compete with you for the bottle."

"Look," Sloan said. "I'm not a rich man, but I'll match what's in the treasury, dollar for dollar."

"That's very kind of you," Weatherlee said a bit stiffly, "but if you should outlive all of us, and that seems likely, you'd get it all back anyhow."

Sloan smiled patiently. "I'll sign an affidavit renouncing all claim to what's in the treasury."

Weatherlee rubbed his neck. "I don't know. I'm not the final authority on anything like this. I'm not even an officer this year, unless you want to count being Custodian of the Bottle. I really don't know what the procedure would be in a case like this. I suppose we'll all have to take a vote or something."

He rose and put the magnum under his arm. "I suppose there's no harm in asking, but frankly I think they'll turn you down."

Sloan put his hand on the hammer. "Better leave this here with me."

Sloan came to Weatherlee's room at nine-thirty the next morning.

He took an envelope from his pocket and handed it to Weatherlee.

Weatherlee nodded acceptance. "To be quite honest, I was a bit surprised that the club decided to accept you. Not without exception, of course. Captain O'Reilly was quite against it."

Sloan moved to the bureau and picked up the magnum of champagne.

Weatherlee blinked. "What are you doing?"

"Taking the bottle with me. You told me yourself that according to the club's by-laws, the youngest member is Custodian of the Bottle."

"Yes, but. . . ."

Sloan opened the door to the corridor. He smiled broadly. "We wouldn't want you to go around asking strange people to break it, now would we?"

When Sloan was gone, Weatherlee locked the door.

He went to the bathroom and began removing the make-up from his face. As he worked, a half century disappeared.

Maybe he could have taken Sloan for more than five thousand, but you never know. Getting too greedy could have blown the whole deal.

He smiled.

Finding the sucker was the hardest part of it.

But once you did, and learned approximately how much he could part with without undue pain, you went about arranging the set-up. That included going to the nearest Old Soldiers' Home and offering to treat a dozen of their oldest veterans to a dinner.

And the old boys did so enjoy an afternoon out.

Two Postludes

by Isak Romun

Desmond Blinn carved a dripping slice of the rare beef, pushed it down on a piece of rye, put another piece of bread on top of the meat, and took great bites, his free hand feeling his stubbled face. A beer was nearby, warm now, poured out too long ago, just before he began wrestling with his thoughts. But he drank it lustily, driblets of pale amber upon his new beard turning into small reflective beads perched on the tips of stiff hairs.

It was a good meal, a good last meal, hearty and rough as his life had been; and simple, simple and direct, as he knew his death was soon to be. A strange man, Bohlmann, the leader; a man for little rituals, careful observances, precise ceremony. The traditional "last meal" of the doomed man's choice, a case in point. What would take place soon?—a quick walk into the courtyard, Blinn's hands tied behind him, two strong boys, each with a paw upon a shoulder, pushing him gently but with no nonsense to his knees; a long wooden slat upon which thick, brushed letters proclaiming the crimes of ingratitude, treachery, and betrayal of which Blinn had been accused and, in Bohlmann's direct, thick-robed judgment, found guilty. And then, one gunshot up through the neck into the brain and eternity would fold out in front of Blinn.

Bohlmann had seen the method in a newsreel: Chinese Reds, the strips of wood calligraphed with records of infamy, executed by Nationalists—or the other way around; and the simplicity, not devoid of a certain economical pomp and high moral tone, was appealing, irresistible to his nature.

"Let us try that with the very next one we shoot," he had said jollily, and Desmond Blinn remembered, with a tremor, for it was he who had accommodated Bohlmann, who bent down, aimed the gun upwards, and pulled the trigger, then stepped back quickly as the two burly boys, like *pas de deuxing* dancers, sprang off to the sides to escape, with Desmond, the squirting blood and the small flying pieces of brain.

And now, he, Desmond Blinn, would again be a participant in this final ceremony. For what? A woman. So foolish, for there were so many women. Bohlmann secured them and spent them like copper coins, and soon Blinn would suffer because he rubbed one while there was some sheen still upon it. The woman had been disposed of, thrown down a well and left to die there. Women did not get to participate in the Ceremony, only men—the ones against whom Bohlmann mounted huge accusations, driving himself up a spiraling curve of vengeful rage until, convinced of the utmost perfidy, he pronounced the awful sentence: the Ceremony.

"Tomorrow," he had shouted at Blinn, his wet red mouth

quivering with anger and expectation. "Tomorrow, at dawn." It was always dawn, another nicety, another line in the format: a chiaroscuro effect cherished by Bohlmann.

But in the meanwhile, thought Desmond Blinn, there's this splendid beef, cut from a cow stolen, slaughtered, and cooked over a great fire that day, and the rough, simple bread, and the beer, though warm, satisfying but almost gone. Might they give him another?

As Blinn went to the door of the cell in the monastery the band had taken over, he felt a keen exhilaration over how well he was taking this whole thing, enjoying the meat and bread, even rattling his agateware cup, chips of its coating flying about, against the short bars of the small opening in the door and shouting down the corridor, demanding more drink. And, by God, see that it's good and cold!

He was certain he could hold out this way, relish what life he had left without indulging in false hopes that somehow it would go on beyond the approaching light, that at the last moment he would receive a reprieve and be welcomed back into the band. No, that would not happen, but Blinn would rob Bohlmann of some of the glee gained through the Ceremony. Hah!—for what was the Ceremony designed? Not to make a man stand tall and stare back upon his persecutor at that last moment, as against a wall to be shot or, rope around his neck, upon a nervous horse. No, the victim was pushed down, his head bent forward, the wooden slat a comical element in a piece already without dignity; and then in this ignominious position, almost fetal (strange, that), the muzzle of the gun was pushed up against the short nape hairs but not fired until Bohlmann, off to the side, fat and squalid in his canvas chair, his torpid face moving rhythmically to the steady chewing of browned sesame seeds, masking his inner elation, gave the signal. (Caligula at the Circus Maximus.) By this time, the miscreant was reduced to a quaking, screaming figure, explaining to Bohlmann, pleading with Bohlmann, assuring Bohlmann that whatever in the world he had done (and perhaps he honestly didn't know), it would never occur again. Never.

If only you'll let me live. That's what they all said, thought Desmond Blinn as his cup ceased its insistent, cadenced ring upon the bars, and his knees felt a certain wateriness when he thought of those wretches, each now in his thoughts, remarkably, with his own face, the fear-stricken face of Desmond Blinn.

He wiped this vision of an uncongenial immediate future from the slate of his mind and struck up again the racket of cup against bars, calling out loudly (too loudly?) for more beer. Then he resurrected the images so recently discarded and ran them through a mental projector so that each, miraculously transformed now, showed Desmond Blinn as staunch, unbreakable, tight-lipped, and not without a trace of annoying wryness playing about his features, robbing Bohlmann of his pleasure.

For now, as one of his guards came padding down the corridor, Blinn knew, *knew,* that he would go through the Ceremony as these last pictures showed him, that he would deny Bohlmann the circus scene he coveted.

But the approaching guard ignored Blinn's demand for more beer and pushed a face against the bars of the small opening and blew his sweetish breath into the cell as he whispered quick and precise instructions to the confined man. The guard was Pardrilone, an old-time member of the band.

Tomorrow it would be over, he told the prisoner, but not for Blinn. For Bohlmann. If the men didn't turn from him now, he said, each would, in time, march screaming to the same fate that their leader planned for Blinn. Bohlmann was mad!

It was, after all, Pardrilone explained, not for a woman that Blinn was to die, but because he represented a threat to the leadership of Bohlmann, just as Bohlmann had been a threat to *his* predecessor. The woman had been emplaced to provide Bohlmann with an immediate cause for ordering Blinn's extinction; and perhaps the woman's as well, for Bohlmann was tiring of her.

This was why Blinn must be the center of the band's revolt against their leader. The others were afraid or, weighted down by the awe in which they held Bohlmann, could not conceive of his overthrow being successful, as if he had been touched by divinity.

Blinn reeled back from the door and fell to his cot,

weakened as much by the prospect of deliverance as others are of death. He had been ready for death. His was a readiness that was absolute, that was devoid of self-deception. He knew that never would he be as ready, that the conditioning of his mind and soul undergone in the hours spent in the dark cell could not be replicated at some future date, could not be turned on, turned off, by some psychic finger pressing a button.

"What's the matter with you?" Pardrilone hissed through the bars. "Are you with us?"

Desmond Blinn nodded as he rose and moved back to the door. "How? The plan. Does Quesada know?" Quesada was a faraway revolutionary figure to whom the band of irregulars owed a tenuous allegiance.

"He'll approve. Later. Here's a gun. Loaded." The guard shoved between the bars an ugly automatic pistol. "The clip is full. One round is chambered."

"I'll kill Bohlmann with this?"

"Yes. When I come to get you, I'll tie your hands loosely. Make sure to wear your woolskin so it will hide the gun. When you're out there, work your hands loose, get the gun out fast, and shoot him as he sits watching."

"Right in his fat, pig face."

"No," Pardrilone cautioned. "Too chancy—you could miss. Place your shots in his chest, around the heart. Can you do it?"

Blinn said he could.

"Good. You will be our new leader. That's the way these things go."

The next day, the plan worked perfectly. But despite what Pardrilone said, Blinn fired at and placed two bullets squarely in Bohlmann's face and watched with satisfaction as the force of the shots toppled the fat man over backwards, his wide buttocks still clamped in the arms of the canvas chair which went over with him as he skidded and rolled to a stop against a car some six feet distant. Some of Blinn's satisfaction was stolen, however, by Bohlmann, who saw, in the instant between the appearance of the gun and its discharge, what was happening and looked at Blinn calmly, a hint of wryness about his lips.

Pardrilone went over to the body, examined it, then growled at Blinn. "You should have fired at the chest. If you had missed, many of us would have been doomed. It was a stupid chance to take."

"I didn't miss—he's dead, isn't he?" Blinn replied matter-of-factly.

Pardrilone pondered this logic, accepted it, turned to the other members of the band, and yelled, "Hail Blinn, our new leader!"

The shouts were ear balm for Blinn, who stood the center of an admiring throng, any one of whose members would have shot him out of hand just moments before. He held his arms above his head, hands cupped in the manner of a champion boxer. Outside the circle—forgotten now even by Evelyn, his latest woman, who now turned her hot, fox eyes upon Blinn—lay Bohlmann, his shattered face a jagged O.

After that, Blinn led the band on many daring raids that garnered them much spoils and a number of casualties. They were richer than ever but disgruntled at the chances they had to take. So, one day, they grasped Blinn, tied his hands behind him, and dragged him to an open field. From the moment they had their hands on him to the moment they fired one sure shot into his head, Blinn, a bag of twitching, sagging flesh, cried and begged for his life. He had few thoughts at the end, but one of them was of how well Bohlmann had died. And how well he, Blinn, might have died that same day.

A Deal in Diamonds

by Edward D. Hoch

It was seeing a girl toss a penny into the plaza fountain that gave Pete Hopkins the idea. He was always on the lookout for money-making ideas, and they were getting tougher to find all the time. But as he looked up from the fountain to the open window of the Downtown Diamond Exchange, he thought he had found a good one at last.

He strolled over to the phone booth at the other side of the plaza and called Johnny Stoop. Johnny was the classiest dude Pete knew—a real fashion-plate who could walk into a store and have the clerks falling over themselves to wait on him. Better yet, he had no record here in the east. And it was doubtful if the cops could link him to the long list of felonies he had committed ten years ago in California.

"Johnny? This is Pete. Glad I caught you in."

"I'm always in during the daytime, Pete boy. In fact, I was just getting up."

"I got a job for us, Johnny, if you're interested."

"What sort?"

"Meet me at the Birchbark Bar and we'll talk about it."

"How soon?"

"An hour?"

Johnny Stoop groaned. "Make it two. I gotta shower and eat breakfast."

"Okay, two. See you."

The Birchbark Bar was a quiet place in the afternoons—perfect for the sort of meeting Pete wanted. He took a booth near the back and ordered a beer. Johnny was only ten minutes late and he walked into the place as if he were casing it for a robbery or a girl he might pick up. Finally he settled, almost reluctantly, for Pete's booth.

"So what's the story?"

The bartender was on the phone yelling at somebody about a delivery, and the rest of the place was empty. Pete started talking. "The Downtown Diamond Exchange. I think we can rip it off for a quick handful of stones. Might be good for fifty grand."

Johnny Stoop grunted, obviously interested. "How do we do it?"

"*You* do it. I wait outside."

"Great! And I'm the one the cops grab!"

"The cops don't grab anyone. You stroll in, just like Dapper Dan, and ask to see a tray of diamonds. You know where the place is, on the fourth floor. Go at noon, when there's always a few customers around. I'll create a commotion in the hall, and you snatch up a handful of stones."

"What do I do—swallow them like the gypsy kids used to do?"

"Nothing so crude. The cops are wise to that, anyway. You throw them out the window."

"Like hell I do!"

"I'm serious, Johnny."

"They don't even keep their windows open. They got air conditioning, haven't they?"

"I saw the window open today. You know all this energy-conservation stuff—turn off the air conditioner and open the windows. Well, they're doing it. They probably figure four flights up nobody's goin' to get in that way. But something can get *out*—the diamonds."

"It sounds crazy, Pete."

"Listen, you toss the diamonds through the window from the counter. That's maybe ten feet away." He was making a quick pencil sketch of the office as he talked. "See, the window's behind the counter and you're in front of it. They never suspect that you threw 'em out the window because you're never near the window. They search you, they question you, but then they gotta let you go. There are other people in the store, other suspects. And nobody saw you take them."

"So the diamonds go out the window. But you're not

outside to catch them. You're in the hall creating a diversion. So what happens to the stones?"

"This is the clever part. Directly beneath the window, four stories down, is the fountain in the plaza. It's big enough so the diamonds can't miss it. They fall into the fountain and they're as safe as in a bank vault, till we decide to get them. Nobody noticed them hit the water because the fountain is splashing. And nobody sees them *in* the water because they're clear. They're like glass."

"Yeah," Johnny agreed. "Unless the sun—"

"The sun don't reach the bottom of the pool. You could look right at 'em and not notice 'em—unless you knew they were there. We'll know, and we'll come back for them tomorrow night, or the next."

Johnny was nodding. "I'm in. When do we pull it off?"

Pete smiled and raised his glass of beer. "Tomorrow."

On the following day, Johnny Stoop entered the fourth floor offices of the Downtown Diamond Exchange at exactly 12:15. The uniformed guard who was always at the door gave him no more than a passing glance. Pete watched it all from the busy hallway outside, getting a clear view through the thick glass doors that ran from floor to ceiling.

As soon as he saw the clerk produce a tray of diamonds for Johnny, he glanced across the office at the window. It was open about halfway, as it had been the previous day. Pete started walking toward the door, touched the thick glass handle, and fell over in an apparent faint. The guard inside the door heard him fall and came out to offer assistance.

"What's the matter, mister? You okay?"

"I—I can't—breathe . . ."

He raised his head and asked for a glass of water. Already one of the clerks had come around the counter to see what the trouble was.

Pete sat up and drank the water, putting on a good act. "I just fainted, I guess."

"Let me get you a chair," one clerk said.

"No, I think I'd better just go home." He brushed off his suit and thanked them. "I'll be back when I'm feeling better." He hadn't dared to look at Johnny, and he hoped the diamonds had gone out the window as planned.

He took the elevator downstairs and strolled across the plaza to the fountain. There was always a crowd around it at noon—secretaries eating their lunches out of brown-paper bags, young men casually chatting with them. He mingled unnoticed and worked his way to the edge of the pool. But it was a big area, and through the rippling water he couldn't be certain he saw anything except the scattering of pennies and nickels at the bottom. Well, he hadn't expected to see the diamonds anyway, so he wasn't disappointed.

He waited an hour, then decided the police must still be questioning Johnny. The best thing to do was to head for his apartment and wait for a call.

It came two hours later.

"That was a close one," Johnny said. "They finally let me go, but they still might be following me."

"Did you do it?"

"Sure I did it! What do you think they held me for? They were goin' crazy in there. But I can't talk now. Let's meet at the Birchbark in an hour. I'll make sure I'm not followed."

Pete took the same booth at the rear of the Birchbark and ordered his usual beer. When Johnny arrived the dapper man was smiling. "I think we pulled it off, Pete. Damn if we didn't pull it off!"

"What'd you tell them?"

"That I didn't see a thing. Sure, I'd asked for the tray of stones, but then when there was the commotion in the hall I went to see what it was along with everyone else. There were four customers in the place and they couldn't really pin it on any one of us. But they searched us all, and even took us downtown to be X-rayed, to be certain we hadn't swallowed the stones."

"I was wondering what took you so long."

"I was lucky to be out as soon as I was. A couple of the others acted more suspicious than me, and that was a break. One of them even had an arrest record for a stolen car." He said it in a superior manner. "The dumb cops figure anyone who stole a car would steal diamonds."

"I hope they didn't get too good a look at me. I'm the one who caused the commotion, and they just gotta figure I'm involved."

"Don't worry. We'll pick up the diamonds tonight and get out of town for a while."

"How many stones were there?" Pete asked expectantly.

"Five. And all beauties."

The evening papers confirmed it. They placed the value of the five missing diamonds at $65,000. And the police had no clue.

They went back to the plaza around midnight, but Pete didn't like the feel of it. "They might be wise," he told Johnny. "Let's wait a night, in case the cops are still snoopin' around up there. Hell, the stones are safe where they are."

The following night, when the story had already disappeared from the papers, replaced by a bank robbery, they returned to the plaza once more. This time they waited till three A.M., when even the late crowd from the bars had scattered for home. Johnny carried a flashlight and Pete wore wading boots. He'd already considered the possibility that one or two of the diamonds might not be found, but even so they'd be far ahead of the game.

The fountain was turned off at night, and the calmness of the water made the search easier. Wading in the shallow water, Pete found two of the gems almost at once. It took another ten minutes to find the third one, and he was ready to quit then. "Let's take what we got, Johnny."

The flashlight bobbed. "No, no. Keep looking. Find us at least one more."

Suddenly they were pinned in the glare of a spotlight, and a voice shouted, "Hold it right there! We're police officers!"

"Damn!" Johnny dropped the flashlight and started to run, but already the two cops were out of their squad car. One of them pulled his gun and Johnny stopped in his tracks. Pete climbed from the pool and stood with his hands up.

"You got us, officer," he said.

"Damn right we got you," the cop with the gun growled. "The coins in that fountain go to charity every month. Anybody that would steal them has to be pretty low. I hope the judge gives you both ninety days in the cooler. Now up against the car while we search you!"

The Last Day of Shooting

by Dion Henderson

By nine o'clock the sun was streaming warmly into the blind and Johnny Tennant's big retriever was asleep on the shooting platform, lying on a hunting coat with his head resting on the rucksack that held the lunch. Blackbirds worked noisily in the bog behind us, their red shoulder patches bright against the dead grass, and once three egrets lumbered whitely down the channel from the rice fields. "Snow geese," someone said quietly back in the marsh and laughed, and the words came distinctly across the water. The sky was very blue and of course the only birds moving out of the refuge a mile away were impossibly high; it would not have been so bad except that it was the last day. It was the last day of the duck season and the last time, for most of us, that we would hunt together, or even meet, except accidentally.

Down in the point blind, Tom Randall stood up suddenly, hooting and thrashing his arms over the sedge and willow that camouflaged the blind, and an alarmed mud hen that had blundered almost into his boat skittered across the channel, peeping wildly. There was subdued laughter from the other three blinds around the point at the familiar performance. It was all very much like other days in other years—with one difference that made it not like any of them at all.

"I wish he had not taken the big gun," Johnny Tennant said. He was sitting on the platform beside the sleeping dog, with his feet down in the boat. He had not smiled at the mud hen's alarm.

"Your 20-gauge will be big enough," I said. "The way the birds are flying."

"I wasn't thinking about the shooting. There won't be any shooting."

"If it really disturbs you for him to have the big gun, I'll row down and get it back."

"If he knew I was disturbed, he wouldn't give it to you."

"That's probably true. He always carried a joke too far."

"Even when it was not a joke," Johnny Tennant said, not smiling.

"It was only a joke, taking the gun."

"No. It wasn't a joke."

"Are things really as bad as all that between you and Tom?" I asked.

"Things have always been that bad," Johnny Tennant said. "But now they are beginning to show, because I do not have much left that he wants."

I did not say anything. I was sorry that he felt bad, and that this last trip was not turning out well for him. Most of us had come because he wanted us to, because he had planned it for us, and because we were sorry for Johnny Tennant— but there wasn't anything we could do, really. The Clam Point Chowder, Poker Playing and Duck Hunting Society was something left over from a long time ago, when we were all a lot younger. Things like that are always more important to some members than to others, and with us it was Johnny Tennant who had inspired it, kept it going, and to whom, now that the shooting didn't amount to much and the members were scattered and the lease had run out, it was important that we get together for one last day of shooting.

I guess that it all became more important to Johnny as it became less important to the rest of us. He took care of the boats, he kept the decoys in repair and spent a good deal of his time in the shack on the point. He was our gunsmith, and reloaded our shotgun shells to a powder-and-shot ratio he had figured out to be most effective for the kind of shooting we had along the channel. Johnny's troubles probably had some relation to all this. They kept quietly overtaking him, one by one: the business that he started with Tom Randall, which did not do well as long as Johnny was in it; the woman who could not make up her mind between them; and then Johnny giving up both the business and the woman. But he did it carelessly, with a shrug, and the only difference we noticed was that Johnny Tennant spent more time at the shack on the point and more time alone, carving minutely detailed miniature ducks for the rest of us to hang up in our dens at home, and working on the inlays and engraving of his own favorite shotgun.

He had started with very complicated checkering of the stock and forearm, and then he had gone gradually into steel engraving, high-relief chiseling, and gold and ivory inlays. He reproduced a scene of the point itself on one side of the receiver, and the channel blind on the other, with ducks flying and the dog retrieving—until the gun itself was a glittering encyclopedia of our times together on the point. Gun engraving is a highly specialized art in itself, and I do not know how Johnny's work compared with the real immortals like Rudolph Kornbrath or Arnold Griebel or Joseph Baver, but the gun was very beautiful.

Now the gun was out in the point blind with Tom Randall, and whether it was just because of thoughtlessness or a poor joke, the hunt was not the way Johnny had planned it; the whole thing was spoiled for him.

It began when Tom Randall dropped his own gun into the marsh. We had eaten breakfast in the shack by lantern light with the windows covered: fried bread, heavy with bacon grease, and eggs and potatoes in a mixture that would kill a man at home in the city, but out here in the marsh would burn just brightly enough in his belly to keep him from freezing to death. Then, bundled up in seaters under the shooting coats, walking clumsily in hip boots, we followed Johnny out into the frosty starlight and down the quarter-mile of trail through the oak scrub to the place where the boats were pulled up under the cypress.

Johnny pushed the skiff out and stepped into it himself. "I'll take the point blind alone," he said. "That way maybe I can turn some of the high fliers coming out of the refuge and bring them in so you all get some shooting."

He uncased his gun and the starlight sparkled on the inlays as he slipped three shells softly and invisibly into the magazine.

"You'd better keep that museum piece covered up," someone said, "or it'll scare the ducks in the next county with its reflections."

"I'll keep it in the shade," Johnny said, chuckling. He sounded very happy then. "It's a pretty thing, though."

That was when Tom dropped his own gun into the marsh, into a foot of water and another foot of ooze. He was trying to push a boat out, holding the piece under one arm, and his hands slipped on the frost-wet gunwale and he dropped the gun. It was not hard to find, but it would take an hour, and daylight, to clean it up so that it was safe to shoot. Randall stood darkly in the water and swore.

"Never mind," Johnny Tennant said patiently, pushing the skiff back ashore. "I've got another gun up at the shack you can use. It's only a 20-gauge that I use to keep the squirrels honest, but it'll do."

He left the skiff and ran lightly up the trail in the darkness while the rest of us stood around uncomfortably, not talking.

"The light is coming up fast," Tom Randall said suddenly. "If we're not in the blinds by first shooting light, we'll never see a bird within range."

"What do you suggest?" I said.

Tom Randall stepped into the skiff and sent it skimming out into the channel. "This," he said. "I'll take old Johnny's boat and shotgun and go on out to the point blind myself. He can shoot with one of you."

"Johnny won't like it."

"Johnny won't mind," Tom Randall said, laughing, although no one laughed with him. "Johnny doesn't mind anything."

He was gone when Johnny came back with the 20-gauge, but it appeared that he was right. Johnny just shrugged and got into the boat with me, and we matched with the others to see who would take the channel blind and who would take the others. Then we poled off into the darkness, feeling for the channels in the grass to the open water.

And of course there had been no shooting. The sun came up clear and full and burned the frost off the marsh. The warm air from the Gulf moved up the river, and the birds getting up off the refuge climbed their aerial staircase straight up into the wonderfully blue sky, and no one truly cared except Johnny.

A little later the mud hen came back across the channel, swimming in narrow suspicious circles, but pressed by curiosity to see what had frightened it the first time. It was forty yards from the point blind, craning its neck, when Tom Randall fired. The charge of No. 4 shot splattered against the water, catching the bird in the center of a lethal pattern four feet in diameter, and presently the bird floated feet up, dead in the water.

"It shoots as good as it looks," Tom Randall's voice said across the water. "I think I'll keep it."

Johnny Tennant sat on the platform in our blind, not smiling. The retriever, awakened by the gunshot, peered out at the distant mud hen, and then, in the absence of a command to fetch, went back to sleep.

"He's a very funny man," I said in disgust.

Johnny Tennant shrugged. "I suppose he had to try it," he said. "He couldn't just look at it."

"I'm really very sorry. We didn't have a chance to stop him."

"It doesn't matter. . . . Maybe he thought it was safer to take my gun than take the one I was getting just for him." He smiled a little this time.

"Sure," I said. "You might have fixed up the 20 just for him, with a nice plug rammed down the barrel, or something."

"That isn't a good idea. A ballistician could tell if a gun blew up because the barrel was plugged."

He smiled again, almost wistfully. "If I wanted to kill a man accidentally in a duck blind," he said, "there are better ways."

The sun was warm in the blind and there was no swell in the channel, but suddenly I felt the touch of a cold wind blowing.

"A worn sear," Johnny said. "Or a cracked bolt in the block, so that the receiver would come right on back into your face after a shot. And when you use hand-loaded shells, it would be easy."

I did not say anything.

"You could make all kinds of mistakes," he went on. "You

could pick up the wrong over-powder wads and block the blow-by just long enough to split a barrel. Or you could measure from a flask of rifle powder, instead of regular nitrocellulose."

He paused, and said, "You remember that just one grain of a nitrocellulose rifle powder can raise breech pressure by almost 10,000 pounds."

He was sitting on the platform, still smiling a little and rubbing the dog's ears, when the dog raised his head abruptly, looking at something in the sky beyond the point. We followed his gaze, from habit, and presently we could see a bird, coming in low, laboriously, head swinging.

"A young goose looking for the family," Johnny Tennant said. "It looks as though he might come right down the channel."

Hearing him talk about the goose made me feel better. The cold wind let up for a moment, and I said: "It looks as though Tom will get the shot. I'm glad he's already fired once."

Johnny Tennant looked at me with a strange expression. "Did I make you nervous, talking about mistakes?"

"I had an odd feeling, while you were talking. I'm really very glad he already fired that gun once."

"That doesn't prove anything," he said, gently. "If a man made a mistake loading a shell, he could only afford one mistake—and there's no way to tell where it would be in the magazine."

The hair rose on my neck and I stood up, but down in the point blind Tom Randall was already up on the shooting platform. The young goose was flaring over him, in easy range, and Randall swung the beautiful gun, the sun flashing on its scrollwork and its splendid inlays. As the goose hung in panic at the top if its flare, the whole top of the blind dissolved in a white flash that was quite distinct before the shattering sound of the explosion swept across the water.

I stood dumbly in the boat, hearing the emptiness after the blast, and then the patter of raindrop-falling shot and metal fragments in the water around us, and then, preposterously later, the heavy sound of the body falling in the point blind.

"Damn him," Johnny Tennant said, in a thick, sad voice.

I looked at him and the tears were running down his defeated face.

"Tom always took everything I wanted for myself," Johnny Tennant said. "Even this."

Blisters in May

by Jack Ritchie

Dr. Kaufmann wasn't sure he'd heard right. "You mean you want a transfer to the road gang?"

"Yes, sir," I said.

He shook his head. "Fred, you have one of the best jobs inside the walls. You're out of the sun and there's no sweat. Don't you like being a medical orderly?"

"Yes, sir," I said. "But . . ." I shrugged. "I guess you could say that I'd like a change of pace."

He thought about it for a few seconds. "How long are you in for, Fred?"

"Life," I said.

He smiled faintly. "All right, Fred. I'll arrange the transfer. But I'm making book that after a few days with a pick and shovel, you'll be begging to come back. Anyway, I'll keep your present job open. When would you like this change of pace?"

"As soon as possible, sir. If you could make it Monday? That's May 1st."

Before I left my job at the dispensary that day, I put a roll of adhesive tape in my pocket. On Monday, after breakfast, I fell in with the outside work crew and we marched to the waiting trucks. The gates opened for us and for the first time in nine years I was outside the walls.

The ride was short and I spent the time taping my hands.

The trucks pulled up in front of a large ramshackle shed which housed the tools and machinery. We got off and waited in formation while a guard unlocked the double doors. He went inside and a con named Mark Hanson followed him.

After a few moments, the rest of us single-filed into the building. Hanson was in charge of handing out the tools. He marked me down for an axe.

We lined up again outside and waited while Hanson went about the business of closing the doors. He was about to snap the padlock when he looked at the guard and grinned sheepishly, "I forgot my shovel."

Yes, I thought, you forget it twice a year.

Hanson disappeared back into the shed and came out twenty seconds later with a shovel. He padlocked the doors and fell into the rear of the formation.

We marched a quarter of a mile to the work site and started the day. It was make-work mostly, clearing the scrub pine and cutting pole wood.

At noon, I got my plate filled in the chow line and sat down in the shade of a tree next to Hanson. He contemplated the contents of his plate and I had the feeling he wasn't going to eat what was there. Not today, anyway. When he put down the plate untouched, I said, "How are the hands?"

He glanced at his palms automatically. Blisters were beginning to form. I got out my roll of adhesive. "Try this."

He shrugged a small thanks and accepted it.

"Kind of interesting about your hands," I said. "Every first of May or thereabouts you develop blisters bad enough to have to be treated at the dispensary. Been that way for every one of the four years you've been here."

He regarded me stonily. "So?"

"So the prison keeps a pretty thorough medical record of everything that happens to you—whether it's a sore throat, lumbago, or blisters. It's put down in your file."

"What's all that to you?"

I chewed a piece of my bread and swallowed. "But the thing that really interests me is your appendix. Two years ago, when Dr. Williams was still the medical officer, he took it out. And what do you know, four months ago Dr. Kaufmann had to do the same thing again."

He made sure that we were out of earshot of the other prisoners and the guards before he spoke again. "The records are wrong."

"No," I said. "They aren't. I'm the one who kept them." I tasted the cold tea in my tin cup. "When Mark Hanson went back into the shed alone for his shovel this morning, he had a small rip on the knee of his uniform. When he came out, the rip was gone."

I smiled and said, "The tool shed is outside the walls. It's locked, but not guarded at night. So you slipped inside last night and hid. Maybe under the floorboards or something like that. And when the Mark Hanson with the rip in his uniform got the chance to go back inside alone this morning, the two of you traded places real quick and you came out. How long are you staying with us this time?"

He studied me for a full minute before he made up his mind to admit anything. "May and June. Like always."

I nodded. "So I guess that makes you the real Mark Hanson. But if you can get the other one to do ten months for you, why not the whole year?"

"He's a family man. A wife and kids. He wouldn't touch this deal if it kept him away for the full seven years of my rap."

"Who is he? Your twin brother or something?"

"No. I used him for my double whenever I was worried about some of my friends and what they might have in mind. When this income tax thing hit me, I had a doctor work on him a little to make him even more like my mirror."

I put aside my empty tin plate. "So you get outside. Why don't you stay out? The world's a big place and they don't extradite from Brazil."

He shook his head. "Maybe so, but I got my business interests in the U.S. and they need my touch. I'm running things from behind a door right now, but in a few more years I want to be able to step out without having the Government tap my shoulder again."

He looked at me. "So now we talked. What do you want? Money? Or you'll toddle to the warden with a story?"

"No," I said. "I don't want money."

He frowned. "Hell, you don't expect me to arrange . . . ."

"Why not?" I said. "You got the connections and you ought to be able to find somebody with my face."

The guards blew their whistles and we got to our feet.

I rubbed at the pain in my back and then picked up my axe. This kind of work really wasn't for me, and I had the hunch that someone using my name would come to the same conclusion after about ten months and make noises about getting out.

I didn't think I'd hear him in Brazil.

The Collector

by Patricia A. Matthews

Allister Hugh loved olden times. He adored the quaint, revered the ancient, and often declared sadly with his hand held over his heart that, "Things today are not the way they used to be."

That is the reason he loved Lenadine Lou Le Clare. Not that Lenadine was old, far from it. She was young and very beautiful. And to Allister she was the embodiment of all the charms credited to the belles of long past years.

Her beauty was of the Dresden china type. Her hair pale gold and simply styled. She took tea at precisely three each afternoon and often fainted when upset.

Every Sunday afternoon Allister called upon her. They had tea upon the terrace and spoke of gentle things.

He presented her with flowers and once—much moved by her rendition of the Moonlight Sonata played upon an old-fashioned spinet—he composed a sonnet entitled "Lovely Hands of Palest Ivory," which he dedicated to her.

All went well. She received him with dignity and poise. Their courtship proceeded as gracefully as a minuet, and Allister was happy. He was certain that ultimately she would be his; a fitting culmination to years of collecting museum pieces.

One lovely afternoon as they sat late at their tea upon the

terrace, Allister decided that this was the moment to declare his intentions.

The breeze was soft, the air fragrant with the scent of flowers from the garden. He sank to his knees beside Lenadine's chair.

"Lenadine," he declared, looking passionately into her sea-green eyes. "Lenadine, I am mad about you. Will you do me the honor of becoming my wife?"

"Oh, Allister," she answered in emotion-choked tones. "Long have I awaited the day when you would offer me your heart."

"My heart," he declared movingly, "my soul, my life, are at your feet."

They were married. It was a lovely old-fashioned wedding and after a discreet honeymoon in Niagara Falls the couple took up residence in the old mansion Lenadine had inherited from her first husband.

Allister found Lenadine all he had ever desired in a woman, and the old mansion was filled with the relics of bygone days which he loved. There was only one flaw. He could not interest Lenadine in his hobby. It was perhaps unrealistic of him to wish to do so, for who expects the collector's item to be interested in the collection of which it is a part? But as many people will who have an absorbing interest, he wished to share it.

One day he said to her, "Lenadine, my love, since you do not share my interest in antiques, perhaps you should have a hobby of your own."

Lenadine smiled sweetly. She always smiled sweetly, it was one of the things he admired in her.

"Oh, I have a hobby of sorts," she replied roguishly; and not a word more would she say on the subject.

He thought it a feminine whim. Women were unpredictable creatures. He let it pass.

Then one day he discovered the locked door. It was a heavy door, well reinforced and bolted. Curious, he asked Lenadine about it.

She was vague.

His curiosity became stronger. He insisted.

She cried.

After that he insisted no more, but his curiosity grew. He decided to break the lock and see for himself what the room contained. He determined to do it that very night, when Lenadine and the servants were asleep.

That evening he was especially attentive to Lenadine, for he felt a trifle ashamed of what he planned to do. She, however, was much subdued that evening.

"Come, my love," he cajoled her. "Why is my little bird so quiet this evening?"

"I did not wish to tell you," she said, "but tonight is the very night that my former husband—" Here she burst into soft sobs which she muffled in her lace handkerchief.

"Ah, my dear," answered Allister sympathetically, knowing that her first husband had died in some vague but tragic manner. "Of course, love. It is natural that you should think of him. I am not offended. Perhaps it would be better if you retired now."

Lenadine smiled gratefully and, kissing him coolly upon the cheek, retired to her room.

Allister was now free to examine the locked room. He secured a candle—he much preferred a candle to a flashlight—and approached the concealing door.

It took him considerable time to force an entry. The lock was extremely difficult. But at last the door stood open and Allister was able to enter the room.

He lit the candle and went in. The door swung slowly shut behind him. The flame from the candle flickered, but its pale light was sufficient to illumine the strange altarlike block of stone with the odd, dark stains upon it and the queer, round jars sitting in precise rows upon a shelf; each of the jars contained an unidentifiable object suspended in liquid.

With a feeling of dreadful anticipation, Allister raised the candle and advanced toward the jars.

The candle flickered perilously, there was a draught as if someone had opened a door. But before the candle went out Allister was able to see quite clearly the contents of the jars.

And in the first frightful blackness after the extinguished flame, he recalled Lenadine's words that sunny afternoon upon the terrace.

"Oh, Allister, I have waited so long for you to give me your heart."

House Call

by Elsin Ann Graffam

She dialed the number and waited. Two rings, three—
Maybe he wasn't in on a Saturday, maybe—

"Hello? Dr. Reed? This is Joe's mother, Mrs. Forte. Yes.
Well, please, you've *got* to come over and see my Joe! He
looks awful bad and I'm so worried. What? Oh, no, he can't
come to your office. He's—he don't look good at all. You
can come here, maybe? You will? In a half hour? Oh, thank
you, thank you so much, Doctor!"

She hung up the telephone slowly and smoothed back
stray strands of gray hair. Her fingers were gnarled, but
strong and muscular from forty years of taking care of her
boys. Her boys. There had been five of them once, but now
all she had left with her was her Joe. A good boy, he was;
nothing bad would ever happen to her Joe. That's why she
had to make the doctor come to her home, had to get
everything taken care of.

She tiptoed down the hall to Joe's bedroom and carefully
opened the door. He was sitting on the edge of the bed, his
body rigid and his face as vacant as it had been the last five
times she'd looked in on him.

"Joe?" she whispered.

He didn't look at her.

"Joe, everything will be all right. You wait and see. I'll
take care of you."

Closing the door as softly as she'd opened it, she looked at
the hands of the old clock in the hall. Twenty-five minutes
to wait. She'd go crazy just sitting, waiting—

Going into the living room, she picked up her knitting
and began to work on the sweater she'd started the week

before. A bright shade of blue, it was Joe's favorite color. He'd be real surprised when he saw it.

"Oh, Ma," he'd say, "you shouldn't have gone to all that trouble for me!"

But he'd slip it over his head and grin at her like a little boy. Yes, her Joe would be pleased with the sweater. It was worth the pain from the arthritis in her fingers to make her boy happy. After all, what's a mother *for*, if it isn't to take care of her boys?

She dropped the yarn when the bell rang and went to the door. Peeking around the side of the curtain, she was relieved to see the doctor standing there.

"Dr. Reed, oh, thank you so much for coming over so quick. I'm so grateful—

He brushed past her and strode into the hall.

"That's all right, Mrs. Forte. Where is he?"

"What?"

"Joe. Where is he?"

"Oh. Well, if you could—if we could just talk for a bit first, in the kitchen, maybe?"

He sighed. "I really haven't too much time, Mrs. Forte. It *is* Saturday afternoon, you know, and my office hours were supposed to be over an hour ago."

"Please, Doctor?"

She stood there, her eyes pleading, and when she turned and went ahead of him into the kitchen he shrugged and followed her.

"A cup of coffee for you, Doctor?"

"No, I—"

"Ah, coffee for the good doctor. No matter how rich and important he gets, he still comes to our house to take care of us. For the good doctor a nice cup of coffee. Here, let me—"

She poured the steaming liquid into one of her two best china cups and pushed it across the table to him.

Sighing again, he picked it up and sipped. "These old women. These *old women!*" he thought with exasperation. " 'A cup of tea? A cup of coffee?' And if you decline their hospitality they get so damned offended."

"Now," he said aloud, "what about Joe?"

"He's in his room, Doctor, just sitting on his bed, staring at nothing. Been like that since he got home last night. He wouldn't talk to me or nothing. Couple of hours ago he sort of came out of it for a few minutes and told me what the matter was, but then he turned his head away. He had tears in his eyes. Tears! My Joe!"

She shook her head with the memory of it.

"You're not drinking your coffee, Doctor," she said then.

"I am. I am. Please go *on*."

"Well, my Joe, he's an important man, really. In this group, you know."

"No, I don't know." He drank the last of his coffee and started to rise.

"Doctor!"

The tone of her voice startled him and he sat down.

"The group," she went on, "they call it 'Our Thing'."

Ignoring the intent look on the man's face, she said, "They—the bosses, they gave Joe a job to do. And he *has* to do it. When they say do something, you do it or else, right?"

"Uh-huh," replied the doctor.

"But my Joe, he's so *sensitive!* He was always the most delicate of my boys."

She smiled, remembering. "When he was only, oh, eight or nine, he fell off his bike and you had to sew up his knee. He fainted, remember? That's how he is, Doctor. A real man, you understand, but so *sensitive*."

Dr. Reed grunted.

"Well, it seems like there's this man around the neighborhood who's been—how did Joe put it?—'horning in on the drug traffic' or something like that. And, see, they told Joe to get rid of him—to kill him, you know. Because they don't like no competition, they don't like that at *all*.

"But my Joe, he just couldn't *do* it. 'Maybe a stranger, Ma,' he said, 'but not—'. And he started to cry. Cry! Think of how I felt, his mother, when I saw them tears running down his face!"

"Ah," said the doctor.

"This man Joe's supposed to kill, he's a real respected man around here. A doctor. . . . Doctor?"

She watched impassively as the doctor slid off the chair and landed on her kitchen floor with a thud.

He hadn't, she noted with relief, broken her china cup in his fall. She picked it up and carried it over to the sink, scoured it and the coffee pot with extra care; then, stepping over the doctor, she went to her son's room.

"Joe? Joe!"

He turned and looked at her dully. "What, Ma?"

"It's all taken care of, just like I said. Come into the kitchen and look!"

That's Ma for you. She always takes care of her boys.

The Adventure of the Blind Alley

by Edward Wellen

Feeling his way through the pea-soup fog, Police Constable Cooper paused at the noise of a struggle. He stared hard to hear. At the first outcry and the noise of scuffling his hand had whisked to his whistle. But before he could blow a blast to frighten off the attacker, he heard the sickening sound of a cosh on a skull, then the thump of a falling body.

He withheld the blast and with heavy caution, in order to catch the assailant red-handed, he lifted his boots towards the rough breathing and the tearing of cloth.

P.C. Cooper smiled tightly to himself. He knew this to be a narrow cul-de-sac and himself to be between the attacker and escape. He had the culprit all but in his arms.

He winged out his cape and moved slowly but steadily into the blindness of the alley. But a kerb leaped out of nowhere. P.C. Cooper's stumble and his muffled oath warned the attacker. The constable blew a savage blast. "In the name of the law, stand fast!"

P.C. Cooper heard fleeing footsteps, the ring of a hob-nailed boot striking an iron mudscraper, then the creak of a door and the snick of a latch. The culprit, then, was a denizen of this unsavoury alley.

The constable swore under his breath. He had his man—and yet he did not have him. He knew there were a half-dozen doors on either hand. Unless the constable located the right door straightway, the culprit would have time to change from his wet outer clothes and to hide what he had stolen from the victim.

The victim. A dozen paces deeper into the alley, and the constable saw the shape of the victim on the cobblestones.

Feeling sudden clamminess and chill, P.C. Cooper stood over the fallen man. He eyed a familiar hawklike profile, a bloodied deerstalker cap, a still-clutched violin case. Rents showed in the victim's clothes where hurried hands had torn away a watch chain and snatched a wallet. That the mighty manhunter should have fallen prey to a common robber!

The victim stirred. A word came forth. "Constable . . ."

P.C. Cooper knelt, careless that his knee touched the wet stones. The blood-blinded face had not turned towards him. How had the man known to call him constable?

The whistle, of course. The habits and skills of a lifetime would not have failed him even in the direst of moments. Though stunned, the great detective would have taken note of some clue, and most likely clung to consciousness now solely to impart that clue.

"Sir, did you see your assailant? Can you describe him?"

A painful shake of the hand.

"Do you know where he ran to?"

A painful nod.

P.C. Cooper's heart surged, but the man only conscious-ness enough to point vaguely and gasp, "A flat . . ."

The constable grimaced in disappointment. The great detective had told P.C. Cooper only what P.C. Cooper already knew.

A flat, indeed! This was an alley of roominghouses—nothing but flats.

P.C. Cooper removed his cape and wadded it under the great detective's head as a cushion. Then the constable rose and duty took over. His whistle guided answering whistles.

Each blast, each echo, ached. It hurt him to think that his colleagues would find him simply standing there, waiting, while the culprit was safe behind one of those unseen doors.

A flat . . .

P.C. Cooper shook his head. Why should those words keep ringing in his mind? They had originated in the poor stricken mind of the great detective.

A flat . . .

Pounding boots pulled up. P.C. Cooper recognised the figure of P.C. Lloyd.

Lloyd was a Welshman, and Welshmen are famous for having perfect pitch.

Swelling with authority, Cooper seized Lloyd's arm and pointed him.

"Man, hurry and kick the mudscrapers with your great hobnailed boots and find the one that sounds A flat."

The Unfriendly Neighbor

by Al Nussbaum

When I sat down at the breakfast table today, my wife had the morning newspaper folded beside my plate as she always did. I took a sip of coffee, then opened the paper to the first page and got the shock of my life. There, staring back at me, was a picture of Elmer Sesler. I read the accompanying article and couldn't keep from laughing.

"What's so funny?" my wife asked.

"It's a long story, honey. It began twenty years ago." Then I told her about Elmer Sesler . . .

I was a freshman in high school when the Seslers moved in next door. There was just Elmer, who was my age, and his parents. His father, who was a minor executive with an insurance company, had been transferred to our city to work in the local office.

Elmer had stood out immediately, and not because of his

jug-handle ears or freckled face. He had his own car. Few seniors had cars, but here was a lowly freshman who not only had a car, he had one that was almost new. A couple of guys tried to throw sour grapes on the situation by saying the car was probably his father's, but I put a stop to that.

"His father drives this year's model," I said. "That one's his, all right."

If anyone was unconvinced, Elmer's actions soon convinced them. He began to take the car apart. One day he'd arrive at school with the hood and trunk lid missing; the next day the doors might be gone. After the first few days, no one ever saw that car completely assembled again. The car *had* to be his. No one could get away with treating his father's car that way.

On evenings and weekends I'd look across the hedge that divided our back yards and see him tinkering with his car or working on something else in his garage. He had a workbench set up and far more tools than I could name. One time he had his car's engine completely disassembled and scattered across the ground with each separate part resting on a piece of clean newspaper. Other times he was hovering over an old TV and a vacuum cleaner he had spread out on his workbench. He seemed to have an insatiable curiosity and a genuine talent for taking things apart.

If it hadn't been for his car, however, he'd have been a social failure. He had all the tact of a kick in the teeth. He always ignored me when he saw me watching him, even though he must have recognized me from school where we had several classes together. Finally I spoke to him, and he walked over to the hedge.

"Yes?" he said in a flat tone.

"I'm Bill Ford," I said, reaching across the hedge to shake hands.

He ignored my hand and kept a level stare on me until I pulled my arm back in confusion.

"Just because we're neighbors doesn't mean you can ride to school in my car," he said.

"Who said anything about riding to school in your car?" I demanded. "*I* didn't say anything about your old car, or about riding in it."

"No, but you were thinking about it," he said.

He turned his back on me and returned to the garage where he had a washing machine torn apart on the cement floor.

I stood there for several minutes, shaking with anger. My fury was all the more intense because he'd been right. I *had* been thinking about how convenient it would be to have a ride to school, instead of having to walk the fifteen blocks every morning.

It turned out I wasn't the only one he accused of having designs on his car. He accused almost everyone, but apparently I was the only one who hated him for it. Perhaps because he was wrong about them, the other kids at school were able to laugh it off, while I resented having my mind read.

From then on I belittled everything Elmer Sesler did, and never passed up a chance to attack him verbally. Though everyone else seemed to consider him some kind of budding, eccentric genius, I made it clear I thought he was just a lunatic.

"He might even be dangerous, the way he thinks everyone is trying to use him," I said. "Just because he can take things apart doesn't mean he's a genius. I see him in his back yard every day, and half the stuff he tears into never does get back together. Take his car, for example—it doesn't look or run as well as it did before he started messing with it."

Nothing I said, though, had any effect. As far as the other students were concerned, Elmer Sesler was going to be famous someday. He was voted the most likely freshman to succeed, while I was given the wet blanket award.

Then, after that one year, Elmer's father was transferred to another city, and I never saw or heard of Elmer again . . .

"So what was so funny in the newspaper?" my wife asked. "Did he invent something?"

"No, he didn't invent anything," I said, "and I guess it's really not very funny. Elmer Sesler murdered his wife. The police found her body in Chicago, and Detroit, and Cleveland, and Buffalo."

A Feline Felony

by Lael J. Littke

Jerome Kotter looked like a cat. However, this did not bring him any undue attention from his schoolmates since almost all of them had an unusual quality or two. Beverly Baumgartner had a laugh like a horse. Bart Hansen was as rotund as an elephant. Carla Seaver's long neck resembled that of a giraffe. And Randy Ramsbottom always smelled remarkably like a dog on a rainy day.

The only person who worried about Jerome's unusual appearance was his father, who quietly set about arming his son to face a world in which he was a bit different. He taught Jerome gentle manners, assuring him that no matter how different he looked he would always get along fine if he acted right. He taught him to recite all the verses of *The Star-Spangled Banner* by heart. He encouraged him to read the Bible. And he taught him to sing the songs from the best-known Gilbert and Sullivan operettas. He felt Jerome was well equipped to face the world.

When Jerome got to high school he became the greatest track star that Quigley High had ever produced, although he had to be careful because the coaches from rival schools cried foul when Jerome resorted to running on all fours.

Altogether, Jerome's school years would have been quite happy—if it hadn't been for Benny Rhoades.

Whereas Jerome was tall, polite, studious, and well-groomed with silken fur and sparkling whiskers, Benny was wizened, unkempt, rude, and sly. His face was pinched and pointed and his hair stuck up in uneven wisps. He hated anyone who excelled him in anything. Almost everybody excelled him in everything, and since Jerome surpassed him in the one thing he did do fairly well—running—he hated Jerome most of all. When Jerome took away his title of champion runner of Quigley High, Benny vowed he would get even if it took him the rest of his life.

One of Benny's favorite harassments was to tread on Jerome's tail in study hall, causing him to yeowl and thereby incurring the wrath of the monitor. Benny tweaked Jerome's whiskers and poured honey in his fur. He did everything he could think of to make Jerome's life miserable.

When it came to Benny Rhoades, Jerome found it hard to follow the admonitions of his father—that he should love his enemies and do good even to those who used him spitefully. He looked forward to the day when he would finish school and get away, for he had to admit in his heart that he loathed the odious Benny. It rancored him to think that Benny was the only person who could make him lose his composure and caterwaul in public, thus making people notice that, despite his suave manner and intellectual conversation, he was a bit different. To keep his temper he took to declaiming *The Star-Spangled Banner* or passages from the Bible. Once he got all the way through the "begats" in Genesis before he took hold of himself and regained his composure.

Just before Jerome was graduated from college, Benny stole all the fish from Old Man Walker's little fish cart and deposited them in Jerome's car, after which he made an anonymous phone call to the police. The police, who had always regarded Jerome as the embodiment of what they would like all young men to be, preferred to believe his claim of innocence; but then again, looking as he did, it was natural for them to believe that he might have swiped a mess of fish.

People began to whisper about Jerome when he passed on the street. They pointed out that although his manners were perfect, he did have those long sword-like claws, and they certainly wouldn't want to be caught alone with him in an alley on a dark night. And wasn't there a rather feline craftiness in his slanted eyes?

Jerome left town after graduation enveloped in an aura of suspicion and an aroma of rotting fish which he never could dispel completely from his car.

Jerome decided to pursue a career as a writer of advertising copy in New York, reasoning that what with all the strange creatures roaming about in that city no one was apt to notice anything a bit different about him. He was hired at the first place he applied, Bobble, Babble, and Armbruster, Inc., on Madison Avenue. Mr. Armbruster had been out celebrating his fourteenth wedding anniversary the night before and had imbibed himself into near-oblivion trying to forget what devastation those fourteen years had wrought. When Jerome walked into his office, he naturally figured him to be related to the ten-foot polka-dot cobra that had pursued him the night before and thought he would fade with the hangover. After ducking behind his desk for a little hair-of-the-dog, he hired Jerome. By the time Mr. Armbruster had fully recovered from his celebration, Jerome had proved himself capable at his job and affable with the other employees, so he was allowed to stay. Mr. Armbruster naturally put him on the cat food account.

Before long, Jerome fell in love with his secretary, Marie, a shapely blonde who thought Jerome's sleek fur and golden eyes sexy. He wanted to ask her for a date, but first, in all fairness, he thought he should find out how she felt about him.

"Marie," he said one day as he finished the day's dictation, "do you like me as a boss?"

"Oh, yes," breathed Marie. "Gee, Mr. Kotter, you're the swellest boss I ever had. You're so different."

Jerome's heart sank. "Different? In what way, Marie?"

"Well," said Marie, "Mr. Leach, my old boss, used to pinch me sometimes. And he used to sneak up behind me and kiss me." She peered coyly at Jerome from under her lashes. "You're a perfect gentleman, Mr. Kotter. You're real different."

Jerome was enchanted and wasted no further time asking her out to dinner.

For several weeks everything was wonderful. Then, unexpectedly, Benny Rhoades turned up. Jerome looked up from his desk one day to see his nemesis standing in the doorway.

"Man," said Benny, "if it ain't Jerome Kotter." He grinned.

"Benny Rhoades," exclaimed Jerome. "What are you doing here?"

"Man, you're the most," said Benny softly. "I work in the mail room, man. You're gonna see a lot of me, Jerome."

Jerome's tail twitched.

"Why did you come here?" he asked. "Why don't you leave me alone?"

Offended innocence replaced the calculating look on Benny's pasty face.

"Why, man, I ain't done a thing. A man's got to work. And I work here." He lounged against the door jamb. "I hear you're a real swingin' cat around here. I wonder how long that's gonna last."

"Get out," said Jerome.

"Sure, Mr. Kotter, sir. Sure. Think I'll drop by your secretary's desk. Quite a dish, that Marie."

"You stay away from her." Jerome could feel the fur around his neck rising. His whiskers bristled.

Benny smiled and glided away like an insidious snake.

From that time on, Benny did what he could to torment Jerome. He held up his mail until important clients called the bosses to complain about lack of action on their accounts. He slammed Jerome's tail in doors, usually when some VIP was visiting the office. Worse of all, he vexed Marie by hanging around her desk asking for dates and sometimes sneaking up to nibble at her neck. Marie hated him almost as much as Jerome did.

Jerome didn't know quite what he could do about it without jeopardizing his job, of which he had become very fond. The other people at the agency liked him, although they regarded him as a trifle eccentric since he always insisted on sampling the cat food he wrote about. But then everyone to his own tastes, they said.

Things came to a head one evening when Jerome invited Marie to his apartment for a fish dinner before going out to a show. They were just sitting down to eat when the doorbell rang.

It was Benny.

"Cozy," he murmured, surveying the scene. He slammed the door shut behind him.

"A real swingin' cat," he said, sidling into the room. He produced a small pistol from his pocket.

"Are you out of your mind, Benny?" said Jerome. "What do you think you're doing?"

"I lost my job," smiled Benny.

"What's that got to do with me?"

"Marie complained that I bothered her. They fired me." Benny's small eyes glittered. "I'll repay her for the favor, then I'll take care of you, Jerome. I'll fix it so they'll think you shot her for resisting your charms, and then shot yourself. Everybody knows a big cat like you could go beserk anytime."

"You're a rat," said Marie. "You're a miserable, black-hearted little rat."

Jerome stepped protectively in front of her.

"Sticks and stones may break my bones but names will never hurt me," chanted Benny gleefully.

Jerome was looking at Benny thoughtfully. "A rat," he said. "That's what he is. A rat. Funny it never occurred to me before." His tail twitched nervously.

Benny didn't like the look on Jerome's face. "Stay away from me, man. I'll shoot."

Before Benny could aim, Jerome leaped across the room with the swift, fluid motion of a tiger. He knocked Benny to the floor and easily took the gun from him.

"A rat," repeated Jerome softly.

Benny looked at Jerome's face so close to his own. "What are you going to do?" he squeaked, his own face pinched and white and his beady eyes terror-stricken. "What are you going to do?"

Jerome ate him.

It took a long time to get the police sergeant to take the matter seriously. Marie had urged Jerome to forget the whole thing, but Jerome felt he must confess.

"You say you ate this guy Benny?" the sergeant asked for the twentieth time.

"I ate him," said Jerome.

"He was a rat," said Marie.

The sergeant shook his head. "We get all kinds," he muttered. "Go home. Sleep it off." He sighed. "Self-defense, you say?"

"Benny was going to shoot both of us," said Marie.

"Where's the body?" asked the sergeant.

Jerome shook his head. "There is no body. I ate him."

"He was a rat," said Marie.

"There's no body," said the sergeant. "We sent a coupla men up to your apartment and there's no body and no sign of anybody getting killed. We even called this Benny's family long distance to find out if they knew where he is, but his old man said as far as they are concerned he died at birth. So go home."

"I ate him," insisted Jerome.

"So you performed a public service. I got six kids to support, buddy. I don't want to spend the next two years on a head-shrinker's couch for trying to make the Chief believe I got a six-foot cat here who ate a guy. Now go home, you two, before I get mad."

Jerome remained standing in front of the desk.

"Look," said the sergeant. "You ate a guy."

"A rat," corrected Marie.

"A rat," said the sergeant. "So how do you feel?"

"Terrible," said Jerome. "I have a most remarkable case of indigestion."

"You ate a rat," said the sergeant. "Now you've got a bellyache. That's your punishment. Remember when you ate green apples as a kid?" He sighed. "Now go home."

As they turned to leave, Jerome heard the sergeant muttering to himself about not having had a vacation in four years.

Despite his indigestion, Jerome felt marvelous. "Let the punishment fit the crime," he said with satisfaction. He took Marie's arm in a courtly fashion and sang softly as they walked along. "My object all sublime, I shall achieve in time, to let the punishment fit the crime, the punishment fit the crime . . ."

"Gee, Mr. Kotter," said Marie, gazing up at him in admiration. "You're so different from anyone else I ever went with."

"Different?" asked Jerome. "How, Marie?"

"Gee," said Marie, "I never went out before with anybody who quoted poetry."

Don't I Know You?

by Henry Slesar

The man was well-groomed, in a sleek, furry way midway in style between Broadway and Bond Street. His hands were buried in the deep pockets of his camel's-hair coat, and he blew a frosty breath of winter past his mink mustache as he waited for the light to change.

The other man, smaller, not so well-groomed, his brown tweed overcoat threadbare in comparison, looked at him sharply, looked away, looked back, and was finally rewarded by an answering stare, equally puzzled and involved.

They crossed the street together, matching stride for stride, and then stopped at the opposite corner and looked at each other again. The mustached man cracked the silence first, with a smile and the words:

"Don't I know you?"

It took the smaller man a longer time to thaw. He said, "I sure as heck think I know *you*. Only I can't remember—"

"Carmody's the name," the mustached man said, in a manner suggesting the click of heels or the presentation of a card. Actually, he didn't move his well-shined shoes or remove his hands from his pockets.

"My name's Siegel," the smaller man said. "Frank Siegel. And if we *do* know each other"—here he finally managed the smile—"must have been a heck of a long time ago. You don't come from Michigan, by any chance?"

"Never been there," Carmody said. "But I've traveled a lot. South mostly, Florida, the Caribbean, southern Europe. I like the sunshine—hate this beastly cold." He said the adjective without a hint of English accent.

"No," Siegel said, "Never been to any of those places."

"School, maybe? No, I suppose not. I went to Washington and Lee."

"City College."

"Must have been some place," Carmody said. "The more I look at you, the surer I am."

"Same with me," Siegel said.

"Look," Carmody said, searching the east and west of the street, "I'm in no great hurry, are you? We could stop for a drink—nice warm bar—puzzle it all out."

"Well," Siegel said uncertainly. But he wasn't in a hurry. "All right," he finished. "One drink."

They chose a small uncrowded cocktail lounge on 50th Street and took a booth in the rear. Carmody had a martini, and Siegel, who didn't like liquor much, had a beer. He was content to let Carmody do the probing of the past.

"Mutual friends, maybe?" Carmody said. "Know anybody named Martin? My life is loaded with people named Martin. No? How about George LeRoy? Carl Kramer? Lillian Dietz?"

Siegel kept shaking his head. He began to feel tired, and even to lose interest, until Carmody said, "Well, I know one thing. We don't have the same occupation." He lifted his glass. The gin twinkled and so did his eyes. "I'm a thief," he said.

Siegel's eyebrows met. "How do you mean that?"

"Why, literally, my friend, literally," Carmody said. "I'm a member of a vanishing species. A good thief. Society thief. Used to be the darling of the fiction writers and Sunday supplements—but no more."

"You're kidding me," Siegel said, in an injured voice.

"No, I wouldn't do that," answered Carmody. "I steal for a living. Steal very nice, pretty things, with high price tags. Only from people who can afford it, of course—that's my one principle."

He took his left hand out of his pocket for the first time. There was a jeweled bracelet in the hand. Rows of neat diamonds made blue daggers of light in the darkened booth.

"Beautiful, isn't it? Belonged to a widow who hasn't worn it in fifteen years. I'm doing everybody a favor by restoring it to circulation."

"And you really stole this bracelet?"

"This morning," Carmody smiled. "It was very easy, really. And of course, now I'll sell it—to anybody who wants it. I'll even sell it to you."

"I couldn't buy something like that," Siegel said.

"Maybe you could. I'd guess that it's worth, oh, five, six thousand dollars. You could have it for five, six hundred, whatever you could afford."

"You really mean this?"

"Of course," Carmody said. "It's the least I can do for an old friend." The smile broadened, showing most of his good teeth. "Even if I can't remember who you are."

Siegel sighed. It was a sigh of regret. He reached into his pocket and took out his wallet. He opened it lengthways to show Carmody something else that glittered, even if dully. It was his police badge.

"I'm a detective," he said, with genuine sadness. "I'm sorry, Mr. Carmody, but I'll have to place you under arrest."

Carmody's facial muscles gave a twitch of surprise. He groaned slightly, and put the "diamond" bracelet into the ashtray. He was plainly distressed, but he forced himself to restore a shadow of his lost smile.

"Of course," he said. "*Now* I remember where I know you from."

Meet Mr. Murder

by Morris Hershman

Roy Worth said, "That's a lot of nonsense! Do you expect your own husband to believe in the supernatural?"

"It's true." Edie Worth put a hand to her heart, as usual when her judgment was disputed. "The man stood in front of Dr. Arbuckle's house all night, and on the next day he died."

"Arbuckle was sick. He'd had a heart condition for years. Sooner or later he was sure to die, only sooner in his case. So was that old Mrs. Culp, who suffered from an aortic aneurism."

"But *he* stood in front of the house."

"You mean the man called Gray because he always wears gray. All you know about him is that when he stands in front of a house somebody in it dies very soon."

"Yes, and you know where that man is right now."

Roy pushed back his chair from the kitchen table and stood up. "I could understand your getting excited about it if we lived in Africa, for instance, but this sort of thing doesn't happen in Lakevale."

"Look outside," Edie suddenly whispered, both hands around her heart area. "You know how sick I am. Don't argue with me, Roy. Just look."

He walked over to the window. A man stood across the road, facing them. The swiss-cheese colored full moon lighted him so that it was possible to see him leaning against a pole with his legs crossed. He wore a gray topcoat, a gray pair of pants, and a hat to match.

"Do you want me to call the police? He's loitering, after all, and I suppose he can be arrested for that."

"Go see Hugo Bradford," she insisted. "He's on the police force. Maybe he'll know what has to be done."

"It's late at night to be disturbing neighbors."

"Please," she said in a choked voice.

Roy glanced angrily at his wife, noticing how much her figure had run to fat. The once lovely bosom had started to sag, the legs had become much thicker, and nobody could have called her face a youthful one any longer.

He shrugged and strode over to the phone.

She said quickly, "Hugo only lives across the street, Roy. I don't want the whole town to know about this."

Glumly he nodded. She wouldn't quit pestering him, he knew. He had been married to her for twelve years.

"I'll be all right here," Edie said. "And please go out the back way so *he* won't see you."

"I'm going out the front way. It's my house and I can do that much if I—"

She said hoarsely, "My medicine, Roy. I need my medicine."

"You always do need it when I want to do one thing and you want me to do another."

But he brought it all the same, along with a teaspoon and a half-filled water glass. Edie swallowed an orange pill from the bottle and settled back.

He went to the closet and put on his coat, jacket, and fur-lined gloves. He was still muttering about a heart condition being used by some patients to get their own way as he walked out the back door. Wind made his skin tingle.

Roy's jaw jutted out when he passed in front of the man called Gray, having changed his route on purpose; Gray didn't look to the right or left. The Bradford doorbell was answered by Hugo Bradford himself, who invited Roy to the living room for a drink. Bradford was a tall, muscular man who'd been decorated for bravery during the Korean war and was now a police sergeant.

"I can guess why you're here," Bradford said, "and I advise you and your wife to take no notice of the man and help smash his racket."

"Racket?"

"Gray has established himself as sort of a harbinger of doom. What he now does is determine who in town is sick and phones the head of the house at work, if at all possible, and asks for two thousand dollars to stay away. You'd be surprised how many people pay up."

"Well, he's varying his method with us," Roy said promptly. "He just appeared and that's all."

"Maybe you'll get a phone call tomorrow, when your wife is more thoroughly scared," Bradford said. "I'll call the boys to take him away, but it'll bring you some publicity, heaven knows. And he'll only come back when he gets out of jail.

"There's really nothing that can be done. No one wants to testify against him. We only heard about his real racket by accident. One of his victims has a nephew who's a stenographer at the courthouse."

"You'd better have him taken away," Roy decided. "For Edie's sake. She really does have a heart condition, you know."

"Okay," Bradford said. "We'll try to scare him out of town, but it won't work with anybody like that guy, you know. He'll come back and take up his stand where he left it."

"I'm tired of being pushed around by him or by—well, never mind. Good night, Hugo. Give my best to Miranda and the kids."

Roy was muttering under his breath when he left Bradford's house. He wondered if it would settle Edie's mind to tell her the truth. Probably not. She had decided on what she wanted and was too stubborn about having anything but her way.

Roy walked to the curb till he was directly in front of the man Gray. It only took a minute. As he passed by he said: "You wasted those phone calls you made to me, buddy, so do the worst to my wife that you can. The very worst."

Roy Worth remembered to wipe the smile off his face as he let himself into his house.

Co-Incidence

by Edward D. Hoch

I first met Rosemary when I joined the editorial staff of Neptune Books, last summer. The job was my big chance, because prior to that time my editing experience had been confined mostly to the pulps and a chain of true crime magazines. For me, Neptune Books was a dream come true—a job with an unlimited future in a fast-growing phase of the publishing industry.

I suppose everyone is familiar with Neptune Books, those dollar ninety-five reprints with a picture of a smiling King Neptune as their trademark. They say in the business that the reason Neptune is always smiling is that he's just seen the latest sales figures. And if it's true, he has plenty of reason to smile.

For in three short years Neptune Books have risen to the top of the field. Their sales are beyond belief, and even their own officers shake their heads in pleased amazement as the money pours in.

The cause of it all, as everyone in the publishing business knows, is Rosemary. At twenty-eight, she is already the brains behind Neptune's smile. The simple fact is that she is a mathematical genius, not just in the usual sense, but in a very unusual sense.

My first meeting with her came, as I've said, the day I started work at Neptune. She was in her tiny office, where she spent most of her time, poring over a list of sales figures from cities all over the country.

She looked up when I entered with Mason, the vice president of Neptune, and as soon as I saw her I knew that the stories about her had not exaggerated.

Sphinxlike, with a somewhat bony face, she was nevertheless attractive—especially when she came out from behind those horn-rimmed eyeglasses. She had the look, the sound, the manner of power. And I sensed then that she was a very unusual woman.

This intuition increased as the weeks went by, and I became one of Rosemary's few good friends. Whenever I could snatch an hour, I'd sit there in her office, discussing new titles we were planning to reprint and listening to her unfailingly brilliant advice. I was even beginning to feel a romantic inclination toward her, but she never indicated any such feelings toward me. I kept my own emotions in check.

But it was in the distribution end of our business that she proved her devotion and fantastic skill. Neptune handled all its own distribution, which meant shipping books to several hundred wholesalers scattered throughout the country. Rosemary had risen to the post of Circulation Manager, a rare job for a young woman and perhaps the most important position in the whole company.

She would sit at her desk for hours, scrabbling over calculations, and then come up tired but triumphant with the solution. "Increase Salt Lake City's draw to 5,000 on this title," she'd order. Or, "Transfer a thousand Westerns from Dallas to Kansas City." I'd look at her in amazement, and sometimes I'd think she was over-reaching herself, but they always did what she said—and Neptune kept smiling on all those covers.

When I'd ask her about some fantastic bit of luck by which she'd transferred the right books to the right place at the right time, she'd simply sigh and say: "Oh, I heard they were having a convention out there, and figured they could use another thousand of that title."

After the first few months I got used to this wizardry, and like the others I stopped asking her. I just read books and helped decide which ones to reprint, and watched the money roll in.

There was only one thing about the job that was unpleasant. And that was Mason, the vice president. The real owner of Neptune Books was some midwest Croesus, whom no one ever saw; for all practical purposes, Mason was the big boss.

We were on the third floor of an ancient building on West 47th Street, and space was at a minimum. Not that the place wasn't big enough to start with; but with billing machines, bookkeepers, files, and the other necessities of distribution taking up so much room, we didn't have an awful lot of floor left for the executive end. Mason had solved his problem by erecting a partition ten feet square and declaring that the space inside the wall was his private office. He was a big, overbearing boor about a lot of little things, and he kept getting under my skin.

About once a week he'd hold what he called a strategy meeting. We'd all crowd into his private office. He'd do most of the talking, outlining company policies and telling us about his foggy future plans. Rosemary, at least, was entitled to a chair at these boring lectures. But I, being the youngest of the editorial staff, usually found myself sitting on the thick green rug that covered the floor.

It was obvious to me from the start that Rosemary and Mason hated each other. Rosemary hated him because he was the only person who stood between her and a place to which she could advance. Mason hated her because he knew her feelings and desires for the vice presidency of Neptune Books. Of course, he couldn't fire her. By that time, Rosemary's word was gospel and her every decision went unquestioned. It was the old law of the jungle: Eat or be eaten.

We all knew that Mason was waiting for her to make just one mistake, but she never made it. The sales figures kept climbing and Rosemary kept on with her necromancy on paper at her desk. Pretty soon it got so that even a poor title sold a half-million copies—and a million-copy sale was considered just average. Rosemary would dash into my office holding a hard-cover edition of some cheap novel that hadn't sold three thousand copies in the trade edition—and she'd insist we reprint it in soft covers. We'd argue that it hadn't sold well at all, but she'd simply say: "That's all the more readers left for us." Of course, we'd finally agree; and, of course, the book would sell around two million copies.

By the time I'd been there six months, my friendship with Rosemary had increased to the point where I was taking her to lunch a couple of times a week. It was at one of these luncheon dates, in a little French place off Fifth Avenue, that I finally persuaded her to tell me the secret of her fantastic skill.

"Well," she said, "I've never told this to any of the other vultures, but somehow you're different." I thanked her quickly and she went on: "It's all done by figuring the percentage of incidents. It took me nearly five years to work out a sort of slide-rule mathematical equation. I've discovered that it's mathematically possible to cause any two objects to meet at a given time and place, provided you know enough about these objects and can exercise enough control over one of them. I aim one angle of incidence to meet another angle of incidence. Result? Co-incidence!"

It sounded even more fantastic to me, but I didn't interrupt.

"In the case of distribution," she went on, "I figure out just where and when the supply and demand will meet, I send books to that spot—and people buy them. It's that simple."

I shook my head and asked for more details.

"Look," she said, "figuring mathematically that five hundred people in Chicago will want one of our new mysteries next Tuesday, I see that that many books get out there. That's all; my equation works it all out for me. It means getting the books to exactly the spot where the consumer is when he decides he wants that certain book."

Her eyes drooped as she added ominously: "I can do the same thing with any two objects, knowing enough about them."

"Why did you choose publishing?"

"I knew it was the best way for me to get to the top fast. The big drawback in publishing has always been, it seems to me, that the books aren't around at the exact instant that most people want to buy them. By the time they see the book they wanted, the purchasing desire has decreased. Put the books into their hands when their purchasing desire is at its peak, and you've got sales."

"And you say you can do this with other things as well?"

"Certainly. Did you ever stop to think that when a man gets hit with an automobile it's because both of them have come together at exactly the same time and place by a chain of events? Think of the millions of events, all unconnected, that have resulted in their coming together."

"And you claim you can control some of these events."

"*Some* of them. I can make calculations. If I can control some of the fractional events, I can bring man and book, or man and automobile, together."

She looked so serious that I laughed a little. "With that sort of power, you can control destiny."

She didn't laugh. "Yes, I suppose I could . . ."

The conversation ended there. Going back to work, I pushed the incident to the back of my mind. We had to line up some strong sellers—five-million-copy sellers—for the big Christmas trade, and I was busy fighting with publishers for rights.

It was one afternoon around four that Rosemary and Mason had their last big fight. It was over a policy matter, concerning exactly what type of books we should concentrate on; and Mason, for once, wouldn't listen to Rosemary.

"I'm still in charge here," he told her sharply. "You haven't got my job yet. And if I have anything to do with it, you won't get it either; I'll keep it if I have to live to be a hundred."

Rosemary's bony face looked frostbitten. She said nothing in return; she simply retreated to her tiny office. I thought that the whole thing had blown over until, a few days later, I happened to walk in and found her gazing out the window, making careful notes on a memo pad. When I asked her what she was doing, she was too absorbed to reply. But I had seen enough to know, anyway.

Rosemary was timing the traffic light on the corner of Fifth Avenue and Forty-seventh Street and ticking off the number of cars that passed.

In the days that followed, I caught her looking out the window several times, writing figures, timing automobiles as they rounded the corner. And she began watching Mason closely, too. He always left the office at three minutes to five. He was the kind of punctual man you could set your watch by; he always walked down the two flights of stairs, rather than wait for the elevator.

Rosemary began staying late at the office, until after Mason left. Then she would run to the window and time him as he left the building and crossed Forty-seventh Street on his way to Grand Central Terminal.

I told myself it was all sheer nonsense, but still . . .

It was on a Friday night, just before five, that she stepped from her office, stood in the hall and called to Mason as he was leaving. He frowned and walked over to her, glancing at his watch; she started discussing some quite irrelevant matter about a wholesaler out in California.

I glanced at the big wall clock as they talked, and I was aware that Rosemary was watching it, too. Finally, when they'd been talking for exactly fifty-five seconds, she suddenly cut the conversation short and retreated to her office, closing the door. Hastily Mason went down the stairs to the street.

I went to my own window and looked out. Slowly but surely an odd feeling crept over me. I wanted to shout out to Mason, to warn him—but I remained numb. What would I be trying to save him from?

I watched him come out of the building and start across the street.

He was halfway across, when a taxi rushed around the corner and struck him head on . . .

Well, shortly after Mason's funeral, word came from the big boss that Rosemary was now vice president of Neptune Books. We were all happy for her, of course, but it wasn't long after that that I left Neptune and went back to my old job on a true-crime magazine.

Oh, I know the whole thing is fantastic, and that Mason's death was just a coincidence, but still I felt a chill about staying around here, near Rosemary.

Suppose I'd fallen hard for her and asked her to marry me. And she accepted. I'd spend the rest of my life wondering when she was going to stop me and talk to *me* for exactly fifty-five seconds!

Alma

by Al Nussbaum

The day Alma Southerly was sent to us, my wife Silvia and I had been caring for foster children for close to twenty years. We were in our front yard, tying vines to a trellis, when the county station wagon pulled to the curb. Mrs. Dunbar of the county probation department climbed from behind the wheel; and Mrs. Snyder of the city welfare department got out on the passenger side, pulling the reluctant Alma after her. The women were big-hipped and considerably over-weight, so there had been little room between them on the seat; however, Alma hadn't needed much space.

We had been told to expect a thirteen-year-old, but Alma Southerly looked more like an undernourished ten-year-old. She was hardly more than four and a half feet of skin and bones, and her flesh was so translucent that blue veins could be seen at her temples and along her bare arms. She had large, sad eyes, like a waif in a painting by Keane, and her straight, shoulder-length hair was such a pale blonde it was almost white. Her lips were trembling and her face was wet with tears when Mrs. Snyder deposited her in front of us.

"I done wrong," she sobbed pitifully. "I done wrong," and our hearts went out to her immediately.

When Silvia and I first began taking children into our home, we had received referrals from both the courts and the welfare agencies. Soon, however, we established a record of success with delinquents, and the children sent to us were invariably wards of the courts with suspended sentences or waived prosecutions in their pasts.

It wasn't uncommon to discover that a child could lie, cheat, or steal effortlessly. Over the years, we found just about every aberration that causes maladjustment in society. Since we'd had no children of our own, we treated each foster child as though he or she were one of the children we'd never had. We gave them love, trust, understanding, and a taste of genuine family togetherness which many had never experienced.

As a result, we became expert at breaking through the facades of even the most hardened offenders, and we did it without reference to their prior records. We seldom read a child's file. We believed that whatever a child had done in the past was unimportant. We didn't feel we had to know of what devilry a child might be capable. If we had a fear, it was that we would someday be sent a child we couldn't help, a child like Alma Southerly.

Silvia and I bent to comfort the little girl and, surprisingly, instead of turning to my wife as the younger children always did, she turned to me. She stood in the circle of my uncertain arms and pressed her tear-streaked face against my side.

"I done wrong," she said between muffled sobs. "I done wrong, an' I awful sorry."

From her manner of speech, it was apparent Alma had spent most of her life in the hills of West Virginia or Tennessee, but if it hadn't been obvious, we would never have known it. Except for confessing she had "done wrong" and professing repentance, she volunteered no information. At the end of two weeks we knew as much about her as we had known a few minutes after her arrival. We hadn't been able to stop her tears and didn't even know how to try.

"Tom," my wife said after breakfast one morning, "you'd better drive down to the Youth Bureau and read Alma's file."

"Yes," I agreed. "I had better . . ."

Alma was on hands and knees, scrubbing the kitchen floor, when she heard her father call, "Al-mah! Al-mah!"

She stood up and wiped her hands on the hem of her dress. Then she hurried into the front room where he was sitting on the couch. He was wearing only his shorts and a sleeveless undershirt; but he seldom dressed during the daylight hours, so Alma thought nothing of it. That morning's newspaper was spread out before him on a low table.

"Come here, child," he said, indicating the seat beside him.

She went to him and sat down. She got along well with her father. He was usually laughing and in a good mood. He was more fun to be with than her mother, who was seldom home, and Alma liked the smell of tobacco and whiskey that clung to him like a sticky cloud. She knew he would have helped her with the housework if he weren't always feeling poorly.

"Yes, Papa?"

He cleared his throat. "Your ma ain't comin' home no more, child. We all alone now."

Alma didn't know what to say. She looked around dumbly for an explanation but found none. The newspaper was open to a story about an unidentified woman who had been found dead from an overdose of barbiturates in a motel room, but that had nothing to do with her ma.

Alma climbed onto her father's lap and put her arms around his neck. "I don't understand, Papa. She just went on a date, like always."

He cradled her in his arms and began to rock her back and forth the way she liked him to do. "There's nothin' t' understand, child. She just ain't comin' home no more, an' we gonna have t' find some new way t' make money."

"Papa, I betcha I could get dates," she offered brightly.

He paused in his rocking, as though considering the suggestion, then shook his head. "No, you're too little. It'll be another couple of years before you'll be big enough for dates. Till then, I'll just have t' think o' somethin' else."

"Maybe we could go home?" Alma asked hopefully.

"No, cain't do that. They just waitin' for your ol' pa to show his face back there. Don't you worry, though. I reckon I'll think o' somethin'."

True to his word, within the week he had thought of something—robbery. Alma listened to him explain her part as he drove his rust-spotted old sedan to the Tall Towers apartment complex in the center of the city. Each apartment tower was twenty stories high and almost self-sufficient. Their bases held laundries, markets, restaurants, and most necessary services. The parking garages were on the third level, and self-service elevators operated from there.

He drove his car up the ramp to the parking area and left it in a space reserved for visiting clergy. Alma followed him, carrying a small, battered case that had once held roller skates, as he led the way to the elevator and pushed the button marked *Roof*.

"Now, remember what I tole you, child. These be all rich folks live here. Why, the newspaper said it costs at least a thousan' dollars every month t' live in these apartments, an' the higher up you goes, the more it costs. We should get enough money tonight t' last us for two –three months."

Alma followed close at his heels to the edge of the roof. She looked fearfully down while he tied a loop at one end of a length of dirty rope and placed it under her arms.

"You see that little balcony jus' below us?"

"Yes, Papa."

"Well, that's where I gonna put you. When you're down, see if the glass door's locked. It prob'ly won't be if the people is home. Then slip outta the rope and wait a couple o' minutes before you slide open the door. Move real quiet across the room, an' open the door t' the corridor for me."

Without further preliminaries he picked her up and dropped her over the edge. Alma swung precariously at the end of the rope for a few seconds, then landed on the balcony below, skinning her knee. She sat on the cool concrete, trying to control her fear, until he shook the line from above to remind her to check the door. It was unlocked. She wouldn't have to swing to another balcony, seeking an unlocked door. With a sigh of relief, she took off the rope loop.

She waited a couple of minutes, listening. Then, shaking with apprehension, she carefully slid the glass door open and paused. She could hear only the ticking of a clock, so she tiptoed across the deep-pile rug to the corridor door. In a moment she had removed the chain latch and quietly eased back the bolt.

Her father pushed open the door and brushed past her. He set down the case he'd used to carry his rope and took his pistol from beneath his jacket. With his free hand he reached out to touch her cheek. "You a good girl, Alma. You did jus' fine," he whispered.

Then he went to the door of the apartment's only bedroom and opened it. Alma followed and was beside him when he clicked on the light.

There were twin beds in the room, and a middle-aged couple had been asleep. The woman awoke when the light went on and sat up, clutching the bedclothes around her. She stared wide-eyed at Alma and her father; then her gaze focused on the large black revolver he held, and her mouth started to open.

"Jus' keep you mouth shut, woman. Don't you say nothin'," Alma's father ordered, and moved forward, holding the pistol ready.

It took only a few minutes to wake the man and tie and gag the pair with strips torn from a sheet. When he was finished, they were lying on their sides with their arms and legs drawn up behind them and bulky gags covered their mouths. All they could do was watch while he and Alma searched the closets and dressing table for valuables.

Alma and her father took turns carrying their loot to the car in the parking garage. Each carried an armload of clothing, a suitcase stuffed with linen, or a small appliance—nothing that would be worthy of notice if they were seen, and which could be explained as donations if they were challenged. He saved the color television for last.

"Alma, honey," he said. "I gonna tote this-here television to the car." His pistol was gone from sight, and he now held a long, thin carving knife she'd seen him pick up in the kitchenette. "There's only one thing left for you to do here, honey, then I want you t' meet me at the car."

"Yes, Papa."

"You 'member how I use' t' butcher hogs back home? I'd hang 'em by their heels an' cut 'em quick an' deep?" He made a pantomiming gesture with the knife.

Alma wet her lips and hugged herself to keep from trembling.

"Yes, Papa."

"Well, I want you t' go into that-there bedroom and do for those folks. If we don't shut them up, they'll tell on us quick as you can spit. They'd have your ol' pa in prison for sure. You don't want that, do you?"

"No, Papa."

"That's my girl," he said, wrapping the fingers of her right hand around the handle of the knife. He gave her a gentle push toward the bedroom doorway. "I'll meet you at the car. You'd best hurry . . ."

"Oh!" Silvia broke in. "How horrible! No wonder the child feels so terribly. After butchering those helpless people, even if her worthless father *did* tell her to do it, it's no wonder her conscience won't let her rest."

I put my arms around Silvia to give her strength. "You don't understand," I said. "Alma's father was identified by the robbery victims and is serving a long sentence in the state prison. When Alma entered the bedroom with the knife in her hand, the people whimpered and cried for mercy behind their gags. She wasn't able to force herself to kill them as she'd been ordered to do. She let them live. *That's* what she's sorry about."

Grand Exit

by Leo R. Ellis

Brett Delane left the key in the front door lock as he hurriedly stumbled down the darkened hallway. Upon entering the study he snapped on the desk lamp. The shaded glow revealed a figure crouched against the wall, the figure of a man, a man who held a gun.

Brett gasped. He opened his mouth to speak, but instead he groaned and fell back against the desk, half doubled over, clutching his middle.

The intruder moved out of the shadows and became a

man, barely out of his teens, dressed in tight pants and a soiled jacket. Scraggly hair hung around his ears. He held the gun pointed.

Still doubled over, Brett worked his way around the corner of the desk and slumped into the leather chair. He reached for the desk drawer.

"Don't go for a gun, dad," the man said.

"Medicine—my medicine." Brett ignored the gun, thrust across the desk, as he feebly lifted out a vial and fumbled off the top. He placed the vial against his lips and swallowed a tablet with effort. Brett collapsed back in the chair, his eyes closed, his face a deadly white.

The man stared at the slight, silver-haired Brett behind the desk. The gunman's trigger finger tightened but there was no shot; instead, the man looked back at the open window. His eyes swept across the pictures on the study wall, photographs of Brett Delane in many of the character roles he had played on the stage.

A moan brought the gun muzzle back across the desk again. Still the man did not fire. He brushed his hair back in a nervous, unsure gesture.

Brett's eyelids fluttered open and his eyes focused across the desk. "What do you want?"

"Loot, man—loot."

"Take what I have then and get out."

The man shook his head. "It don't work out that way now, dad. I figured to blow when I thought you were gone, but you messed things up by coming to life again. Now I've got to blast you."

Brett sat upright. "You can't mean you're going to kill me!"

"You get the idea real good. I don't like witnesses— witnesses get a guy pinched." The man raised the gun and Brett collapsed in the chair. "Cut the faking," the man said angrily. "You ain't dying. I saw you take your medicine."

Slowly Brett opened his eyes. "But I am dying," he said in a low voice. He reached out and touched the vial. "This medicine has kept me alive so far, but someday, someday—poof." He gave a sardonic chuckle. "Perhaps it would be a blessing if you did shoot me. It would be sudden, no drawn-out suffering."

"This ain't meant as no favor, pop."

Brett nodded slowly. "Death is something to dread when it comes slowly. But murder, now that would be a more fitting climax to the career of Brett Delane." Brett leaned forward and pulled himself to his feet. "Yes, then I would have headlines for my obituary—Noted Actor Dies in Mystery Slaying. Very nice."

The man backed away. "Man, you're a nut."

"No, I'm an actor. It is highly important to an actor to make a grand exit, you see." Brett raised his arm. "I want my final scene dramatic, packed with emotion and suspense." Brett dropped his arm. "No actor could ask for more, and since I am to die anyway, I feel that murder would serve as an excellent vehicle in which to frame my passing."

"Man, you are a N-U-T, a real, genuine filbert." The man's gun had drooped, but now it snapped back up as Brett started for the door. "Stand where you are, dad. You ain't leaving."

"But I insist this scene be done right. I'll need the proper wardrobe and I want to get my maroon dressing gown. I don't suppose you would allow me time for a shower first?"

The gunman jabbed the gun while he clawed at his face with his free hand. "You *can't* be that nutty," he yelled. "Nobody could be nutty enough to fix up for his own murder." He stopped and his eyes narrowed. "I get it, you're pulling a fast one. You've got this setup rigged somehow." His eyes darted around the room and stopped at the desk. "A tape recorder—you're putting this down on tape." The man dashed across the room.

"I use that machine to study my diction," Brett said calmly. "You'll find it quite empty."

The gunman shoved the recorder to the floor. He made sure the telephone was firmly in the cradle, then ran back to run his hand over the wall. "I got it now, the room's bugged. You're trying to stall me until the cops get here." He whirled and pointed the gun. "It won't work, I'm going to blow your head off right now."

"Please, not the head. Shoot me in the body. And there are no hidden microphones."

The young man's mouth worked as he tugged at his long

hair. "You're trying to sucker me into some kind of a trap. You *want* me to kill you, but I'm too smart for that. I'm not buying any murder rap." He ran to the window and threw one leg over the sill. "You'll have to die a natural death on your own, dad." The man slid outside and disappeared.

Brett Delane had finished the second of his two telephone calls when the front door opened and his wife entered. Brett kissed her on the cheek. "Frightfully sorry I had to leave the dinner so abruptly, dear. I should have known that blasted curry would tie my stomach into knots, and I had left my ulcer medicine in the desk drawer."

Brett helped his wife with her coat. "We had a prowler," he said. "It was quite a dramatic scene, and I gave a magnificent performance. You'll hear all about it when the reporters get here. Now be a good girl and hold them while I shower and put on my maroon dressing gown."

Hunting Ground

by A. F. Oreshnik

It had rained earlier in the day. Dark gray clouds filled the sky and seemed to press ominously close to the ground. Gusts of chill northern wind chased dead leaves across the damp grass. Without exception, the wire frames that had been set up to hold floral wreaths at some grave sites had been blown over, spilling dying flowers and brightly colored satin and nylon ribbon onto the wet grass or muddy, raw earth.

Wilson Block stood with the collar of his dark topcoat turned up and the brim of his black hat turned down against the cold. The weather was terrible, but even on sunny days cemeteries were cheerless places. During his sixty-three years, Wilson Block had buried over forty wives, so he was an expert on cemeteries. Mount Calvary outside Buffalo, St. Louis' Oak Grove, San Diego's El Camino, and a few dozen others had received business as a result of his activities.

There had been a time when almost every grave had an elaborate headstone or piece of statuary sitting atop it. Now that was seldom permitted except in the older sections. One was allowed to mark a loved one's location in the new areas, of course, but the stones usually had to be small and flush with the ground. Grass-cutting equipment could then be driven directly over the graves, thereby reducing maintenance costs to the minimum. It was all very unfeeling, and Wilson Block was repelled by it. Although he was a multiple murderer, he was not insensitive.

He held a silver-mounted, ebony walking stick in one gloved hand. He had owned it for over thirty years. There was a time when he had strolled jauntily along the boardwalk at Atlantic City, spinning the stick like a baton. When he had gone to New York City to visit his broker he had liked to stride purposely through the financial district, gripping the head tightly and reaching out to tap the sidewalk every fifteen or twenty feet. Now, however, the stick had become less of an ornament and more of a necessity. He would never walk anywhere unless he had the stick to lean upon and furnish support.

The woman was standing beside a fresh mound in the next section. She was about forty, five-foot-two and weighing a rounded and matronly 130 pounds. Her long, dark hair had a streak of gray. Because of the ban against large markers, Wilson Block had a clear view of the woman despite the fifty yards that separated them.

This was her fourth visit to the grave site in a week. She always came alone and never seemed to know what to do with herself. Sometimes she'd stand, shifting her weight from one foot to the other; sometimes she knelt and pulled out the weeds that were taking root.

After seeing her for the second time, Block had waited until she left, then approached the grave. There was no marker yet, but he was sure she had lost a husband. The woman's nervous activity was the tip-off. He had noticed that women stand quietly beside children's and friends' graves, but seem driven to movement by a dead spouse.

Perhaps it was because they were merely spectators of the lives of children and friends, while the loss of a husband left a giant void in their lives that had to be filled.

Block had no way of knowing how accurate his theory was, but its application had made him extremely wealthy. It was a tool that worked for him and that was the only test that mattered.

When he had committed his first murders forty-odd years before, he had found his victims through lonely-hearts advertisements in newspapers and magazines. Soon, however, this became both time-consuming and dangerous. Many amateur fortune hunters and inept murders began to compete with him for the more promising victims. This was hardly satisfactory, so he was forced to look for something different.

He found his next method of selection by chance. He had moved to a new city—immediately after a funeral—and had wanted to establish himself as a young widower as quickly as he could. There was a church a few blocks from the home he had rented, so he began attending services. Within a month he had been introduced to half a dozen widows and twice that many spinsters. All he had to do was choose.

Churches made an excellent hunting ground; nevertheless, they still fell short of being perfect. For one thing, the women he met were seldom wealthy or even comfortably well-off. The spinsters were invariably almost destitute; and the widows, even those who had collected modest insurance claims, as often as not had spent the money before Block got to them.

Despite the weakness of churches, Block might have continued to use them if it hadn't been for the invention of the computer. Before computers, it had been a simple matter to give himself a new name and insure his wives, carefully selecting a different insurance company each time; but as soon as electronic data-processing became widespread, the companies began to pool their claims information and investigate beneficiaries more carefully. It was no longer possible to change his identity every time he moved, and it was no longer safe to collect the insurance of his wives. If he did either, the new electronic marvel would quickly single him out for human attention.

He could no longer marry a woman for her own insurance money, so he had to do it for her former husband's. What better place to find a fresh widow than a cemetery? He figured, and that's where he began to stalk them. If a woman had an insurance policy of her own, and most of them did, he always had her sign it over to a charity or close relative, thereby alleviating the possibility of suspicion later. He took whatever real estate, stocks, or cash there might be and considered the loss of the woman's insurance money as a necessary operating expense.

The woman at the grave in the other section straightened her shoulders and seemed to take a firmer grip on her handbag. Wilson Block had wondered how long she was going to stand there. He was chilled to the bone. He turned and started down the walk toward her at the same moment she left the grave and began to walk in his direction. He timed it so that they reached the intersection at the same time and turned toward the entrance together.

The woman seemed a bit startled to find him walking beside her. She glanced up at his face and then quickly away.

"You do not have to be frightened," Block said. He had a very deep and mellow voice that women had always found comforting. "I have been visiting my wife."

The woman nodded without saying anything, but she made no effort to increase her pace. Then, as they reached the entrance, she blurted, "My husband is buried here," and hurried away.

Wilson Block watched her go. As first contacts went, that had been about average. What was unusual, however, was the fact that he had found her very attractive. No woman had stirred him quite so much since he was in his twenties. Another positive factor had been the woman's clothing. Her coat, shoes, and handbag had been new and very expensive, but they hadn't been so new that they could have been purchased with sudden, recent insurance wealth. She had been used to comfortable living even before her husband died.

The following day Wilson Block exchanged a few more words with the woman, including their names. She was Mrs. Elizabeth Ayer and her husband had been dead a month. So far, so good.

Within a week, Block was riding back to the city in her car instead of using a bus or taxi. He had a perfectly fine sedan of his own, but he never used it at times like this unless his target didn't have transportation.

He invited her to lunch one day and she accepted. From then on, his progress was swift. Block had always been able to fascinate women. He played whatever role they seemed to need. He prided himself that all of his wives had died happy. Soon there was no more "Mr. Block" and "Mrs. Ayer." It became Will and Betty.

He found her to be a thoroughly charming woman. Unlike all of his previous conquests, she didn't exert a silent pressure to be entertained, and she didn't whine about her misfortune, or try to play upon his sympathy. She held up her end of every conversation with ease and seemed to make every effort to have him feel comfortable.

The day Wilson Block took her hand in his and said, "Betty, I love you and want you to marry me," he meant every word. He always did. Acting is believing.

Neither of them had relatives or friends, and they had only a few acquaintances. There was no need to delay the wedding for the sake of appearances. Betty never even suggested it. Wilson had already filled the void left by her dead husband. He was sure she saw marriage as the next logical step.

Wilson also told her he'd like to move to another town. This way, as he explained it, they could leave the past behind them, and their honeymoon cottage would also be their new home.

"A wife's place is wherever her husband wants to be," she answered and kissed him.

More from habit than design, Block checked to see if the new community had a medical examiner. He found that it did. Had he been planning an immediate murder, that would have been a problem. He far preferred cities and towns with elected and untrained coroners. A coroner will often diagnose brucine or strychnine poisoning as a heart attack, but no trained medical examiner would. For a medical examiner, Block had always had to arrange carefully staged accidents, something he found extremely bothersome.

Happily, for once in his life he wanted a wife more than a funeral. Betty was everything his other wives had never been, and he suddenly realized she was everything he needed. He was sixty-three. He had all the money he would ever need. It was about time he retired, and he couldn't pick a better time. Betty hung onto his every word, catered to his every whim. He'd never had it so good.

He found himself enjoying domestic life. If his first marriage had been half as satisfying, he might never have hastened its end. Betty had absolutely no faults. She cooked to rival a *cordon bleu* chef. She kept a spotless house, but never nagged him for his sloppy ways, and she baked well enough and often enough to keep a constant stream of neighborhood children at the rear door.

The only household duties she reserved for him were the ones that traditionally fell to the male: he fixed leaky faucets, replaced blown fuses, and carried out the garbage at night.

One evening three months after they moved into their new home, he picked up the bag of kitchen scraps and took it outside. He carefully descended the concrete rear steps, but placed his foot on a child's roller skate that had been left on the walk. His leg flew out from under him, the bag of trash soared high, his arms went wide and he toppled backward. His startled cry ended abruptly when his head struck the edge of a concrete step with a sickening thump.

Betty stood at Wilson's grave and felt very unhappy. She hated cemeteries. During her forty-one years she had buried over fifteen husbands, so she was an expert on cemeteries—but she didn't like them.

The Big Trip

by Elsin Ann Graffam

This was the part of the day that Nancy liked best. Dishes done, place straightened, time to rest in bed, sip a cup of tea, watch TV and have a cigarette.

Being alone wasn't such a bad thing, she'd come to think. No man to order her around, no children to cause her grief. Just two aloof cats, a small apartment, and her TV. The last of life for which the first was made. She was alone the first part, she'd be alone the last part. And that was fine with her. One thing she had come to treasure was her independence. Other women her age had ties. Not Nancy. Her life was her own, every minute of it, and that was exactly the way she wanted it.

Carefully, frugally, all these years she had saved her money for the Big Trip to Europe. It had become a joke at the office, the extent to which Nancy would go to hang on to her money. Once she had heard June say, "If old Nancy can't take it with her, then she's not going!"

Let them laugh, she thought. When they were old, living on a pension, they would remember her—Nancy and her Big Trip Around the World. Yes, let them laugh, they who had no thought for the future, who lived from day to day, spending their money as fast as they got it.

Now she was having the joy of planning the trip, going to travel bureaus on her lunch hour, deciding on the clothes she'd buy. Oh, the countries she'd see! Switzerland, for sure. And Spain, the Netherlands, England, Italy—the world would be hers!

Retirement in two short months—and then the fun would begin! The money was ready, safely tucked away in her mattress, hundreds and hundreds of dollar bills. Just two months to wait!

She shut her eyes, smiling, thinking of the moment she'd get on the airplane, when the Big Trip would finally begin . . .

"What's she blabbering about now?"

The other woman shrugged. "Same old thing. How she's going to go to Europe and see everything. I kinda feel sorry for her, you know?"

"Uh, uh. Don't go feeling sorry for them, Joan. You gotta harden your heart or you'll go crazy working here, you should excuse the expression."

The woman laughed. "Yeah. Anyhow, I guess she's happy enough. I mean, look at her, off in that dream world of her own."

"Funny thing about her," the woman mused. "I was here when they admitted her, ten years ago. Seems she was just as normal as you and me until one night she fell asleep smoking in bed. Neighbors got her and her cats out in time. She wasn't burned much at all, but by the time the firemen got there, her apartment was ruined, every bit of furniture burned to a cinder. You wouldn't think that would make someone go insane, would you?"

Dutch

by William F. Nolan

Dutch got the idea when we were in Beverly Hills. It was late, almost midnight, and the whole town was quiet as a grave. All the fancy stores were dark and we could hear our own footsteps like clapped hands on the pavement. Me and Dutch and Rosa. She was one of his chicks. Dutch had plenty others.

Rosa was seventeen, a real little doll, like you find on the shelf of a toy store, all in blue and pink. She always dressed real nice when Dutch asked her out.

Dutch was eighteen and he looked like a movie star. I mean, handsome in a dark, curly-haired kind of way. The chicks flipped over him. Rosa, for instance.

Me, I'm Eddie Conners, and in the looks department I don't score. Year younger than Dutch; short, with thick glasses. Dutch always used to tell me that my eyes looked like two crazy fish swimming around behind the lenses. The chicks pass me by, and I guess I don't blame them any. Sometimes Dutch would fix me up with a cute chick, but she'd spend more time looking at him than she would me when we double-dated.

Anyway, on this particular night Dutch got the idea we should cop a couple of new irons and have ourselves a little dice over Mulholland Drive.

"Me against you, Eddie," he grinned. "You game, boy?"

"Sure," I said. "Why the hell not! Only let's be sure we get two alike. You could walk away from me in some souped-up short."

"Then let's start lookin' around."

Rosa put up no objections. What was okay by Dutch was okay by her.

We found a couple of new Fords near Martindale's bookstore. Dutch was a real cool operator when it came to a deal like this. He told us to wait over in the building shadows and keep our eyes open while he got the cars started. Dutch didn't need keys, not the way he worked. In about two shakes he had both engines purring like a pair of big cats. We were all set to go.

"Now, listen," he said to me. "You follow my iron over Coldwater to Mulholland. Then, we'll line up even for a run. I claim by the third turn you'll be outa sight behind me!"

"We'll see, Dutch," I said.

Rosa got in front with him and they glided away from the curb with me in the other Ford right behind. I sure like the way a new car feels—powerful and ready to do anything you want it to.

I felt pretty great tooling along smooth and easy, like some big high-class banker maybe, or some big office president out for a spin in his new car. My folks are tramp-poor and everything I make at the warehouse goes to the family. I couldn't afford a car of my own.

Then I pretended that Rosa was sitting next to me instead of next to Dutch. Real close, with her head on my shoulder. That was damn nice. I could almost smell that sexy perfume she wore and see her smile just for me. Yeah, Rosa was a real gone chick, and no mistake.

We were taking it easy around town because we didn't want any cops on our tail. Beverly Hills is lousy with cops at night. I saw the turn-indicator blink on in Dutch's Ford; he was swinging into an all-night gas station. What the hell was wrong with the guy, anyhow? Why risk being pegged in these hot buggies? I was plenty sore when I got out.

"You *nuts?*" I demanded, keeping my voice down. "What's the lousy idea?"

"Tires," he said. "What if the tires are low when we hit that cliff road? Hell, boy, we'd go on our heads for sure. You check 'em while I hit the can. Thirty-two all the way round should be okay."

I waved the station guy away and began to check pressures.

Rosa stayed in Dutch's car, fixing her face, touching lightly at her hair. She was always primping around Dutch, trying to look prettier than she did already. She didn't need to. Rosa looked plenty good to me all the time. She had natural blonde hair and a hell of a figure and she *really* knew how to walk.

"How were they?" Dutch asked me.

"My left rear was low," I said. "Good thing we checked."

"Damn right. I just don't like taking chances is all."

We climbed back in the Fords and got going. As long as we kept it at twenty-five we were okay. We'd done this before, taken a couple of hot irons out for a joyride. No dice then. Just a ride. Afterwards we took 'em right back where we found 'em and nobody knew the difference.

I snapped on some dance music. Rosa was sure a wonderful dancer. Once, in Gardena, when Dutch was pooped, Rosa asked me to hoof it with her. I remembered how light and airy she felt in my arms that night, how soft and warm she'd been. *Damn!*

We'd crossed Sunset, taken the long climb up Coldwater and I got ready for the sharp right-hand turn onto Mulholland. Easy to miss if you're not on the ball. I followed Dutch around, taking it slow. He waved me up, and I pulled my Ford alongside his.

"This is it, Eddie." He was smiling in that handsome crooked way of his. "We dig on three. Rosa will do the counting."

"Wait a minute," I said. "Rosa's weight adds better than a hundred pounds to your iron."

"So?"

"So I don't want any advantage. Either we start equal or it's all off."

The road stretched away ahead of us, narrow and treacherous and misted with fog.

"Okay, okay." Dutch reached across and opened Rosa's door. "Wait here for us, baby. We'll make the run down to Laurel Canyon and back."

"Right, Dutch," she said, sliding out. "But, be careful, hon."

Her voice was soft and husky and I figured she must practice talking that way, knowing how sexy she sounded.

"Nervous, Eddie?" Dutch asked, grinning at me from the open car window. He jazzed the Ford's mill and it was mean. Real mean.

"Hell, no," I snapped, lighting a cig. I was lying. Sure I was nervous. Who wouldn't be with a set-up like this?

Rosa was standing to one side, her arm raised, ready to flag us off. She looked like a little pink doll in the bright glare of our headlights.

Dutch was grinning, the way he always does when he's real sure of something. He was sure he'd cream me on this stretch. Mulholland is a bitch at night, with the fog hanging low over those hairpin turns, and a long drop waiting for you if you goof. He'd driven it a lot more than I had, and he knew the road pretty well. He was used to irons, too; he could stomp through the turn and broadslide like a pro. Sure I was nervous.

"Get ready, fellas," Rosa shouted.

I stubbed out my cig on the Ford's dash and tried to relax. I juiced the engine to make sure she was firing right and got all set behind the wheel.

"One . . . Two . . ."

I could feel the sudden sweat on the palms of my hands. God, but I wished it was all over! The whole thing was crazy and unreal.

"Three!"

We were off like twin jets, engines screaming, our tires sliding on the damp asphalt. I gave the Ford all the pedal she'd take in first and held Dutch, but when I snap-shifted into second he was by me and moving for the first turn. It was a fairly rough one and I eased off a little, watching Dutch throw his car in. He fishtailed like mad and his Ford was all over the road. He was really pushing.

I got through without much trouble and we headed for the next turn. He pulled away from me on the short straight and I let him go. Hell with it! No use risking my own neck on this kind of road.

The second turn wasn't bad at all—just a bend really—but the one coming up was a lulu. I remembered I'd almost gone off there once myself in my cousin's Chevy—and I hadn't even been dicing then.

Dutch was going like a crazy man, booming through the bend, ragged and swaying with speed. I knew he'd never make it through the hairpin.

And he didn't.

The whole rear end of his car broke loose and slid sideways. I could see him fighting the wheel, but it didn't help. He was in the kind of a slide that ends only one way.

Dutch went over.

I saw his Ford jump the little raised hump at the edge of the road, hover for maybe a split second in the air, like it couldn't make up its mind which way to go, and then drop out of sight.

I'll never forget the long roar it made going down, bumping over rocks and brush and trees, clear to the bottom.

Pulling over, I cut the engine and got out.

I was trembling. I snapped loose a cigarette and lit it; the smoke felt good. I began to relax.

Dutch was dead. That was for sure. Nobody, but *nobody*, could live through one like this. Besides, I could hear a dry crackling sound, like cellophane being crumpled up, and I knew the car was burning down there. Yeah, Dutch was finished all right.

What really got me was how dumb he'd played things. When he made that first rough turn and felt the whole car going he should have known something was haywire. But, he wouldn't stop in the middle of a dice, not Dutch. The fever was in him, and that's what I'd counted on. Anything to beat me. In racing or in pool or with chicks. Beat ole Eddie. Make him look like a damn fool.

Well, Dutch, this time *you* lost. Because not even you could corner at speed with only fifteen pounds of air in your back tires!

I killed the cig and fired up the Ford. I'd better hurry. Rosa would be wondering what had happened.

Loaded Quest

by Thomasina Weber

Tony Graybill stepped out of the bus, his joints stiff from the long ride. It was eight-thirty on a warm July evening, but the Florida air was pleasingly fragrant after the air-conditioned atmosphere of the bus. The cigar smoker who had been his seatmate for the last two hundred miles had not helped matters.

Reclaiming his duffel bag from the luggage compartment, Tony headed for the motel he had noticed a few blocks from the depot. The night was young and, after cleaning up, he would still have an hour or two to look for Millie.

The room he was given was clean, but far from luxurious. Compared to where he had been, though, it was paradise. He never wanted to see another jungle. He relished the hot shower, letting gallons of water revitalize his weary body. He wondered if he would ever feel rested again.

He still had not grown accustomed to the fact that he was his own man, with no more orders and living with filth and death, grateful every time a bullet whizzed past his ear to a less fortunate target. Now he could do exactly as he pleased. At the moment, he had one goal in mind, the goal that had kept him alive, day after hellish day.

Maybe that explained ghosts, he reflected, as he locked his motel room door behind him. They were probably dedicated persons who had died before achieving their goals. It seemed logical. Death would not be strong enough to quench *his* fire. He could readily picture himself as a dedicated ghost. A smile touched his lips and it felt strange, like something he had forgotten how to do.

The main street did not look familiar to him, but he had been away a long time, and towns change. People change too, he mused grimly. You can't blame a town; but a person, that's different. A faithful, worthwhile person does not change, not the way Millie did. So what did that make Millie?

Other wives waited, even though it wasn't easy. It wasn't easy for the men, either, but knowing they had someone to go home to made it bearable. Millie hadn't even given him that. He should have known something was wrong when her letters stopped coming. When he finally did get a letter, it was not from Millie but from her lawyer.

Before the ink was dry on the divorce papers, Millie had married again. That was all he knew. He did not know whom she had married, but he was willing to bet it was someone with money. When Tony and Millie had married, they had less than fifty dollars between them. At first Millie had thought it was a lark, sitting on a plank laid on concrete blocks and eating off lap trays. Rent and food, those were all his wages as a gas-pump jockey supplied.

The novelty soon wore off, for Millie was not the grin-and-bear-it type. Millie was strong, but in Millie's life, Millie came first. Her parents were well-to-do, and she was used to an easy life. When Tony was drafted before their first anniversary, he had the feeling Millie was happier than she let on at the prospect of moving back into her parents' home. His only consolation was that even if he had not gone off to war, chances are their marriage still would not have survived.

So her new husband must have money. It followed, then, that they would live on the wealthy side of town. Every town had its Snob Hill, so he headed in that direction.

It was a waste of time, he discovered half an hour later. The houses were set well back from the streets and many of them were unlighted. The Party Set, of course. Those families that were at home had discreetly drawn their drapes. He would have to come back tomorrow, when it was daylight. Just as well; he was tired.

Next morning he had breakfast at The Diner and no one recognized him, but that was not surprising. He did not recognize them, either. It was probably under new management. Businesses were always changing hands, and waitresses never stay in one place very long. Besides, these waitresses looked as though they had still been in school when he went away.

He set out once again for Snob Hill. Refreshed by a good night's sleep and a satisfactory breakfast, Tony covered the neighborhood systematically. Another man might have been discouraged by the apparent futility of his quest, for very few people showed themselves, but Tony was determined to find Millie. He knew beyond a doubt that the intensity of his feeling would flush her out. It was his belief that by concentrating on what he sought, he emitted electromagnetic waves which attracted electromagnetic waves emitted by the object sought. This would bring them together.

Whether that was the case or not, Millie did emerge from a $200,000 house just as he was walking by. Thanks to the distance between the house and the sidewalk, she did not see him. Averting his face, he hurried on. He was not yet ready to confront her. He would know when the time was right.

He watched her for a week. He saw her in shorts, in slacks, in mini-skirts, in suits, in every sort of outfit money could buy; all expensive, nothing but the best. Millie had had a good figure, but it had never looked that good in the clothes she wore when she was married to Tony. He remembered with a pang how he used to run his fingers through the long red hair that was now bleached blonde and piled on top of her head so elegantly. His Millie—the same Millie—yet so different.

There were no children, he was glad to see. He didn't think he could have endured his Millie being mother to another man's children. It was bad enough that she was another man's wife. He wondered vaguely if her husband had done his part to defend his country. Probably not; money like that does not have to fight.

He wondered what she would say when she saw him. Would she cry? Back there, squinting through sweat and grime, he had thought he could not possibly wait another day to see her. Now that they were practically together, he could afford to wait. Everything had to be just right; he would not allow haste to spoil it. He would approach her when he was ready, and not a moment before. He had all the time in the world.

He watched her sunning in the yard and swimming in her pool. He followed her when she went shopping, even took a seat a row behind her in a movie one afternoon, watching her profile instead of the film. Her husband must have been out of town, for one evening a cab delivered a big, well-dressed man carrying an attaché case. She opened the door for him and he enfolded her in his arms. Tony watched the house all night; the man did not come out again.

The husband was about what Tony had expected—close to fifty, showing the effects of too much rich food, with a way of carrying himself that indicated years of commanding bellhops, porters, and other lesser mortals. Money must have meant more to Millie than he realized.

It was toward the end of the second week that Tony knew the time had come. Apparently her husband had gone off on another business trip several days before. It was early evening, not quite dark, although the full moon was already visible. Millie came out of the house wearing a gold bikini. Concealed behind the hibiscus that ringed the pool, Tony followed her with his eyes as she seated herself on the edge of the pool, swinging her legs in the water. Hands flat beside her, she gazed downward into the green depths. Soundlessly, he came up behind her.

"Hello, Millie," he said as he grasped her shoulders and pushed. He had to go in with her, for, fighting wildly, she started to scream. That would have spoiled everything, but she didn't scream long. He left her there, a shimmering stone on the bottom of the green pool.

Tony Graybill stepped out of the bus, his joints stiff from the long ride. It was nine o'clock on a hot August evening, but the Texas air was refreshing after the air-conditioned atmosphere of the bus.

Reclaiming his duffel bag from the luggage compartment, Tony headed for the motel he had noticed on the way into town. The night was young and, after cleaning up, he would still have an hour or two to look for Millie.

Hand in Glove

by James Holding

"The man was a blackmailer," said Inspector Graves, wrinkling his nose in distaste. "There's nothing nastier. Therefore, in my opinion, the person who killed him deserves a vote of thanks, not censure and a possible prison term."

Golightly, standing with his back to the fireplace and jingling his change in his trousers pocket, looked at the inspector with surprise. "A blackmailer?" he inquired. "The newspaper report of the murder made no mention of that."

"Naturally not," said the inspector, "since it was one of the few clues we had to work with in the case. Releasing it to the press would have complicated matters enormously."

"I can understand that," said Golightly. Then, curiously, "What I *can't* understand is how you concluded Clifford was a blackmailer."

The inspector said, "Quite simple, really. We found a list of his victims in a wall safe behind a painting in his bedroom—with the amount of blackmail each one had paid to Clifford, and at what intervals. It was a very revealing document."

"I daresay." Golightly nodded agreement. "It also answers a question that has puzzled me ever since you knocked at my door a few moments ago, Inspector."

"Why I am here, you mean? Yes, Mr. Golightly, your name is on Clifford's list. He was into you for a rather staggering amount, wasn't he?"

"You could say so." Golightly looked bleakly about his once luxurious flat. Everything had a slightly shabby and uncared-for look now. "I make no secret of the fact that Clifford's murder made me a happy man."

"As it did every other victim on his list," acknowledged the inspector. "And all have admitted it readily, once they realized we were onto Clifford's dirty work. We have, of course, contacted them all. They comprise a ready-made list of suspects, as you will appreciate."

"But you have not been able to discover the murderer?"

"Each of Clifford's other blackmail victims has an unshakable alibi for the evening of Clifford's murder, as it happens," said the inspector sadly. He gave Golightly an expectant glance. "Are you also provided with one, Mr. Golightly?"

Golightly seemed taken aback. "For last Saturday evening?"

"Friday evening. From ten to midnight, approximately."

"Friday, yes, let me see." Golightly frowned in the act of memory, then smiled. "As it happens, I, too, have an alibi, Inspector. I would prefer, however, not to give you her name except in the ultimate extremity. She is what Clifford's blackmail demands on me were all about. I can tell you this much: she is a lady of high station and—thus far—unblemished reputation. Do you see my dilemma?"

The inspector sighed. "Perfectly," he said. "Yet if our other line of investigation proves a dead end, we may very well come to your ultimate extremity, Mr. Golightly. It is only fair to warn you."

"Thank you." Golightly bowed. "You do have other clues, then?"

"Only one. A full set of bloody fingerprints on the sill of the rear window by which the killer made his exit from Clifford's home."

"Bloody fingerprints, you say?"

"Yes. As the newspapers reported, Clifford was stabbed with a paper knife, a letter opener. There was a great deal of blood about."

Golightly looked baffled. "Perhaps I am dull," he said, "but if you have a set of fingerprints to work with . . . Aren't they infallible in establishing identity?"

The inspector nodded. "If they are clear and unsmudged, they are infallible. But our bloody fingerprints were far from clear, I regret to say. They were badly smeared. Even without the smearing, they presented certain difficulties."

"What difficulties, Inspector, may I ask?"

"Whoever left bloody fingerprints on Clifford's window-sill was wearing gloves."

Golightly started. "Gloves! Then no wonder it was impossible to learn anything from the prints."

"I said difficult, not impossible," murmured the inspector. "As a matter of fact, I was able to deduce certain basic information from the prints, even though the fingers that made them were gloved."

"I shall never cease being astonished at police technology," said Golightly. "What could you possibly deduce from prints made by gloved fingers?"

The inspector ticked off his points on his own fingers. "One, I deduced that the gloves worn by Clifford's murderer were of a type that would be very expensive. Under high magnification, the prints showed that the gloves worn by the killer had been string gloves—you know, the woven or knitted type. And not just knitted of the ordinary kind of cotton, but of fine silken thread. Two, some seam stitching showed quite plainly in one of the glove prints, and it was so fine and so carefully contrived that our laboratory had no hesitation in pronouncing that the gloves had been hand-made; custom-made, if you prefer. And by a very expensive glove-maker."

"You astound me, Inspector."

"I sometimes astound myself," the inspector said comfortably. "In any event, these and other characteristics of the glove smudges indicated to us that they might provide a feasible, even a fertile, field of inquiry."

"And you followed it up?"

"Just so. I, myself, after a city-wide search, unearthed a custom glover in a byway off Baker Street, Mr. Golightly, who admitted to producing gloves of this particular kind. His testimony is available if needed."

"He must have made such gloves for scores of clients," Golightly suggested.

Inspector Graves shook his head. "Such was not the case. This glover had made only a single pair of gloves like the ones I described to him. One pair only. Several years ago. Yet by great good luck, his records still contained the name and address of that client."

"Indeed?" said Golightly. "That *was* good luck, Inspector. For you, if not for me." He shrugged his shoulders. "I suppose," he went on with a wry smile, "that your investigation's success now depends rather heavily upon a show of hands, does it not?"

Inspector Graves nodded regretfully. "If you please, Mr. Golightly."

Golightly stopped jingling his coins. Slowly he withdrew his hands from his trousers pockets and held them out for Graves' inspection.

His right hand had six fingers on it.

The Slantwise Scales of Justice

by Phyllis Ann Karr

Were I five years younger, Hal, I had killed myself for bringing such shame upon your memory. But now, let me be content to set all down in this paper, and bury it in the earth above your grave. And pray you, also, be content with this much, for here has been enough of bloodshed.

That your father was a hard man, my husband, who should know better than you? Had his lordship your father been willing to lay aside his quarrel with Camden, this six years past come Shrovetide—had he bethought himself that it was his only son's life which hung in the balance, and summoned Camden who was the nearest surgeon—but no, having sworn to ruin Camden's repute, he must needs send to Saltash for Trevane, for sottish, worse-than-useless Trevane—and that when your pressing need was for physic that same night! So now we lie apart, with cold earth and sod and stone between us, when you might have been still in my bed.

I pray you, Hal, do not judge me in haste. I have a horror

of judgements which can not be undone. This present disgrace took its root when you and I were little more than children, in 1616 when your father sued and won his unjust judgement against Thomas Penhallow; and when Penhallow would have appealed, the Justice replied to him in the words King James had used to the Star Chamber, that "it is better to maintain an unjust judgement, than ever to be questioning after sentence is passed." So that Penhallow was ruined, losing house and lands and all, and it was rumoured his child starved and his wife left him because of this, too. He had reason enough to hate your father, Hal, but he dropped from sight, and for fifteen years his lordship had no thought of him save to gloat now and again over those words of his late Majesty, which could be turned to such convenient use.

Only, some while after you were buried, your father went to work at Master Carnsew and Sir Edward, and by wearing them down and wearing them down he was able, last year, to buy out both their shares in the Wheal Nancy. But one day going to see his new mine, he stood there looking on whilst the men were drawn up out of the shaft, when up came one who, on stepping into the light of day, stood and stood looking back at his lordship. Then your father, peering more closely, saw beneath the grime and ore dust and coating of years, and knew this man to be Thomas Penhallow.

We searched and made enquiry (for after Master Harkness refused to stop longer in Wilharthen House, your father had made of me, though a woman, a sort of secretary; a clever economy it was for him, seeing he need pay me no more than food, gowns, and chamber in Wilharthen, which he must have provided me in any case; nor could I leave him, having no where to go). But all we learnt was that Penhallow had been three or four years in the Wheal Nancy, working as a tributer, for a share of the ore he brought to surface, and a good man for finding out new lodes; and the mine captain thought he had come from the Great Pelcoath when it filled with water, but how long he had been at Pelcoath, or where he lived before that, the captain could not say. Your father privately fed a hope that Penhallow, now he had seen his old and powerful enemy, would leave of his own will, but when Penhallow did not do so, his lordship began to cheat him of his earnings: your father had learned well enough, Hal, the arts of juggling accounts and corrupting assayers. To my shame, I also helped him cast up his columns of false figures—there are so many little persecutions a man may put upon his daughter-in-law day by day, she living alone under his roof. But Penhallow did not leave, only his pile of ore grew less, which diminished a little your father's profits from the mine. Then, in the next fortnight there was a cave-in that shut up the new tunnel, and although no men were trapped therein, yet no ore could be got from it for three days while they dug it out again. At the last, his lordship went again to see how he might have more tin out of the miners, when Penhallow's core, having come up after their morning's time below, and playing at quoits, a quoit flew astray and narrowly missed your father, who would believe no otherwise but that it had come in malice from Penhallow's hand.

Whether indeed Thomas Penhallow meant your father some bodily mischief, or your father merely chose to believe it was so, his lordship now made up his mind he must see to the man he had wronged fifteen years ago, before that man saw to him. There was a certain worthless fellow called Ned Curnow working at the Nancy, or rather signed on to draw his month's pay, for little ore he ever brought to surface. They said that by some traces in his speech and bearing he must be some gentleman or gentleman's son fallen into low estate, and scarcely a day passed but Curnow was in mischief of some sort, and often serious mischief. The mine captain pointed him out to your father, that same day of the quoit, remarking he wished to turn this Curnow out of the mine. His lordship questioned the captain more closely, and ended by telling him to have the fellow come round to Wilharthen House.

He did not come round until two mornings after, and being let in by Bosvannion (our new steward, Hal; old Parsons died a fortnight after you, of a kick he had from Thomson's jackass), and finding us in the parlour, Curnow bowed, and looked at me as a man looks at a woman, past my thirtieth year as I was, and still in the mourning I have vowed never to lay aside. Then taking an apple from the bowl on the table, he sat in the oaken armchair, which had used to be your favourite, and put his feet on the settle. Three weeks before, this vagabond had been whipt through the streets of Saltash, and had stood in the pillory, and cared not who knew it, and yet he bore himself as if Wilharthen were an ale-house, and your father his drinking companion. Only to me, Hal, did he shew respect. I sat on and sewed. Your father had brought me far enough into his confidence that, though he did not tell me in so many words all that was in his evil heart, he cared little whether I went or remained.

His lordship told Curnow of certain enquiries he had made. "It was only by the grace of Sir Edward Chilwidden," said he, "that you were not banished to the galleys when you would not say the name of your home parish, and it is only the lightest thread holds you from the Stannary Gaol now."

"Send me up, then," said Curnow, "to galleys or gaol, whichever you will." The rogue had, I think, washed his face before coming up, and perhaps even his hair, which fell long and golden on his shoulders; but his beard was untrimmed and the rags he wore left the dust of the mine on all they touched, and he was like a man who has lost all joy and desire and hope, so that he no longer cares how long he lives or when he dies.

I too, Hal, I had lost all joy, all desire and hope, and there have come lines into my face, and silver hairs in with the chestnut. I would look very seldom in my glass, but that it was your gift to me.

So your father talked for some minutes to Curnow, sounding him, as I have seen him sound the mettle of a mare before buying, or the honesty of a judge before bribing, whilst Curnow sat and ate his apple. The colour of Curnow's eyes was between green and grey, and he looked at your father as I think he might look at a long deep shaft in the mine. At length his lordship came to the point, and offered Curnow fifteen pounds to do away with Thomas Penhallow.

Curnow put back his head and laughed. "So I am to murder a man," he said, "and be paid for 't too. How if I were to go to the magistrates with this tale?"

His lordship replied that "I have the magistrates in my purse, and judges too."

Curnow threw the core of his apple into the fire. "I misdoubt that," said he, "if you pay them in proportion as you offer to pay me."

Then they haggled over the blood money as if Penhallow had been a pound of fish or a pile of ore, and at length Curnow settled for thirty pounds. His lordship gave him ten, and told him to return when he had done the thing, and to come at night. Curnow bowed to me again in leaving us, and looked once more into my eyes, as a man looks at a woman. I dropt my eyes to my seam. (Your father had money enough, Hal, I could have sewed with good thread, that was not forever knotting and breaking.)

I had no power to stop this thing, Hal, but what great difference was there, after all, between how your father had dealt with Thomas Penhallow fifteen years ago and how he would deal with him now? In any case, whatever we keep hid from outsiders and strangers, it is no life to go about in ignorance and suspicion of those under the same roof with you, those on whom you depend; and I judged it better I should know, than only suspect.

This was why I sat up with your father into the night, to see the play run out to its end. His lordship had sent the steward on some errand to Launceston, and ordered Betty to her room an hour before sunset, to stay there all the night as punishment for some pretended fault in sweeping her kitchen. All so that we would be alone; and I much thought he meant to settle all likelihood of Curnow ever telling what he had done.

There had come no word nor even rumour from the mine during the day, and we did not know whether Curnow would return on this night or another—or indeed, I thought, ever. Your father sat and studied over his accounts. You remember how he loved his accounts, Hal: as others love their coin, and more, for there was ever the hope of catching some mistake I had made in casting them up, for which he might take me to task. I nodded over my book, and as the hours passed I rose to pour out a glass of wine from the silver bottle which had been your mother's pride.

"I would advise you against it, Margery," said your father.

I smelled the wine. It was hippocras, sleep-heavy with many spices. I brought back the glassful and set it at his elbow, rather than my own, and saw that he did not drink. "Why did you not find some means of killing Penhallow by your own hand?" I asked.

"Penhallow would not have trusted himself near enough my hand," said your father. "Nor would I have trusted myself near his."

"Perhaps Ned Curnow will not trust himself near your hand again, neither," said I.

"I took the man's measure," said his lordship. "There is twenty pounds in the balance. He will come."

I thought that your father had but applied his own scale to Curnow, while that insolent man with neither hope nor desire nor fear in his grey-green eyes had likely taken better measure of his lordship. But I did not speak this thought, and so we waited. Somewhat after midnight a storm broke, and, thinking Curnow would not come, I might have sought my bed, but every moment I delayed would lengthen out into another moment, and yet another, and so I sat on, scarce thinking, with my book open in my lap. Your father had laid aside even his accounts, and all was still, excepting only the thunder and rain without. A mouse ventured into the middle of the floor. Your father said, "We must find another cat," and at the sound of his voice the mouse scurried away.

Close on to one, Curnow came, knocking at the door in the pattern they had arranged. His lordship sent me with a rushlight to bring in his hireling. Curnow was wrapped in a ragged sodden cloak, and trailed mud and filth wherever he stepped, yet on seeing me, he gave me a greeting which shewed he had indeed had gentle breeding once.

When we were come again into the parlour, his lordship stood already with the silver bottle in one hand and a fresh glass in the other. "Have you done it?" he asked.

Curnow unwrapped the cloak and tossed it down on the bench. Beneath it he carried in one hand his miner's pickaxe of iron. The rain had wetted him through cloak and all, but had not utterly rinsed away the blood and bits of hair from the flat-headed end. Curnow stepped forward to shew it his lordship at closer hand.

His lordship looked shrewdly at the blood, and nodded. "There is your twenty pounds, safe in the purse," said he.

"But drink you a glass of hippocras before you go, to warm you against the weather."

"Tom Penhallow told me much about you before he died," replied Curnow, "and there is one thing which I owe his soul." And turning the pickaxe to the sharpened end, he drove it into your father's skull. The poisoned wine mingled with the blood and streams of filthy water, and the silver bottle took a great dent as it fell.

Curnow let fall the pickaxe with your father's corpse, and turned to me. He smiled. "Here is enough of murder for the day, my lady," he said. "But do not follow me, lest you take a chill in the storm."

I smiled at him then as a woman smiles at a man. "There will no one come until the morning," I said. "Time enough to take off your clothes and dry them by the fire."

Hal, your father never did but one good work in the whole of his life, and that was the begetting of you, and that he undid again the night he let you die for his stubborn heart. Yet he was your father, and my father-in-law, and murdered, and he had at least the bowels to leave me better provided for by his death than he had in his life. Let his slayer go out into the night and the storm, and by morning was it likely they could find so much as his trail?

Forgive me, Hal, my husband, my love, but how else could I keep Ned Curnow until the morning, when he could be taken, save in my bed?

Child on a Journey

by Fred S. Tobey

The big jet had scarcely lifted off the runway at Los Angeles Airport before the passengers began to busy themselves with the things that would pass the time on the long flight to Boston. Some turned their eyes to the TV screen, waiting for the movie; others took out books and magazines. A Hollywood actress drew a script from her handbag and began leafing through it. Two elderly men opened a pack of cards and started playing rummy.

Dr. Gordon Prince, sitting by himself in a window seat in the coach section, waited until the airliner was well above the clouds before he took his nearly completed treatise on medieval history from his briefcase and laid it on the little table that he had lowered from the back of the seat in front of him. The lengthy document, on which he had labored for weeks, was to be published in a distinguished journal, and the youthful professor of social science meant to spare no effort to perfect the syntax and punctuation. By great good luck, the two seats beside him had not been sold, and he was taking an almost sensual pleasure in the thought of the quiet hours of undisturbed concentration that would be his. He thought he might even pass up dinner, and work right through.

Midway through page two, as Dr. Prince raised his eyes to ponder a fine point of grammar, he became aware of a small figure standing in the aisle beside his seat. He brought his eyes into focus and saw that it was a girl of seven or eight. She was staring at him steadily with large blue eyes. A pair of auburn pigtails hung primly down the front of her blue denim dress.

"Hello," she said. "My name is Suzy. Are you busy reading?"

Dr. Prince was a very literal man. "Not exactly," he said. "I'm writing something."

The child's eyes grew even bigger. "Oh, that must be wonderful," she said. "I'm going to write when I get older. Do you write for movies?"

"This is a different kind of writing," the professor said. He supposed it was not surprising that a writer boarding in Los Angeles should be suspected of turning out froth for the screen. "This is history. Important things that really happened."

Suzy dropped into the aisle seat. "I guess I'll sit here a minute," she said. "Unless you don't want me to."

"Well . . ." Dr. Prince began; then, rather lamely: "Won't your mother be wondering where you are?"

"Mummy—" Suzy paused and looked appraisingly at Dr. Prince, as if wondering how much she should confide in this stranger. Then she shook her head. "Mummy's dead," she said. "Mummy and Daddy were killed in a car accident, and Uncle takes care of me."

Dr. Prince looked at the child with increased interest. What a shame that one so young should lose her parents! The professor was not married, but he expected to marry someday when he found time, and if there were children he hoped they would be like this one: bright, neat and well-spoken.

"My big brother was killed, too," Suzy offered. "He was driving the car and he and Daddy were having a big fight about money, and he went too fast and hit a tree. I was lucky because I was in the back seat and only got hurt a little, and I went to the hospital but I'm all right now."

"Well, you poor kid." Dr. Prince looked around. "Where is your uncle sitting?"

"Uncle didn't come with me. He said he was too busy."

"You mean you're traveling by yourself? A little girl like you?" He knew that children sometimes were handed over to the care of stewardesses, but to his conventional thinking it seemed a strange way of life.

Suzy nodded. "Uncle put me on the airplane and went home to get drunk."

Before Dr. Prince had a chance to respond, a stewardess who had been watching came toward them.

"Is the little girl being a bother?" she asked. "I said I'd try to keep her amused, but we've been kind of rushed today. But if you're busy—" She nodded toward the manuscript on the table in front of him.

"Oh, no, it's all right," Dr. Prince said.

The stewardess smiled, patted Suzy's head and went away.

"Who is going to meet you in Boston?" Dr. Prince asked.

"Uncle said his brother will take me home to stay at a mansion and give me a maid all for myself, and I can go out on a big yacht whenever I want. But I don't believe him. I don't think anyone is going to meet me at all."

"Oh, come, Suzy! Of course someone will meet you. Your uncle wouldn't say so if it weren't true."

"Yes, he would. Uncle Lucifer wants me to get lost and die, because he wants my money. When Uncle gets drunk he always says, 'I hope you die, you little brat, and then I'll get your money.'"

The information was coming too fast. "Lucifer?" said Dr. Prince. "His name isn't really Lucifer, is it? What do you mean, he wants your money?"

"Of course his name is really Lucifer! Uncle says there's always been a Lucifer in the family. Daddy left tons of money for me, but I can't have it until I'm eighteen, and Uncle can only spend little bits of it to take care of me, so he wants me to die and he will get it."

Dr. Prince looked speculatively at the little girl. How much of this was fantasy? She did seem an imaginative sort. On the other hand, of course, there certainly *were* people like the uncle that Suzy was describing. Dr. Prince made a mental note to watch and make sure someone *did* meet Suzy in Boston. Meanwhile, of course, there was his manuscript, which was being sadly neglected. He turned back to it and picked up a page, hoping Suzy would take the hint.

"I wish I had my teddy bear," said Suzy, sighing.

Dr. Prince thought he saw an opportunity. "Why don't you go back and sit with Teddy for a while, then?" he said. "I think they're going to serve dinner now, and you ought to be with Teddy when you're having dinner."

"His name isn't Teddy, it's Smoky, and he didn't come with me. He was in the suitcase but Uncle Lucifer took him out and put in a box of candy instead, because he said there isn't any candy in Boston."

"That was a foolish thing to say. There's all sorts of candy in Boston, even some famous candies . . ."

Suzy nodded. "Uncle lies to me all the time. Anyway, it isn't all candy, I know. There's a clock."

"A clock?"

Suzy nodded again. "I heard it going 'tick, tick' in the box when Uncle went out of the room for a minute, and I told him I heard it, but he just said, 'Shut up, you little brat!' and locked the suitcase."

Dr. Prince felt a prickling at the back of his neck, and it seemed to him his forehead had suddenly become moist. He took a handkerchief from his pocket and dabbed at it.

"Listen to me, Suzy," he said. "Where is the suitcase now? Is it back at your seat?"

Suzy shook her pigtails. "Uncle gave it to a man at the airport and the man put a little tag with my ticket and said I could get the suitcase with it when I got to Boston."

The public address system of the airliner came on with a sharp click. "This is your captain speaking," said a confident, pleasant voice. "We have leveled off at our cruising altitude of thirty-six thousand feet. We have a good tail wind, and our ground speed is six hundred and—"

Dr. Prince cast a furtive glance around the plane. *All these innocent people!* he thought. *How could anyone be so utterly unscrupulous!* Fighting panic, he thought incongruously of his precious manuscript, saw, in his mind's eye, the pages gliding and fluttering down, like autumn leaves, toward faraway earth.

Pull yourself together, you fool, he thought. *With luck, you've found this out in time. There must be an airport we can get down to in a hurry.*

He saw a stewardess in the service area, ten rows or so ahead, and he scrambled over Suzy and started up the aisle toward her. Then, turning back, he grasped the child's hand and pulled her along with him. Better to have her there to repeat the story.

As they reached the service area, Suzy pulled her hand

out of his grasp abruptly and went to sit down in a seat just ahead, in a rear row of the first-class section.

"I guess I'll stay here a while," she announced.

The frightened professor hurried toward her and tried to take her hand again, but the child pulled away and shrank toward the woman in the seat beside her. It was the Hollywood actress.

"Dammit, Suzy, honey!" said the woman, putting her manuscript down with a gesture of exasperation. "Where in hell is that stewardess who was going to keep your busy little mind occupied for a while? I *told* you all about my new movie, *Uncle Lucifer*. Now can't you leave Mummy alone for a *minute* to study the script?"

The Witches in the Closet

by Anne Chamberlain

Except for the witches in the closet, Catharine was the wife John had thought she would be. She was companionable and neat, she played an expert hand of bridge, and she was really interested in cooking. She liked, or pretended to like, the movies, the magazines, and most of the people he liked. It did not occur to him to worry about the witches until some weeks after his marriage. He did not think of them, in fact, until he and Catharine were looking for their first apartment.

"Remember, darling," she said, with a chuckle at her own foolishness, "we must find one with the proper bedroom closet."

John had to think a moment before he did remember. The problem had not come up in the hotel where they had been staying, and John had almost forgotten the evening when Catharine had told him about the witches. He recalled how she made a small point of telling him, soon after they were engaged, and of how at the time he had thought tenderly of what an innocent child she was. He had not been uneasy at all because, with the telling, she gave a plausible explanation.

"You see—" she had pressed his hand confidingly. "I really must warn you before we're married. It wouldn't be fair not to warn you about my phobia."

"Every smart person has at least one phobia these days."

Catharine mused, resting a small bright-tipped finger on her lips.

"Maybe it isn't a phobia; I'm not sure about those terms. Anyway, when I was ten years old I was real sick with a high fever and chills and all, and one night I woke up and saw three witches in the bedroom closet. I screamed and screamed—really, I did!" She smiled reminiscently. "I was such a silly thing, and you know we had a big bedroom closet in that house, a big, deep dark one. Well, I saw three witches there. Well, since then . . ."

"You're always expecting to see them again," he interrupted, not because he was uneasy but because he thought they had more important things to say.

She clasped her fingers.

"Brace yourself, darling. I was going to tell you. As a matter of fact, I do see them. I still do see those witches once in a while." Her eyes narrowed, as though she were pondering an irritating puzzle. Then she laughed and shook her head. "Of course, a good deal depends upon the closet."

That was all that they said about the witches until they were looking for their first apartment and Catharine demanded brightly that they find one with a closet that was small, shallow, and had a light in it. They made a little joke of this, telling each other that the landlords probably thought they were finicky bores for inspecting the apartment so carefully. When they had rented a place that exactly suited Catharine's specifications, John almost, but not quite, forgot about the witches again.

"You're not the imaginative type," he observed lazily the evening after they had moved. "It's funny you think you see such things. Of course, it's a business of hallucinations." He looked at her and laughed. She was sitting on the edge of the bed, brushing her fine black hair. In a few minutes she would meticulously tuck a hairnet around the curls, cleanse her face with a thick white cream, step out of her yellow kimono, and turn out the light. She looked to be the last person in the world to have hallucinations.

"Oh, I know that," she said, a bobby pin between her teeth. "I know it's perfectly silly, and probably a good psychiatrist could explain it all away. But then he might not."

"I can see myself telling the office that I'd just dropped my wife at a psychiatrist's."

"It's nothing to worry about," she answered casually. "I hope there's enough breakfast cereal; I forgot to buy some."

"You haven't seen anything of them since we were married, have you?"

"Oh, no," she gave her little smile. "No, I imagine I'll tell you when I do."

"Maybe it all had something to do with sex."

Catharine giggled.

"I bet that's what a psychiatrist would say." Her eyes were suddenly mysterious. "Maybe."

One night, seven months after their marriage, John returned late from his poker club. He had told her he would be home by one, but he did not make it until after four. He entered the apartment softly, and was surprised and irritated to find all the lamps turned on. He had thought her much too sensible to wait for him, angrily awake, and he walked from room to room, calling "Sweetheart?" in a loud, belligerent voice. When she did not answer, he stalked into the bedroom, flung off his coat, and began explaining as he undressed.

"I couldn't get out very well when I was taking everyone in the house; it went on like that all evening . . ."

He glanced toward the bed, and started. She was curled in a tight, covered hump in the middle. The hump was shivering, as though she had been crying for hours.

"Catharine!" He leaned over her, weak with remorse. "Were you that worried? You could have phoned."

She pulled an inch of cover from her face.

"Oh, darling." She sat up, suddenly cheerful. "Darling, they've been there for hours. It must have been hours ago I saw them."

"Saw what? Oh my God!"

She laughed happily.

"I really didn't mind you staying out. It wasn't that. But several hours ago I knew they would be there, so I got up and turned on all the lights. But I was afraid to turn on that light. I was nervous, you see, and I did feel so silly."

"My God," he repeated. "Is *that* what had you down?"

"Please don't think you can't stay out because of it. I would hate you to think that." She accepted a cigarette and leaned for a light. "Really, I did see them, though."

He did not know whether to believe her or not. The timing seemed too apt. But Catharine was certainly not the melodramatic type, and in his memory she had never been too possessive. She was not sly nor subtle and her gay lack of sentimentality had pleased him more than it had troubled him. When he looked at her now, suspiciously, he thought her smile seemed too honest and her eyes too strange. He spoke carefully:

"Now you look here. You've got to stop indulging yourself. You know and I know how ridiculous it is. Why, you're not neurotic, darling." He waited, and then said again, "You're not neurotic, not at all."

She was rearranging the wrinkled hairnet around her curls.

"Do you remember a Russian children's story about an old witch?" Her voice was gossipy. "And a little girl named Magda who ran and ran away from her? Well, I read that when I was little. Come to think of it though, they're more like the witches in *Macbeth*." She shivered slightly. "Only it's 'when shall we *four* meet again.' "

"Some women would invent a thing like this to keep their husbands at home. What'll you do when I'm drafted? What'll you do then?"

She patted his hand.

"Don't worry, please don't worry. I got along by myself for years." She shrugged. "They don't do anything, you see. They just appear." Sighing, she leaned close to him. "Maybe I shouldn't have told you about them. I won't tell you next time."

He clutched her shoulders harshly.

"Yes, you will. You'll tell me every time; you've got to tell me. And for heaven's sake," his voice grated, "get that funny look out of your eyes!"

He suggested the next morning that they move to another apartment. In the small sunlit kitchen, the conversation seemed so incongruous that he could not help smiling when he said:

"We don't need a psychiatrist at all. All we need is a place without a bedroom closet. Let's look for one today."

Catharine smiled back as she poured the coffee.

"Wouldn't that be hard to find? Besides, if they weren't in the bedroom, I don't know why, but I'm sure that they would move somewhere else."

The thought of sending her to a psychiatrist stayed with him. He hated to suggest it seriously. He was afraid she would be hurt, or angry, and would behave as though there were no real provocation. When several quiet weeks had passed, he began to think that the problem was absurd. Some men he knew hated spiders, and since a fall when he was four years old, he had always secretly feared unlighted stairways.

He did not got out often in the evenings. When he did, he always turned on the light in the closet just before he left, and he did not allow himself to think of the witches while he was away. But he went out less and less often. He dropped the poker club, and Catharine observed:

"I thought you liked to play, darling. And it's nice for men to get out by themselves once in a while."

"It was something to fill a bachelor's evening." He looked at her closely, and was sure that she did not realize why he was staying home.

They entertained or went out together, and the evenings they spent alone were relaxed and companionable. She was fond of sewing, and he liked to watch her, over the edge of his magazine, as she neatly whipped the needle in and out. The weeks stretched into months. The draft crisis passed when John was rejected because of a compound skull fracture that was not too solidly healed. He had forgotten about the boyhood accident, but now he could not help being glad of it. They said patriotic things and settled down to a smooth married life. Then John was obliged to go on an overnight business trip.

He did not think of the situation as an emergency until, well-settled on the train, he remembered that he had not turned on the closet light. He resolved immediately to return at the earliest possible hour, putting the other thoughts out of his mind. He did not even tell himself why he was boarding the train the next morning at the unbearable hour of five.

When he opened the door of the apartment, he was trembling and sick. His heart bounded with relief when he found the lights turned out, the morning seeping softly through the dusky rooms. He tiptoed into the bedroom and dropped his coat on a chair. Humming softly, half hoping that his voice would wake her, he walked over to the bed.

A chill crawled up his spine. At the foot of the bed, completely covered, the curled-up lump of her body shuddered convulsively. In a fury, he whipped off the blankets.

"Catharine!" he shouted. "What the devil's wrong?"

He seized her wrists and pulled her to a sitting position.

"Don't you feel well? What's wrong?" He repeated the question arrogantly, closing his mind to what he knew was wrong. Her eyes looked out of black circles. After a moment, she shook her head and began to rearrange her hairnet.

"Aren't you going to give me a kiss?"

"You've got to stop this, Catharine." He strode to the closet, snapped on the light, and returned. "If it means you have to go to a psychiatrist, you've got to stop. Do you hear me?"

She smiled placatingly.

"I didn't even have time to turn on the lights," she chattered. "As soon as I walked in here—it was twilight—I had a feeling it would happen. But I got into bed all right and read for a while, and the feeling went away. I turned out the bed lamp and looked up . . ."

"Don't talk. Tomorrow I'll find a good psychiatrist."

She made a sad little face.

"Darling, I'll never go to a psychiatrist. I decided that a long time ago."

He slapped her cheek. She drew back, her eyes wide between her fingers.

"Darling, please don't do that."

"We must stop it," he said gently.

"We can't," she said with equal gentleness. "You see, if a psychiatrist shouldn't be able to do anything—if it shouldn't work out, I mean—I'm sure that everything would get worse." She stared at the closet. "They might come out."

He sat for a long time on the edge of the bed. He did not know how long he sat there. The morning grew brighter and brighter in the bedroom. The light in the closet shone through the sunlight like a jaundiced eye. Once in a while, John looked at Catharine. She was wearing a pink satin nightgown with lace over the bodice; fatigued as she was, she looked fresh and darkly caressible, and her eyes met his with loving confidence.

She smiled the smile that implored him to be amused with her at her foolish whims. But she was different. He saw a wickedness about her lips, a strange glee in her eyes. He did not speak or move toward her. This morning he felt that he would never want to touch her again.

Setup

by Jack Ritchie

McNalley picked up the phone. "Hello?"

The voice was a man's. "Mr. Amos McNalley?"

"Yes."

"My name is Hamilton. James Hamilton. I am a vice-president at the First National branch bank in the South-view Shopping Center."

McNalley was tall and thin and in his middle seventies. He nodded. "That's my bank."

"Yes. Mr. McNalley, I've heard that you are a respected citizen in this community. A man who can be trusted."

"I guess so. Why?"

"I . . . *we* would like your help, Mr. McNalley. Your cooperation."

"What's your trouble?"

"We have an employee—a teller—at our bank who . . . how shall I put it . . . of whom we are . . . *suspicious.*"

"What's he been up to?"

"We think he's been doctoring his records. When a depositor withdraws one thousand dollars from his account, for instance, this teller marks the withdrawal as being eleven hundred, pocketing the extra one hundred himself."

"Sounds pretty simple-minded. Why isn't he behind bars?"

"He is very *very* clever, Mr. McNalley. Somehow he manages to cover up these shortages before we can check on his books at the end of the day. It's all very *technical,* Mr. McNalley, and would take a long time to explain. However, we—the officers of the branch and I—have decided that the best . . . the most *direct* . . . way of catching this criminal would be while he was in the *act* of committing the crime."

"I suppose so," McNalley said. "But where do I come in?"

"You have . . . let me see . . . I have your records somewhere here on my desk . . . something like $10,000 in your savings account?"

"$5,256 and some odd cents," McNalley said. "And the rest in savings certificates. Can't touch any of that but once in six months. Been thinking of putting everything into savings certificates."

"A very sound idea, Mr. McNalley. However, for the moment . . . Ah, yes. I have the records now. $5,256. And those extra pennies. But they do add up, don't they?"

"Which teller is it? There are three or four, as I remember."

"I don't think I ought to mention his name. You know how courts are these days about the silliest little thing. However, if you go to the window where you'll find a young man in his late twenties, with black hair, and a mustache . . ."

"Oh, sure," McNalley said. "You know, I never did trust him. I know you can't judge a book by its cover, but I just don't like him."

"Perhaps your instinct is more accurate than you suspect.

Now, sir, it is just after 9:00 A.M. We—the officers of the bank and I—would like you to go to this teller's window at exactly ten o'clock and withdraw $5,000 from your account."

"Five thousand dollars?"

"We are not asking you to go through all this trouble for *nothing*, Mr. McNalley. We will see that you receive two hundred dollars for your cooperation in apprehending this criminal."

"Two hundred dollars?" McNalley rubbed his jaw. There was a pause. "If I withdraw $5,000, then what?"

"You put the bills into an envelope and leave the bank. You walk to that little park in the shopping center."

"Darrow Square?"

"Yes, that's the one. Anyway, you go and sit down on one of the benches and wait for me. I should be there in five or ten minutes."

"Should I sit on any particular bench?"

"Any one will do. I'll recognize you. When I join you, you give me the envelope."

"Give you the envelope?"

"Yes, you see that is *evidence* and we will need it."

"But . . ."

"You have absolutely nothing to worry about, Mr. McNalley. Our bank is *bonded* to cover the entire amount. It's just a *technicality* to satisfy the law, but we need the money when the police make the arrest. I will return the money to you immediately after. The whole operation shouldn't take more than half an hour. And remember, we'll give you *two* hundred dollars for your cooperation. Not bad interest for the loan of $5,000 for half an hour, now is it, Mr. McNalley?"

"You want me to stay in Darrow Square until you come back with the money?"

"Exactly, Mr. McNalley. You stay there until I get back."

In the phone booth, the man who had identified himself as Hamilton waited exactly three minutes and then dialed McNalley's number again.

McNalley answered. "Hello?"

Hamilton had a talent for disguising his voice. "Is Bill there?"

"Bill? There's no Bill here."

"Isn't this 674-4778?"

"No. This is 674-4779."

"Sorry, I must have dialed the wrong number."

He waited another three minutes and then dialed McNalley's number once more. When he heard McNalley's phone ring, he hung up.

Good. The line hadn't been busy either time he dialed.

If the suckers didn't phone the police within the first five or six minutes, the chances were that they had been hooked.

Hamilton went back to the bar and ordered a whiskey and sweet soda.

Sitting on this particular stool, he could watch the front of McNalley's three-story apartment building. He always liked the extra insurance of being able to do that. More than once he'd seen the squad car draw up when the pigeon got suspicious later and phoned the police.

Hamilton sipped his drink.

Why did they fall for it so often?

Ignorance, stupidity, old age. Sometimes all three?

Yesterday, Hamilton had spent the morning in the lobby of the First National branch in the Southview Shopping Center. He had kept an eye on the deposit window. It was the second day of the month and that was usually a busy time, what with pension and social security checks being deposited.

He had selected Amos McNalley.

McNalley fitted the pattern. In his seventies or more. Good clothes. Neatly groomed.

Hamilton had followed him when McNalley left the bank.

McNalley covered four blocks at a brisk pace before he turned into the three-story apartment building.

Hamilton, one block behind, found himself puffing when he entered the small foyer and studied the names on the glassed mail compartments.

Evidently the mail had just been delivered. There was mail in all the slots except one. Amos McNalley had apparently picked up his before going up to his apartment.

Now Hamilton glanced at his watch as he saw Amos McNalley leave the apartment building and begin walking toward the shopping center.

Hamilton quickly downed his drink and followed. He was

puffing again when McNalley entered the First National branch building.

After approximately ten minutes, McNalley came out of the building. He blinked for a moment at the green square and its park benches. He sat down on one of them.

Hamilton waited another five minutes and then approached. "Mr. McNalley?"

McNalley looked up. "Hamilton? The vice-president of the bank?"

Hamilton nodded. "You have the money?"

McNalley took an envelope from his inside coat pocket. "You said something about two hundred dollars?"

"Of course." Hamilton brought out his wallet and removed two one hundred dollar bills. "Here you are, sir. And the bank wishes to thank you for your assistance."

Hamilton glanced into the envelope. The money was all there. "Now I'll go back to the bank and we'll get after that scoundrel immediately. I should be back in half an hour."

He took a dozen steps before he felt a tap on his shoulder. He turned to face what instinct told him were plainclothesmen.

The taller of the two spoke. "You are under arrest. You have the right to remain silent. If you do not choose to . . ."

Hamilton closed his eyes and listened to the bitter end.

McNalley joined them and spoke for Hamilton's benefit. "I waited *fifteen* minutes before I used the phone." He grinned. "I spent forty years on the force before I retired and the last ten were as head of the Bunco Squad. I think I learned a few things about Pigeon drops in that time."

Hamilton sighed. Every five years or so he had a day like this. It made him wonder if it was really all worthwhile.

A Very Rare Disease

by Henry Slesar

Spiro got to the restaurant first, and sat silently on a plump semicircle of leather cushions, sipping a cold, dry martini and listening to the lunch talk. Big talk, little talk, deal, deal, deal; it was just like the talk he'd heard in every restaurant in every city where the selling business had taken him and his black suitcase. But today, the talk jarred. Today, Spiro had big worries.

O'Connor showed up at 12:30. He said: "Welcome home, Joe. You knock 'em dead in Chicago?"

Spiro edged over for his lunch partner and picked up a spoon. "Yeah, I knocked 'em dead, all right." He rapped the spoon against a glass and rang a clean sweet bell that made the waiter look in his direction. "You want a martini, right?"

"You got it," O'Connor grinned. "Tell you the truth, Joe, I kind of think you're lucky. I hate being stuck behind a desk. Me, I like to travel."

"I like it all right," Spiro said.

"Then what's wrong? You look worried."

"I am."

"Bad trip?"

"No, good trip. Best three weeks on the road since last year. It's no business worry. It's a health problem."

"No kidding? You having trouble, Joe?"

Spiro slumped in his seat.

"No, not me. It's Katherine."

"Your wife?"

"Yeah. I guess the worst is over, but she really had me scared for a while. I been through hell these past three days—"

"Well, what happened?"

"It must have started a couple of weeks ago, when I called her from Chicago, just to say hello. She complained of a headache, some dizziness, nothing very serious. But that's the way this thing is—hardly a symptom at all. That's what's so frightening about it."

"About what, for Pete's sake?"

"About this disease. I forget what it's called exactly— mono, monotheocrosis, something like that. It's a very rare disease, one of those medical freaks that show up once in a hundred years. The symptoms are practically nonexistent; the doctor told us some people don't realize a thing until it's too late."

O'Connor's jaw slackened. "Until it's too late? You mean this thing's *fatal*?"

"That's right. If you don't catch it in time—" Spiro snapped his fingers crisply, "—that's it."

"But she's okay now? You found out in time?"

"Yes, thank God. It was pure coincidence that saved us. My doctor came to our house on Thursday night to play some bridge. I told him about Kathy's cold, and he looked her over. He thought she was looking funny, so he decided to take a blood sample; that's when he found this crazy bug. It's a damn good thing he did—for both of us."

"How do you mean?"

"This monotheocrosis—it's catching as hell. A couple of nights more, and I would have had the damn thing in my system, too."

O'Connor's drink arrived, and he gulped it gratefully.

"But what did you do about it? Is there a cure?"

"That was my first question, too. My doc was a little baffled by the whole thing, but luckily he remembered the name of a man who made a study of the disease. A Dr. Hess, on the third floor of the Birch Building. We shot right down there and saw him, and he was very comforting. He said they might not have been able to do anything ten, twelve years ago, but now they had drugs that could do the trick. I was so relieved I almost cried."

"Boy! No wonder you look so beat. That was quite an experience."

"It sure was," Spiro said, downing the rest of his drink.

They left the restaurant at two, and Spiro said good-bye to O'Connor on the corner of Fifty-eighth and Madison. Then he stepped into a cab and gave the driver the address of the Birch Building.

He was there in ten minutes. In the lobby, he stopped at a newsstand and bought a pack of cigarettes. He lit one, and entered the elevator. "Three," he told the operator.

The corridor was bustling with people settling back into the afternoon work routine. He lounged near the elevator for another ten minutes, and the hallways emptied.

At 2:30, O'Connor stepped off the elevator, looked up and down the hall, and then headed left.

Spiro called out: "O'Connor!"

O'Connor whirled, looked bewildered, and then walked up to his friend.

"I just wanted to be *sure*," said Spiro, "you son of a bitch." Then he drew back his fist and drove it into O'Connor's cheek. O'Connor yelped and fell sprawling to the marble tiles. Spiro, feeling better than he had in a long time, pressed the Down button.

Two Small Vials

by Elsin Ann Graffam

He awoke at 6:55, five minutes before the alarm was to sound. Turning on his side, he gazed with dispassionate interest at the woman who lay sleeping beside him.

Such a cow, he thought, When he thought of who he could be sleeping next to—

Sighing, he sat on the edge of the bed and pushed the alarm button in.

"Is it seven already?" Joanne asked sleepily. "I'll get breakfast. Hotcakes O.K., honey?"

"Sure," he said, not looking at his wife.

Her banal chatter at breakfast was almost suffocating.

"And this woman who won the jackpot was rich, from Great Oaks—can you imagine! How come poor people never win?"

Cow, he thought, rising. "I'd better get going," he said, slipping on his topcoat.

The ride to work was pleasant. Peaceful, after a breakfast with Joanne.

He tuned in his favorite FM station and drove slowly, thinking of Chris. Chris, with her long golden hair, her youthful figure, her blue eyes.

"You'll get over her, Bill," Joanne had said a hundred times, humoring him, forgiving him. The placid, long-suffering wife. Cow! he thought.

He turned the car into the immense parking lot of the Willsin Chemical Plant and parked at the spot marked MR. REED.

It was nice, he thought, to be only twenty-seven years old and a production manager with his own private parking spot. Willsin Chemical Plant was relatively new, but growing fast. Maybe in five years, ten at the most, it would be rated Triple-A, Dun & Bradstreet.

He'd had the best—college, good connections, looks, ambition; everything but the right wife.

He could never have his colleagues and their wives to dinner. They'd sit down to one of Joanne's insipid dinners—tuna casserole, say. She'd open her mouth and say, "And this woman who won the jackpot was rich, from Great Oaks—can you imagine!"

Wincing, he locked the car and headed for his office at the front of the plant.

I could have bought her off, he thought. I could have given her money and seen her through an abortion. But not Mr. Nice. I marry her.

And she loses the baby. And I'm stuck. With a *cow*! A—

"Good morning, Mr. Reed."

"Morning, Susan," he said to the bookkeeper.

"We're getting a rush of orders for that new explosive. Harper Construction Company, Mideast Construction, Fallstaff." She flipped through a stack of orders.

"Well, it's good, cheap, does the job."

"And you have to use so little of it," she said.

Suddenly he felt light-headed. He sat down.

"Is something the matter?" she asked.

"No. I just thought of something, that's all."

Joanne glanced at the skillet clock on the kitchen wall. Five of ten. In a few minutes her TV programs would begin. She poured herself a glass of soda and padded to the living room to turn on the set. Drawing her fuzzy-slippered feet under her, she settled down.

In seven hours Bill would be home. Maybe. The week before he'd come home late three nights in a row. How late, she hadn't known; she'd been asleep. He no longer bothered to call to say he'd be working late. He simply wouldn't show up. In frustration she'd eat her meal—and his. All fifty-five of her overweight pounds, she reflected, were his fault.

She was willing to put up with his tomcatting. Someday he'd settle down and realize what a comfortable, homey place she'd created for him. Realize, more importantly, that he still loved her as he once had. He'd come to his senses. All she had to do was wait.

The first show, *Mister Dollar,* was on. Leaning back, she immersed herself in the program.

"You're tense tonight, honey," Chris said, drawing on her robe.

"I've got a lot on my mind."

"Poor Lumpkin."

"It's just—a lot of pressure at work."

"Well, I've got my problems too."

"I know, I know." Bill lit a cigarette. Sometimes she nagged him a little too much for comfort.

"I mean, I don't want to wait so long for my ship to come in that my pier collapses."

He smiled, despite his mood. "It won't be much longer. One of these days Joanne'll see the light and give me a divorce."

"And one of these days I'll win the lottery."

"Oh, come on, Chris. Be patient. We still have each other, haven't we?"

"Sure," she said. "How about a drink?"

He nodded. His mind returned to the two small vials tucked into his jacket pocket. Getting them that afternoon had been absurdly simple. Now all he had to do was figure how to combine the two chemicals.

The telephone rang.

"Damn," she said, going to answer it. "I'll bet it's Mother, *again.*"

The alarm went off at 6:30. Quickly he reached over and silenced it. Joanne was still asleep, he saw, relieved. Easing himself out of bed, he tiptoed from the room and went down the carpeted stairs to the kitchen. The two vials were at the back of the cutlery drawer where he'd left them the night before.

The beauty of the new explosive was not only that such a small amount was needed to do the job, as Susan had said, but that just the slightest vibration—like the ringing of the telephone—would set off the explosion. Apart, the two chemicals were inert. Combined, he guessed most of the downstairs would be blown to a powder. And Joanne with it.

He knew that she sat down fatly on the sofa at ten in the morning to start watching her precious TV shows. The telephone was on the end table next to the sofa. At ten-fifteen he'd dial his home number. The vibration from the ring would be more than enough to do the job.

For a moment he clasped his hands together to stop their trembling. Then, the phone cover removed, he placed a drop of dioxorb and one of riantrin on the bell.

Did he hear her coming down the stairs? Holding his breath, he listened. No, it was just the thumping of his heart. Gently—*gently*—he replaced the cover of the telephone. There. It was—

She'd been thinking about him and his "Be patient" all night, unable to sleep, more infuriated with each passing hour. He had been stringing her along for far too long. How was she supposed to explain her time to her mother, her sisters, her brother, her friends?

Well, an early call *at home* should let him know how serious she was! *When* her call finally got through. She raised her finger from the cradle button and dialed again.

Sweet Remembrance

by Betty Ren Wright

"I blame those dreadful books for his death," Miss Mackey told the sergeant. "Indirectly, of course, I'm liberal in my thinking, I assure you, but I do think that publishers have a responsibility. Have you *seen* the kind of trash being sold in every drugstore and supermarket at this very moment?"

She didn't look like a liberal. The sergeant watched her thin white hands, expert among the tea things, and felt nostalgia for an age he had never known. In the short hours of their acquaintance he had become very fond of Miss Mackey, and he could not understand why. Certainly she was nothing like his mother—his noisy, moody, cheerfully vulgar Ma—nor like any of his noisy, cheerful, vulgar sisters and aunts. Perhaps that was it, he decided, forgetting for a moment the dreary purpose of his visit in the pleasure of watching her pour tea into pearly cups. Perhaps he loved her because she was the other side of his moon, the unresolved, even unrecognized dream of what a female should be.

"Now, about Mr. Higgins," she said with endearing directness, after he had taken his first sip of tea. "He is a simply heartbreaking example of what I mean. If he didn't read those books—if he didn't think those thoughts!—I venture to say he would be alive at this moment."

The sergeant set his cup back on its saucer. "I don't see—" he began gently, but she was quite ready to explain her theory.

"He always had one of those dreadful books in his overalls pocket," she said. "You know, the ones with the *covers*. He was always snatching a moment to read them—

I've seen him—and all that nastiness aroused his prurient curiosity. Prurient curiosity, young man." She passed him a plate of tiny cookies, which he refused. "Why else would he have been lurking behind my draperies?"

"Robbery, perhaps," the sergeant suggested, but Miss Mackey would have none of it.

"Nonsense! As the janitor of this building he had keys to every apartment, and he knew that I go to my book club every Tuesday afternoon without fail, and buy my groceries every Friday morning, so he had plenty of opportunity to come in if he simply wanted to take something." She shook her little white head decisively. "No, Sergeant, carnal appetite was his problem, and guilt was what did him in. When I saw him and screamed, he turned and climbed out of the window as though he had taken leave of his senses. He was the very picture of a guilt-ridden man."

It was one more delight that Miss Mackey saw nothing strange in Mr. Higgins choosing to spy on her instead of on one of the younger women who lived in the building, the sergeant decided. He put aside the tea regretfully. "Well, I won't bother you any longer," he said. "You've been very kind and helpful, and I'm sure you're tired after your bad experience. Thank you for the tea."

She followed him to the door. "You are not at all the way one usually imagines a detective to be," she said. "You're very young. And you have a certain—grace."

The sergeant stiffened for a moment. How his parents would have roared at that, how his brothers and sisters would have jeered! *Grace,* he thought, and then decided he liked the sound of it as long as no one else had heard.

Westerberg was waiting in the lobby. "Well?" he asked.

"An elegant old lady."

"Who pushes janitors out of windows."

The sergeant led the way to the car, feeling very much on the defensive. "So a few people heard her scolding him for reading dirty books," he said grumpily. "So this makes her a killer? She admits she spoke to him about it—for his own good. She thought she was doing her duty."

"She threatened him," Westerberg said patiently. "He told people in the apartment about it, thought it was a joke. She told him he'd be punished if he kept up his sinful ways, that his evil thoughts were showing in his face. She sounds like a nut."

"She's a nice old lady trying to set the world straight," the sergeant told him. "Anybody who wants to magnify that into a criminal act is going to have his hands full."

He thought about Miss Mackey while he shaved, mentioned her guardedly to his date at dinner, and that night he dreamt he was fighting a duel under an oak tree that was festooned with Spanish moss.

In the morning there was a report on his desk at the station, and Westerberg was waiting in the chair by the window, a cup of coffee in his hands. When he had finished reading the report, the sergeant sat for a long time staring at the crack that marred the brown-egg wall in front of him.

"I was never as young as you are when I was as young as you are," Westerberg said finally, when the coffee was gone and the silence had become too oppressive to be borne. "Do you want me to go get the old lady while you patch up your shattered illusions?"

"Go get her!" the sergeant repeated sharply. "Why should you get her? You want to send her to the chair because this damn sheet says someone died in the last apartment she lived in, too?"

"Not just *someone*." Westerberg set the coffee cup on the windowsill, adjusting its position slightly to coincide with the stains already there. "A window-washer; a wholesome, clean-living fellow who supported a wife, a mother, a sister, and the sister's two kids. Been washing windows for seventeen years, and there was never a complaint about him not minding his own business until Miss Mackey moved into the building. She reported him twice as a peeping tom—and the third time he was doing her windows he fell seven stories to the ground and broke his neck."

The sergeant slouched in his chair and thought of gallantry in the shade of a giant oak. "You can't arrest a nice old lady for being around when two people died," he said, "whether she happened to like them or not."

"Tell me one thing," Westerberg said with irritating gentleness. "Did the nice old lady mention the window-washer to you? Did she tell you Mr. Higgins was the second man to leave her elegant presence in a great big hurry?"

The sergeant looked at him with something close to hate. "No," he said. "She didn't happen to mention it. She probably assumed we'd look at it the same way she did—as a nasty coincidence."

"Good grief!" Westerberg said, but he didn't go on with the discussion.

They spent the rest of the day talking to residents of the apartment building. Most of them had known Mr. Higgins casually; none of them had thought there was anything odd about him, though they all agreed that he had been seen with lurid paperbacks in his hands and was always well-informed about, and eager to discuss, the latest sensational murder. Three residents reported having received anonymous letters in the last couple of months: a bachelor who had a painting of a nude delivered to his apartment; a model who had posed in a bikini for a slick magazine; and a young actress who had been accused in her letter of letting a man stay overnight in her apartment. Each of the letters had been a warning of punishment to come; none of them had been taken seriously. The recipients remembered that they were written on pale gray, tissue-thin paper in fine script.

As he looked over his notes, the sergeant wondered why he found it impossible to believe anything bad of Miss Mackey. Who was to say, actually, that her righteous innocence did not become a twisted, perverted passion behind those bright blue eyes? His mind simply would not accept it. He moved angrily through the long day, and at the end of it he visited her again, wondering at his own sense of homecoming as he sat down in the parlor.

Parlor, he thought. The word prompted a picture of plush and velour and china figurines; a Seth Thomas clock; books bound in muted leather, stillness tucked protectively around every object. Then he remembered that when he was twelve he had asked his seventh-grade teacher a question about Browning and, in an ecstasy of gratitude—how many seventh graders had ever asked her about Browning?—she had invited him to stop in at her home that evening and pick up a book.

The house was a treasure of towering gingerbread where she had lived first with her parents and then alone. The boy had entered into a dream when he stepped through its door. The crowded kitchen, center of life at home, had faded from his consciousness as if it had never been, and with it the bursts of laughter, the slaps, the curses, the tears that were the music he lived by. Dignity, dry wit, and, most of all, orderliness were what he found in the teacher's old house, and he had gone back again and again making mental lists of subjects to ask about the next time as his eyes moved over the ceiling-high shelves of books.

"You look tired, Sergeant." There was a tiny crease of concern between Miss Mackey's eyes. "I don't think I'll offer you tea this time. I have a better idea." She crossed the room to a glass-doored cabinet and took from its glittering depths a crystal decanter and two glasses on a tray. The glass was like a small bubble in his hand; he held it gingerly and let the brandy restore him.

"How is your case developing?" she asked as he settled back in his chair. "Have you learned what you needed to know about that unfortunate man?" She might have been asking about the weather, or his indigestion, or where he was going to go on his vacation.

"Well," he said, "it seems to be getting more complicated instead of less so. We're beginning to wonder whether there's some connection between Mr. Higgins' death and another one that occurred some time ago."

She took a tiny sip from her glass. "I don't understand."

"Your theory," he told her, "may be the right one."

She leaned forward with a tiny smile of triumph. "Twisted thoughts," she said. "Evil influences lead men to do things they would not otherwise do."

"Twisted thoughts," the sergeant agreed. "Of the murderer, however, rather than the victims'. There's someone living in this building, Miss Mackey, who is very mixed up indeed."

She watched alertly as he put down his glass and went to the window. "I hate to keep going over this," he said, "but I have to be very sure of the facts." He opened the window as far as it would go. "Now," he said, "when you came into the room you saw Mr. Higgins standing there, partly hidden by the drapery. You had no idea till then that he was in the apartment."

"That is correct," Miss Mackey said, and the sergeant seemed to hear again his seventh-grade teacher's voice.

"You're sure you didn't call Mr. Higgins in to fix a window?" he went on. "Some of your neighbors report having heard voices in the hallway minutes before Mr. Higgins fell."

"Certainly not," Miss Mackey said.

"When you caught sight of him, you screamed and ordered him to leave," the sergeant went on.

"Exactly." Miss Mackey put down her glass and came over to the window. "He seemed to panic. He crawled out on the sill, looked back over his shoulder at me, and then he fell forward and was gone."

"Like this." The sergeant then climbed cautiously onto the sill and crouched there, balancing himself with his fingertips. He looked back in time to see her small, reproachful face close to his shoulder, and then he felt her hands on his back, pushing with great purpose, and he was hurtling out into space.

"Like that," he heard Miss Mackey say very closely behind him.

It was an astonishingly long way down. The sergeant thought of his Ma, and of the cheerful, sometimes ribald girls he had loved as he grew up. He saw, in kaleidoscope, the dark places of his life and the churning colors, the chronic grand disorder of being alive. When he landed, bouncing twice in the great lap of the safety net, it was as if he had resigned himself—committed himself—forever to the way things actually were.

Westerberg helped him down.

"You want to go up or should I?" he asked sympathetically.

"You go," the sergeant said.

He waited in the dark courtyard until Westerberg had disappeared into the building. Then he straightened his coat and went around the side of the building to where the patrol car was parked. He took out his pipe. He knew they wouldn't be down for a while. Miss Mackey would want to wash the brandy glasses and put them away, powder her nose, and close the window before she went to the station.

A Dip in the Poole

by Bill Pronzini

I was sitting in a heavy baroque chair in the Hotel Poole's genteel lobby, leafing through one of the plastic-encased magazines provided by the management, when the girl in the dark tweed suit picked Andrew J. Stuyvesant's pockets.

She worked it very nicely. Stuyvesant—a silver-haired old gentleman who carried a malacca walking stick and had fifteen or twenty million dollars in Texas oil—had just stepped out of one of the chrome-and-walnut elevators directly in front of me. The girl appeared from the direction of the curving marble staircase, walking rapidly and with elaborate preoccupation, and collided with him. She excused herself. Bowing in a gallant way, Stuyvesant allowed as how it was perfectly all right, my dear. She got his wallet and the diamond stickpin from his tie, and he neither felt nor suspected a thing.

The girl apologized again and then hurried off across the padded indigo carpeting toward the main entrance at the lobby's opposite end, slipping the items into a tan suede bag she carried over one arm. Almost immediately, I was out of my chair and moving after her. She managed to thread her way through the potted plants and the dark furnishings to within a few steps of the double-glass doors before I caught up with her.

I let my hand fall on her arm. "Excuse me just a moment," I said, smiling.

She stiffened. Then she turned and regarded me as if I had crawled out from one of the potted plants. "I beg your pardon?" she said in a frosty voice.

"You and I had best have a little chat."

"I am not in the habit of chatting with strange men."

"I think you'll make an exception in my case."

Her brown eyes flashed angrily as she said, "I suggest you let go of my arm. If you don't, I shall call the manager."

I shrugged. "There's no need for that."

"I certainly hope not."

"Simply because he would only call me."

"What?"

"I'm chief of security at the Hotel Poole, you see," I told her. "What was once referred to as the house detective."

She grew pale, and the light dimmed in her eyes. "Oh," she said.

I steered her toward the arched entrance to the hotel's lounge, a short distance on our left. She offered no resistance. Once inside, I sat her down in one of the leather booths and then seated myself opposite. A blue-uniformed waiter approached, but I shook my head and he retreated.

I examined the girl across the polished surface of the table. The diffused orange glow from the small lantern in its center gave her classic features the impression of purity and innocence, and turned her seal-brown hair into a cascading black wave. I judged her age at about twenty-five. I said, "Without a doubt, you're the most beautiful dip I've ever encountered."

"I . . . don't know what you're talking about."

"Don't you?"

"Certainly not."

"A dip is underworld slang for a pickpocket."

She tried to affect indignation. "Are you insinuating that *I* . . . ?"

"Oh come on," I said. "I saw you lift Mr. Stuyvesant's wallet and his diamond stickpin. I was sitting directly opposite the elevator, not fifteen feet away."

She didn't say anything. Her fingers toyed with the catch on the tan suede bag. After a moment, her eyes lifted to mine, briefly, and then dropped again to the bag. She sighed in a tortured way. "You're right, of course. I stole those things."

I reached out, took the bag from her and snapped it open. Stuyvesant's wallet, with the needle-point of the stickpin now imbedded in the leather, lay on top of the various feminine articles inside. I removed them, glanced at her identification long enough to memorize her name and address, reclosed the bag and returned it to her.

She said softly, "I'm . . . not a thief, I want you to know that. Not really, I mean." She took her lower lip between her teeth. "I have this . . . *compulsion* to steal. I'm powerless to stop myself."

"Kleptomania?"

"Yes. I've been to three different psychiatrists during the past year, but they've been unable to cure me."

I shook my head sympathetically. "It must be terrible for you."

"Terrible," she agreed. "When . . . when my father learns of this episode, he'll have me put into a sanatorium." Her voice quavered. "He threatened to do just that if I ever stole anything again, and he doesn't make idle threats."

I studied her. Presently, I said, "Your father doesn't have to know what happened here today."

"He . . . he doesn't?"

"No," I said slowly. "There was no real harm done, actually. Mr. Stuyvesant will get his wallet and stickpin back. And I see no reason for causing the hotel undue embarrassment through the attendant publicity if I report the incident."

Her face brightened. "Then . . . you're going to let me go?"

I drew a long breath. "I suppose I'm too soft-hearted for the type of position that I have. Yes, I'm going to let you go. But you have to promise me that you'll never set foot inside the Hotel Poole again."

"Oh, I promise!"

"If I see you here in the future, I'll have to report you to the police."

"You won't!" she assured me eagerly. "I . . . have an appointment with another psychiatrist tomorrow morning. I feel sure he can help me."

I nodded. "Very well, then." I turned to stare through the arched lounge entrance at the guests and uniformed bellboys scurrying back and forth in the lobby. When I turned back again, the street door to the lounge was just closing and the girl was gone.

I sat there for a short time, thinking about her. If she was a kleptomaniac, I reflected, then I was Mary, Queen of

Scots. What she was, of course, was an accomplished professional pickpocket—her technique was much too polished, her hands much too skilled—and an extremely adept liar.

I smiled to myself, and stood and went out into the lobby again. But instead of resuming my position in the baroque chair before the elevator bank, or approaching the horseshoe-shaped desk, I veered left to walk casually through the entrance doors and out to Powell Street.

As I made my way through the thickening late-afternoon crowds—my right hand resting on the fat leather wallet and the diamond stickpin in my coat pocket—I found myself feeling a little sorry for the girl. But only just a little.

After all, Andrew J. Stuyvesant had been *my* mark from the moment I first noticed him entering the Hotel Poole that morning—and after a three-hour vigil I had been within fifteen seconds of dipping him myself when she appeared virtually out of nowhere.

Wouldn't you say I was entitled to the swag?

Doctor's Orders

by John F. Suter

The pain, the pain is everywhere. No, not everywhere. But I throb in places where there is no real pain. And now it is only an ache and a tired feeling. It seems as if there is no time, no space, nothing but this. But I am a little stronger than I was. So little. But I *am* stronger. I have to get well. I intend to get well. I will get well.

"Mr. Shaw, I think she'll come out of it all right. As you know, it was either your wife or the baby, for a while. But she's improved, I know that. Of course, there will always be the weakness. We can't correct that."

"I understand. Just to have her well again is all I care about."

I had better open my eyes. Jeff isn't here. I can't sense him. But I can stand the white room now. I no longer have a wish to die. No, even though he didn't live. I could cry and cry about it. I wanted to when Jeff first told me. But there is no strength in those sorts of tears. I will get well.

"You did tell her that the baby died?"
"Yes, Doctor. It was hard for her to take at first. Very hard. Then I told her that it had been a boy. That pleased her, in spite of—of what happened."

There. The world is back. So much sunshine in the room. So many flowers. I wonder if Jeff—

"Did you tell her that the child is already buried?"
"Not yet. If you're sure that she's stronger, I'll tell her today."
"You don't think she'll hold it against you, Mr. Shaw? For going ahead with the funeral, I mean."
"Jessie is very level-headed, Doctor. She'll understand that we couldn't wait. And—if you don't think it's out of style to say so—we love each other."

I'm sure Jeff has done whatever is best. If only it—he—had lived until I could have seen him. . . . How long have I been here? Where is Jeff? Is he being sensible, as I begged him to be? Is he at work? I hope so. The job is so important to him. Oh, I do love him! And I do so want to give him fine children.

"Perhaps, then, Mr. Shaw, it would be better for you to tell her the rest of it. Better, I mean, than for me to do it. It might be easier for her to believe someone who loves her. Sometimes people think they know more than doctors do."
"That part won't be easy."

I hope the children will look like Jeff. I'm not ugly. But I'm so—plain. Jeff has the looks for both of us. That's one of the reasons they all said he was only after my money. But he's refused to let me help him. He's independent. He keeps working hard managing the sporting-goods department. And why? He wants to support us. Neither of us would ever have to work again, if we didn't want to. I must get well, for his sake. I will get well.

"Easy or hard, Mr. Shaw, it has to be done. Someone has to tell her. It will come best from you. She must never try to have a child again. Never. It will kill her. Make no mistake about it—having another child will kill her."

"I'll take the responsibility, Doctor. You needn't say a thing to her. I think I can convince her. Perhaps I can even persuade her to move away for a while. A room's all set up for the baby. Those things shouldn't keep haunting her."

I'm glad I made my will before I came to the hospital. I'm glad I made it in Jeff's favor. He doesn't know about it. And it wasn't necessary, as it turned out. But I'm glad. He's been so good to me that now I'm sure of him. . . .

The door swung inward, silently. She turned her head, slowly. A tired smile crept across her white face. A tall young man with crinkled blond hair was in the doorway.

"Jeff."

He was at her bedside, kissing her hand. "Jessie."

When they both could speak, she gripped his fingers. "Jeff, I've been lying here thinking. Everybody has troubles of some kind or other. We can overcome this. I'm going to get strong, fast. Then we're going to have another baby. Just as quickly as we can. Aren't we?"

He smiled proudly. The truth was exactly the right answer.

"We certainly are, sweetheart. We certainly are."

Mrs. Twiller Takes a Trip

by Lael J. Littke

Old Mrs. Twiller ran a gnarled finger over the inexpensive wrist watches on the display card and smiled tremulously at the salesgirl.

"Could I try that one on, Miss?" she said, her voice quavering a little. "The one with the pretty brown band?"

"Why, certainly," the salesgirl said, smiling back at Mrs. Twiller. "These are very nice watches for the price." She strapped the watch on Mrs. Twiller's frail wrist.

"Now, isn't that pretty?" Mrs. Twiller said, stretching out her arm and twisting it around to admire the watch from all angles. She cleared her throat. "How much is it, my dear?" she asked hesitantly.

The salesgirl beamed. "Would you believe it? They're only $9.98. A special, this week only. Shall I wrap that one up for you?"

"Oh, mercy, no," Mrs. Twiller said. "$9.98? Oh, mercy." She fumbled at the buckle on the wristband, trying to undo it.

The salesgirl looked perplexed. "It's very reasonable," she said. "Really, it's a bargain for the price."

Mrs. Twiller looked up brightly. "Oh, it's just lovely," she assured the girl, "but with everything so dear these days—oh, my, I couldn't possibly spend all that on a watch. Thank you anyway, Miss."

The girl blinked a little as she helped undo the watch. "I'm awfully sorry, ma'am."

"That's all right, dearie." Mrs. Twiller patted the girl's hand. "It's just that a body can't help wishing now and then." She held the watch in her fragile hand and gazed at it with one last sympathetic look as the girl turned to another customer.

With a quick motion, Mrs. Twiller dropped the watch into the large shopping bag at her feet.

There, she thought. With the transistor radio and the electric shaver she already had in the bag, that should be enough for one day. The money Mr. Simpson would give her for them would feed her army of stray cats for several days.

As she stooped over to pick up her bag, Mrs. Twiller noticed a man watching her from two counters away. A floorwalker, no doubt. She grasped the handles of the bag and straightened up, tottering just a little not so much as to make the floorwalker come to her assistance, but just enough to make him think tenderly of his own dear old mother. She fluttered a hand to her chest and saw the suspicious look on his face fade away and be replaced by a benign smile.

Well, that took care of him. Now if he saw her drop something into her bag he would merely chalk it up to her absent-mindedness, which was certainly forgivable in a lady of her age.

It was time to leave, but first Mrs. Twiller wanted to visit the basement floor and pick up a few more plastic bowls for the new cats who just that week had found out about the private welfare center she ran. They did so appreciate their own dishes, and she liked to afford them that small dignity.

On the way down the escalator she checked her coin purse to see that she had the necessary cash. She wouldn't think of filching anything like the dishes. That wouldn't be ethical. She only took the other things because she just couldn't stretch the tiny check she received weekly from her son—certainly could not stretch it to cover all the cat food she put out each day. Besides, her son kept close account of how she spent the allowance he sent her.

Actually, she thought, the department store would probably be quite proud of the humane project they were supporting, if only they knew.

Suddenly Mrs. Twiller realized she had been on the escalator for some time. She should be down to the basement floor by now. Maybe the escalator was broken. No, it was still moving. Then why was it taking so long?

Mrs. Twiller squinted into the darkness. Darkness? Why was it dark? Was there another power failure like the ones in 1965 and 1977? No, the escalator would have stopped if that were the case.

For a moment Mrs. Twiller was alarmed, then she breathed a sigh of relief when she saw a glimmer of light far down in the mists at the bottom of the escalator. Mists? Mists in a department-store basement?

The light became brighter as she descended toward it. The mists began to look more like smoke and she could detect a faint sulfuric smell. In the distance she could see what looked like vast fires. And then she caught sight of a colossal gate, topped by a spectacular sign whose flaming letters spelled out: HELL. Underneath was a smaller sign which read: Entrance.

"My stars," marveled Mrs. Twiller aloud. "So that's where it is, right here under the Hardware Department."

She didn't have much time to wonder about it because she was about to be met by an uncomfortable-looking individual who appeared to have a bad sunburn.

"Follow me, lady," he intoned without introducing himself, which Mrs. Twiller regarded as especially bad manners. But then, she reasoned, what else could you expect in Hell?

She decided she had better follow the man since it seemed safer than trying to escape into the smoky terrain that stretched out on all sides. He led her into a seared building beside the imposing gate, and Mrs. Twiller found herself in a large room decorated sumptuously in vivid colors— scarlet, tangerine, and blood-red, among others. There was another fiery-looking individual seated behind a huge table which Mrs. Twiller took to be a reception desk, but when she headed toward it her guide said curtly, "Sit down," and disappeared through a crimson door.

Mrs. Twiller chose a cherry-colored sofa and sat down heavily, jarring her poor old bones until they rattled. Despite its soft appearance, the sofa was hard as a rock— which was only logical, Mrs. Twiller thought, since on closer examination it turned out to be made of petrified lava. She settled herself as comfortably as she could and glanced at the man behind the desk; but he was occupied with some business of his own involving a large book into which he seemed to be burning notations. Since he seemed in no way hostile, she relaxed a little and let her gaze roam around the brilliant room.

Mercy, she thought, it was a nice place to see but she certainly wouldn't want to live here. Not that it wasn't beautiful, in its own fashion, with its startling colors and stunning art objects scattered casually about. But to Mrs. Twiller's way of thinking it was overdone and even rather vulgar, as if the owner were trying to impress someone by displaying the valuable things he owned. Still, she caught her breath as she leaned closer to examine a small gold figurine of an imp which reposed on an obsidian table next to the sofa. There was also a ruby statue of indeterminate shape and a small vase studded with huge diamonds. She was admiring a solid platinum Mt. Vesuvius when a deep voice addressed her.

"Mrs. Twiller."

She turned quickly to see an elegant dark-haired gentleman attired in a shiny-black cutaway coat with a copper-red vest and tie, and striped trousers. He wore a well-trimmed goatee and managed to look distinguished in spite of being a brilliant shade of red.

Mrs. Twiller gulped, then stiffened her back. "How do you know my name?" she asked, standing up and eyeing him belligerently.

"I make it my business to know the names of people like you," he said, smiling sardonically.

Mrs. Twiller clutched her shopping bag in both arms, it being the only familiar object in this frightening situation. "What do you mean, people like me?" she demanded somewhat weakly.

The fiery-faced gentleman shrugged. "I hate to apply so harsh a term as thief to so lovely a lady. Shall we say pilferer?"

"I don't know what you mean," Mrs. Twiller whispered, her voice trembling. She let her left hand flutter to her throat in the gesture that never failed to make strong men turn squishy with concern and sentiment.

The red individual raised his hand. "Please, dear lady," he said, "spare me that. I am well aware of your wiles and I also have a record of every item you have ever appropriated for your—ahem—worthy cause."

Mention of her project gave Mrs. Twiller new courage. "Who would feed all those starving cats if I didn't? I'm just trying to do a little good in the world the only way I know how." She blinked her eyes and tried her best to squeeze out a tear or two.

The man in the cutaway, which had turned wine-red, strode to a window whose black shade he raised to reveal a landscape of fire and smoke. "Dear lady," he said, "you seem to forget where you are. We are not concerned with the good you do. Quite the contrary!" He turned and pointed a slender finger at her. "You are running up a very bad record, Mrs. Twiller, and I have brought you down here this time just for a warning. Mend your ways or you may end up down here for good—or rather, I should say, for bad."

"This time?" Mrs. Twiller was cheered. "You mean I'm not really here to stay?"

Her companion gave a short laugh and turned back to gaze out of the window at his domain. "I hope to frighten you enough so that we can burn our records on you, Mrs. Twiller. What would happen if we started taking in little old ladies like you down here? In a short time we'd have frilly curtains at our windows and sweet daffodils all around our fire pits." He swung around. "This is a last warning, dear lady. No more stealing from department stores or you'll wind up down here, and none of us would like that now, would we?"

Mrs. Twiller's courage had returned. "Oh, I don't know," she said, running her hand over an emerald statuette of the god Pan. "It doesn't seem to be that bad down here."

"You've noticed my collection," the scarlet man said, a note of pride creeping into his voice. "Of course there are compensations to this job or no one would want it, not even me. I can truthfully say that I own the most priceless objets d'art in existence." He stopped and sighed. "The hell of it is, there's really no challenge to getting them. All I have to do is wish for them and they're mine."

"Oh, that is too bad," Mrs. Twiller clucked sympathetically. "Takes all the fun out of it if you can't outsmart someone."

"Yes, it does," grumbled the fiery one.

Mrs. Twiller made a small cooing sound and patted his arm, which made him jerk it angrily away.

"Now cut that out!" he bellowed. "See what I mean? Get a sweet little old lady down here and within ten minutes she has me all soft and mushy. I won't have it, do you hear?"

"Oh, mercy, yes," Mrs. Twiller said, retreating a couple of steps. "I hear."

The man's eyes glowed crimson. "Swear, then, that you won't take any more merchandise from any store up there."

Mrs. Twiller swallowed. "I swear. Oh, my, yes."

"Then go," roared the Master of Hades. "And see that you don't have reason to come back."

Mrs. Twiller went, clutching her shopping bag and scuttling along toward the escalator as fast as she could. She had a moment of panic when she discovered that the escalator moved only down, but she did find a narrow, almost unused stairway which she ascended as quickly as she could; and she didn't stop until she reached the department-store's street floor.

"Missed the basement again," she puffed, but decided against going back down. She was already late for her weekly appointment with Mr. Simpson. She could pick up the cat dishes somewhere else, although she did like to give this store her business.

As she hurried toward the door, a display of silver flatware caught her eye. It was always easy to slip a few pieces of flatware into her shopping bag. But after a moment's hesitation she walked on past. After all, a promise was a promise. She would miss these shopping trips, though. There was something decidedly heady about seeing what she could get away with. But of course there would really be no need for any more forays. Oh, mercy, no, not with what she had in her shopping bag.

Just before entering the revolving door, Mrs. Twiller paused long enough to peep into her bag at the platinum Mt. Vesuvius, the ruby statue, the diamond-studded vase, and the emerald Pan. If she was any judge of value, her cats would be well taken care of for the rest of their combined nine lives.

Humming softly and a little breathlessly to herself, she closed her bag and hurried from the store. Mrs. Twiller had had a good trip.

Such a Lovely Day

by Penelope Wallace

Little Treddington is the prettiest village you could hope to see. It nestles in the Cotswolds and the guide books describe the Church of Saint Andrews as "a little gem," as indeed it was.

I well remember the first time I saw the village. My late husband, the Reverend Charles Framley, drove me down to see his new parish. The departing vicar, Mr. Wyland, showed us the Church and pointed out all the tourist attractions. (I am afraid that he was rather a worldly man!) He also showed us the postcards and booklets which were on sale in the church porch, but I could see that poor Charles did not approve, and so could Mr. Wyland, for he very tactfully led us across to the Vicarage. He was a bachelor but I must say that he provided a splendid tea and the house and garden were quite beautiful.

I so looked forward to living in this beautiful place and moving from the rather depressing Manchester suburb where Charles had his present parish. The thought of seeing, everyday, green fields and those neat golden cottages instead of dirt-grained houses, sustained me during the drive back to Manchester. It would almost be like going home; for I had been born and brought up in the soft lands of Surrey and to me the North would always be "alien corn".

That was ten years ago.

We moved to Little Treddington in the autumn and soon it was the Carol Service and Christmas and taking sherry with Lord and Lady Dawson at the Manor House; then Easter and Whitsun, and then every waking minute getting ready for the Church Fete. It was always held on the second Saturday in August and opened, of course, by Lady Dawson so it had to be between the time she returned from the Riviera and before they went to Scotland—Lord and Lady Dawson are both excellent shots. I remembered that the Vicar (Mr. Wyland that is, not my husband for he never made a joke!) had said Lady Dawson really chose that day to mark the last appearance of her second-day Royal Ascot hat! Fortunately, Charles did not hear.

There was so much to be done for the Fete and so many little jealousies to be sorted out, but I do pride myself on being rather good with people, and really I felt I could take quite a lot of the credit when I looked around the Vicarage garden and saw so many happy faces behind the stalls and all the children—such a happy day for them—with their pennies and sixpences clutched in one hand while they threw coconuts or delved in the lucky dip, and Lady Dawson most beautifully dressed . . .

And then—quite without warning—down came the rain! I was sure that Lady Dawson's hat was quite ruined, but she took it very well and we all ran as fast as we could into the Vicarage.

The rain stopped as suddenly as it had started and back we all went to the garden—except for Lady Dawson who had "called it a day" (as she put it) and driven home. Of course, it was rather muddy round the coconut shies and the bran in the lucky dip was a little squelchy and poor Mrs. Wills was very upset because young Millicent had left her "guess-the-weight cake" in the rain and all the icing colours had run! But there, I always say, "These little things are sent to try us."

Poor Charles is not so philosophical and he was most upset, and the following year he started to worry about the weather long before the Fete. That year there was no rain and I thought all would be well, but it made no difference—sometimes it rained and sometimes it was fine—but every year for two weeks before our "D-Day" on the second Saturday in August, Charles would study the Weather Reports.

"Oh, I do hope it will be a fine day for the Fete," he would say (so gloomily too), and then for the last week before the Great Day he would stand in the Vicarage doorway scanning the skies.

I remember once Dr. Brown (such an amusing man, but very irreligious I am afraid) asked him whether he was looking for rain clouds or a sign from the Almighty! My husband was not at all amused and when Dr. Brown went on, "The Devil sends sin and the Lord sends the weather and I should have thought He could have arranged one fine afternoon in return for all the work you do for Him," poor Charles was really most upset.

"Charles," I would say (I would never have called him Charley for I think these abbreviations are such a pity), "Charles, why do you worry so much about the weather? If it is wet we can always hold the Fete in the Village Hall." But his answer was always the same.

"No, Maude," he would say in his sad voice. "You know how that upsets Miss Gosling; she has such a job afterwards getting it ready for Sunday School the next morning." And indeed it was true that on the one occasion when we did use the Hall, Miss Gosling complained for weeks!

Even after Miss Gosling died, quite suddenly, at the end of July three years ago, it was as if her ghost haunted him for he still insisted that the Fete be held out of doors.

Day after day he would open *The Times* and read the Weather Report (before he'd even cracked his boiled egg). Day after day he would "Tut Tut" and say, "Oh, I do hope it will be a fine day for the Fete." Day after day he would scan the skies . . .

He died suddenly, last year—just four days before the Fete.

Dr. Brown was most surprised—but I cannot say that I was.

They tried to say that I was mad—wasn't that silly of them! I am glad to say that they didn't succeed. (And luckily no one found out about poor Mother.)

Because, you see, there was Miss Gosling too; at the time they thought she was what they call "natural causes", but

after my husband's death they dug her up! (Such a distaste-
ful practice, I feel.)

They said that my husband was well-insured; but that was
not the reason at all, as you can imagine!

Today is such a lovely day for a Fete—or a hanging.

Matinee

by Ruth Wissmann

"It isn't my fault I fell in love with you," Carla said. She
placed her elbow on the pillow, her chin in her hand and
gazed at the man on the bed beside her. "I didn't want to. I
really didn't want to become involved like this. It just—
happened."

He smiled and rumpled her hair. "But you aren't sorry,"
he said. "I know you aren't."

She sighed, sat up and swung her legs from the side of the
bed and, after a moment of quiet reflection, said, "No, I'm
not sorry, Alan, but I'm not happy either."

"It's one of those things, baby," he said. "You'll get over
it—the worry, I mean. That's what you're referring to
again. Right?" She nodded.

"Sometimes," she said, "I look at Tom and get the most
God-awful feeling that he knows about us."

"I should hope not! Aw—he *couldn't*."

A frown shadowed her face. "I know. At least, I don't see
how . . ."

"We've been careful." He spoke in a relaxed, contented
tone of voice.

"Yes. Careful and foolish and selfish and—"

"Come on now. No self-contempt, please."

Looking around the motel room, Carla said, "I'm always
afraid someone I know will see me driving in here. I've even
had nightmares about it—and about being followed, too."

"Let's hope you don't talk in your sleep." An amused smile played around his lips and eyes.

"Oh, lord! I should hope not. Alan, aren't you ever worried about Lisa finding out about *us*?"

He laughed and shook his head. "She'd kill me, baby. I don't let myself think about it. This is a chance we have to take, honey. But I believe that everything is chance. Life itself is a chance. What the hell! We can't worry all the time about what *might* happen. It would spoil these afternoons for us—these matinées."

"True." She sounded uncertain as she stood up. Then, frowning at her wristwatch, "It's getting late. We'd better shower and be on our way. I have to get home in time to cook dinner and . . ."

"Okay, my sweet. If you have to, you have to."

It was Carla who opened the shower door. It was Alan who gasped and clamped a hand over her mouth before the scream really exploded. What they saw would be stabbing their minds for the rest of their lives.

The limp form lying there stared at them with sightless eyes, a bullet hole in its forehead. Here was a deathly white, bloody red shock dressed in black trousers and a gray shirt. Carla was not conscious of Alan's closing the shower door, but he had. Yet she could still see the grotesque, gruesome body. There was no stopping the wave of hysteria that surged to the surface.

Above the torment wracking her mind she heard his words. "*Please! My God!* Someone will *hear* you! Be *quiet!*" He held her to him while his eyes circled the room quickly as if looking for an escape route where there was none. "*Jesus!*" he said with disbelief. "What'll we do? What in hell are we going to do?"

She was shaking and crying, and he felt her skin turning cold and clammy. "Get dressed, Carla," he said in a voice that had become tense and sharp. "We've got to get the hell out of here fast as we can."

"I know," she sobbed. "I know, I know!" When he released her, she found that her arms and legs seemed to have turned to water, her fingers to icicles. "It's so *awful!* So ghastly! That—that *man!*" Her heart was thrashing inside her chest, her throat, her ears. Her face was without color. "Alan—I—I think I'm going to—faint."

"Listen to me," he said, gripping her shoulders in his cold hands. "This is no time to black out. We've got to run for it, and don't panic. Just don't panic."

"Yes, but—" she stared at him with tortured eyes, "—shouldn't we call the police—or someone?"

He looked at her incredulously as he reached for his clothes. "The police?" he said. "You've got to be *crazy!* I don't think you realize the jam we're in."

"But, Alan—that man's been *murdered*! He's been shot in the head!"

"Oh, *God!*" He turned his eyes toward the ceiling. "I know you're not overly bright, but—just get yourself dressed and hurry." He paused and frowned at the shower door, his eyes dark with apprehension. "We've got to think," he said as though speaking to himself. "Yeah—wait a minute. We . . ."

"We can think later," she told him as she tried to brush at her tears and fumbled with the zipper of her skirt. "After we get away we can—"

He shook his head. "It's not that simple. We *can't* just leave here. We can't just walk out and leave a dead body behind us to . . ."

She swallowed with effort and the horror of their predicament began to twist in her mind. "*Alan!*" she gasped. "We'll be *caught,* won't we? And it'll all come out about us. The manager of this place will tell, and the police will come after us, and there'll be questions, and Tom will find out, and then—"

"Shut *up*! I've got to *think*. I can't think when you're talking."

"But Alan, I've got to get *out* of here. I don't want to get mixed up in a murder. I don't want Tom to—" Then the tears flowed again and she heard Alan speaking, and there was no sympathy in his words.

"What about *me*? You think *you're* in trouble—what's this kind of publicity going to do for me at the studio? Let alone with Lisa and that temper of hers."

Now his eyes seemed to be looking at Carla without seeing her. Watching the lines that fear was etching in his face, she said, "You're scared. I don't like to see a man scared. Oh, Alan! Think of *something*! We have to get away from here—from that . . ." She swallowed with difficulty and found her throat had become dry and nearly paralyzed, that it was difficult to speak.

He shook his head and finished dressing in silence.

"Alan, whoever was in this room before us must have killed that man, so why don't you just go to the office and tell the—the manager the truth. Tell him what we found and—"

"Good God!" He spoke with disgust. "Why do you think he'd believe me?"

"Well, I don't know—but he'd have the name of the person who checked into this room before we did, so—"

"Names, hell! Probably as phony as the one I've used. Oh, why? Why did *we* have the stinking luck to find that stiff?"

She shuddered and reached for her sweater. "Alan, I'm going home. I *have* to be there before Tom arrives. I—I'm leaving."

His face darkened quickly. "You just wait one damn minute," he snapped. "You're not going to walk out of here and leave me with *this* on my shoulders. You're in this jam as much as I am, you know."

Her eyes widened with alarm. "But I *can't* stay here!" she wailed.

"Keep your voice down. These walls are thin. Someone will hear you."

Carla looked at the room around them as though it were a prison. Seeing Alan pace the floor like a caged animal, she croaked, "We're trapped, that's what. We're trapped in this ugly place with that—that—"

"Shut up. I'm trying to think of everything—of every angle."

"Like what?"

He turned on her with narrowed eyes. "Well, suppose— just suppose Tom does know that you've been with some- one, and—"

"*No!* Don't *say* that. I won't listen. I just *won't!*"

"You'll listen and you'll listen good. How do you know you don't talk in your sleep? How can you be sure that he hasn't followed you here? Maybe he thought that . . . Look, suppose he came here and found that guy in this room and thought he was me—thought *he* was the one you've been meeting here."

"*No!* Oh, *no!*" She shook her head quickly.

Again Alan paced the floor. Then he walked back into the bathroom, opened the shower door, grimaced and closed it again. "Jesus! That's horrible! Whoever did that was god-damned mad—insane." Now he stood still, frowning thoughtfully and hitting a fist against his open palm.

A long, agonizing moment of silence followed before he walked back into the bedroom, took a deep breath and said, "There's only one thing we can do. It's a hell of a chance, but we've got to take it."

"Leave here?" she asked. "Just get into our cars and drive away?"

"How can you be so stupid?" he said, spitting out the words. "The manager here would recognize us anytime, anywhere, because we've been here so often."

"But he doesn't know your name."

"This," he said, pointing to his face. "This he'd recognize, describe. Yours too. No doubt he's taken a good look at you more than once. He could identify our cars, too. Did you ever think of that? He may have our license numbers."

She was trembling again. "I want to go home. I have to get out of here. I wish I'd never come here in the first place, I wish . . ."

He dropped into a chair, closed his eyes and rested his chin on clenched, white-knuckled fists that looked like marble. Then he finally nodded. "Yes, all I know is to wait until dark, put that stiff in the trunk of my car, take him somewhere and dump him."

She caught her breath and then said, "You're right. Yes—you do that. I'll leave now, and after it gets dark, you—" She saw him cast her a long and thoughtful stare. "Don't look at me like that, Alan. You make me feel guilty."

"Do I?"

"Alan—I *have* to leave here. I can't help it that soon Tom will be home, and that he'll be worried about me. He'll wonder where I am. He'll call the neighbors and our friends. How can I ever explain where I've been? It'll be late and dark and—"

"Funny," he said, "but suddenly I'm thinking about a rat leaving a sinking—"

"What do you expect me to *do*?" she cried.

"Nothing."

"But, Alan, you know I can't wait any longer."

He watched her silently as she walked to the window, parted the Venetian blinds a little and looked through. "The sun's going down," she said. "In winter, you know it gets dark early. You won't have long to wait."

"Thanks. That's most encouraging."

"Alan, where will you—put him?" she asked in a tight little voice.

"On your front porch. Where else?"

"Oh, Alan! You can't blame *me*. You can call Lisa and tell her you've been delayed, but I can't. There's no logical reason for me to be late. Tom would—"

"Look, he said, pointing a finger at her. "If I'm caught dumping that body . . ."

"Dammit," she said. "What do you want me to do?"

"Testify for me if I get caught," he told her. "That's what you can do."

"But you didn't kill that man, so they couldn't . . . *Could* they?"

"You think not? Carla, if I get caught dumping this body—or if his murder is traced to me—you're going to have to come forward and swear that we arrived in this room at exactly the same time. Understand? I don't want anybody to know that I got here before you did. Remember that."

"But then Tom will . . ." She stared at him while perspiration trickled down her forehead. "I can't believe it," she said. "I can't believe that all this is happening to me. Alan, if you cared for me, you wouldn't want me dragged into this horrible mess. You would try to protect me, keep my name out of it—if you loved me."

The air thickened with the heavy silence, and then he said, "Carla, whatever made you think that I did?"

"*Alan!*"

"For God's sake, what does that matter now? What does anything matter but to get ourselves out of this jam? I mean—we're in *real* trouble."

"It matters," she said slowly.

"Jesus! There's a dead man in that shower. There's no one to pin the blame on but us. *Us!* You and me!"

Carla's cheeks had turned from white to a fiery red, and

her voice rose as she said, "I'm getting out of here. Alan, don't call me. Don't try to contact me—ever—in any way. I'll never help you. You should have told me that you didn't love me. Do you know what I hope? I hope you burn in hell!"

She was gone, and he was staring at the door she had slammed behind her. He heard her start her car, kill the engine, start it again. He stood like a stone pillar as she drove away. Then he went outside, looked around swiftly and, seeing no one, opened the trunk of his car, pulled out a raincoat and hurried back into the motel room.

He went directly to the shower, reached inside, and dragged out the lifeless form. Hastily he wrapped his coat around it as he said, "We've done it again, good old George. Now it's back to the prop department for you."

Big Mouth

by Robert Edmond Alter

Hardesty had just got his eggs going well in the bacon fat with the three bacon strips crackling around them, when his old enamel-chipped coffee pot leaped off the rock and spilled itself, grounds and all, in the sand. Then he heard the flat *whap* of a rifle.

He sprawled in the sand beside the bullet-drilled pot and raised his head. About a hundred yards up the slope, west of his camp, was a hardwood ridge. He figured a good rifleman could get a clear shot at him from there. He hunched up his knees, preparing to crawl to his tent for his Winchester.

The second slug hit the smoking frying pan and sent it into a spin. Hardesty ducked his head away from the spattering fat. His eggs went all to runny goo when they hit the ground, and for a moment the pool of hot fat continued to sizzle and spit in the sand. He looked around as his canteen jumped with a *toomp* and started to bleed a silvery guzzle of water through its bullet wound.

Figured he missed me on that first shot, he thought. *But a man don't miss another man with a rifle three times running—not and hit a coffee pot and a frying pan and a canteen. Fella up there knows what he's doing.*

Hardesty knew what he was doing, too. Nothing. He was pinned down proper and there was nothing he could do except stay that way and wait his turn.

His enamel drinking cup was on his tin plate on top of the packing box he used as a table when he wasn't using it for something else, and he watched the cup spin away as the hidden rifle *whapped* again. *That was a good shot,* he thought. *A damn good shot.*

A tin of peaches, standing on the box next to the place where the cup had been, fell over with a moist *thop.* Next, a really sweet shot sent the tin plate skimming off in a crazy oblique, and finally a hole appeared in his dishwater-gray tent.

There was a sense of hesitation as he stared at the opening in the tent. Abruptly, the fore pole snapped in two and the forward section of the tent crumpled like a skirted old lady falling to her knees.

Figured so, Hardesty thought. *That lick he gave the tent flap was the first time he missed. Takes some shooter to pick off a tent pole at that distance.*

He craned his head to the left and looked down an alley of scrub at Shingles, his mule. *If he goes to drill her,* he thought, *then I'll kill him. Don't care what it takes, I'll get him.*

He started crawling towards the tent. He thought he had it figured now. It wasn't a killing; it was a joke, western style. Most of the Indians and the gunslingers and all the rest of that lawless bunch were long gone now, but occasionally you still came across a rowdy who was a hangover from those old ripsnorting badmen days—one of that wild restless breed who hadn't quite been able to make the transition from the nineteenth to the twentieth century.

They, the restless ones, went drifting across the plains daydreaming about the Kid and Jesse and Earp and, in the monotony of their frustrated loneliness, a sort of simple-minded, outraged madness gripped them, and they figured the only way they could assuage the fury was by busting loose. That's what the fella on the ridge was doing now, busting loose, giving himself a good laugh.

Thing was, though, Hardesty wasn't a joking man, had no sense of humor at all. He crawled up to his baggy tent as a bullet went *phut* in the sand right in his face, and he blinked and spat, and crawled on under the canvas and reached for his Winchester.

But the game was over. He could hear the muted *clack-clack* of hooves moving off down the stony draw beyond the hardwood ridge. He went over there, anyway, just for a look around. Didn't discover anything, though; no clue as to who had shot up his camp. The few U-shaped hoofprints in the sand told him nothing. And the prankster had had enough sense to gather up his empty cartridges.

Hardesty went back to camp to change to his town trousers and shirt and jacket.

He went to Stag, which he and all his isolated neighbors called "town." But it wasn't. It was simply a ramshackle landmark whose existence depended solely upon the needs of the men of the desert. It sold; it did not give. It did not have a church or any civic buildings or any homes. You either brought money to Stag or you stayed away. It had that much honesty.

Hardesty went into the store which had the sign "Post Office" tacked on it and answered, "Um-hm," when the storekeeper said, "Hello, Hard. How's the pickings?"

"Want a new coffee pot, pan, canteen, cup—"

"Getting yourself a new outfit, hey? You must've struck a pocket out there," the storekeeper said without a hope of an answer, because he knew Hardesty was an uncommunicative, if not inarticulate, man.

"Tent pole, too," Hardesty said, and he put down some money and turned on his heel and went through the open doorway into the adjoining saloon where four or five men were playing poker at a table.

They said, "Hello, Hardesty," and "Want to sit in?" and he nodded, saying, "Um-hm."

It was a quiet game, because that was the unintentional

influence the tall, gaunt, mute, mildly angry, deliberate man had on people. He had very little to say during the game. Sometimes he said, "A card," or "Check," or "Call," or "Raise."

The game shuffled and chipclicked through the coyote night and the black morning and the chill dawn, and then it broke up. Hardesty's luck had been in. He pocketed nearly $200. He didn't have anything to say about it.

He went over to the little hotel and said, "Want a room," saying nothing when the Mexican clerk said, "Joe tells me you got yourself a new outfit, Hard?" He went upstairs and gave himself a bath and a shave and went to bed.

It was dusk when he returned to the saloon. He bought himself a steak and a bottle and, for about an hour, he sat off in a shadow-pooled corner by himself and worked on the bottle. He left the saloon without any visible alteration in his taciturn disposition.

Hardesty hung around Stag for three days, nursing a few pints, playing a little poker. Then he paid off the hotel, collected his gear from the storekeeper, and he and Shingles went back to his claim.

Hardesty was hunkered over his fire and he had his eggs going, with the bacon fat popping around them, when he heard the *thup-thuppity-thup* of a rider coming. He looked up and watched the distant man and mount for a moment, and reached behind him and picked up his Winchester and leaned it against a rock near his right hand. After that, he shifted his gaze from the eggs to the rider, until the man was near enough for Hardesty to recognize. Then he ignored him.

It was Tope Jenkins, a young wrangler from over the ridge west of Hardesty's claim. The cowpoke slowed his bay to a dainty step and let her pick her way into the camp. He smiled amiably at Hardesty.

"Hidy, Hard. Coffee smells good."

"Um-hm."

"Hear you had some trouble last month, huh?" Tope said. "Stag folks tell me some joker shot up your camp for a laugh. Bet a quart it was one of them sheepmen south of the valley."

Hardesty had nothing to say. He lifted his crackling pan

from the fire and set it on a flat rock. Then he removed his hat and placed it crown down on the sand and picked up his Winchester and levered the cartridges into the hat. He leaned the empty rifle against the rock again, picked up the hat and scooped all the shells out of the hat and put them in his jeans.

Tope sat up there with his hands folded one on top of the other over the saddle horn, and watched him with a blank expression. Hardesty walked over to the bay and reached for Tope's rifle with a smooth, seemingly unhurried movement; drew it from the boot and stepped back and began levering the shells into the sand.

"Hey! What're you doing?"

Hardesty said nothing. He took the rifle by the barrel and raised it over his head and swung the stock against a rock. Then he pitched the barrel into the scrub.

"You crazy coot! What the hell you—" Tope shut up as the tall, gaunt, mute, quietly angry man walked back to him, rubbing his work-grained palms on the sides of his jeans. All at once those hands flashed upward and outward and caught Tope by the belt and levered backward and to the left, hauling him clear of the saddle and dumping him head-and-shoulders into the sand.

Hardesty slapped the nervously stepping bay with the flat of his hand, saying, "Git," and the bay bolted out of their way, rearing its head and backrolling its off eye.

Tope, outraged, spitting sand and wet curse words, got up on one knee and started accusing Hardesty of a vivid and varied list of vice.

Hardesty hit him in the face and nearly somersaulted him into the fire. He went after the wrangler, getting him by the front of his corduroy jacket and hauling him to his feet and planting a left deep in Tope's wind, jack-knifing him, and then straightened him up with a right uppercut and followed that with a left-cross, and Tope went into the sand again.

"You crazy old bastard! Why you poundin' *me*? What I ever done to *you*?"

"Because I never *told* nobody, damn you!" Hardesty cried, losing his temper at last. "You hear me, big mouth? I never told *nobody*!"

The Weathered Board

by Alvin S. Fick

Why they dug their pit at the base of the little hill I don't suppose we will ever know. Maybe it was because there was a scrub pine which provided a bit of shade, a rarity in this section of Wyoming range country where the land starts to rise in anticipation of making the mountains which divide the continent.

Perhaps they were just riding along and stopped to rest the horses. Or they might have been arguing for days, and this spot of dry and seared plains with its greasewood and black sage happened to be where the talk erupted into something more deadly. The territories were not tranquil places.

It could be they sat and smoked in the taciturn manner common to range hands, each hoping for a cooling of blood. But it was not to be. In the end they dug the pit in the loosest soil they could find, probably loosening it further with a piece of pointed rock and throwing the soil out with their hands. They both worked at it, shirts off and the sweat drying almost as soon as it surfaced on the skin. The wind blew little dust devils off the top of the pile of dirt beside the pit.

The sun was low and the shadows were long when they finished. The horses, restless now and eager to move on, nickered and pulled at the reins looped around a branch of the pine.

When the pit was chest-high in depth and oval in shape, they stopped digging. It is likely they climbed out to rest and smoke. When they got back in, they fought with knives, silently.

Only one man crawled out. He slid back in twice on top of the other man, for he was grievously hurt. The smell of blood spooked one of the horses. With a wild tossing of head and rolling of eye it broke loose. The man watched the spurts of dust rise from each hoofbeat as the mount ran off.

Some weeks later a rider drew rein at the spot where a small mound of stones, wrenched from the rib cage of the hill, marred the otherwise featureless aspect of the plain. He dismounted slowly, tethered his horse to the pine, and took down from the back of the saddle a board attached to a stake.

He worked with one hand. His right arm hung down, and swung loosely when he walked. A raw scar the color of fresh liver began at his temple, ran down the side of his jaw, under an ear, and disappeared beneath his collar. From time to time he stopped to rest, hunkered on his heels with his good hand pressed to his side under the nerveless arm. He had to prop up the stake with stones in order to drive the sharpened stake with a piece of rock held in his left hand.

When he was finished he rolled a cigarette, spilling two papers of tobacco down his shirt front before he succeeded. It hung unlighted in his mouth. He fished for a match but found none. It took him a long time to reach into his right-hand pants pocket with the good arm. The unsmoked cigarette still dangled from his lips when he rode off.

The section of the Wyoming territory where the men dug their pit is on the edge of the upper Sonoran continental life zone of North America. It is dry country, but it is almost on the verge of the Transitional zone. Sometimes rain washes the sage and the air has a clean sharp bite in the nose. You might come on the grave in the morning after just such a spring rain. Small bright blossoms of wildflowers will spangle the brown sod between the jagged rocks of the hillside.

Wood seldom rots in this dry land. If you ever find this lonely spot, you will still be able to read the legend carved into the weathered board nailed across the stake:

LAFE THOMAS
1882
HE LOST

Before you leave, be sure to notice how the drops of water on the needles of the little scrub pine catch the sunshine, breaking the light into glass-like shards which pierce the eye, even as a knife might pierce the heart.

Lot 721/XY258

by R. L. Stevens

It takes more than hatred to make a murderer.

William Willis had hated his wife almost from the day of their marriage seventeen years ago, but the thought of murder had never once crossed his mind. He was quite content to live out the days of his life without complaint, driving to the office each morning, returning each evening, and simply shutting his ears to the constant drone of her voice.

In her late thirties, Constance Willis had lost almost all the youthful beauty that had first attracted Willis to her in college. She was flabby of body and mind, hardly ever bothering to read a newspaper or pick up a book. Her days were spent in random shopping excursions with girl friends, at a weekly bridge club, and in countless hours on the telephone. But for all his hatred, William Willis had never thought of murder. In fact, he did not even think of divorce until he met Rita Morgan in the apartment downstairs.

Willis and his wife had no children, so they'd remained for many years in the pleasant garden apartment close to the downtown expressway. It was convenient to his office, and the surroundings had taken on the comfortable feeling of home. The apartment was one of the few things in their marriage that William and Constance agreed on.

When Rita Morgan moved into the apartment below

them, Willis' evenings and weekends immediately perked up. Rita was a twenty-five-year-old schoolteacher with long blonde hair and the sort of quiet beauty that couldn't have passed unnoticed even among her fifth-grade pupils. Willis helped her move in, carrying a few cartons of books up from her car, and they became friends immediately. She was everything he'd seen in Constance seventeen years before. But more important, she was intelligent and witty.

"Were you down in Rita's apartment again?" Constance asked one Saturday afternoon.

"One of her faucets was leaking," he explained. "It only needed a new washer."

"There's a janitor to take care of those things."

He sighed and opened a beer for himself. "You know she'd have to wait a month before he'd get around to it."

Constance grunted, but he knew she was unhappy about his attentions to Rita Morgan. She need not have worried quite so much, for Rita was a virginal young lady—at least as far as Willis was concerned—who treated him only with neighborly good will.

Nevertheless, it was Rita's presence on the scene that came first to Willis' mind when he read in the afternoon paper about the food contamination. A twelve-year-old boy had died of botulism in Chicago after eating canned peaches that had been improperly sterilized. As a rule, peaches were rarely affected by botulism, but these had been processed in a special manner, making them more susceptible to the deadly spores.

Reflecting on the blind fate that had killed the boy, he could not help speculating on a similar fate befalling Constance. Driving home that night, his recent daydreams of divorce and marriage to Rita shifted focus. Now he imagined Constance dead, killed by some trick of fate like an automobile accident or contaminated food.

Constance did not mention the news of the botulism scare, and it passed from his mind for the night. She kept up so little on current events that he'd often had to explain at length some happening on the foreign scene or some new face on the political horizon. Her interest in events, and in people other than her own circle of friends, had virtually ceased the day she left college to marry Willis.

But he was reminded again of the canned peaches when one of the secretaries at the office mentioned it. The afternoon paper had further details, including word that all of one lot was being recalled by the canner. Can o' Gold Fancy Prepared Peaches, lot 721/XY258.

Then the daydreams returned. He knew Constance ate canned peaches during the summer, often having them as part of her dessert. And he knew that she sometimes bought the Can o' Gold brand.

He poured over the newspapers that afternoon, even walking three blocks to a store where he knew he could buy a Chicago paper. He read more about the boy's death, and about the deadly effects of botulism poisoning, and the fantasy continued to grow in his mind. By the evening paper all Can o' Gold fruit products were being recalled, and consumers were being warned to avoid lot 721/XY258.

That evening at home, while Constance chatted on the telephone with some friend, William Willis glanced over the cupboard shelves, inspecting the canned goods. There were two cans of peaches, and one of them was Can o' Gold. His heart skipped a beat as he peered in at the lot number embossed on the lid. It was lot 721/XY258. Studying it more closely, he noticed that the can was bulging a trifle—an almost certain sign of gases produced by the bacterial activity inside.

There, standing on a shelf in the cupboard, was one of the deadly cans of peaches.

He said nothing to Constance, but that night in bed the possibilities paraded through his mind. All he had to do was say nothing, and sooner or later Constance would eat the contaminated peaches and die of botulism. Everyone would be most sympathetic. No one would suspect a thing.

And William Willis would be a free man.

He rolled over on his side and gazed into the darkness, thinking of Rita Morgan downstairs.

On his way out in the morning he saw Rita washing her car with a hose. "Hello, there," he called out. "I didn't think teachers ever got up this early in the summertime."

"I'm going on a picnic," she answered, beaming a smile his way. "Trying to get some of the dirt off this thing first."

"If I didn't have to go to work I'd help you out." He stood

chatting with her for another few moments, until he noticed Constance watching them from an upstairs window. "Gotta be going," he said finally. "Be seeing you."

That day in the office he tried not to think about it. But after lunch, while reading the latest newspaper account of the can recall, he let the idea of murder cross his mind.

If Constance died from eating those peaches, was he guilty of murder?

No, no—he refused to accept that. He had not even touched the can. Constance had purchased it, Constance would open it, Constance would eat it—possibly during the day when he wasn't even at home. How could it be his fault?

Accident. Or death by misadventure, as the British liked to say. But certainly not murder.

William Willis went back to work and tried not to think of the can of peaches waiting on the shelf for Constance.

When he got home that evening the first sight that greeted him was Constance sitting at the kitchen table eating peaches and ice cream.

"Won't that spoil your dinner, dear?" he asked a bit stiffly.

"It's too hot to cook dinner in the apartment. I thought we might just go out for a sandwich later. All right?"

On any other night he might have grumbled, but this evening he simply said, "Sure," and walked behind her back to the cupboard. The Can o' Gold peaches were still on the shelf. She was eating the other brand.

They talked very little that night and for the first time in many years he found himself getting through the hours with Constance without feeling the old hatred. When they returned from dinner, Rita came upstairs to borrow some milk, and Constance greeted her in a friendly fashion and even invited her in for coffee. Willis went to bed that night feeling good.

The feeling persisted the next day at the office and he wondered if he might be mellowing toward Constance. He made a point of buying the New York and Chicago newspapers, where the story of the botulism scare was still very much alive on the inner pages. One paper carried a detailed account of the boy's death agonies, of the gradual impairment of various parts of his brain until finally he simply stopped breathing. Willis read it grim-lipped, imagining

Constance as she might be during those long hours of dying.

He grabbed the telephone and dialed his home number, but the line was busy. She was chatting with a girl friend again.

His hands were trembling when he put down the phone, and he knew he must get a grip on himself. He'd been only an instant from warning her, from telling her of the contaminated can and thereby revealing the dark presumptions that had run through his mind. He must control himself. He was not a murderer. He was not even an instrument of chance.

And yet—if Constance died would he ever be able to look at himself in a mirror again? Would he ever be able to love Rita Morgan without the memory of Constance's death to haunt them?

He picked up the phone and dialed his number again. The line was still busy.

"I have to go home," he told his secretary. "Emergency."

He got the car out of the lot and headed for the expressway. It was nearly midafternoon and he knew she sometimes had her peaches about this time of the day. The drive home seemed longer than it had ever been at rush hours. Driving fast, almost recklessly, he imagined finding her stretched out dead on the kitchen floor—even though he knew from the newspaper articles that botulism took several hours to show its first symptoms.

He turned into the drive next to the apartment house and parked in his usual spot. The second-floor window of his apartment seemed the same, the place itself seemed unchanged. Perhaps he'd made the drive for nothing, and he'd have to explain it to Constance. And somehow get that can out of the house.

"Dear! I'm home early!"

There was no answer and he went into the kitchen seeking her. The first thing he saw was the open, empty, discarded can of Can o' Gold Fancy Prepared Peaches by the sink. That, and an empty dish, with its dirty spoon and telltale juices.

"*Constance!*"

She appeared then, coming from the bathroom. Her face

was pale and somehow a little strange. "What are you doing home?" she asked.

"I wasn't feeling well."

"Oh."

"Constance, did you eat those peaches?"

She glanced at the empty dish and the discarded can by the sink. Then her eyes met his and there was something in them he'd never seen before.

"Oh, no, dear. That nice Miss Morgan came up to borrow something, and she stayed and chatted, and I persuaded her to have a little snack."

Thirteen

by Edward D. Hoch

Renger looked up from the crude map on the table before him and studied the newcomer with critical eyes. "You're Hallman?"

"That's right."

"They tell me you're a good man with a gun."

"I get by."

"Then I guess you're the man we need for this job. Ever used an automatic carbine?"

"Plenty of times."

"Like this one?" Renger asked, bringing out a new Plainfield carbine very much like the standard military weapon. "It uses thirty-shot clips. All right?"

"Fine." Hallman glanced around at the five other men in the room. The only one he knew was Asmith, a part-time heroin pusher who'd been in and out of prison. He nodded to him and waited for Renger to introduce the others.

"That's Crowthy and Evans and Asmith and Galliger and Yates. A damn good team for this job. But we needed a good man with a gun—somebody who's not afraid to use it."

"That's me," Hallman said. He had earned the reputation.

"Good! We'll have smoke bombs and stuff, but I'm not kidding myself that we're going to get in there without killing a few people."

"What about guards?" Hallman asked. "And patrol cars?"

Renger pushed back his graying hair and stabbed at the map with a pencil. "The only guard you need to worry about is right here. Take him out and it's smooth sailing. Now, a patrol car comes down this street about once every hour. We're timed to miss it, but we can't be sure. All I can tell you is that Crowthy here will be covering you from across the street. If the patrol car surprises us, you'll have to deal with it."

"I understand," Hallman said.

"Your job is to take out this guard, get into the place, and fire a few shots. Create confusion. Make them think we've got a whole army out here. Then I'll toss a few smoke bombs and the rest of us will move in."

Asmith spoke up from his corner. "What about the getaway?"

"We'll leave the truck at this point and go the rest of the way on foot. Afterwards each of you will have to get back to the truck on your own. Evans will stay with the truck as a lookout. But at ten o'clock we pull out. Anyone not back to the truck by ten, we figure they're caught. Any questions?"

As they went over the plan step by step, Hallman found his attention wandering. He was twenty-four years old, and already he had the reputation of being good with a gun. Anyone who bothered to check his record would know he was equally good with a knife. The first man he'd ever killed had been with a knife, and he still remembered the expression of shock in the man's eyes as Hallman's blade slid deep between his ribs.

That was the way it had been the other times, too, though he remembered that first one best of all. Sometimes he had not even seen the men he'd killed. They'd merely been figures to be gunned down at a distance, or sometimes men to be blown up in their beds by a well-tossed bomb. And people knew that Hallman was an expert. They came to Hallman when the killing had to be neat and swift and efficient.

"All right," Renger said. "It's set, then. We go at dawn."

The men nodded silently and left the room. There was very little conversation, and Hallman was glad of that. He was not much of a talker.

The early morning was usually best for a job of this sort, Hallman had discovered. It was especially good if you could hit a place just a few minutes before eight, when people were arriving for the day's work. The patrol cars were generally off the road then, too, changing crews for the day tour.

This morning was especially good, because a light mist from the river hung over the streets of the town. Evans had parked the truck an hour earlier, and they'd come the rest of the way on foot, moving singly to avoid attracting attention. The town was quiet, with only a few people moving about, when Hallman poked his head around a tree across the street from their target.

The first thing he saw was the uniformed guard by the gate. He seemed to know everyone who entered, though occasionally he glanced at a pass when it was held out to him. The holstered revolver at his side presented no difficulty to Hallman, who could have, if necessary, killed the man from across the street.

Hallman broke from cover and walked directly toward the guard, carrying the carbine casually in his left hand, pointed at the ground. The man didn't notice him until he was almost up to him, and then the guard's hand dropped uncertainly to the holstered revolver. "You need a pass here," he said. "A pass."

Hallman smiled and kept walking toward the man, as if he didn't understand the language. When he was close enough he brought his right arm up quickly to the guard's throat, plunging his knife deep into the flesh. The man went down with the gurgling sound they always made. Already, before the guard hit the ground, Hallman swung his automatic carbine up to cover the doorway ahead of him, and that was almost a fatal mistake.

From behind him he heard Crowthy shout a warning,

and he whirled to see the patrol car traveling fast down the street. They'd already spotted him and screeched to a stop. Crowthy fired a quick wild shot and retreated toward the woods. Two officers jumped out of the car and one of them fired three rapid shots at Crowthy's retreating back. Hallman saw him topple in the dirt as Hallman brought his own weapon up. He fired a quick burst, dropping one officer in his tracks as the other dived behind the patrol car. A third man, the driver, started out his side and then fell back, bleeding from the shattered windshield.

Hallman moved backward into the building, firing as he went, and saw the second officer fall over. Then he was inside, running down a dingy hallway, ramming another 30-shot clip into the weapon. He hoped the others would be coming soon.

A man appeared ahead of him at the end of the passage, like a pop-up target in a shooting gallery, and Hallman sprayed him with bullets. Then he ran on, into the first room, firing quick shots to clear the way. He'd got the rhythm of it now, the half-forgotten feel for killing that left him at times but always returned.

In the second office a screaming woman was hunched in one corner, covering her face. Hallman paused only an instant, and then fired a short burst into her body. She slid down the wall, torn and bleeding and already without life. She was the first woman he'd ever killed, and he was surprised at how little it bothered him.

He smashed out the window in a front room, seeking the others, and saw two more uniformed guards running around the front of the building. He fired fast, cutting them both down with a line of bullets across their backs. Then he saw the others break from the cover of the trees. Renger was in the lead, running with his gun ready, and he hurled a smoke bomb as he crossed the road. Then someone on the floor above cut loose with three quick shots and Hallman saw Yates stagger and go down in the street, just before the smoke obscured him.

Hallman found the stairs and started up. A figure appeared at the top and Hallman let go with the rest of the clip. Before he could reload, a second man fell on him with a roar, toppling him backward halfway down the steps. He felt the carbine slide away from him, but he rolled over and managed to get his knife out. He plunged it into the fleshy man's side, heard his grunt of pain, and plunged it again. The man went suddenly limp, and Hallman rolled his body down the stairs.

There was shooting below him now, and he knew Renger and the others were past the gate. He made it the rest of the way to the top of the stairs, finding his weapon and then reloading it as he climbed. He burst through the door at the top landing and killed the man at the window with a sudden spray of bullets. Two others—short, frightened men— raised their hands and backed against the wall. Hallman shot them both.

He could feel the warmth of blood on his lower lip now, and he realized the man on the stairs had landed some damaging punches. But there was no pain. The exhilaration of the moment had blotted it out. He glanced out the window, but the smoke was too thick to see anything.

Leaning against the wall, he tried to remember how many he'd killed. The guard, and at least two of the three in the patrol car, and the man in the passage. And the woman. The two guards out the window. And the two on the stairs. And three in this room. That made twelve, in just under five minutes. Fast work. Good work.

He took out his knife again and made sure they were dead. He was on his last clip of bullets, so he couldn't waste any more. Then he heard someone coming up the stairs, calling his name. It was Renger, carrying two suitcases. Hallman licked the blood from his lip, savoring it, and went to meet him.

"You did a damn good job," Renger told him. "You're a regular one-man army!"

"I said I was good with a gun. How many men did we lose?"

"Crowthy and Yates. The others are all right. Let's plant these explosives and get the hell out of here!"

They did their job, working fast, and then left the building with the others.

"Damn!" Renger said as they started across the muddy road toward the shelter of the woods. "I'm going to see that you get a medal for this, Hallman!"

"Thank you, Major."

"When they hear back home how you led an attack on the enemy's forward command post and helped destroy it, almost single-handed, they'll make you a hero. How many did you kill?"

"Twelve."

"Damn good shooting!"

They passed the enemy patrol car, parked at a crazy angle on the road, and Hallman saw that the driver was still alive, gasping for breath behind the shattered windshield. He raised his carbine with one hand and killed the man with a single shot.

"That makes thirteen," he said, and walked on.

Operative 375

by Gary Brandner

When the creature walked in the office door, Gus Blattner stopped cranking the printer and stared. The apparition wore a trench coat and a thrift-shop fedora pulled low over a pair of orange eyebrows. The eyes and mouth were concealed behind purple shades and an unlikely black moustache.

"Aren't you supposed to say trick or treat?" said Gus.

With a flourish the trench-coated figure whipped off the hat, glasses, and moustache to reveal a grinning young man with orange hair to match the eyebrows. He stepped to the counter and announced, "I'm Dudley McBean."

"So?"

"This *is* the Universal Academy of Investigation, isn't it?"

"Yeah," Gus admitted.

"Well, I'm Dudley McBean," the young man repeated. "Operative 375."

Gus wiped his hands across his ink-smudged sweat shirt. "I think you better talk to my partner," he said and retreated to the rear of the office and into a plywood-partitioned cubicle. Inside, a round-faced man sat at a card table with a pile of envelopes in front of him. He was slitting these open with a nail file and removing cash and checks, which he stacked in tidy piles.

Gus said, "Secret Agent X-9 or somebody like that is out front. I've got a terrible feeling it's one of our students."

"What does he want here?" asked the man at the desk.

"How would I know? I'm just the muscle in this operation. All I do is crank the stupid machine."

"Don't sulk, partner," the other man said. "You know how important it is that we keep turning out the lesson booklets. I would gladly spell you out at the machine, were it not for my old lacrosse injury. Shoulder stiffens right up."

"I'd just like to get out of here once in a while, even if it's only to go to the post office."

"Now, Gus, the only reason I pick up the mail is because I have to be out anyway making the necessary personal contacts. That is, after all, my specialty. Besides, what difference does it make how we split up the work? The money goes fifty-fifty, and take a look at what came in just today. You never did this good sticking up gas stations."

"Ah, don't mind me," Gus said. "I'm on edge from worrying about Natalie. I think she's playing games with some other guy. If I could just catch her at it, then I could kill both of them and get it off my mind."

The other man stood up and walked around the table to clap his partner on the shoulder. "That's the curse of being married to a beautiful woman," he sympathized. "While I go out and talk to our visitor, you sit down and count some money. Maybe that will help cheer you up."

Adjusting his butterfly bow tie, the round-faced man left the cubicle and strode to the counter where Dudley McBean waited, smiling hopefully.

"Good afternoon, my friend. I'm Colonel Homer Fritch. What can I do for you?"

"Pleased to meet you, sir. I'm Dudley McBean." The young man waited for a reaction, got none, and went on. "Operative 375. From Snohomish. I took your course in how to be a private detective."

"Of course!" Colonel Fritch exclaimed. "From

Snohomish. One of our very best students. What brings you to Los Angeles, Dudley? You *do* know that our classes are strictly home study?"

"Oh, yes, sir. But now that I've completed the course, I wanted to come down in person to pick up my solid bronze investigator badge and handsome embossed diploma. I brought the extra ten dollars for handling, like it said in your ad in *Fearless Action* magazine."

The colonel searched the guileless blue eyes for a trace of mockery. Finding none, he said, "I think I can fix you up, young man." He reached under the counter and brought up a badge in the shape of a shield with an eagle perched aggressively on top. It bore the words *Official Private Investigator*. Colonel Fritch laid it reverently in front of Dudley. "Wear it with pride," he said. Reaching down again, he produced a printed sheet of stiff paper. "There wasn't time to have your name embossed on it, but if I may borrow your pen I'll take care of that. I have been told I write a very fine hand."

Dudley passed over a ballpoint pen, and the colonel carefully stroked the young man's name in the blank space on the diploma. He added a touch of rococo scrollwork and slid it across the counter.

"There you are, my boy, and godspeed back to Snoqualamie."

"It's Snohomish, Colonel Fritch, and I'm not going back."

"You're not?"

"No, sir. I figure there are probably more opportunities in the detective business here in Los Angeles than there would be back home."

"I daresay. Now, if you'll excuse me . . ."

"So I'd like to get the free job-placement assistance like it said in your ad."

"Hmm, yes, right your are. Sharp-eyed lad. Very promising. I'll take care of that right now."

The colonel tore a sheet out of a spiral notebook and wrote rapidly:

This will introduce Mr. Dudley McBean. He has my personal recommendation for a position as Private Investigator.

Col. Homer Fritch

"There you are, my boy," he said. "Just take this note to

any of the larger detective agencies in town and they'll have you out on a case before you can say Continental Op."

"I don't know how to thank you, Colonel."

"Tut-tut, lad. Good luck to you and good-bye."

With the new badge pinned discreetly inside his lapel, Operative 375 cinched up the belt of his trench coat and replaced the hat, shades, and moustache. "Lesson Eight— The Art of Disguise," he explained, and slipped furtively out of the office.

Colonel Fritch sighed heavily and headed back to the plywood cubicle. Gus Blattner came out to meet him.

"Didn't you lay it on a little thick?" Gus said.

"It doesn't do any harm," the colonel said, "and it made the boy feel good."

"How will he feel when he finds out that your name at the legitimate detective agencies carries about as much weight as Daffy Duck?"

The colonel shrugged. "I am afraid the young man will be disillusioned, but he will have learned one more valuable lesson—Be Wary of Strangers."

"That won't help much when the cops come for us."

"There is nothing to fear from the police. We have made good, to the letter, on all offers put forth in our advertisement. Try to remember, Gus, that we are honest businessmen, so stop your worrying."

"Sure, if you say so," Gus muttered, and resumed cranking the machine.

The next afternoon the colonel and Gus were stuffing handsome embossed diplomas into mailing envelopes when Dudley McBean entered their office again—undisguised this time.

"Hello, there," the colonel said coolly. "I didn't expect to see you back here."

"I think I need more assistance," Dudley said. "I took my diploma and your personal note to every detective agency in the Yellow Pages. Some of them laughed at me, and the others weren't that polite."

"I'm sorry to hear that, my boy, but I've done all I can for you."

"So I decided to go into the business on my own," Dudley continued, as though there had been no interruption.

"I see. Well, best of luck." The colonel returned to stuffing diplomas.

"I thought you might want to put up the money to get me started."

The jaws of Gus Blattner and Colonel Fritch dropped in unison, and they stared at the orange-haired young man. When the colonel found his voice, he said, "What gave you that preposterous idea?"

"It would be a good investment for you," Dudley said. "I've learned a lot about detective work. For instance, how do you think I found your office? All the ad gave was a post office box number."

Colonel Fritch started to answer, then his eyes grew suddenly thoughtful and he turned to his partner. "Gus," he said, "how about running down to the stationer's for some more of these envelopes?"

"What for? We got two boxes in the back."

"It wouldn't hurt to have two more."

"Oh, all right," Gus grumbled, and walked around the end of the counter and out the door.

When he was alone with Dudley, the colonel asked, "Tell me, my boy, how *did* you find our office?"

"Lesson Three," Dudley said proudly, "Shadowing and Surveillance. I waited at the post office until somebody—it turned out to be you—came to pick up the mail from the box. Then I trailed you, just for practice."

"Very enterprising."

"But you didn't come straight here from the post office. You stopped at an apartment on Franklin Avenue where you visited a blonde lady for one hour and twenty-two minutes."

The colonel dabbed at his forehead with a crisp white handkerchief. "Dudley," he said, "I have reconsidered and decided to finance you after all. If you will step back into my private office, we will discuss the terms."

"I sure appreciate that, Colonel Fritch," the young man said. "Some coincidence, isn't it, how that blonde lady has the same last name as your partner."

He'll Kill You

by Richard Deming

I said, "I think I'd better report Ellen missing tomorrow. If we wait any longer, the police may think it strange."

Margot's freckled face spread in the grin I had grown to love. She always laughed when I mentioned Ellen, and while I loved the sound of her deep, good-humored laughter, her jollity on this subject upset me. I suppose humor was the sanest attitude toward Ellen's departure, and I for one certainly felt no regrets, but somehow Margot's laughter indicated a lack of delicacy I would not have expected from her.

It was the laughter and the wide, unaffected grin that first drew me to Margot. When we moved to Bradford, the faculty house assigned us was next door to hers, and my study window looked directly into the broad windows of Margot's sun room, where she kept her phone. She was fond of phone gossip, and often I would see her there, her sun-freckled face animated with laughter, and one lean, strong hand making wide gestures as she talked. When she phoned Ellen I particularly enjoyed watching her, for in the hall I could hear Ellen's part of the conversation, and from Ellen's words and Margot's gestures, sometimes piece together what Margot was saying.

Almost from the first we were attracted to each other—as early as the faculty tea given in my honor as the new head of the English Department. Miss Rottell, the dean of women, introduced us, saying in her precise, inhibited drawl, "Professor Brandt, Miss Margot Spring. She's Music," and moving away to leave us together.

I remember bowling formally and saying, "An appropriate name, my dear. You have the look about you of nature's fairest season."

She laughted. Why, Professor! I do believe you're a romantic."

It started as simply as that, and grew as the months passed into a deep but quiet love. Oh, on the surface we were merely good-natured friends, for in a college town gossip can be fatal to careers, and Margot chose to accept my compliments as laugh-provoking jokes, even when no one was nearby to hear. I too was meticulously careful to arouse no comment. Not once did I even so much as kiss her on the cheek, restraining my physical love-making to an occasional accidental touch—my fingers brushing against her hair when I held her coat as she prepared to leave after a visit with Ellen, or lightly managing to touch her hand as I passed her a cup at a faculty tea.

But the depth of understanding that springs from mature love made my innocent words and gestures as meaningful to Margot as though I held her in my arms, just as her apparently joking replies had a meaning for me that a less perceptive nature might have missed entirely. As a matter of fact, it was best that no one aside from me understood her sublety, for she had a breathtaking flair for danger and seemed to love making me shudder at the risks she took. She had a trick of brazenly stating her true thoughts as though they were rather clumsy jokes, such as the time she lightly remarked to Ellen, when Ellen first began to plan her visit home, "You better hurry back again, or you may find I've stolen your romantic husband." But Ellen only laughed, and I pretended Margot's remark was a great joke.

I waited until two days prior to Ellen's scheduled departure before even mentioning what opportunities her absence would leave us, and even then I brought it up to Margot casually. But she surprised me with the blunt frankness of her reply.

"It's too bad Ellen means to stay only two weeks," I remarked.

"Ask her to stay a month," Margot said. "I'm sure if you explained you wanted to elope with your next-door neighbor, Ellen would be glad to cooperate."

Margot's habit of affixing a completely fantastic suggestion to a sensible statement was another twist her odd sense of humor sometimes took, and I knew of course she had no expectation of my explaining any such thing to Ellen.

I asked, "Would you like it if she stayed away permanently?"

"You mean bury her body in the cellar?" She dropped her voice to a conspiratorial whisper. "Is there enough insurance to finance our honeymoon?"

I said patiently, "I meant ask her to get a divorce."

"And have a campus scandal?" Somehow she managed to grin and look horrified at the same time. "No, Theodore. The safest way is the cellar." She closed one eye and made a cutting motion across her throat.

I said, "I've never even killed a chicken."

"There's nothing to it," Margot said. "Read the papers. Husbands do it all the time. I'll phone Ellen tonight and ask her to stand still."

"Now please don't make clever comments to Ellen," I told her. "I know Ellen misses the double meaning of your jokes, but it's an unnecessary risk."

But Margot disobeyed my request when she phoned Ellen that evening. From my study I could see Margot's wide smile and loosely gesturing hand, and in the hall behind me I could hear Ellen's restrained laughter.

"It amazes me that you find Theodore so excruciating," Ellen said. "I've never been able to detect the slightest sense of humor in him."

I knew then that Margot was brazenly describing our conversation to Ellen, and even though Ellen was obviously enjoying it as a joke, I was irritated at Margot for indulging her bizarre sense of humor against my specific request.

It was a week after Ellen's trip was supposed to have started that I suggested to Margot I inform the police I had not heard from her. We sat in my study sipping a Sunday afternoon cup of tea.

"You've never shown me where you buried the body," Margot said, grinning across her cup like a good-natured spaniel.

I said, "I thought you'd rather not know. However, come along. I'll show you."

I rose and led the way through the house with Margot chattering behind me. Getting my flashlight from the kitchen, I preceded her down the cellar steps.

Holding my flash on the floor behind the furnace, I indicated the freshly laid cement. "There," I said simply.

She turned toward me, a peculiar expression beginning to form on her face, and all at once she was so desirable my restraint fell away and I took her in my arms. She stood stiff but unresisting when I kissed her, and her lips were cool.

Immediately I realized it was a mistake to let down the barriers so soon, and the wisest course was to retain our surface amiability until the police lost interest in the case. I moved back a step, bowed and apologized.

Margot's stiffened face gradually drained to the color of paper. It was an interesting example of delayed psychological reaction. Obviously the sight of fresh cement for the first time fully impressed on her what we had done, and that it was not a matter for laughter.

She climbed the stairs ahead of me slowly, swaying slightly from shock. When we reached the parlor, she turned to face me and her expression was a study in terror. Without a word, she took her coat and stumbled toward the door.

From my study window I can see her talking on the phone now. But her boyish face is not laughing as usual and that eloquent hand is strangly still. Her expression is one of dull horror, and I am worried that she may transmit some of her feeling to whichever of her innumerable friends she is phoning. But she loves the phone, and perhaps a little womanly gossip will help cure the delayed shock reaction.

I wish she would grin.

Caveat Emptor

by Kay Nolte Smith

The wish first occurred to Judson Wick while he was attending the opera.

An opera box was not his normal milieu, but he could not pass up the chance to escort the elderly widow who glittered with diamonds and influence; so, masking his lack of interest and knowledge, he kept an attentive look on his handsome, if rather bland, face and bent his sleek, dark head in response to the widow's frequent nudges. It was during such a moment, when he did focus on the performance, that the wish occurred to him. He smiled ruefully and dismissed it.

It came back to him the next day, during his yearly lunch with the manager of Wick Industries. The man always recited lists of figures—this year they showed the declining value of the company's stock—and reminisced at irritating length about the years when Judson's father had built and run the company. It was Judson's practice to keep his manner aloof and unconcerned; but this time, when the manager made pointed references to "the leisurely life," the manner began to show fine cracks, like battered safety glass—until the moment was saved by the sudden return of the wish.

That evening it returned once more when, as a guest of the director, Judson attended the opening of a Broadway play and the party that followed. He ate smoked oysters and listened while the rave reviews were read aloud; over the rim of his champagne glass he watched the director, with whom he had gone to school, standing in the spotlight of success, and the wish came back so forcefully that the champagne soured in his throat and he left the party.

He barely had returned to his apartment when the doorbell rang. His spirits lifted at the thought that the red-haired actress had changed her mind about a nightcap, but the person at the door was not female, and the hair was quite gray. The suit was gray too, in both color and spirit, drooping on the man's shoulders and rounding over his knees. Everything about him seemed tired and sad except for his tie, a strip of vivid orange silk that ran down his shirtfront like a tongue of flame. "Good evening," he said. "I am advised by my firm that you have some property for sale."

"I think you've got the wrong apartment."

"I think not. You are Judson A. Wick, you are forty-one years old, and you are interested in selling the balance."

"Of what?" asked Judson cautiously.

"Last night you attended Gounod's opera and made a wish, which you have repeated twice. Therefore you are requesting an arrangement similar to Doctor Faust's. May I come in?"

Judson moved aside mechanically while his mind struggled for comprehension. "I think you're putting me on."

"Mr. Wick," sighed the man, "if I were not what I claim to be, how could I have known about your wish?"

"I don't know," said Judson finally. "But you don't look the part. Who ever heard of you as the man in the gray flannel suit?"

"But I am just a salesman, a mere servant of the firm. Call me John, if you like." The man shot his cuffs and smoothed his tie. "This is the twentieth century, Mr. Wick. We are no longer a Middle Ages barter service but a modern business corporation. Naturally we don't ask you to take us on faith. We offer, in fact we insist upon, a twenty-four-hour period in which you sample our merchandise free of charge, with no further obligation. Now, for what did you wish to negotiate? Power? Knowledge? Eternal Youth?" When Judson frowned, he added, "Then there is our most popular offer, Fame and Influence."

"Ah," said Judson. "Yes."

"In which field would you want it?"

Judson shrugged. "I wouldn't care. No, wait a minute." Into his mind bubbled the memory of champagne and rave reviews. "Make it show business. Broadway. No, make it bigger. Hollywood."

The man took out a small, gray pad, made a note, and rose. "When you wake up tomorrow, the twenty-four hours will begin. Incidentally, we'll be observing you, to insure that satisfaction is achieved. Then I return at the end of the period, with a contract for you to sign."

Judson's gaze wavered and slid around the room. "All right," he said finally. "What have I got to lose?"

Something flickered for a moment in the man's gray eyes, like matches at the ends of two tunnels. Then the orange tie dimmed out, and he was gone.

When Judson awoke at ten, he heard a voice that seemed to be located in his ear. "Good morning," it said in metallic, asexual tones. "The observation has begun. We are ready to grant your wishes." After a moment there was an odd sensation inside Judson's head: a faint, not unpleasant, echoing, rather as if someone were listening on a telephone extension. "They mean it," he said softly. "What the hell do you know about that?"

The words made him smile; he lay in bed for some moments grinning, but finally he began to consider what his requests should be. Self-consciously at first, because he was aware of the inner listener, and then with growing pleasure in the fact of an audience, he thought of some of the important film people he had met in the past, during the years when he had been married to Shelley and she had not yet catapulted to fame. He could, he thought, choose to be like any of them—to be one of those who moved on the edges of the limelight but in the center of power, or even to be an actor, perhaps the top male box office star in the country. Or the world.

The pale green phone on his nightstand rang. In a rather puzzled voice a man introduced himself as a reporter from *Variety,* said he had just heard there was an important story to be gotten from a Judson Wick, and inquired what it might be.

It took all of Judson's skill to convince the man there was a story but that it could not be divulged yet; when he hung up, he was sharply aware that the inner listener was still listening. He got into the shower and made a careful list of people he might call, narrowing it to three, one of whom was his director friend of the night before, but finally rejecting all of them. While he was shaving, the thought that Shelley was in town promoting her latest picture kept pulling at his mind. He nicked his chin, swore, and suddenly laughed aloud: why should he worry about finding an excuse to call? Shelley would call him—if he wished.

When he reached the restaurant two hours later, Shelley was just arriving in a cloud of reporters. He detached her and led her to a table, where he insisted that she talk about her new film throughout their first drink. "All right," she finally said. "I'm the one who called you, God knows why, so I must want to hear what you've been up to all these years."

He took her hand, and a deep breath; it seemed to him that the interest of the inner listener had quickened. Picking his way among the words, he said, "I'm on to something big. Very big. Something that's going to lead me straight to your town."

"Something in pictures, you mean?"

"What else do you do in Hollywood?"

"But you don't know anything about the industry."

"Shelley," he said softly, "I'll be able to do anything I want. Anything."

She studied him, her violet eyes narrowing to points of black light. "Are you serious? You're going to produce a picture?"

"Yes, I guess you could say that. Of course. That's what I'm going to do."

"What picture?"

He raised a hand for the waiter, wishing for him to come immediately, and ordered more drinks. Then he leaned back and said carefully, "Let's put it this way. I'm in the market for ideas."

"Are you? That's a coincidence." Shelley tapped her glass slowly with one mauve and perfect nail. "There's a book that Global is planning to buy for Lisa Gordon. But it would be so right for me. If someone else got it, that is. If someone else were able to get it."

"That's a coincidence." He smiled boyishly, the smile she used to say she liked. "Because what I had in mind was to make a great picture for Shelley."

When he returned to his apartment, there were eighteen

hours left of the twenty-four. Despite the successful lunch, there was a fist of tension at the back of his neck that would not uncurl. He made a martini and sat staring down at its olive eye. Then he picked up the phone and called the elderly widow whom he had escorted to *Faust*. Adopting the bantering manner she liked, he inquired about the charity ball she was staging, automatically wangled an invitation, and finally extracted the true object of his call, a telephone number.

He dialed it, adjusting his mental posture to one of deference; to the famous film critic who answered, he posed as a graduate student researching the adapting of novels to the screen. He sought the critic's opinion of several recent films, and then casually mentioned the novel Shelley had suggested. When the critic spoke of it enthusiastically, he asked, in a casual, speculative manner, which writers and directors would be most capable of translating such a property to the screen. He hung up with a half smile that could not seem to grow; he sat fingering the back of his neck, and told himself that he needed to get out.

An hour later he headed for an art gallery on Madison Avenue. The crowd at the opening was already so dense that there was no way, or need, to see the paintings; he thrust himself in among the bodies and soon had collected enough comments to deliver them to the artist as if they were his own tribute. Then he was free to turn to the real business of the evening.

Moving among the crowd with studied aimlessness, he talked to a Senator's mistress and the president of a Fifth Avenue store, telling them that he was going to make a film; the sudden interest in their eyes became a glint in his own. He told the wives of three industrialists that Shelley Garnett would be starring in his picture; the warmth in their voices became a cool assurance in his own. He told two art critics of the major literary property he was going to buy and the screenwriter and director he planned to hire; the attentiveness in their manner became a certainty in his own veins.

By nine o'clock the crowd had thinned, but its power was still with him. With the insolence of confidence, he attached himself to the painter and to the man's plans for dinner with a few influential clients.

When he got home at two o'clock, he did not know

whether his exultation was the racing of his own pulse or the throbbing attention of the inner listener. He paced the living room in wide, jagged arcs; finally he took a sleeping pill and forced himself to lie on the bed.

Around five o'clock his staring eyes closed, but behind their lids a dream began almost at once: at the end of a flame-colored carpet, down which he walked for dozens of triumphant yards, he was greeted by a massive figure in red.

John wiped his face with a gray handkerchief and turned to the last entry in his notebook. He was making his daily report to the gentleman known simply as M, who sat behind a battered desk in an office that had seen better centuries. M wore a gray cape as thin as smoke, and a chronic scowl.

"Merchandise check on Judson A. Wick," John read. "Requested Fame and Influence. Field: none. When pressed, subject chose the film industry, a desire inspired by watching a friend's success. Here is the printout on his mental processes: Settled on becoming a producer, a notion which he got from his ex-wife. Decided to produce a certain novel, an idea which came from the same source. Determined that the novel was brilliant, by checking the opinion of a noted film critic. Selected a screenwriter and director, names he also got from the critic. Subject ended the trial period feeling confident and self-assured, a state which he induced by seeking out the reactions of influential persons at a fashionable cultural event."

M glowered. "Do you mean there wasn't even one of his own? Not one opinion or desire?"

"No, all were derived from other people. I believe he even got the idea of selling his soul from the Gounod opera."

"Damnation!" roared M. "There are too many like him! They're ruining my business! I need some kind of consumer protection. It's fraud, that's what it is—people trying to sell me borrowed merchandise. If I didn't check them out first, they'd bankrupt me." He sighed, in a shower of sparks. "Why are the ones without a soul of their own always the most eager to sell?"

John smiled wryly. "I'll have the incident erased from Wick's mind."

"What mind?" snarled M. "Just suppose I took people

like that. Where's my profit? Where's my pleasure? Turn them into servants, procurers of other souls, and they'd feel right at home. No agony at all." His glance darted hotly over John's face. "Not like you, eh, Doctor?"

"No, not like me."

"Well," sighed M, "get back out into the field. And see if you can find me someone like you. Someone with clear title to his property."

Something in the depths of John Faust's eyes glowed in pain for a moment. Then he closed his notebook and left the office wearily and sadly.

The Facsimile Shop

by Bill Pronzini and Jeffrey Wallman

James Raleigh had just finished stenciling with gilt spray paint the words *The Facsimile Shop* on the narrow front window when the two men came in.

Raleigh, a plump jovial man with silvering hair, wiped his hands on a chamois cloth and approached them, smiling politely. It was almost three o'clock now and they were the first customers of his first day. "Gentlemen," he said, "May I assist you?"

Neither man spoke immediately. Their eyes were making a slow circumspect inventory of the small shop, taking in the copy of Sesshu's Winter Landscape on the wall beside the door, the gold-painted, delicately amber-inlayed replica of Pectoral of Lioness from Kelermes, the fake gold and ivory Cretan Snake Goddess from the Sixteenth Century B.C., the imitation Egyptian Seated Scribe, of red-hued limestone—each of which, among other items, adorned the single row of display shelves in the center of the shop.

The taller of the two men, dressed in a conservative gray sharkskin suit and a pearl-gray snapbrim hat, picked up the Seated Scribe and rotated it in his hands. He had craggy features and a cleft chin, and he studied the synthetic work of art with cool hazel eyes. After a moment he said conversationally, "Nice bit of craftsmanship."

Raleigh nodded, smiling. "Its prototype dates back to 2500 B.C."

The man looked at him quizzically. "Prototype?"

"Why, yes. You see, everything in my shop is a facsimile of the original *objet d'art*. I specialize in genuine imitations—sculptures, paintings, and the like."

"In other words, junk, Harry," the second man said affably. He wore a Glen Plaid suit that was cut too tight across the shoulders and a green felt hat with a small red feather in the band. His nose had been broken at one time and improperly set, and his ears were large and distended.

"Now, Alex," Harry said in a mild voice, "that's no way to talk."

"Sure," Alex said. He looked at Raleigh. "What's your name, pal?"

Raleigh did not care for the man's tone, but he said, "James Raleigh. Really, gentlemen, if there is something I can—"

The man called Harry continued to study the Seated Scribe, frowning thoughtfully. Finally he glanced at the other man. "What do you think?"

Alex shrugged.

"How much is it, Mr. Raleigh?"

"Forty-nine ninety-five."

"Alex?"

"Too damned expensive."

"I believe you're right," Harry said. He turned toward the display shelves, and then seemed to spread his hands, allowing the sculpture to fall at his feet. It shattered with a dull hollow sound on the hardwood floor.

Raleigh stared down at the shards, feeling heat rise in his cheeks. It became quiet in the shop. At length he raised his head and looked at the two men; they returned his gaze steadily, expressionlessly.

"Why did you do that?" Raleigh asked.

"An accident," Harry answered. "It just slipped out of my hands."

"I don't think so," Raleigh told him evenly.

"You don't?"

"No. I think you dropped it deliberately."

"Now why would I do a thing like that?"

"That's what I'm asking *you*."

Harry turned to the second man, Alex, and shook his head sadly. Then he produced a wallet from the inside pocket of his sharkskin suit and took a small white business card from it. He handed the card to Raleigh. On it were the words *Sentinel Protective Association* in black script. Below the words was an embossed drawing of a uniformed soldier with a rifle, standing at attention.

Harry said, "Accidents happen all the time to small businessmen such as yourself, Mr. Raleigh. There's nothing you can do to prevent them. But there *is* something you can do to prevent a lot of other costly business hazards— vandalism, burglary, wanton looting. This is a very bad neighborhood, you know—out of the way, poorly policed. The Sentinel Protective Association eliminates all such hazards here—all except, of course, simple accidents."

Raleigh smiled faintly. "And how much does the Sentinel Protective Association charge for this service?"

"There is a membership fee of one hundred dollars," Harry said. "The weekly dues are twenty-five dollars, payable on Fridays."

"Suppose I choose not to become a member?"

"Well, as I told you, this is a very bad neighborhood."

"Very bad," Alex agreed. "Why, just last week poor Mr. Holtzmeier—he owns the delicatessen on the next block— poor Mr. Holtzmeier had his store all but destroyed by vandals in the middle of the night."

"I suppose Mr. Holtzmeier wasn't one of Sentinel's clients."

"He was," Harry said. "But he had decided to discontinue our services only three days before the incident. An unfortunate decision on his part."

Raleigh moistened his lips. "They call this kind of thing 'juice,' don't they?"

"Beg pardon?"

"These protective association shakedown rackets, like the one you're working here."

"I really don't have any idea what you're talking about, Mr. Raleigh. The Sentinel Protective Association was formed on behalf of the small businessmen in this neighborhood and it operates solely with their interests in mind."

"Of course it does," Raleigh said.

"May we put you down on our membership list?"

Raleigh did not answer at once. He glanced around the little shop; it was a comfortable old place, one that suited him perfectly, and the rent was moderate. The thought of being forced out of it was not an appealing one.

After a time he turned back to the two men. "Yes," he said slowly. "I haven't any choice, have I?"

Harry's expression was guileless. "I knew you were a reasonable man," he said.

"I suppose you'll want the money in cash?"

"Naturally."

"I can have it for you by noon tomorrow."

Harry shook his head. "We're sorry, Mr. Raleigh, but we couldn't possibly offer you any protection until we receive at least a down payment on the membership fee."

Alex reached out to the display shelf and began to tilt to and fro a sculptured replica of the Eleventh Century head of Divinity. "A lot of things can happen before noon tomorrow," he added meaningfully.

Raleigh sighed. "How much do you want now?"

"I think fifty dollars would be an equitable sum," Harry said. "A guarantee of your good faith."

Raleigh worried his lower lip for a long moment. Then he sighed again, in a resigned way, and said, "Perhaps it would be better if I paid one month's dues in advance, along with the membership fee. I wouldn't want anything to happen unexpectedly."

The two men exchanged glances. Harry raised his eyebrows. "Why, that's very wise of you, Mr. Raleigh," he said. "Most prudent."

"Yes," Raleigh said. "I have some money in my safe. If you'll excuse me for a moment?"

"Certainly." The two men smiled.

Raleigh turned and disappeared through a door leading into a storage room at the rear of the shop. After several moments he emerged and stepped to the small check-out counter, where he placed ten twenty-dollar bills on the vinyl top. "Well, there you are," he said. "Two hundred dollars."

Alex came forward and counted the currency. Then he nodded in satisfaction, put the bills into a leather executive wallet, and removed a receipt book and a ballpoint pen from his coat. Laboriously he wrote out a slip and presented it to Raleigh.

"Congratulations on becoming one of Sentinel's clients, Mr. Raleigh," Harry said. "You can rest assured that your cooperation is appreciated, and that you won't have any trouble whatsoever."

Raleigh nodded.

"Goodbye for now, then," Harry said in a pleasant voice, and the two callers walked out leisurely.

As soon as they had vanished from sight, Raleigh hurried to the front door, locked it, and drew down the shade. Then he went quickly into the storage room.

He sighed a third time, wistfully now, as he set to work. It really was a very nice location—but then, he was reasonably certain, he would have little difficulty finding another quiet, side-street spot, perhaps in another state, where he could set up his Facsimile Shop—and the Old Heidelberg printing press that he was now beginning to dismantle.

He smiled only once during the lengthy task, and that was when he thought of the inferior-quality throwaways he had run off for testing purposes that morning; and of what would happen when the Sentinel Protective Association tried passing those particular genuine imitation twenty-dollar bills.

A Corner of the Cellar

by Michael Gilbert

"And don't forget the boiler," said Mrs. Cotton. "I opened it up so that we can have a nice bath. It'll need two scuttles of coke."

Sam Cotton groaned.

When they had moved into the Old Rectory at Marlhammer, he had felt in his bones that he was making his last move. He was only forty-nine. But the time comes in every man's life when he will settle down to enjoy the fruits of his toil.

Starting as an unskilled, untrained, almost unpaid assistant to an assistant in a shaky firm of chartered accountants, he had worked. How he had worked! Twelve, fourteen, sixteen hours a day—in his spare time, at night, during the weekend. Now he was a qualified accountant, a partner, a director of four companies, and a rich man.

Too fat, not healthy, seldom happy, but rich.

The Old Rectory had cost money. It was a plain, Georgian house, of dark red brick and darker red tile, with more solid wood in its window-frames and box shutters than a builder would put into a row of houses these days.

It stood back a little, isolated by beech trees from the road. It had its private path to the little church, but it was nearly a quarter of a mile from its nearest human neighbour.

"It's pretty," agreed Mrs. Cotton, "but it's got too many rooms."

This, like most of Bertha Cotton's deceptively simple remarks, was true. The house had been designed for and occupied by old-fashioned country parsons. It had many bedrooms and vast box-rooms. It had a pantry, which the Cottons used as a kitchen. A kitchen, which they had used as a storeroom. And range upon range of stores and sheds and cellars.

"I wonder how the Grundsells managed?" said Mrs. Cotton. She referred to their immediate predecessors, who had purchased the house from the last incumbent some five years previously.

Mr. Grundsell had been a small, happy, cheerful person, popular in the village. Not nearly as rich as Sam Cotton, but perhaps happier. His wife, older than he by some years, had been something of a mystery at first. A heavy, dark, foreign-looking woman, who seldom spoke.

However, nothing is hidden for long from the legion of charwomen and daily helps, and it became known— whisper it softly—that she drank. Seldom, but my, how deeply!

"A cupboard full of bottles," reported Mrs. Tyzer. "Gin. And another pile—so big—buried in the paddock."

However, Mrs. Grundsell had not lasted. Perhaps she found the house too isolated. She spoke wistfully of Blackpool. Mr. Grundsell, who gave in to her in everything, gave in to her in this. One night of dark and storm when no one was about, he packed her and her belongings into their big, closed car and drove her off. Or so he reported, when he mentioned it later.

Marlhammer saw her no more. Shortly afterwards, Grundsell had decided to sell.

"Not surprised, really," said Mrs. Tyzer. "A great big house, and him all alone in it."

That was how the Cottons had come to buy it. A handsome house, full of large, cheerful rooms, rooms still redolent of the line of sober, god-fearing clerics that had inhabited them with their industrious wives, their contingents of servants, and their quiverfuls of children. Against the edge of one bedroom door Sam Cotton had found their heights recorded, starting with Benjamin, a mere two-foot-nine off the ground and running up, through eight others, to Ruth.

A cheerful house, with one reservation.

He could not get used to the cellar.

Well, it was not really a cellar at all. It lay down two steps only at the end of a series of pantries, dairies, and wash-houses. A sort of sunken cul-de-sac. It had been designed as a game-larder. As you shone your torch upwards—the electric light did not reach so far—you could see the great steel hooks, deep-rusted now, in the beams of the roof. It had a floor of badly cracked concrete.

"Just the place for coke," said Mrs. Cotton.

It was late summer when they moved in, but, warned by her experience of the winter before, she had ordered four tons. And had got them.

Mrs. Cotton usually got what she wanted in the end.

As autumn turned into winter and winter into spring, and Sam Cotton made his nightly, dreaded pilgrimage, sometimes one scuttle, sometimes two, the huge pile diminished. As it diminished, a curious fancy grew in Mr. Cotton's mind.

There was something evil about the cellar. And the evil lay in the far corner where the coke was piled deepest.

He got into the way of calculating how long, at his present nightly rate of progress, it would be before he uncovered this corner. Two months. One month.

He said nothing directly to his wife, who was not an imaginative woman, and inclined to be impatient of her husband's fancies. But he did suggest, casually and tentatively, that they might perhaps take on a resident servant. At the moment they had only Mrs. Tyzer, who worked like a giant by day, but deserted them at six o'clock.

"I could never stand anyone living in," said Mrs. Cotton. "They'd get on my nerves."

"We could afford it," said Sam.

"It isn't a question of money," said Bertha. "And anyway, it's quite unnecessary. Do I ever ask you to do anything except get the coke at night?"

It was true. She was a splendid manager. Twenty years younger than Sam, and five times as healthy.

"I don't even ask you to wash up," she said.

"I wouldn't mind washing up," said Sam. But he had left it at that. It would have been too difficult to explain. And it would soon be summer—and the last of the coke would be gone.

A fortnight. A week.

He had noticed lately that a crack in the floor seemed to lead directly into the corner. It grew larger as he uncovered it.

That there was something in the corner, he was now certain. He had lived a great deal of his life by instinct, and now all his instincts told him so.

As the pile of coke diminished, as he bent, night after night, to fill the two steel hods, nearer and nearer and nearer to that corner, the corner to which the crack pointed, a prickling sweat broke out all over his body. His heart thumped, and he felt curiously light-headed. He had never felt quite that way before, but it reminded him of an occasion when, as a boy, he had fainted from overwork and lack of food.

There *was* something in that corner. Something inevitable, something deadly that would become apparent when the last scuttle of coke was removed.

But how would it be if the last scuttle—the very last scuttle—was removed by someone else? Like everything in life, it was simply a matter of calculation. The daily woman filled four scuttles during the day. He filled two at night. It was like one of those card games when you have to arrange your play so as to avoid holding the last card.

When he had seen the coke the night before there had been, he calculated, about sixteen scuttles of it. Four would have gone. He would take another two—then Mrs. Tyzer would take four more—

"You've been doing sums to yourself for ten minutes," said his wife. "What's wrong? Money?"

"Nothing's wrong," said Sam.

"Then hurry along and get the coke and we can get off to bed. I don't know about you, but I'm dog-tired."

"We shall have to be ordering some more soon," said Sam, cunningly. "I don't suppose we've enough left for three days."

"We haven't that," said his wife, briskly. "I lent a bit to Mrs. Tyzer. She's right out. You ought to be able to scrape up enough for tonight, though. They're delivering a ton in the morning."

With a curious leaden feeling which centered on the top of his stomach and the bottom of his chest, Sam Cotton walked heavily out to the cellar.

It was as his wife had said. A pathetic remnant of coke and coke-dust covered the corner. The crack gaped, so wide now that he could almost put his fist into it. Two blocks of the cement flooring looked almost as if they had been taken up and carelessly laid down again.

Sam picked up the shovel and bent down.

It had come now. It had to be faced. As he had faced and outfaced other things in his hard life.

His heart was pounding so that it nearly choked him. One scuttle. Then the other. The coke which was left would exactly fill it.

He stooped again and scraped the shovel on the floor. A blinding red light. An uprush of dizziness. He was on his knees. Then on his face, his nose an inch from the crack . . .

"Murder," said the young doctor, savagely, to his partner. "Plain murder. Letting him go out, night after night, with his heart in that state, and grovel for coke and lift weights. But not the sort of murder she can be hanged for—more's the pity."

Every Fifth Man

by Edward D. Hoch

You probably wonder why I'm still alive after all that has happened, and I suppose it *is* quite a story. I'd been living and training with the exiles for two years before the attempted coup, knowing—as we all knew—the penalty for failure. There were months of hand-to-hand combat and paratrooper training and even some explosives practice before we were ready for the big day, the day we returned to Costanera.

I'd lived the twenty-five years of my life in the cities and towns and jungle villages of Costanera. It was my country, worth fighting for, every inch of it. We left with the coming of General Diam, but now we were going back. We would drop from the skies by night, join the anti-Diam military, and enter the capital city in triumph.

That was the plan. Somehow it didn't work out that way. The military changed their minds about it, and we jumped from our planes into a withering crossfire from General Diam's forces. More than half of our liberation force of sixty-five were dead before we reached the ground, and the others were overrun quickly. By nightfall we found ourselves prisoners of the army in the great old fortress overlooking Azul Bay.

There were twenty-three of us taken prisoner that day, and of these one man—Tomas—had a bad wound in his side. We were crowded into a single large cell at the fortress and left to await our fate. It was hot in there, with the sweat of bodies and a mustiness of air that caught at my throat and threatened to choke me. I wanted to remove my black beret and shirt and stretch out on the hard stone floor, but I did not. Instead I bore it in silence and waited with the others.

A certain custom has existed in the country, a custom which has been observed in revolutions for hundreds of years. Always faced with the problem of the defeated foe, governments had traditionally sent down the order: *Kill every fifth man and release the others.* It was a system of justice tempered with a large degree of mercy, and acted as a deterrent while still allowing something of an opposition party to exist within the country. Of course, the eighty percent who were released often regrouped to revolt again, but the threat that hung over them was sometimes enough to pacify their activities.

This, then, was the fate that awaited us—twenty-three prisoners in a gloomy fortress by the blue waters of a bay. We had reason to hope, because most of us had the odds on our side, but we had reckoned without the cold-blooded calculation of General Diam. The order came down early the following morning, and it was read to us through the bars of the cell. It was as we had expected: *Every fifth man will be executed immediately. The remaining prisoners will be released in twenty-four hours.*

But then came the jolting surprise. The officer in charge

kept reading, and read the same message four times more. General Diam had sent down five identical executive orders. No one was to survive the executions.

I knew something had to be done, and quickly. As the guards unlocked the cell door I went to the officer in charge. Using my deepest voice I tried to reason with him. "You cannot execute all twenty-three of us. It would be contrary to orders."

He looked down at me with something like scorn. "Be brave, little fellow. Die like a soldier!"

"But the first order says that every fifth man should be executed immediately. It means just that. They should be executed before you read the second order."

The officer sighed. "What difference does it make? The day will be hot. Who wants to die under the noonday sun? At least now there is a bit of breeze out there."

"You must obey the orders," I insisted. "Each order must be executed separately."

You can see, of course, the reason for my insistence. If the five executive orders were lumped together and carried out at once (as General Diam no doubt intended), all twenty-three of us would be shot. But if they were carried out separately, the orders would allow nine of us to live. I'd always been good at mathematics, and this was how I figured it—every fifth man would be taken from the original 23, a total of 4, leaving 19. The process would be repeated a second time, killing 3, leaving 16. On the third round another 3 would die, and 13 would be left. Then 2 shot, 11 left. A final 2 shot, and 9 of us would walk out of the fortress as free as the air.

You say the odds were still against me? Not at all—if the officer agreed to my argument, I was certain to survive. Because consider—how would the fifth man be picked each time? Not by drawing straws, for this was the military. We would line up in a single column and count off. And in what order would we line up—alphabetically? Hardly, when they did not even know our names. We would line up in the old military tradition—by height.

And I had already established during the night in the cell that I was the shortest of the twenty-three prisoners!

If they started the count-off at the short end of the

line—which was unlikely—I would always be safe, for I would always be Number One. More likely, they would start at the tall end, and for the five count-offs I would always be last—numbers 23, 19, 16, 13, 11, and 9. Never a number divisible by 5—never one of the doomed prisoners!

The officer stared down at me for what seemed an eternity. Finally he glanced through the orders in his hand once more and reached a decision. "All right, we will carry out the first order."

We lined up in the courtyard—by height—with two men supporting the wounded Tomas, and started the count-off. Of the 23 of us, 4 were marched over to the sea wall and shot. The rest of us tried not to look.

Again—and 3 of our number died against the sea wall. One of the remaining 16 was starting to cry. He had figured out his position in the line.

The officer formally read the third executive order, and 3 more went to the wall. I was still last in the line.

After the fourth order 2 of the 13 were marched to their death. Even the firing squad was beginning to look hot and bored. The sun was almost above us. Well, only one more count-off and then 9 of us would be free.

"Wait!" the officer shouted, as the first man began to count off again. I turned my neck in horror. Tomas had fallen from the line and the blood was gushing from his side. He was dead, and the 11 was suddenly reduced to 10.

I was the tenth one as the last count began!

The fifth man stepped out of line—then *six, seven, eight, nine, ten*. I didn't move.

"Come, little fellow," the officer said. "It is your turn now."

You ask how I come to be sitting here, when I was so surely doomed, when my careful figuring had gone for nothing. I stood there in that moment, looking death in the face, and did what I had kept from doing all night and morning. I knew the officer would obey General Diam's order to the letter—to execute every fifth man—and that was what saved me.

I took the beret from my head, let my hair fall to my shoulders, and showed them I was a woman.

The Pro

by Robert H. Curtis

Mrs. Henrietta Marshall looked at herself in the faded mirror. The reflection did not please her. In her bathrobe and out of her girdle, she appeared to herself fat and old. Usually an inborn optimism and energy would have prevented any sort of self-pity, but she felt sad now about leaving New York. The depressing hotel room itself played no part in her feelings. Midtown commercial hotels had been familiar to her for over forty years, and she stayed at places like this all over the country. But she always regretted her departures from New York. She saw so many old friends in this city. Mrs. Marshall spent more time on the road than in the small Iowa town where she lived—hardly a place people would visit on vacation.

"Oh well," she mused. "I've got at least ten years before I have to call it quits completely." She scanned the room and sighed as she contemplated her half-packed suitcase lying like an open-faced sandwich on the bed. She looked at her alarm clock—11:15 A.M. Two hours until plane time and, tomorrow morning, back to work in Chicago. She looked into the mirror again and noticed the doorknob turning and the door slowly opening. The reflection revealed a thin, sallow man in his thirties. Mrs. Marshall was about to tell him that he was in the wrong room, but before she could get one word out the man said, "Be quiet!" in a voice chilling in its hatred. "I want money and jewelry. In exchange for your cooperation, you get to keep all your teeth."

"Nothing I have is valuable," she protested. She was standing now, hugging her bathrobe tightly to herself.

The intruder placed his attaché case on the bed and

opened it. "Listen, you!" the man said. "Don't waste my time. Hand me your purse."

Mrs. Marshall did as instructed, and the man held the purse in his left hand as he rapidly went through her suitcase. He was angry at finding nothing of value. Now Mrs. Marshall watched helplessly as he emptied the contents of her purse on the bed. He picked up her wallet and counted the money. "Two hundred and fifty-three dollars. Stupid women like you always carry a lot of cash. That's cause you can't travel with your mattresses." He stuffed her money into his own wallet which he replaced in the inside pocket of his jacket. Then he put Mrs. Marshall's small gold compact into his case.

"You're not even leaving me cab fare," she complained. "I'm going to the airport in half an hour."

"Don't con me. You got travelers checks right there." He pointed. "You're just lucky that forgery's not my bag. Nothing much from you," he muttered, "but sometimes hitting a dump like this pays off. Look!" He touched the case. Mrs. Marshall saw only some burglar tools and a thin jewel box. But then, the man opened the box and Mrs. Marshall gasped. Outlined against the black velvet was the most beautiful necklace she had ever seen. Made from perfectly matched natural pearls, it glistened so hypnotically that she felt an almost palpable need to touch.

The man laughed unpleasantly. "All your dough wouldn't have bought you three pearls from this baby." He closed the jewel box and then the attaché case. Moving to the dresser, he rifled through the drawers but found nothing. "You don't have any jewelry at all? That's hard to believe."

"You've taken everything from me. Isn't that enough?" she asked as her eyes darted to the closet and back again.

Her eye movement did not go undetected, and the man walked to the closet and pushed each dress to one side after a brief inspection. Finally he spotted a cameo brooch. He tried to remove it but had some difficulty with the clasp.

While the man was struggling with the brooch, Mrs. Marshall eased towards the table and silently removed something from it. Just then, and as the man was about to rip the pin from the dress, the clasp released and the man pocketed the brooch. As he came to pick up his attaché case from the bed, he was almost knocked off his feet as Mrs. Marshall tripped on the rug.

"Oh, I'm sorry," she said.

"Idiot! the man snarled. His face was only inches from hers. "I'm leaving now. You make a move for the phone or call out in the next ten minutes and you'll *really* be sorry." Mrs. Marshall believed him.

The burglar ran to the stairwell and raced down two flights, entering the crowded lobby unnoticed. He calmly walked to the revolving door and disappeared into the noon crowd along Lexington Avenue. A half hour later, he entered the elevator of an apartment house on Third Avenue in the mid-90's. He got out at the fourth floor, let himself into his room, and sat down on the sofa. He paused for a moment, anticipating the joy he would feel when he surveyed the spoils of his most successful morning. Now he was ready. He pressed the latch of the case and opened it. At first he couldn't believe what he saw but then he let out a moan. Gone were his tools, gone was the gold compact, and gone was the thin box with the pearl necklace. Only a black book lay in the case. He felt panic for a moment but then realized that he must have placed the necklace in his inside pocket. He reached in his jacket and broke out in a cold sweat. Not only was the necklace not there but his wallet was missing. Hurriedly getting back to the attaché case, he picked up the black book and turned it over. It was a Gideon Bible. He opened it and found, between the cover and the flyleaf, a sheet of heavy writing-paper, half of which was occupied by a slightly gaudy lithographic heading. It showed a number of men in old-fashioned evening clothes cowering before a younger, slimmer, but easily recognizable Mrs. Marshall, who smilingly held aloft a double handful of watches, vests, suspenders, and wallets. The caption read: *Madame Henrietta, The American Sorceress. Conjuress-Illusionist-Prestidigitator. Bookings Available.*

Nobody, That's Who

by William F. Nolan

Look, Danny, you're my lawyer, aren't you? Can't you get me *out* of this? Hell, it's all crazy, it's a frame. Sure, I can go all over it again for you if that'll help. Sure, right from the beginning outside her apartment.

Well, like I said, I didn't really have anything *definite* to go on. I mean, I had this kind of hunch is all. Just a feeling that she was playing house with some other guy while I footed the bill. When I get a strong hunch on something I usually play it out. So that night I decided to stick around after leaving her apartment. Just in case. I kissed her like nothing was wrong and pretended to leave. But I only took the elevator down one floor, then climbed the stairs back to her apartment. I posted myself down at the end of the hall where it was plenty dark, where I figured I wouldn't be seen. And, by God, I didn't have long to wait, either. Maybe ten, fifteen minutes. Then along comes this guy. Like I told you, I never did get a look at his face. Wore a hat pulled down low and the collar of his topcoat was turned up all the way round, so I couldn't make out any features. Just a tall guy in a dark blue outfit.

Anyway, he tapped on the door, quiet like, two shorts and a long, and she opened it while he slipped inside. Now that was two o'clock on the nose. I checked my wrist watch, because I wanted to see just how long he'd stay in there with her. Hell, I felt like rushing in there and catching the pair of them at it, but I'd have the break the damn door down to do it and by that time he'd be long gone down the fire escape outside her window. So I decided to see just how long he'd stay.

Figured I couldn't hang around in the hall. Too suspicious in case the house dick came along, or maybe another hotel guest or somebody. I knew this guy would have to cross the lobby on his way out, so I took the elevator down and planted myself in a leather chair by the doors and waited. Just waited it out for him. I didn't know, right then, just what the hell I'd do when he finally showed. I was boiling, I'll admit. I hate being played for a sucker. That really ate into me. I mean, after the way I'd set her up and all. I just sat there in that chair and boiled.

Finally, two hours later, the elevator door slides back and he steps out. Same guy. Same dark blue outfit, hat and all. And, damn it, I *still* couldn't make out what he looked like. My chair was too far back and the lobby was pretty dark by then. I would have had to catch him and knock off that hat of his to really get a look, but what the hell, *she* was the one I wanted, not him. So I let him go. That was my first big mistake.

Then I got the idea about scaring her. I mean, I wanted to teach her a lesson. Shake her up good. Not hurt her, understand, just scare her. Sure, I had every right in the world to work her over for two-timing me, but I decided not to lay a hand on her. I figured why play it dumb and get myself in hot water with the law.

So I took the stairs up to her apartment. Four flights, just enough to wind me, get me to breathing hard like I was half nuts, you know. Figured that would help.

I tapped on her door, soft, the same way he had. Two shorts and a long. I knew she'd be plenty surprised to see me—and she sure was. She thought her lover boy had come back until she got a look at me. Then she tried to shut the door in my face, but I just pushed hard and forced my way inside.

"Whatta you want?" she says, and starts backing away from me toward the bed.

I didn't say a damn thing, just stood there looking mean, breathing hard and ragged. She let out a gasp, a kind of little choking sound. Then she dropped on the bed and curled up there, watching me like I was some kind of animal.

I locked the door behind me, then went over to the open

window and shut and locked it. Like maybe I was going to do something that I didn't want anyone else to hear.

Oh, she was scared, all right, *plenty* scared. She didn't know what the hell I'd do next. I could see her eyes shining out at me from the bed, wild and wide. She had on a pink and blue shortie nightgown and her legs were all drawn up under it. She looked like a rabbit you catch in the headlights of your car, kind of frozen with fear.

I eased down into a chair by the window, where she could see my face in the reflection of the outside neon. Then I thought of a beautiful touch.

I began to scrape my fingernails. You know, just sitting there quiet in that chair, with the red and yellow neon lighting my face, breathing slow and hard—and scraping each nail with one of those sharp little silver files. Listen, that threw the fear of God into her. She figured I was just waiting till I finished the last nail before I went for her, so she was as still as a cat. Just her eyes moved, watching me.

Well, this went on for maybe ten minutes. Then she began to see I was bluffing, that I wasn't going to try anything. She sat up and dug out her cigarettes. She lit one, with the pillow propped up behind her. Then she tried some bluffing on her own.

"What's the idea?" she said. "Why the big spook routine?"

"I know all about your boy friend," I told her. "I saw him come in and I saw him come out."

"So what?" she snapped. "So a guy spends a couple of hours in my apartment."

The goddam nerve of her! Here I'd set her up in this place of her own, bought her some nice clothes and things and always treated her fine. And this is what she gives me. I'm telling you, it knocked me out. Then I asked her if she denied sleeping with this guy.

"He made a few passes and we wrestled around some, that's all," she told me.

Oh, sure. I believed that was all like I believed there wasn't any moon in the sky.

When she saw I wasn't having any she got sore. Her whole face changed. I mean, she suddenly turned hard, like some two-bit hustler. All the softness went fast and it was like I was seeing her for the first time with the shell off. She knew the game was finished and she didn't give a damn.

Then I got the full treatment. She began to laugh at me like I was a fool.

"You're not very bright," she told me in that new hard voice of hers. "Sure I had some kicks with this guy. Why? Because I'm fed up with playing around with you, that's why."

Then she told me that this other guy was a real *man*—not just a weak excuse for one—and that one like him was worth ten of me.

God, but she had nerve! Wasn't afraid of me at all by then. Not at all.

And I didn't intend to touch her. She wasn't worth it. Maybe I *was* the dumb cluck she made me out to be. Maybe I deserved what I was getting. I was as sore as hell at myself for playing along with her.

"I'm finished," I said. "This is the end of the line for us."

She just kept on laughing. Told me the sooner I got out the happier she'd be.

And here's where the crazy part starts. I was on my way to the door when it opened—and there, outlined against the light from the hall, was this guy of hers in the blue coat. And right away I saw something glint in his hand and I knew he had a gun.

It was all real freaky. He'd done the same thing I'd done. Come back, I mean. He'd probably seen my car parked in the hotel lot and recognized it. Had come back up and heard our voices outside the door. Figured she was playing *him* for the chump. Hell, it was all mixed up ten ways from Sunday.

Well, this guy didn't give either of us a chance to say a damn thing. Just stood there for a split second, long enough to make out the girl good and clear. Then he just pumped two slugs into her, one, two. Just that quick. Slammed the door and he was gone. Only first he tossed in his gun and it landed right at my feet on the rug.

That's when I *really* played it dumb. I actually picked the damn thing up and looked at it. Now, I've seen guys do that in the movies maybe fifty times and I always figured it was phony. No innocent party, I told myself, would ever pick up a murder weapon and get his fingerprints all over it. But I swear that's just what I did. Who knows why? Shock, I guess. The shock was terrible, the kind you get after a real bad auto accident. I was trembling, I remember, and weak all over.

I knew she was dead without even walking over to her. Nobody could miss at that kind of range. So I just stood there holding on to that damn gun and looking down at it while the outside hall filled up with people.

Next thing I know, somebody is pounding like hell on the door and yelling for me to open up. Oh, I dropped the gun quick enough then, all right. I knew I was a goner if they found me in here with her body, so I unlocked the window and took off down the fire escape.

What else is there to tell? The cops were waiting for me when I dropped into the alley—and I guess I sure looked guilty enough. I told them about the other guy in the blue get-up, but they just grinned and treated me like I was already on my way to the chair.

Hell, Danny, can't you find this guy? *He* killed her, not me. I never even touched her that morning. I don't know what this guy looks like, but he's *got* to be found. What chance have I got without him? Who's going to believe my story?

I'll tell you. Nobody, that's who.

Start looking for this guy, will you? He could be almost anybody. A mutual friend maybe. Hell, Danny, *you* knew her—and I've seen *you* wearing a dark blue topcoat. And . . . the guy's about your height, too.

Just do one thing for me, will you? Quit grinning like that. That's the way the damn cops grinned at me.

Will you *quit* it?

Pigeon

by William F. Nolan

When Vince Thompson entered his apartment, he saw the small white square of paper under the door.

Well, he thought, it's about time. Been a month since the last one.

He locked the door behind him and unfolded the paper. It was like all the others: a phone number and the letter R typed at the bottom. Nothing else. Vince ignited the edge of the paper with his lighter and watched the number blacken and curl into ash. Then he dusted his fingers and reached for the phone.

"Vince?" R's voice was cold and metallic over the wire.

"Yeah. I just got the message."

"Ready to go to work?"

"Just fill me in."

"It's tonight. Top of Bel Air Road off Sunset. You follow it all the way up. To the left, at the summit, you'll see a stretch of open ground. About a hundred feet in is a small white stucco house set into the hill with a two-car garage in front. You station yourself inside the garage. Door's unlocked, so you'll have no problem getting in. Your pigeon should arrive by eleven. You be there by 10:45 just in case."

"Fine. What's my boy look like?"

"Tall. Fairly slim build. Around forty or so."

"This one for the usual?"

"Maybe more if the job's real clean. We'll see."

"Anything else I need to know?"

"That's it, Vince." The voice clicked off.

Thompson replaced the receiver and leaned heavily back

on the couch. He grinned to himself, thinking of a quick two grand for one night's work. Wilma would be real pleased to get that coat he'd been promising her. Tomorrow night they'd celebrate, go dancing, drink some good champagne . . .

Vince lit a cigarette, drawing the smoke deep into his lungs. R was sure some operator. Like a ghost. Nobody sees him, nobody knows who he is. As he'd told Mitch, Vince didn't like the feeling you get working for a guy with no face. A square of white paper, a phone number, some orders, a dead man—and a couple of thousand bucks. No problems. No loose ends. But sometimes it made Vince jumpy. He'd been asking around, among some of the wise boys, but no one seemed to know anything. R was just a voice. Well, for the kind of dough Vince was getting he could keep his curiosity curbed. Actually, with R figuring all the angles, it was a perfect set-up.

Vince checked his watch: 9:30. He estimated a half hour to reach Bel Air, another ten minutes to the top. Which meant he still had time to stop downstairs for a couple of quick ones.

The place was packed. Full house for a Friday night. Vince managed to push his way to the bar. He ordered a scotch and water, and looked over the crowd.

Here I am, he thought, ready to kill a man tonight and it might even turn out to be one of you guys. He sipped his drink slowly.

How many jobs had he done for R? Ten? A dozen? It didn't matter, really. To Vince Thompson, killing was a business and it was up to R to keep the books. A year ago, when he hit L.A. from Frisco, his old pal Mitch had put in the good word on him to R, and he was in.

His gaze swept the room once more. Jerks! Poor dumb jerks pushing trucks for a living or delivering milk or sweating over a desk in some seedy office. Hell, he'd make more tonight with one shot than these dummies would make in three months!

He finished his drink, had another.

When he left the bar, he felt just right: not high, but brought to a fine cutting edge. He knew he could handle the job without any trouble and be back at his apartment by midnight. He might even give Wilma a late buzz and tell her the news.

Just at the entrance to Bel Air Road, under the tall, wrought-iron gate off Sunset, Vince pulled his car to a stop. Nobody around, no other cars. Quickly he reached under the dash and unstrapped the slim Italian Beretta he always carried there. He flipped out the magazine, checked it, and eased the gun into his coat. He sighed, feeling whole once more.

One of the toughest rules Vince had to accept, when he started working for R, concerned the Beretta. None of R's boys packed a gun before a job. That way, according to R, they were always clean if the cops picked them up between jobs. For Vince, the rule seemed all wrong. Without his Beretta he felt half-naked; he'd carried it since he was sixteen; he was never fully at ease without it.

Bel Air Road twisted up sharply past the rich hillside homes, and Vince felt the Merc slide a bit on the turns. He backed off. It was no use pushing it because the road was dark and narrow and he didn't want to get tangled up with another car on the way down.

The climb was a steep one. At the top, he pulled the Merc far over on the dirt shoulder under some trees and cut the engine. His car would be out of sight here. Below him, stretching for miles, Vince could see the glittering lights of Beverly Hills and Hollywood.

He got out of the Merc and stretched. Chilly as hell up here, Vince thought, feeling the cold wind against his face. He looked around.

As usual, R had arranged a perfect set-up for the job. No other houses nearby, a long stretch of open ground between the garage and the road. If anybody heard the shot, it would sound like a car backfiring on the steep grade. Perfect.

Vince checked his watch again. 10:44. He'd better get moving. When he reached the garage, a low modern structure with a sliding door, he nodded. No lock, just as R had said. The door slid up quietly under his hand.

Inside, near the far corner, he saw several stacked

cartons. Vince allowed the door to slide down behind him as he moved toward the boxes.

He eased down on the cool concrete, his back against the wall. When the door opened, his pigeon would make a perfect target against the lights of the car.

Minutes ticked by. A cigarette would be too risky, he knew, so he quit thinking about a smoke. He slipped the thin Beretta into his right hand, letting one finger curl slowly around the trigger. One shot. That's all he needed to do the job. He'd earned a marksmanship medal in the service, and he'd had plenty of practice since. *Plenty.*

Vince Thompson stiffened at the sound of a car on the road below him. The high whine of the straining engine increased in volume. He eased forward, transferring his weight to the balls of his feet; the Beretta was up and ready.

He heard the car pull off the road and bump over the open stretch of ground.

His pigeon all right.

Vince pressed close against the stacked cartons, waiting. Outside, he heard a car door open, the dry scuff of shoes against the ground.

Any second now . . .

The garage door began to slide upward and Vince sighted along the Beretta's thin barrel, ready to squeeze the trigger.

Vince swore, drawing in his breath sharply.

No one was there.

Just the bright cones of two powerful headlights in the open doorway.

Vince felt his mouth go dry and his heart begin to pound inside his chest. He squinted into the glare. Nothing.

Only the lights, the smooth sound of the car's idling engine, and the wind.

Suddenly he was remembering the metallic voice of R: *"Tall. Fairly slim build. Around forty or so."*

Which, Vince realized, was a thumbnail description of *himself.*

Sure, it all figured. His bitching about working for a faceless man, quizzing Mitch, nosing around the boys for information he didn't really need . . .

He was becoming a risk—and R didn't believe in risks.

Okay, then, Vince told himself, get the hell out of here. If you can reach the Merc you've got a chance. But first, fix those lights.

Two shots and the twin beams winked out in a soft shower of glass. In the thick darkness, he was up and running.

Ahead of him, the way seemed clear. He twisted past the car in front of the garage and struck out across ground, crouched low, the Beretta poised for action.

Then Vince Thompson went blind.

A dozen bright flashlight beams dipped up from the dark ground, slicing into his eyes.

God! They were all around him!

If anyone heard the sudden roar, it must have sounded like a car backfiring on the steep grade.

The Prisoner

by Edward Wellen

He absently brushed a few specks of dust from the desk but did not really feel in the mood to get down to work. He looked around the cluttered office. There was so much to do. And, God knew, he desperately wanted nothing to go wrong.

But on impulse he quietly—any sudden loud noise would bring a guard running—opened the bottom right drawer and took out his binoculars. The binoculars were a way of escape. He kept to one side of the window, out of sight of the guard he heard coughing and shifting below the window, and peered out beyond the gate.

It was just past dawn, and traffic was light in the streets outside his prison. He focused the binoculars. At the nearest intersection came the young paper boy riding his bike no-handedly. He could not hear, of course, but from the cant of the head he knew the boy was whistling or singing.

Suddenly a car shot into sight, taking the turn too swiftly, too sharply. It struck the bike, toppling the boy and his basket of papers. The car slammed to a shivering stop.

Instinctively he burned the license-plate number into his mind.

The driver's door opened. The driver got out and with the exaggerated sobriety of the truly drunken walked back to the still form, looked down at it, then with a shock into true sobriety looked wildly around, hurried back into his seat, and drove off.

Watching it all, he himself felt a shock into something beyond sobriety. He should have recognized the car on sight, for he had seen it before, had more than once from this same window seen Pardee breeze by with the top down. And each time he had smiled a twisted smile knowing the thought that must have gone through Pardee's mind as he passed by: by God, *he* was inside these walls of gray sandstone painted white and Pardee was *outside*.

He started guiltily from his trance, hearing the siren of an ambulance, nearing, nearing, then on the spot and moaning into silence. He had known instantly, by the terrible fling and the ragdoll fall, and by the mangled bike, that the boy was past saving. Still he felt thankful someone had quickly sent for help. It was now out of his hands.

Grimly he put back the binoculars and started to work. Someone else must have seen Pardee, just as someone else had seen the still form in the street and summoned the ambulance.

But no. As the day wore on, he managed to listen to the local news broadcasts and learned the police had no leads to the hit-and-run driver.

His mouth tightened. He could not remain silent. But it would be impossible for him to speak out. He thought wryly how much easier it would've been for him to identify Pardee. The man was someone he didn't know.

He could not go into court and permit a clever defense lawyer to cross-examine him and make capital of the dislike he and Pardee had for each other.

"Isn't it a fact that you and Mr. Pardee have been known to be enemies for years?"

He would have to say yes. It was the truth.

But even if he got off with merely giving a deposition, the shadow of suspicion would linger—more than a shadow, a stain—the suspicion that private spite had lurked behind public spirit.

He looked around in frustration at the walls that closed him in.

Then voices broke in on him, voices from the yard outside. He had forgotten. It was a Visitors Day.

The people passing in through the gate were usually a distraction, but now their hushed intensity was a convicing reminder of where he was.

He eyed the phones on the desk ruefully. One disguised call to the local police would suffice; but he could hardly make an anonymous call from here.

Then he had it. The least he could do—and the most—was to write an anonymous note. The time was now, while he thought of it and had this rare chance.

He stepped back to the desk, drew a piece of stationery toward him, stood leaning over it, and picked up a pen to begin. No. First things first. He took up a ruler, covered the letterhead, then lifted the bottom of the sheet to tear it off below the letterhead. But as he did so, light passed through the paper, outlining the watermark. He let the sheet fall flat. All the stationery on the desk bore that revealing letterhead and watermark.

The scratch pad. He took up the ballpoint pen again and printed his message painstakingly in characterless block letters. No one would ever find out he had written it or that it had come from within these walls.

But what now? Even if he found a plain envelope he would never be able to smuggle the letter out. He might manage to pass through the mail room, but how could he slip the envelope into the outgoing mail without someone noticing? He was always being watched.

Cross that bridge when he came to it. He was wasting time. He whirled his glance around the room and saw a book on a shelf in a plain dust wrapper. He grabbed the book and pulled. It was tightly wedged in and pulling it out caused a book alongside to fall to the floor.

The thump of the book on the carpet had an echoing thump in his heart. He waited frozen for a guard to rush in.

No one came. He let out his breath slowly. The carpet had a deep pile and the thump had seemed louder to him than it really was.

He took off the dust wrapper and spread it out on the desk. He found a used envelope stuffed with some news clippings, dumped the clippings into the wastebasket, and pulled the side and bottom flaps of the envelope unstuck. Using the spreadeagled envelope as a pattern, he cut the dust wrapper to its shape and matched the folds. Now he had a plain envelope. He shoved the letter inside, sealed all the flaps with dabs from a small stick of glue, then printed an address on the envelope.

All that had taken only a few minutes. The group of visitors was off to one side still admiring the garden. Now to distract the guard under the window.

He tossed a pen—there were lots of pens—into a bush off to the right. The alert guard whipped around, reaching for his gun in the same motion, and headed for the bush.

Quickly now, while the guard's back was turned. He sailed the envelope out to the left. He agonized over its flight—rather, its fall; watched it tilt and plummet like a broken-winged bird until a swirl of wind carried it out into the open near the path.

The guard came back to his post, shaking his head.

Time passed. The sky darkened. It was clouding up to rain, and rain would beat the address on the envelope into soggy illegibility. The guard had still not noticed it.

Then the man coming on to relieve the guard saw it and picked it up.

"What's this?"

"Dunno. Let's have a look."

They frowned over the address.

"Guess one of the visitors left it there. I better take it right in."

Listening to them he smiled. Then a thought struck him and he stepped quickly away from the window and went to the desk.

He could barely make out the shadow-edged imprint of his message on the top sheet of the scratch pad.

I WITNESSED THIS MORNING'S HIT-AND-RUN ACCIDENT BUT I CAN'T GET INVOLVED.

The message ended with the car's license-plate number.

Hurriedly he tore off the top half-dozen sheets, made a spill of them, lit a match, and burned the sheets to char in the ashtray.

Just in time. There was a buzz. He pressed a switch.

"Yes?" he said, his voice calm.

"Sorry to break in on you, Mr. President, but something politically touchy has just come up—"

Politically touchy, yes. They had done a quick check on the license number. But no one—not even Senator Pardee—could reproach him for forwarding an anonymous letter to the Chief of Police for the District of Columbia.

The Sooey Pill

by Elaine Slater

It was the pill society. There was the morning-after pill, of course, which the government had made obligatory after the first child. Yet even so, the population growth was alarming, and overcrowding was becoming desperate. Then there were the multitudes of tranquilizer pills in almost every color, size, and shape that helped one to cope with the tensions caused by the almost total lack of privacy, by the constant noise, polluted air, continual abrasive physical contact with crowds, and by the harsh and ugly sights of a superindustrialization devoid of trees or greenery of any kind.

Then there were the food pills. One took them three times a day. The endless wheatfields, pastures, grazing lands, and vegetable farms of former days had become ancient history. Even the Grand Canyon was now filled to overflowing with sweating humanity, jostling endlessly for living space. The food pills were processed in huge floating factories, and consisted of compressed algae and seaweed, and plankton. They had a sort of unpleasant fishy taste, but could be swallowed whole with a glass of desalinated water, and they provided all the nutriments necessary to go on living.

But the most important pill of all was affectionately called the Sooey pill. It was the only one that came in a lavender color with a stamp on it resembling a clenched fist. Every person was issued one of these on his or her twenty-first birthday. If one lost the Sooey, another would be issued—but only after much red tape; and, of course, one's name was permanently placed on a "Suspects List," to be consulted every time someone was murdered by misuse of the Sooey. These suspects automatically came under police surveillance and were questioned at great length, and one knew oneself to be at best a possible unwitting accessory to murder. For this reason, and others, people took great care not to lose their Sooeys.

Basically the entire society was built around the Sooey pill. It was not only the individual's escape hatch, but society depended on it as a regulator in a world where nature's own regulators seemed to have fused out, or gone haywire. There had been much talk—and the Radical Demopubs had actually tried to force through a bill to issue the Sooey pill at age thirteen or younger—of issuing the pill before childbearing age. It was a desperate measure, attempting to deal with a desperate situation. But the Demopubs were overruled by the conservative wing of their own party, who joined with the opposition in saying that it was an inhuman solution, and that the situation was not yet *that* desperate—an indication, some people muttered, in itself, of things to come.

But perhaps it would not become necessary ever to pass that bill, as living conditions were indeed fast becoming so intolerable that the Sooey, or suicide pill, was being used with ever-increasing frequency. People rarely reached forty before using it, and then desisted only because of an excessive love for their child and a desire, more sentimental than reasoned, to help the child reach adulthood. Parents who felt less responsible or loving were using the Sooey in greater and greater numbers—in their thirties, when the child was likely to be a teen-ager, or even younger. This was a great help to the government despite the large number of orphans.

But the government did not of course sanction murder as a solution, as this would have opened the gates to total chaos and anarchy. Therefore, when thirteen-year-old Billy Overton was found dead of Sooey poisoning, the police went to work as they always did—to seek the perpetrator of this heinous deed. The boy had been a happy, healthy, loving child, and his parents were beside themselves with grief.

The "Suspects List" was immediately consulted and the computer was put to work. It came up with only three names—all people who had lost their Sooey, of course, and who, in addition, had somehow been near the scene of the crime or had known the murdered boy. All three seemed most unlikely suspects, but the police were determined to track down every clue.

One was a taxi driver, who had lost his Sooey some eight weeks ago, and whose only connection with Billy was that he had dropped off a passenger three blocks from the Overtons' apartment an hour or so before the crime was committed. As it would have taken him about that long to drive to the Overtons', he became a prime suspect. But the fact remained that he insisted he had never laid eyes on Billy Overton, and all objective evidence seemed to bear out his contention. And what possible motive could he have?

The second suspect turned up by the computer was a woman who lived within walking distance of the Overtons, had lost her Sooey pill three months before, and was just about to have a new one reissued. She knew the Overtons vaguely, but never remembered having met Billy, although she may have passed him many times on the busy, frantically crowded street; and surely, she said, she had no wish to kill the young boy. She was married but as yet had no child of her own. And what possible motive could she have? She was known to be a quiet almost apathetic type.

The third suspect seemed even more remote than the other two. The computer turned up the name of Bobby's first grade teacher who had lost her Sooey three days previous to the murder; but she now lived three hundred miles away, and since any type of transport had to be reserved months in advance, she couldn't possibly have been at the scene of the murder even in the highly unlikely situation that she had somehow conceived a hatred for Billy in first grade and, harboring this dislike, had resolved seven years later to kill him! It was utter nonsense and the police knew it. But Billy was dead and someone had killed him.

Inspector Fenner was nearing forty-two and only his deep attachment ot his sixteen-year-old daughter kept him from using his own Sooey. His wife had used hers the year before, after writing him a heartbreaking farewell note begging forgiveness for leaving him to bring up their Hannah; but she could bear the stifling tension no longer. Inspector Fenner had held her in his arms as she gratefully breathed her last, so he knew the suffering of the bereaved.

He now regarded the Overtons with great compassion. Billy's father, while obviously grief-stricken, was trying to console his wife, but she was beyond consolation. Her eyes were red-rimmed, swollen, with dark black circles underneath. She sobbed continually in great gasping tearless sobs.

"Billy is better off, my darling," her husband told her. "You know that. How often have we spoken of the horrors of this world, of the horrors that awaited him, that more and more were enveloping our Billy as he grew older and came to realize what the world is like. You, who never wanted him to stop smiling. You, who protected him and built an imaginary world around him—you must know and be grateful that he is released now from the ghastly, gray, grim unrelieved life that we live."

Inspector Fenner could bear no more. He left. But the call to duty was too strong, too deeply ingrained in him. He returned the next day and in the gentlest of voices asked the Overtons to show him their Sooey pills.

"What!" said Billy's father, in anger. He was afraid the police officer wanted to take them away. Reassured, he brought forth his precious little lavender pill with the clenched fist stamped on it. Mrs. Overton just stood staring at the Inspector.

Three months later, after the trial of Mrs. Overton, the Inspector leaned over his sleeping Hannah, sleeping among hundreds of others in the unmarried-women's dormitory of their apartment complex, and kissed her good-bye. That night he gratefully used his own Sooey pill, unable to bear the reverberating screams that kept resounding in his ears—screams that he had heard that afternoon—screams of Mrs. Overton after the sentencing.

Until his last breath he heard her shrieking dementedly to the Court, "Have mercy! Have mercy! I did it to save him. I loved him so dearly! Don't make me live! For God's sake, don't make me live!"

But the Court refused to reissue her Sooey.

Backing Up

by Barry N. Malzberg

So I show him the gun. This is the great leveler, the great persuader. "I must tell you," I say in my mellow voice, "that we have been dissatisfied with the collections for a very long time." The gun is a point forty-five caliber precision job, not that this really matters since it is not the make of the guns but their function that interests most laymen. "You are five thousand dollars behind," I add. "Not even allowing for the matter of interest."

He looks at me with calm sad eyes. His name is Brown. I believe that I've got that right, and there's no need to look on the card to check as I'm definitely in the right office. He says, "I told you, I need more time. I'm doing the best I can. Furs is a seasonal business, an erratic business, and this is not our season." It is February, I should point out, although a very mild and springlike February. My forehead in this small room is veritably jeweled with sweat. "Next month," he says, "next month I will have something for you."

"Next month is not sufficient," I say. "My instructions are

not to leave without a down payment now. Two thousand dollars is suggested."

"I don't have two thousand dollars," he says. He looks down at the floor, then up at me with curious brightness. "Anyway," he says, "I don't think you have the nerve."

"What?"

"I said I don't think you have the nerve. The guts." He puts his palms flat on the desk, raises himself to military posture. "I don't think you have the guts to blow my head off at high noon on the seventh floor of this building with at least forty people on the same floor right now. The walls are like paper here. Corners are cut in the construction business something awful. The whole place may hear the shot, up to the fortieth story. You wouldn't think of it."

"Don't toy with me, Brown," I say. I focus my mouth into a snarl. "I don't like being toyed with and I have a vile temper, to say nothing of a job to do."

Brown shakes his head. "We all have a job to do," he says, "but I don't think you have the nerve to do yours." He stares at me from his rigid posture. "Go on," he says, "blow my head off. I don't have five thousand dollars. I don't have two thousand dollars. I have nothing to give you so you're just going to have to carry through your threat." His eyes glint disturbingly. He is exactly right about the construction business. Roadways, churches, automobiles—nothing is built the way that it used to be. Corruption and the cutting of corners prevail. Even the silencer on the pistol is flimsy; I don't trust it.

"Come on," he challenges. The position he has taken seems to have given him a sense of release. "Come on, do it. I have nothing to give you."

He is quite right. My orders don't provide for the contingency of defiance. Whether I have the nerve is another issue, but I don't have to consider that now. Reluctantly I lower the pistol. "I'll be back," I say. "Soon. Maybe today. Certainly tomorrow. You can't run. I know where you live—your wife, your children."

Brown's face leers with sudden power. "You won't do it to them either," he says. "You won't do it to anyone. You've lost the fire. You've acquired scruple. You're like all the construction people now, all the contractors. You just want an edge without risk."

"I don't have to take this kind of abuse," I say. I put away the pistol and leave his office quickly. My footsteps clatter in the hallway; the whisk of elevators is audible at fifty paces.

What is the raw material of these modern office buildings? Chewing gum?

Considering the issue of scruple, I make my way crosstown and find in his accustomed place the bartender whose gambling losses are now in excess of fifteen thousand. He is alone behind the counter at this difficult hour of a February afternoon, but his face does not light with pleasure when he sees me. Quite the opposite. "I told you yesterday," he says, "and I told you the day before that too. I don't have it. I need time to get it together. At least a month."

"They don't want to wait a month."

"That's their problem," he says. He dries his hands noisily on a towel. "I have to ask you to leave," he says. "You hanging around here creates the wrong kind of atmosphere. Customers might be disturbed."

"I'll have a rye and soda."

"No," he says, "I don't want to serve you."

I reach my hand into my pocket in a menacing gesture. "Come on," he says, "this business with guns no longer fascinates. I tell you, I don't have it. I have personal problems, medical bills. Maybe by June I can work something out. Right now I can't do a thing."

"You're in no position to make that statement."

He flings the towel down the length of the bar. "Come on," he says, "eighty-six it. I've had enough of this."

Striations and laughter float from the television set—an afternoon celebrity quiz or something. The level of television has deteriorated as much as everything else, I think as I back away from the bar. Nothing works quite as it used to. Nothing can quite be trusted. Quality levels go down. Strapped gamblers and bankrupt fur manufacturers take a dictatorial position and there seems no way to deal with them. None of this would have gone on five years ago. It is part of urban rot, I think.

"And stay out of here," the bartender says as I go through the door.

Who do these people think they are?

I phone in to tell them that collections have not gone well. They grumble if the message comes direct, but for the fourth day in a row it is the answering service and the answering service, of course, assumes a neutral posture. Sometimes I wonder if the messages are even passed on. Sometimes I wonder if they are out of the office permanently. Sometimes I wonder if I need this job, but then common sense prevails; at my age and stage of life there are few new careers open to me. It is one of the hazards of an overly liberal education; I should have learned a trade.

I take the train north and come in at the usual time. Lydia's face is clamped with tension but at least the children are out for the evening—having dinner with their friends, I am told. "Pour your own drink," Lydia says, "I'm not any servant. I've had a bad day myself." I can see from her expression that it is going to be a difficult evening. We will be up until at least midnight and it will be necessary for me once again to explain to her the meaningfulness of life in the suburbs. Since I no longer believe in that, I will find it tedious and agonizing. "If you want dinner you take me out," Lydia says. "I didn't feel like cooking."

"Restaurant food isn't home cooking."

"We can go to the Major."

The Major is the local chain motel. "Franchises are no good," I say. "Franchising has destroyed the nation. Everything is the same and nothing is very good."

Her eyes, infinitely weary, look up at me. "I don't want to hear that now," she says. "Please don't start up on that with me now."

Who does the woman think she is, anyway? What has happened to the institution of marriage?

Wide O—

by Elsin Ann Graffam

Maybe I'll put my head under the pillow—no, that's no good. I can imagine him, whoever he is, sneaking up on me. Okay, that does it! I'm going to get up and stay up, put the lights on in the living room, turn on the television.

Oh, I hate going into the dark...there! Overhead light on, floor lamp on, TV on, nice and loud. Now I'll just sit down and relax and watch the—

Hey, what was that?! Oh. Old houses creak, remember? If it creaked when Bill was here, it'll creak when he's away, and it's just—just something in the house. It's only your imagination, old girl, that's what it is. And the more sleepy you get, the more vivid your imagination will get.

All the doors are locked, right? And all the windows, ditto. Okay, then. So I feel like an idiot, trying to stay up all night. Well, sitting here in the living room is a lot better than doing what I did the *last* time Bill was away overnight! Locking myself in the bathroom and staying there until dawn, for heaven's sake—

Oh! Oh, the furnace clicked on, that's all *that* was! Calm down, girl, calm down! The trouble with you is, you read the papers. You should read the comics and stop there. No, I have to read MOTHER OF THREE ATTACKED BY INTRUDER and WOMAN FOUND BEATEN TO DEATH IN HOME. But, oh, they were so close to us! That old lady lived—what was it, only three, four blocks away? But she lived alone, and nobody knows I'm alone tonight. I hope.

What *is* the matter with me?! I'm acting like a child. Other women live alone—for years, even—and here I have to stay by myself for just one measly little night and I go all to pieces.

Sure seems cold in here! The furnace was on—still is on, in fact. Must be my nerves. I'll go into the kitchen and make myself a nice hot cup of tea. Good idea! Maybe that'll warm me up!

Now, where *is* that light switch... there... well, no *wonder* I'm cold, with the back door standing wide o—